husband and wife

A NOVEL

LEAH STEWART

Author of *The Myth of You and Me*

"Brilliantly written. . . . A deeply human book: funny, tender, smart, self-aware."
—ELIN HILDERBRAND, *New York Times* bestselling author of *THE CASTAWAYS*

Praise for Leah Stewart's *Husband and Wife*

"An unflinching look at what happens when one's identity is shattered, and 'what-ifs' and past choices come back to haunt the present. . . . Stewart's graceful prose and easy storytelling pull the reader into caring about what happens to the struggling heroine while exploring the many gray areas of life and marriage."

—*Publishers Weekly*

"Stewart's book does what real life doesn't always allow: It gives the woman a voice." —*Raleigh News & Observer*

"[Stewart] is a perceptive writer with a keen grasp of contemporary culture and domestic life whose depictions of marriage and motherhood are pitch-perfect in tone and detail." —*Booklist*

"Leah Stewart's brilliantly written novel, *Husband and Wife,* is a deeply human book: funny, tender, smart, self-aware. When you read it you will laugh, you will cry, you will recognize others, you will recognize yourself."

—Elin Hilderbrand, author of *The Castaways* and *Barefoot*

"Hilarious, heartbreaking, and wise, *Husband and Wife* is a novel to savor. Stewart's bright heroine is faced with an impossible choice—and I couldn't put the book down until I'd followed her story to the end."

—Amanda Eyre Ward, author of *Love Stories in This Town*

"This narrative voice is so alive and specific that it moves past the idea of 'narrative voice' to become a human woman speaking to you. Sarah Price tells the story of how her life cracks open one day and of how she has to consider each piece of it in order to know which parts of herself she wants to keep, which parts she wants to reclaim, and what to do next. I cherish this wry, funny, aching, intelligent character and this book!"

—Marisa de los Santos, author of *Belong to Me* and *Love Walked In*

© Carolyn Ebbitt

ABOUT THE AUTHOR

LEAH STEWART is the author of two previous novels, *Body of a Girl* and *The Myth of You and Me*. She lives with her family in Cincinnati, where she teaches in the creative writing program at the University of Cincinnati.

ALSO BY LEAH STEWART

The Myth of You and Me

Body of a Girl

husband and wife

A NOVEL

leah stewart

HARPER

NEW YORK • LONDON • TORONTO • SYDNEY

For my parents

HARPER

A hardcover edition of this book was published in 2010 by Harper, an imprint of HarperCollins Publishers.

HarperCollins books may be purchased for educational, business, or sales promotional use. For information please write: Special Markets Department, HarperCollins Publishers, 10 East 53rd Street, New York, NY 10022.

FIRST HARPER PAPERBACK PUBLISHED 2011.

Designed by William Ruoto

The Library of Congress has catalogued the hardcover edition of this book as follows:

Stewart, Leah
Husband and Wife: a novel / Leah Stewart.—1st ed.
p. cm.
ISBN: 978-0-06-177450-8
1. Married people—Fiction. 2. Authors—Fiction. 3. Adultery—Fiction. 4. Books and reading—Fiction. 5. Domestic fiction. I. Title.
PS3569.T465258H87 2010
813'.54—dc22
2009035473

ISBN 978-0-06-177447-8 (pbk.)

11 12 13 14 15 OV/BVG 10 9 8 7 6 5 4 3 2 1

PART I

CHAPTER ONE

My name is Sarah Price, and I'm married to a fiction writer. He's published a couple of books, and one of them did quite well, so you might recognize his name if I told it to you, which I won't, because I don't want you thinking, Oh yeah, that book, I read that, it was good. This is not about that.

I am—or maybe was—a writer, too. For a long time I called myself a poet. As a child I concentrated on rhyming *fun* and *sun*, and then in high school I devoted myself to metaphors featuring storm clouds and the moon. For college workshops I wrote sonnets about what I saw as the real subjects—time and death and the end of love, although what did I know, what did I know, about any of that. Both my notions and the poems that emerged from them were ludicrously abstract. By the time I went to grad school I'd given up the effort at profundity and gone back to writing free verse that was more or less about myself. That I proved to be good at. I published in *Poetry*, won a prize and a grant, got a note that read, "Try us again" from the *Paris Review*.

Now I'm thirty-five, and these days most people would call me a working mother, a term I don't much like. That I have a job and two small children is a better, if less succinct, way to put it. Someday I'll look back and thirty-five will seem much younger than it does now. I don't feel old, exactly, though I do, at times, feel weary. But in the last couple of years I've begun to experience the signs of impending age. The stray white hair and the inability to drink more than two beers without a hangover. The bad knee and the cracking in my hip joint and the desire to say "Oof" when I sit down in a chair. The whims of my increasingly agitated hormones. And, most disturbingly, the dawning conviction that such infirmities will only increase in number. Judging by the way these things surprise me, I must have believed age would never happen to me. For a long time, perhaps longer than I should have, I thought of myself as young. My adolescence was prolonged, in the way all the magazines have been insisting, by the fact that I waited until my thirties to get married and have children, that I waited so long to get a regular job and start worrying about my credit card debt. I'm a grown-up now. There's no disputing that, especially not to the two small people who call me Mommy.

I take back my claim that at twenty and twenty-one I knew nothing of time and death and the end of love. I shouldn't offer up such a commonplace untruth. It's easy, isn't it, to fall into the trap of devaluing what we once knew and felt, as though the complicated and compromised experiences of adulthood are somehow more authentic than the all-consuming ones of youth. Certainly I knew the pain and vulnerability of the end of love. Of course I did. Most of us learn that early.

■

We were late for a wedding, or if not late yet, in imminent danger of being so. And as usual I was ready and my husband was not. I'd been ready for half an hour, during which time he'd spent twenty minutes worrying about a small red wine stain on the tie that matched his suit, and ten minutes locating one of his shoes. The children were in the kitchen with the babysitter, a teenager whose blank youthfulness made me nervous. I could hear the baby crying, and I was as clenched as a fist, because I was still breast-feeding and the hormones made it painful to hear him cry. I wanted to go get him, but I knew if I picked him up he'd want to nurse, and I was wearing a dress already—a silk dress, at that, easily stained by breast milk—and besides I'd been thinking for half an hour that surely my husband would be ready to go any minute and I didn't want to hike up my dress and settle down with the baby only to have him say, "Oh, you're not ready to go?" and then disappear to his study to read music reviews online.

So I was annoyed with my husband, and getting more annoyed by the minute, but I was trying to keep that in check because I'd been looking forward to this wedding. I didn't want to fight in the car all the way there and then spend the whole wedding struggling against the urge to make dire comments to the other guests about life with a man. Life with *my* man, in particular, which at that moment consisted of crawling around on the floor in my dress, searching for his missing shoe under the furniture and the discarded clothes and the pile of *New York Times* he'd left there since Sunday. Meanwhile he sat on the bed holding the one shoe he'd been able to locate, staring blankly at the wall. I remember thinking, Why in God's name doesn't he put that shoe on?

"Sweetie," I said. "Why don't you go ahead and put that shoe on?"

He didn't appear to have heard me. I sighed. Let's just get out the door, I told myself. Let's have a good time. On the floor in front of me I saw one of my daughter's makeshift baby beds—this one holding her tiny stuffed pig, whose name, inexplicably, was Hemp All. I felt a rush of amused motherly affection. After a moment I realized that I was looking at my husband's shoe, transformed by a burp cloth into a bed for a pig.

I dislodged the pig, jumped up, and presented the shoe to my husband with a flourish. He took it, still with the blank expression, looking like he had no idea what the thing was for. "Let's put the shoes on," I said. "Let's go, let's go."

"Sarah," he said, "I have to tell you something. Something about the book."

When you live with a writer you know what he means by *the book*. He means *his* book, the one he's working on, or, as in this case, the one he recently finished, the one that had arrived that very day in the form of advance reader copies. Three of them in a big padded envelope, with shiny covers and my husband's picture on the back. We'd exclaimed over them. We'd showed them to our daughter, and laughed at how little she was impressed. We'd high-fived, only half joking, over the note from my husband's editor: "This is going to be the big one!"

"What about the book?" I asked.

He took a breath. "Not all of it is fiction."

"What do you mean?" I asked. I asked, but I already knew. I knew what he meant, though that knowledge was contained not in my brain, not yet, but in a space that began to open inside my stomach, slowly, a black circle, expanding like an aperture. I'd read the book. I'd edited it, for God's sake. I knew it intimately, word by word. But I wouldn't even have had to read it to know what he meant. It was right there in the title: *Infidelity*. I knew what he meant before he said it, and knowing, I would have liked to stop him, but he said it before I could.

He said, "I cheated on you."

"What?" I said, because knowing is different from believing. And then, "We have to go to a wedding." That seemed relevant at the time.

And there you have it—the beginning of the end, as people like to say, as though there were such a thing, as though the beginning and the beginning of the end weren't one and the same.

■

I was not a stay-at-home mother, in case all this talk about feeding the baby and dressing my husband has given that impression. I was, in fact, the primary—or at least the most consistent—breadwinner, working as the business manager in the Department of Neurobiology at Duke. We'd managed, since the kids, to cobble together a schedule that gave my husband time to work—Mattie went to preschool in the mornings, so he had the baby's naptime to himself, and I took the kids all day Sunday and sometimes on Saturdays so he could write. The plan had been for him to write in the evenings, too, but he was often too tired, so we were looking for someone who could come in a couple mornings a week. He was frustrated by how much his progress had slowed since the babies came.

He was frustrated, yes, but he was nevertheless a good stay-at-home parent. He was good with the kids, and he did a lot around the house—far, far more, he liked to tell me with a self-righteous air, than most men. Why, spending so much more time in the house than I did, he could never find anything that was in it—that was a mystery neither of us could solve. But let's stay focused, for now, on his transgression. On my own strange reaction: "We have to go to a wedding." You keep thinking you have a life together, you know, a life whose primary story and struggle is parenthood and its pleasures and difficulties. You keep thinking that even when you've just been told differently. It turns out you go on thinking that for quite some time.

He said, "I cheated on you," and I said, "What? We have to go to a wedding."

"I don't deserve you," he said. "I don't deserve for you to find my shoe." And then he started to cry. He looked small, and faintly ridiculous, hunched over at the end of the bed, clutching his shoe. He's a slender man, my husband. You might say skinny. This gives him an unfairly boyish appearance, that and the fact that he wears his hair a little on the shaggy side, and that it curls at the nape of his neck in a way I'd always found adorable. I could see those curls clearly at that moment because his head was bowed, and I wondered if she'd liked them, too, this unnamed woman whose name I never wanted to know. He wears glasses, but he wasn't wearing them then, because he'd put in his contacts in anticipation of going out, and on the whole he looked very nice in his suit and the blue shirt I'd bought for him. His eyes are the sort that can look blue or gray or green depending on what he's wearing, and I'd bought this shirt specifically to bring out the blue. The hair on his neck was a little overgrown, and I wondered if he even knew that. If he knew that he had a mole on the lower left side of his back. If he knew that his lips moved slightly when he was thinking about something he was writing. I knew his body better than he did. I'd known him a long time. He was my husband.

He was really, truly crying, his whole body shaking. I shushed him, worried about the children, but he couldn't hear me over the sounds he was making. Sentimental to the core, he'd been known to tear up at movies and weddings and, after we had the kids, commercials with babies. But the only time I'd ever seen him cry like this was when his grandmother died. The sound he was making was a death sound. That alarmed me even more than his admission. He was crying like this was the end. I wasn't. I thought how easy, how obvious, the response to this sort of news seemed when you were watching guests on a talk show, when you weren't the one receiving it.

"So which one was it?" I asked, and when he looked at me like he didn't understand, I said, "Which story is about you?" The book—*the book*—was about three extramarital affairs among a group of interconnected people. It was the kind of book that inspired reviewers and fellow writers to words like *generous* and *genuine* and *human* and *heart*. The endorsements had poured in, all of them raves. And he'd been delighted, of course, and so had I, and his editor, and his agent, everyone. It was his best book yet, we all agreed. Here's what we were thinking: glowing reviews, big sales, movie deal. From here on out a better life. All because my husband, as one blurb had said, possessed a deep understanding, and, so possessing, granted his characters the full range of their humanity. Well, good for him.

"They're all about me, I guess," he said.

There was a blanket chest at the end of our bed. An antique, likely brought to America on a boat from somewhere. He'd given it to me one year for my birthday. I sat down on it, and it creaked under my weight. "You had three affairs?"

"No, no, no," he said. "Of course not. I mean, none of them are strictly true. It's just that what . . . what happened . . . I guess it informed . . . it went into all of them."

"Oh, of course, you didn't have three affairs. Of course not," I said. "Just one. One teensy little one."

He was mute.

"And it inspired you, is what you're telling me. You're telling me where you got your 'deep understanding.' I guess I should have realized you didn't just pick it up at the mall."

Still mute. He sat there and endured me. He probably would have let me knock him down. How could he have done this to me, when I'd chosen never to do it to him? How much force would it take to knock him down? "So when did this happen?" I asked. "This inspirational affair?"

"Summer before last," he said. "At the conference. I was drunk. I know that's no excuse, but I was drinking way too much, and—"

"She's a writer?"

He nodded. How easily the scenario unfolded in my mind. He'd spent two weeks that July at a writers' conference, one of those places they go and booze it up and sleep with each other, and then go home and write their he said, she said poems or terribly delicate little short stories with epiphanies both beautiful and sad. I knew all about it. He'd been drunk on alcohol, yes, and also the heady conversation and the free-floating romantic yearning, and she'd looked at him with eyes awash in profound understanding, she'd seemed to appreciate the beauty of his language, which the reviews had never mentioned. And so my husband—all right, his name is Nathan—had fucked another woman. That was what he'd done, and in doing so he'd doomed us to become characters from a book. But would we be characters out of his novel, with the full range of our humanity intact? Were we characters out of his novel already, and if so which ones? Or were we perhaps figures out of a contemporary short story by a middle-aged writer of the male persuasion? He could be the divorced dad who'd admit he screwed up and yet resent me, the ex-wife, for dating my inevitably dull new boyfriend, and for folding my arms and leveling at him a look of weary contempt when he arrived late to pick up the kids for the weekend. And then he'd ply them with pizza and amusement parks and express regret in that self-righteous manner that suggested really it wasn't his fault, because he was a man after all, and what can you do? Meanwhile I'd be the ex-wife. The ex-wife, that figure of longing and resentment, that personification of promises betrayed. I'd barely gotten used to being the wife. "Hi, I'm Nathan's wife." After four years it still seemed like a strange thing to say.

His name, his full name, is Nathan Bennett. I kept my own, my original, name, in part because I'd published a few poems under it. In part because I just wanted to. I wanted to stay myself, though it was hard to say what I meant by that, or whether I succeeded, or whether that was even an achievable goal in the first place. "I don't feel like myself," my friends said, after motherhood. "When am I going to feel like myself again?" When Nathan and I married, I was a poet. When we met, I was a poet. When Nathan confessed, I was a mother, a business manager, a wife. I'm not saying I held this against him. I'm saying he held it against me.

"Stop crying," I said. "Stop, stop crying."

He struggled to obey. He looked exactly like my three-year-old did when given the same directive. His lips trembled. His body shook. His eyes were both mutinous and tragic, and very, very blue.

"I can't believe this," I said.

"I'm a terrible person," he said.

"Are you?" I asked. "Am I married to a terrible person? Is the father of my children a terrible person?"

"What do you want to do?" he asked. "I won't publish the book if you don't want me to. Just tell me, and I'll make them stop. I don't know how exactly, but I'll find a way. I'll do anything you want."

I realize he was asking what I wanted to do about his book, about our life. Our more or less happy life, about which suddenly some decision had to be made. But at that moment all I could think about was what I wanted to do right then. I considered my options. I imagined dismissing the sitter. I'd have to pay her anyway, that much was certain. What would I tell her? That he was ill, suddenly ill? The baby would ramp up his crying at the sight of me, because I was his favorite person in the world and that was how he said so, and then the sitter would hand me the baby, and he'd stop crying and smile at me, that beautiful gummy smile, exclaim, "Ga!" and dive into my bosom like a duck after a fish. He'd make his milk cries, "Huh-huh, huh-huh, huh-huh," and then the sitter would walk out the door and my daughter would say, "Where is she going? Why is she going home? Why are you not going to the wedding? Will you do a puzzle with me? Can I watch TV? Where's Daddy?"

and I'd be standing there with the baby wanting something and the child wanting something and my husband sobbing in the bedroom and no idea how to answer my daughter's questions, not even whether she could watch TV, because the answer should be no, she'd already used up her hour, but how else, by myself, would I keep her from misbehaving while I nursed the baby, how else would I help her through the abrupt change in plans that is so hard for a child her age, and apparently for me as well?

"I wish you hadn't told me this right now," I said. "I wish you'd waited until we got home. Or, no, not right before bed. I wish you'd told me tomorrow. Though I guess then I might have said, 'Why did you let me go to that wedding and have fun with all our friends when the whole time you knew you were going to tell me this the next day?' I wish you'd told me in a couple of days."

He said nothing. We both knew there was no good time to tell me. He didn't need to say that. But certainly this was a particularly no-good time. I wished he hadn't told me at all, ever. Why did I need to know this? Why was I the one who had to decide what to do? Why was I always the one who had to decide what to do?

"I guess I want to go to the wedding," I said.

For just an instant, the normal Nathan surfaced, and he shot me the look that always preceded the question, "Are you crazy?" Then he was gone, and this new, sad—shattered, as if I'd dropped him on the floor—Nathan said, "All right. I'll put on my shoes."

I didn't wait. I left the room. I wanted to close the door behind me, and it took some effort to leave it open. Then I went, for no reason I recognized, into the baby's room. It was the coldest room in the house, maybe because the floor was linoleum, the same crappy linoleum as the kitchen. We'd meant to replace the linoleum but never had, because the room had been my study before the baby and it didn't much matter then. The room had had built-in bookcases and a built-in counter, where I used to sit, ostensibly to write, looking at the field in front of our house and the big tree to the left that I was worried might have some kind of fungus and the hummingbird feeder, which reliably attracted a number of the tiny birds, as long as I remembered to refill it. Our friend Alex had ripped out that counter when I was pregnant—she was handy in a way neither Nathan nor I were, and so confident in her abilities she'd started the task with no better tool than a kitchen knife. So that was gone, and in its place the white crib, slightly the worse for wear, and a wicker dresser that had been a hand-me-down from a friend. The bookcases were still there, but now they held a stuffed green sea horse and *Owl Babies* and an old wooden train I'd found at a secondhand toy sale and would probably never let the baby play with because I was afraid the paint had lead. I'd boxed up my poetry books, and they were currently sitting in those boxes in a corner of Nathan's study. Nathan still had a study. All of this might sound heavy on the symbolism. I couldn't help but think so, when I was boxing up those books to make way for the baby, but really giving up my study was the practical choice. Nathan still wrote, and I didn't. I'd been going in my study from time to time in the last couple years, on weekends, but not doing much more than reading celebrity gossip online, an activity that made me feel tawdry and useless. Sometimes I could hear Mattie asking, "Mama? Mama?" and Nathan saying, "She's working," and I wasn't, and Mattie went on saying "Mama? Mama?" the question both hopeful and despairing, and I went on sitting there, failing to produce a single word. And then Nathan would ask me if I'd been writing, and I would lie and say I had. Maybe I was doing it for him, keeping up appearances, because he'd married a poet and I thought he still wanted to be married to one. Maybe the other woman was a poet, this woman whose name I never wanted to know.

It really bothered me that the baby's room was so cold. Nathan and I had had several fights about it in the baby's first three months, not because he didn't agree that it was cold but because he said I was excessively anxious about it. Once I said, "What am I not excessively anxious about? Would you rather I went back to worrying about SIDS?"

He sighed. He said, "Touché." For some reason that struck us both as hilarious, and we laughed a long time.

I heard Nathan's footsteps in the hall, and so I emerged from the baby's room, nearly colliding with him. I'm sure I'd startled him, but he didn't have to look so terrified. He practically flattened himself against the wall to let me go first.

The children and the sitter were in the kitchen. The kitchen was the largest room in the house, and the sunniest. There was a window at one end, a door to the porch with a pane of glass at the other, and glass doors into the backyard in between. When the white floor was clean, the room looked bright and cheery, crappy and scratched as the linoleum was. It wasn't clean now. I wondered where the Swiffer was. Did I have time to clean the floor? No, I did not.

Mattie was sitting on the floor by the glass doors, reading *The Cat in the Hat* aloud to the baby doll in her lap. Her hair was in her face, as always, because I didn't want her to have bangs and she always pulled her barrettes out. Her hair was the exact shade of Nathan's, brown with a shimmer of gold. Neither one of the children had gotten my hair—black, curly—or my green eyes, or the shape of my face, or my Mediterranean skin. They both looked exactly like Nathan, as though I existed merely to return his genes to the world.

When I say Mattie was reading, I mean she was making up her own story, a mishmash of what she remembered from bedtime readings of this book and a few others, plus her own embellishments. She said, "Her mother said, 'The fish doesn't want to fall.' Her mother said that. Why did her mother say that?" She put a lot of stress on the word *mother*.

The baby was in the high chair, the sitter spooning something orange into his mouth. "Hi, Rooster," I said. We called him "Rooster" because Mattie was named for the protagonist of *True Grit*, one of our favorite books, and Rooster Cogburn was another character in the book. His real name was Binx, after the main character in *The Moviegoer*. Nathan and I had admitted to each other, just a couple weeks before, that we had some doubts about naming him that. Nathan and I had doubts. Nathan and I. Nathan and I.

The baby smiled when he saw me, jerking his arms as his whole body expressed his delight, then immediately began to fuss, banging his hands against the tray. The sitter, who was used to this routine, put another spoonful in his mouth. "Y'all leaving?" she asked brightly. Had she heard Nathan crying? There was no way to find out without asking, and if I asked, I'd give her the very information I didn't want her to have.

"Yes," I said. My voice sounded strange, flat. I tried to mimic the sitter's bright tone. "Mattie," I said, "can I have a kiss?"

She looked up. “No, I’m reading!” she shouted. She threw the book across the floor. She looked at the doll in her lap, considering. Then she threw the doll across the floor.

“No throwing,” Nathan said without conviction. Normally I would’ve crouched down, looked Mattie in the eye, told her that she knew better and she needed to pick the things up and say she was sorry or she’d lose TV time tomorrow, and so on and so forth. But I did nothing. I was gripped by an image of a possible future: me, smoking cigarettes on the couch, the baby in a dirty diaper on the floor, Mattie eating french fries in front of some mind-melting cartoon.

There was nothing I needed to tell the sitter, but I asked, as usual, if she had our cell phone numbers and as usual she said she did. I kissed the baby on his warm head. I wanted to scoop him up, clutch him close, run off into the woods to make a new life, just me and him. He smiled at me again. I palmed the top of his head like a ball, rubbed his downy-chick hair. “OK,” I said. “OK. We’re going.”

Nathan followed me to the door. I had it open when Mattie changed her mind. She barreled toward us, and when I bent down she threw her arms around my neck. “You’re a sweet mommy,” she said. “I’m glad that you love me.”

“I’m glad you love me, too,” I said, and her little arms tightened. She pressed her face against my cheek in her version of a kiss. Outside, after Nathan had kissed her and I’d shut the door behind us, I said, with maudlin self-pity, “I’m glad somebody does.”

Nathan turned on me those tragic eyes. “I love you,” he said. “I do.” We got into the car.

We had a longish drive ahead of us because we lived in the country—out in the county, as Nathan and I liked to say, with just the slightest inflection of a redneck accent—about ten miles from Chapel Hill, between it and another small town called Hillsborough, where several famous southern writers lived in large historic houses. We lived out there, instead of in Chapel Hill or Durham, where I worked, because we'd rented the house sight unseen eight years before, when we were moving from Austin to Chapel Hill for a one-year job Nathan had at UNC. Nathan had wanted an outbuilding. A friend of his had worked briefly as an assistant for a well-known writer who had transformed an outbuilding into a dream of a studio. Nathan had been to visit this friend and seen this studio, and though we were a long way from well-known he had the notion that somehow a studio of our own would make us so. From Austin he searched the Chapel Hill rental listings for a couple of months, until the word *outbuilding* leapt out, and he called the rental agent, who warned that the house was about to go to another couple. So Nathan, in a frenzy, faxed her our application and overnighted her a deposit even though we'd never laid eyes on the place. It's not like he did those things without my consent, as I'm making it sound. I don't know why I'm doing that.

Anyway the outbuilding proved to be a workshop built by the owner of the house out of spare parts, including logs and garage doors and a glass door that had been hoisted up and turned sideways and transformed into a window. The owner had insulated about half of it, but squirrels had pulled out some of the insulation to make nests, and spiderwebs glistened in every corner. I knew the instant I saw the place it wasn't going to be a studio, not while we lived there. We couldn't remodel ourselves because when it came to the mechanical we were utterly inept, and we couldn't pay someone else to do it because when it came to the financial we were totally broke. With Nathan, romantic notions die a little harder. He walked around the place, talking about how, see, it was wired for electricity and phone and wasn't the view of the woods amazing and it would be perfect, just perfect, until he stopped suddenly in a corner and said, in a new and radically altered voice, "That's a funny-looking web."

It was, indeed, a funny-looking web, because it was the home of a black widow spider, who, as we leaned in, hustled over to an egg sac and clung to it. Looking back, now that I'm a mother, the image gives me a twinge of guilt, because we killed that spider with a stick and squashed her egg sac. She died in vain, because we could never get past the conviction that where there was one black widow spider there might be more. When we walked out of the outbuilding that first time, Nathan was still talking of transformation, but I probably don't even need to say that the place today is exactly what it was back then, except with less insulation in the walls and more on the floor, courtesy of the squirrels, who are doing their babies no favors by snuggling them down in fiberglass. At any rate we remained the renters, and, eventually—when the owner wanted to sell and we were too lazy to move—the owners of a house in the country that had the distinction of looking like a trailer without actually being one.

The two acres we owned had once been part of a family farm. Our house was up on a hill, at the end of a quarter-mile-long gravel drive, and across the field from our front windows you could see the original farmhouse, and two trailers, all inhabited by members of the original family. The son of the people who lived in the green trailer at the road had been the owner of our house, and after he sold us the place, because he'd decided not to come back from California, his parents seemed standoffish for a while, as though in our very persons we represented the death of a dream. The parents—hardy country people in their seventies—had been friendly again for so long now that I couldn't quite remember when that hadn't been the case. They'd offer us okra and collard greens from their garden, and since the children came they'd dropped off little gifts on our porch from time to time, shyly, never ringing the bell. They hadn't set foot inside the house since we'd moved in, despite our invitations, and in general we had the feeling that they, and their relatives, adhered to a strict moral code that we didn't understand but did admire. Once, when a van full of our musician friends drove up to the house, Mr. Dodson had come out waving a gun, and though such behavior, and gun ownership, was generally against our principles, we'd found that the episode left us feeling protected, rather than indignant or alarmed.

We, we, we. The first person plural is a hard habit to break. We rode down that bumpy driveway, on the way to our friends' wedding, and when we saw Mrs. Dodson outside, taking her wash off the line, we waved, and when she motioned for us to stop, we did. I rolled down my window and shouted hello. Mrs. Dodson was a small woman with sun-weathered skin, a practical haircut, and surprisingly broad shoulders. Her voice was so soft and her accent so thick that sometimes I didn't understand her, though I had a policy of not asking her to repeat herself more than once in a given conversation. On this occasion she said, "Y'all be careful tonight. It don't look good," and I stared at her openmouthed until she twitched her chin at the sky—which was bright, almost golden—and I understood she was talking about the weather.

"Is the forecast bad?" I asked. I hadn't thought to check.

She shrugged. "Don't know," she said. "Just looks bad. Looks like how it did when my cousin up the road was just sitting on his couch, lightning came in the window, killed him. You know Danny's ex-wife was blown clean off the porch of y'all's house when lightning struck it."

She'd told us these stories before. As a result I had a phobia about lightning, which had increased since the babies came. When I was alone in the house with them during a storm, I'd take them to sit in the narrow hall outside what should have been the linen closet but was instead the kitty litter closet, the only windowless space in the house, redolent with cat pee.

Mrs. Dodson's expression changed. "How's that baby?" she asked. She loved small children.

"He's good," I said. "He's trying to crawl."

"I ain't seen him in a while," she said. "I bet he's getting big." I heard longing in her voice and felt my eyes tear up. "Well, y'all get going," she said abruptly, turning toward her trailer.

"Mrs. Dodson," I called. She stopped and turned back halfway toward me. "How long have y'all been married?"

"Fifty-three years," she said. I heard no inflection in her voice. Was this fact a good thing? A bad thing? Just a fact? She didn't seem curious about why I'd wanted to know, or if she was, she didn't show it. She kept on moving toward the trailer.

Nathan and I had been together for ten years, married for four. We kept on moving, in silence, toward the road.

CHAPTER TWO

I think we're very confused, Americans, about the whole idea of adulthood, and I don't just mean my generation and the ones after me. "Grow up," we tell each other, voices dripping with contempt, but we go around endlessly celebrating those of us who never do. We say that growing up is all about disappointment, even as we insist to our young that anything is possible. "Follow your dreams," we say, and then we spend our free time making fun of the blinkered contestants on *American Idol*. "I followed my dream," they bleat, as the security guard escorts them away. An interesting lesson I've learned from reality TV—when asked why they deserve to win, most people say, "Because it's my dream." Why should you get what you want? the world asks. And we stand there and say, with sweet sincerity, "Because I want it."

Adulthood was not conferred naturally upon me, as I'd always imagined it would be. My grandmother used to say, "You do what you have to do," but she was a child of the Depression. Me, I was a child of the good times. Somehow I made it into my thirties with the notion that you do what you want. I made a decision, sometime after Mattie arrived, to do what I had to do, although at times it didn't seem to me that that particular version of adulthood fit me at all. But I had adopted it anyway—I had the marriage and the children and the house and the job and the occasional party at which I allowed myself to drink too much and behave with my friends just as I did when we were twenty-five. Sometimes I was so exhausted by my life, I fantasized being hospitalized—a bed, a TV, a glucose drip that removed even the imperative of hunger. Sometimes, angry at Nathan, I played in my head a game I liked to call Whose Husband Would You Rather Have? Other times, in a melancholy mood, I took the copy of *Jesus' Son* I'd had since grad school from its place in my desk drawer. It was my madeleine, that book—I touched it, and life in Austin flooded back.

I saw Nathan for the first time at a party, thrown by one of the second-year students in our MFA program to welcome the first-years. It was mid-August and hot, hot, hot, and the party took place at one of those cheap, generic apartment complexes with a pool in a dubious shade of blue. I'd come with my new friend Helen. Helen was a Hollywood-small Korean woman with firm opinions, a confident manner, and an enviable ability to wither with a look. But she had an easy smile and a bubbling, girlish laugh that belied her crisp, all-black ensembles, the sardonic way she raised her eyebrows at you over the plume of her cigarette. She could be goofy. I liked that about her, this promising combination of wary cool and open silliness. She and I were drinking a strange pink concoction we'd found in a punch bowl on the snack table. In the thirty minutes or so we'd been there, we'd backed out of the way of hungry and thirsty revelers so many times that we were now lodged between the snack table and the wall. "I mean," said somebody, "the woman uses the word *postmodern* without any irony." Somebody else said, "Oh fuck that shit. Let's go find some cocaine."

"This is the writing life," I said to Helen.

"Apparently," she said.

"God help us," said a male voice, and we turned to see a guy wearing an old Pixies T-shirt and grinning at us. Nathan. His hair was long then, to his shoulders, and he had facial hair that might have been the deliberate beginnings of a beard or might have been just a few too many days without a shave. "Can I join you behind the table?" he asked. "I don't like it out here."

Obligingly we edged farther behind the table to make room for him. He surveyed the food on offer, cheap graduate student fare—chips and salsa, nuts, Goldfish crackers. "What are we, five?" he asked, spotting the bowl of crackers. He picked it up and offered it to us, and we each took a handful and crunched. "They're actually pretty good," he said. He poured himself a cup of the pink stuff and washed down his crackers. "This is *something* alcoholic anyway," he said, holding the cup up to the light. "So." He looked us each in the face, seriously, as though taking our measure. "Who are your favorite writers?"

"We're poets," I said.

He laughed. "Poets are writers, aren't they? You use words. You write them down."

"Actually," I said, "I type them. I'm a typer."

"On a typewriter?" he asked.

"God, no," I said.

"This is the computer age," Helen added.

"I write on a typewriter," he said. "That's why I asked." He moved his fingers like they were on a keyboard. "I like the clackety-clack," he said. It was incredibly dorky and yet endearing, and, too, there was something attractive about the sort of confidence Nathan had, the kind that allowed him to be incredibly dorky in a way that suggested that he knew he was being dorky and just didn't care.

"You should talk to the guy who lives here," Helen said. "He's a typewriter romantic, too. There's one on the kitchen table, an old manual. He typed a line of poetry, and he wants everybody to contribute their own."

"I can't decide," I said. "Is that cool, or is it pretentious and stupid?"

"It's cool," Nathan said. "Even if it's pretentious and stupid. I mean, come on, this guy is so into poetry he's making it communal, he's making it a party game. You could say he's doing it self-consciously, but who cares? I'd rather see somebody self-consciously trying to share a love of language and be an artist than self-consciously refusing to do anything that's not one hundred percent cool."

"Are you scolding us?" I asked.

"Was I?" He looked genuinely alarmed. "I didn't mean to. Here, let me fill your cups." He grabbed the ladle from the punch bowl. "Drink up, drink up," he said, slopping out more pink stuff. "Then you'll forget anything I said. You might even start to think I'm cute."

"You are cute," I said, and then I grinned at him. I could feel the smile on my face, and I knew it was the biggest, most genuine version I had.

"You know," Helen said, her mind still on our host, "he's still trying to be cool. He's trying to be bohemian cool, Left Bank cool, instead of 'I refuse to be a poseur' cool."

"You're right, you're right," Nathan said, but his eyes

stayed on me, and his smile, too, I could tell, was his best and brightest one.

■

I wrote poems about him, for God's sake. I even brought them into workshop, thinking somehow that nobody would know what they were about, even though it was a small program and everybody knew we were an item. I remember a line from a poem about Nathan just out of the shower: "Warm, warm and wet, his soft furred belly." Embarrassing stuff. The poet teaching our class that semester was thrilled. She loved the sensual in poetry—she said "sensual" with an unsettling emphasis on the *s*'s, as though the word itself stirred her blood—and I got a lot of unwarranted praise for my work just by virtue of being unable to turn my attention to subjects other than my new boyfriend. The way his eyes crinkled at the corners when he smiled. The space on his neck that was so sensitive he cringed away, laughing, before my lips even touched it. The curls in his hair, which snagged and held my fingers. I loved him madly, and I loved the poetry I wrote about him, and so did he. He loved that I inspired his stories, which he wrote feverishly in the middle of the night. How lucky we felt to have found each other. How deeply understood and understanding we felt. My God. The reverence with which we gazed into one another's eyes.

I don't know what it's like to be in your twenties and not want to be an artist, but I can tell you that when you're in your twenties and you do want to be an artist and you find a community of like-minded types, it's a pretty heady time. It's all hope and anticipation and a conviction of your own potential greatness, and you know that nobody reads poetry anymore, but you think maybe somehow in some inchoate way you haven't bothered to articulate to yourself that your poetry might change all that. Helen said to me not long before Nathan broke his awful news that adulthood had been all about a gradual lowering of her expectations, and I agreed, but when I thought of all of us at that unsuspecting time, I didn't feel sorry for us. I didn't think we were fools. I didn't want to go back there either, but I suspected that Nathan did. After I found out he'd cheated, I was certain I was right. I imagined that he'd said to this woman, as he'd once said to me, "Literature is my religion," and she'd gazed at him with the intense understanding of a fellow zealot, instead of saying, "Did you feed the baby a snack? Why not? Why do I have to remind you every single time to feed the baby a snack?"

When I learned that Nathan had cheated on me, I supposed that if I were still a poet, my subject would again be him. For several years it wasn't, and then of course I stopped writing. But even if I'd been writing at the time, it wouldn't have been about him. It would have been about my children, I thought, or what had become of my body, because I'd always been inclined toward the personal. Or maybe I would have taken to writing what Helen and I called "flowerpot poems" about the hummingbirds at the feeder outside my window, or the fungus tree. But the cheating—that would have made me go back to writing about Nathan. The way he held his shoe in both hands when he told me. Or maybe I'd have changed that detail. I didn't know. What was the best way to talk about heartbreak? Would it be better if the detail was more in keeping with the content of the moment, if I gave him something unavoidably symbolic, like a knife, to hold? Or was the contrast of that insignificant shoe to those significant words the way to go?

I wondered how my old poetry teacher would feel about my work, if I still wrote it, if Nathan was still and once again all I could talk about. We gain love, we lose love. We tell what stories we have.

CHAPTER THREE

Before Nathan's confession, my primary concern about the wedding, besides our inevitable lateness, had been that I looked fat in my dress. I still had ten pounds of baby weight to lose, but more importantly my second pregnancy had stretched out the skin around my midsection in a way I feared was grotesque, but which Nathan swore was normal, and fine, and no reason for immediate and expensive plastic surgery. Just a few days before the wedding I'd been flipping channels and seen a promo for an afternoon talk show about postpartum bellies. They'd shown photos of the guests' stomachs, wrinkled as crumpled tissue paper, and the audience gasped in horror—genuine horror—at the sight, as if the photos were of deformed babies, or victims of a war. This intensified my feeling that what had happened to my body was a shameful, terrible secret, had somehow made a monster out of me—just in time for me to put on a dress and go out in public among people who would no doubt discuss how I looked, not because my friends were especially superficial but because all people discuss how other people look, especially women. And I cared what they would say. And it made me angry that I cared. And now I felt like this discussion of how I looked would be augmented by discussion of whether my appearance had any relationship to Nathan's infidelity, even though that infidelity had happened more than a year before, and in all the mental confusion I started to feel angry at Nathan for drawing more attention to my shape.

"Don't tell anyone about this," I said to Nathan. We were still in the car, about halfway to the wedding, and this was the first thing either of us had said since we pulled out of the drive. "I don't want people thinking about whether you cheated on me because of the way I look."

"That's cra—" He stopped, seemed to think better of it.

"I'm allowed to be crazy," I said. I gripped the door handle as if the ride was wild, which it wasn't. Nathan is a very safe driver. He can be counted on for that.

"You're right," he said.

"You just wrecked my life," I said. "I'm allowed to be crazy."

"I'm sorry," he said.

"Don't tell me I'm crazy," I said. "Don't tell anyone what's going on."

"I won't," he said. "I won't."

"Good," I said. Out the window the sky went on looking bright and golden, and the trees dropped their leaves as we rolled by.

There was another, more important, reason that I didn't want anyone to know, but it was a reason I didn't want to voice to him. If he didn't leave, if I didn't leave, if I kept him and he kept me, if we were able to keep each other—and at that moment, despite everything, I wanted this so badly

I thought the wanting might turn me inside out—I knew just what sort of talk this would provoke among our friends and family, and I shuddered at the thought. Should we or shouldn't we, they'd ask, and would he again, and was I weak to stay with him or was I strong, and how could I, and well, the children, and on and on it would go, as we became a small-time tabloid sensation for everyone we knew. I'd known that a book called *Infidelity* would make people ask, if not us, then each other, whether Nathan might have strayed. I had joked about it, and Nathan had laughed, and I would have noticed, wouldn't I, if there had been anything pained in that laugh? It was one thing to laugh, to shrug, at the notion of everybody's wrong idea, and entirely another to imagine the way they would read that book if they knew, the way they'd search it—as I was doing in my head now, as I knew I'd do later with the book in my hands—for evidence, for truth. They'd wait for it like those eager readers of the nineteenth century had waited for the next installment of Dickens.

I looked fat in my dress, and I wasn't a poet anymore. I had a role in the world, OK, sure, but not in the writing world, not anymore, not like in grad school when it didn't matter that a fiction writer might make money someday and a poet never would, when we were all writers and that was what mattered, we were the same. Now I was Nathan's wife. His betrayed, blinkered, stretched-out wife. If the truth came out and that book came out, everyone would look at me, and that was what they'd see. I couldn't let him publish it, not if I stayed with him, not if people knew. Maybe he could publish it if I left him. Because if it sold like the publisher thought it would, that money would help support our children, and could I take that away? Could I allow myself to take that away? Maybe he could publish it and I could stay with him if nobody ever knew, if I could manage to pretend that *I* never knew. Fiction, fiction, all of it was fiction.

"Oh, God," I said, as all of this hit me like a wave. I couldn't breathe. I felt hot and cold at once. I thought, I'm going to have to divorce him, and simultaneously I thought, I can't, I can't. I struggled against those two opposing currents. I drowned. Then, thankfully, the wave receded. I told myself everything would be all right. We could work it out. We'd always worked things out. Over and over in the days before my day job I'd thought us on the brink of financial ruin, and yet we'd never been ruined. Perseverance was the key, perseverance and faith.

"Do you still love me?" I asked, as though I was just now following up on what he'd said as we got in the car. Two hours ago it wouldn't have crossed my mind to ask this question. Now I heard how tremulous my voice sounded when I did. I stared at his profile. The corners of his mouth turned down, as in a child's drawing of a sad face.

"Of course I do," he said, but this time he didn't sound sure, and I said so. "It's just . . . " He shot a look at me, gripped the wheel with both hands. "Sometimes, part of me wishes I didn't."

"What do you mean?"

"I wish I could say I didn't love you, or we were unhappy, or I was in love with her. At least then I'd have a reason for doing what I did."

"Yes," I said. "That would be *much* better." "You're gazing at me adoringly!" I used to cry, when I caught him looking at me, and he'd deny it, and then I'd insist that he stop, that he was freaking me out, and I'd pretend to flee his presence, and he'd chase me and tickle me and fix me with wide eyes, a goofy smile, and say, "I love you, I love you, I love you, you can't get away."

"Let me go!" I'd shriek, laughing and squirming. "Let me go!"

"I'm sorry," he said now. "I don't know what I'm saying. I don't really mean any of that. I love you. I just feel so bad."

I said nothing, though what I wanted to say was, Yes, you love me, you do, and how could you ever for one moment wish that away? I wanted to list every profound or merely pleasant moment I could think of in the last six months. I wanted to remind him of the birth of our children. I wanted to make a speech on the enduring value of our marriage, the importance of our family—because it wasn't just about us, we were a *family*—and that desire reminded me that at the wedding we were supposed to give a toast, the two of us, together, because our friends the bride and groom had asked us to.

I'd forgotten, when I'd been envisioning how awful it would be to send the babysitter home, to envision how awful it would be to stand in front of a hundred people with Nathan and attest to the joys of marriage, taking turns reading lines of the toast we'd written, which was both humorous and sentimental and which Nathan had been editing up until that very morning. I thought, I don't think I can give that toast.

"Everything's such a mess," Nathan said. "I don't think I can give the toast."

There are things that are wonderful until they're awful, and our tendency to think the same thing at the same time was suddenly one of them. He had no right to know what I was thinking, not when I'd so radically failed to know what was on his mind. Abruptly I was as annoyed with him as I'd been thirty minutes before, when I still believed our relationship secure. I was disgusted and scornful and sharp as a tack. "If we go to the wedding, we have to give the toast," I said.

"Then I don't want to go to the wedding," he said. "I can't give that toast." His eyes were welling up again. "I'll feel like a fraud. I'm a terrible person. I've hurt you, I've hurt the children. All I ever wanted to do was—"

"All you ever wanted to do was what?" I snapped. "Was what?"

"I'm sorry," he whispered.

"Let me tell you how it's going to be," I said. "We're going to stand up and make this toast and act like there's nothing on our minds but how much we love our friends and how happy they're going to be. We're going to read every line just like we wrote it because we are not going to ruin their wedding with our problems. And after that we'll go home and we'll work this out, we'll work all this out, we just have to work it out." I was using the matter-of-fact voice I used to calm the hysterical at work, as though fixing the mess he'd made were equivalent to making changes to the budget or finding extra classroom space, calling someone to come fix the copier again. The problem we had was just a problem, and we would solve it. If I believed that, I could stay calm, could endure this wedding, could make this toast. Could smile. If I believed otherwise, then the life I thought I had had been nothing but a thin layer of ice over a bottomless despair, and with one wrong step we'd plunge so far down we'd never see the light again. And if that was the case, then all there was to do was sink.

Sink, I thought, and then something new occurred to

me. "Nathan," I asked, "if you don't publish the book, will we have to give the money back?" By "money" I meant his advance, of which he'd already received $50,000, much of which was gone, gone, gone.

"Oh, God," he said, and I knew that he, too, had failed to think of this. "Oh, God," he said again. "I think we would."

■

We were actually responsible for this wedding. We'd been friends with Alex; we'd been friends with Adam; we'd introduced them. One morning after a party at our house that had lasted well after I'd gone to bed, I found them entwined on our couch. They were tall people—both of them topped six feet—and our couch was small, so this was a sight to see. I was several months pregnant with Binx. My back hurt. My hips hurt. My feet were starting to swell. When I saw them on my couch, clutching each other even in sleep, for a moment I fell out of time. I might have been in graduate school, I might have been in college, I might have been curled up on a couch with Nathan, clutching him just like that. I remembered how that felt. What brought me back to the present was the thought that I didn't want my two-year-old to see Mommy and Daddy's friends clinched half-naked in the living room in a John-and-Yoko pose. I was a mom. That's when I knew it. Not Mama, as you are at first, when having a baby doesn't preclude wearing a funky T-shirt to the food co-op, baby kicking her feet in the Bjorn. Mom. Mom who gets handed the used-up gum on car trips. From now on that was me.

The wedding was outside, at an old farm now rented

out for events. Alex and Adam had chosen the location largely because they could have a live band there—Adam was a musician, as were many of his friends, and a number of them were to play—and because the climate was temperate enough in North Carolina that an outdoor wedding in October seemed a good bet. By the time we arrived, though, hustling through a field from the dirt parking lot, the gold in the sky was darkening, the clouds standing up like belligerents considering a fight, and I feared Mrs. Dodson had been right about the weather. The rows of white folding chairs were set up under a canopy, the food inside the small barn, but if the skies opened up, the ground would turn muddy and the music would have to move inside, and the guests would get wet going between the tent and the barn. The vision Alex and Adam had had for their wedding—of sunset giving way to the twinkling light coming from globes strung between the trees, guests drifting through the field with drinks in hand while light breezes toyed fetchingly with the women's skirts and hair and musicians sang songs of love—would come to naught. "I hope it doesn't rain," I said to Nathan, a normal comment I would have made if we were still living our normal lives.

He turned to me, his face distraught, like he was lost in a city where he didn't speak the language. "What?" he said. I didn't repeat myself. I didn't ask what he'd been thinking about.

The bassist in Adam's band was sitting in front of the rows of chairs, playing Cat Stevens on his acoustic guitar. The minister stood with her arms at her sides, smiling beatifically. Everyone was in their seats except us and Erica and Josh, another perpetually late couple who were right behind us. Erica's heel sank into the earth, and when she stepped out of her shoe she let out a startled, muffled scream, loud enough to make the wedding crowd turn to stare at us. Coworkers, parents, aunts and uncles, college friends—this motley assortment of people gathered once and never again—they looked at us as one and thought, Who the hell are *these* people? I knew it was some brand of hallucination—I knew many of my own close friends were among that group—but none of those faces looked familiar, and not a one looked friendly. They could see what we brought with us, smoke trails of unhappiness, one enormous dose of bad luck.

We slipped into back-row seats. Erica gave me a sheepish, commiserating smile, and I did my best to return it, hoping my face conveyed no other concern but that we were, once again, late. I always blamed Nathan for our lateness, but we'd been together so long I no longer truly remembered whether I'd been prompt without him. I supposed if I were right, and we divorced, I'd start being on time. If not, I'd be divorced, and late, and wrong.

Alex and Adam had no attendants, and nobody gave anybody away. They walked up the aisle together, not even arm in arm but hand in hand—"like hippies," Alex had told me, quoting her mother. We, the guests, stood, the way we always do, and I smiled in the general direction of the aisle, in case Alex happened to look over and see me. I was having trouble experiencing the proper emotions—the rush of romantic feeling, the aesthetic pleasure of seeing people in dress-up clothes. Alex did look beautiful. Her dress was long and strapless and white. Earlier that day, when I'd taken her to get a pedicure, she and I had laughed and laughed because her friend from Germany had asked, "Are you going to wear white, like a *real virgin*?" I remembered the laughing as though it had happened a very long time ago, and yet it had been only a few hours earlier, which meant that time, the time before Nathan told me, was still accessible, still present, still possible. The hem of Alex's dress was collecting dirt, and the wind picked up.

The storm held off a few more minutes, until the vows, at which point the skies opened as though God himself were objecting to the marriage. The wind whipped itself into a sudden frenzy that pulled the tent stakes from the ground. A couple of men were clinging to the tent in an effort to keep it from becoming airborne. I think a woman was screaming, although I may have been hearing a desperate, frightened human voice when it was only, after all, the wind.

I had a narcissistic conviction that my emotions had been made manifest. Except that the weather was more like what I should have been feeling. To match my actual feelings it should have been one of those humid days when there's no movement in the air and the sky is cloudless but tinged with gray, the whole world dulled and waiting.

Adam held onto Alex as though the wind might blow her away. A few petals lifted off her bouquet and spun wildly in the air. I dropped my head to my knees, like a child of the 1950s in a nuclear-disaster video. I didn't even realize I'd done it until I felt Nathan's hand on my back. I realized this was the first time he'd touched me since he told me. Why was he doing it? To comfort me? To protect me? To apologize? I tried to pretend his hand wasn't there, but even though the wind summoned goose bumps on my bare legs and the rain slanted in under the tent to give us cold, hard kisses, the weight of his hand was all I could feel.

I don't know how long it lasted. When it was over, it was totally over, the storm gone, poof, magic, as though a chorus of voices sang "Ahhhh," the clouds parted, and a golden light shone down from heaven. A murmur of relief went through the crowd. People righted their clothes as though they'd been engaged in a fight, or hasty, backroom sex. They turned toward the front to find the bride and groom, if not their hairstyles, intact. "Welcome to marriage," the minister said.

■

And then it was the cocktail hour, when all the guests hit the open bar and Alex and Adam posed for endless snapshots of marital bliss. A lawyer friend of Alex's who wanted to be a writer and so always cornered Nathan showed up to corner him, and though in the normal course of things I would have attempted a rescue, I took the opportunity to slip away to the bar. I got myself a vodka martini with a twist and some company—Erica and our friend Sally, who were sitting on a bench on the outskirts of the party, their high heels already kicked off, bare feet in the grass. They both looked wrung out, as though they should have been sprawled beside a basketball court in sweaty gym shorts, rather than sitting in cocktail dresses with their knees pressed together, highball glasses sweating in their hands.

"Kids keep you up last night?" I asked, addressing either of them, or both, and together they said, "Yes."

I joined them on the bench. We talked about our kids, and how Erica had read an article about pedophiles and had what she thought might have been a panic attack, and how Sally felt like she should have another kid even though she didn't want to because she didn't want her daughter to be an only child. We were all good friends, but we didn't see each other as often as we once had, partly because Sally and I worked and had no time and Erica had taken to hanging out with the women in her moms' group. I used to see Sally as indomitable, but lately she seemed flattened, as if her life was a car that had run her over. Erica, on the other hand, had been spiky with anxiety ever since she had her kids. I wondered how I seemed to them. How had I changed? From the time I was eighteen until I got pregnant I smoked cigarettes, and even after we started trying to conceive I smoked them, sneaking them on the way to work with the windows down. If Nathan ever smelled them, he pretended he hadn't. And then I got pregnant, and the faintest whiff of cigarette smoke tortured my nose, my mouth, my stomach. Every puff I'd ever taken seemed to float before my eyes like a tiny ghost prophesying emphysema. I'd tried to smoke, once, after Mattie was born, looking to recapture that old, lost pleasure, but it was a joyless experience, the burn in my lungs, the sharp ashy taste in my mouth, the nauseous buzzing in my brain. Which was the essential self? The self who smoked cigarettes? The self who wanted to, but couldn't, so she just stopped wanting to?

Erica had eaten the cherry out of her drink, and now she sat twirling the stem between her forefinger and thumb. "Do you know I used to be able to tie a knot in a cherry stem with my tongue?" she asked.

"Of course," I said. "You used to do that all the time. It was your party trick."

She looked at me with astonishment. "Really?"

"You don't remember that?"

"Yeah," Sally said. "Every time you got drunk you used to do that. Don't you remember that bartender who used to call you Cherry?"

"That is so weird," Erica said. "I don't remember that at all. What has happened to my brain?"

"We thought he was creepy," Sally said.

Erica held up the stem, squinted at it. "I can't do it anymore," she said. "I don't know why."

■

When dinner was served, Nathan came for me. Erica and Sally had already wandered off in search of their husbands. Nathan held out his hand as if to help me up from the bench, and after a moment of staring at him like I'd never seen him before, I took it. We ate in the barn, crowded together at picnic tables. I got hot and took my sweater off, and then tried to keep one arm crossed artfully over my thickened midsection. The entire length of my thigh was pressed against Nathan's—given the seating, I couldn't avoid this—but I did my best to ignore him, talking to everybody else. I was like a manic-depressive cycling at an alarming rate, one minute talking loud and making everyone laugh and the next staring blankly into space as an invisible hand squeezed my throat. As the meal wound down, Alex's brother appeared at the front of the room, tapping the top of a wireless mic. The people who noticed him began to clink their silverware on their glasses, and the noise of the crowd rumbled into silence.

"Oh, God," Nathan said beside me, and I turned to look directly at him for what seemed like the first time in days. Beneath the table his leg began to jiggle, and the table shook in response. I put my hand on his knee, automatically, to stop him, and he turned to look at me. "I can't do it," he said.

"We have to," I said.

Alex's brother made a joke about the weather—the crowd laughed loudly—and then started talking about his sister. I caught the word *childhood*. I caught the word *love*.

"Do you love her?" I said.

"Who?" he asked. "Kate?"

"Don't tell me her name!" My voice shot up, and Erica glanced my way. I caught her eye, waved, smiled. Everything okay here. My heart was pounding like Nathan had just told me the day I was going to die.

"And now," Alex's brother said, "we'll hear from Nathan and Sarah." In two strides he was in front of me, holding out the microphone. I took it. I stood. Nathan didn't. I didn't look at him. I looked out at the audience. That woman there—I didn't know her, but I recognized her from Alex's photos as a college friend. Just recently Alex had been telling me some awful story about that friend's life, how her husband left her in the hospital after their son's traumatic birth to go to a football game, so when she began to bleed out he wasn't there, and if the nurse hadn't come in, she might have died. And I'd felt pity for her, and self-righteous indignation of the *Damn, I'd never put up with that* variety. Now I had an absurd urge to wave at her.

How long had this silence been going on?

"Nathan," I said into the microphone. The word boomed back at me. I'd said it like the beginning of a sentence, the start of something. They were all waiting. Nathan what?

"Nathan," I said again, but this time to him. I risked a look at him. He looked at me like I was the teacher and he was a student who hadn't done the reading. I smiled at him, made my voice low and amused. "Are you ready to talk about marriage?" A low rumble of laughter from the audience. They thought this was part of the act, and I hoped it was. A small but maniacal part of me rooted for turning the moment into a scene from a female-empowerment movie, in which I'd announce that Nathan had cheated on me, then call for a toast, snatch somebody's glass off the table and then somebody else's, until I'd drained a roomful of champagne. "Nathan and I have been married four years," I said. "We have two small children, and we're waiting for Alex and Adam to join us in propagating the race so that they'll start to understand why we never return their phone calls, why we want to go out to dinner at five." More tittering.

I looked again at Nathan, who was still sitting down, and I knew the second my eyes met his that my ability to walk the line between playful and embarrassing had just exited the building. The next thing I said into that microphone was going to be hopeless and unhinged. He must have known it.

He said, "But that's not the subject of the toast."

I said, "What do you mean?"

He stood, leaned into the microphone. He said, in a stage whisper, "But that's not what the toast is about, remember?"

"What's it about?"

Nathan looked at the crowd, shook his head, playing it big. "We're supposed to talk about the *love*."

"Oh," I said. "Right. The *love*."

"We've known Adam and Alex a long time," Nathan said, "and we've spent a lot of time in their various homes." This was the opening line of the speech we'd written.

"So when we were thinking about their relationship," I said, on cue, "we started talking about the kind of home Adam and Alex have already started creating together.

We'd like to offer some of our predictions about what that home will be like."

"You will always find, on the back of every toilet, a Robert Christgau consumer guide."

"Unlike in our house, all the copies of the *New Yorker* will have actually been read."

"Adam will make sure that in the kitchen, the trash can is placed in a sensible relationship to the refrigerator."

"And that Alex always puts cut-up onions away in the proper container."

"Alex will make sure the bathroom never again looks like it did when Adam lived alone."

"There will be an abundant garden."

"And abundant guacamole."

"There will be good beer."

"And spirits."

"You will find music by the following ten thousand artists . . ." I took a breath, as though to begin listing them, and as we'd planned, Nathan leaned over and pretended to whisper in my ear. "Nathan says there's not time for that. But one of the artists is Dwight Twilley."

And so we went on, as if we'd spent our lives treading the stage, as the toast segued from funny to sentimental. We mentioned their cooking, their tastes in books, their storytelling. We said that any child born into their house would be lucky, and tall. And then we were almost at the end. I said my second-to-last line: "When Nathan and I are at Alex and Adam's house, it can be guaranteed that at some point in the evening I'll look up and see Nathan and Adam standing side by side reading CD liner notes." I used the future tense.

Nathan said his line: "And that at some point Adam and

I will glance up from reading CD liner notes, see our wives talking passionately on the couch, and think to ourselves, 'After all this time, isn't it nice that we married women who get along so well.' " He used the future tense.

I said, "And we'll know that, in the way you are when you're with really good friends, we're home." Future tense.

Nathan said, "Here's to Alex and Adam," and when he lifted his glass he looked at me, as though it was me he was toasting. *Future tense*, I thought, willing him, now, to think the same thing at the same time. *Future tense*. We clinked glasses. We drank.

People applauded as we dropped, exhausted, into our seats. I felt somebody's hand clap my shoulder—for a moment I couldn't even remember who was sitting next to me—but I kept my head down. Nathan leaned forward like he wanted to kiss me. He put his hand on my thigh. I felt his breath against my ear as he said, "No, I don't love her. In my whole life I've never loved anybody but you."

I put my hand on his but said nothing. They were still applauding, and I thought about the picture we must be making to people ready and willing to be moved, our heads together, my fingers tucked loosely over his.

"I'm so sorry," he said. "I couldn't be sorrier. And whatever happens next is up to you."

"OK," I said. I tilted my head, let it bump lightly against his. "OK."

"Anything you want," he said.

"And now," Alex's brother said, "the first dance, to 'Hallelujah,' " and I looked up.

"I'll do anything you want," Nathan said.

Alex and Adam advanced hand in hand onto the dance floor, her skirt so long she seemed to float. They rotated toward each other, placing their hands with a practiced, military precision that made them both laugh. When the music started and they took those first few steps, they smiled at each other like co-conspirators.

"Honey," I said. "Could you get me a drink?"

■

I had two more martinis, which I shouldn't have, because after pregnancy and months of breast-feeding my tolerance was nil. For a while I felt expansive and euphoric, prone to sweeping generalizations and declarations of affection, and in this mode I persuaded myself that my problems were eminently solvable, and was even tempted to tell my friends that, as if a public declaration would make it true. At some point I lost track of Nathan, for which I wasn't exactly sorry, as his actual presence was a hindrance to my drunken narrative of harmony and forgiveness. I danced with my friends, noting that I was drunk enough not to feel inhibited by my unhappiness with my physique, feeling that that was a good thing until a number of bright flashes of light slowly alerted me to the presence of the wedding photographer, at which point I left the dance floor and went walkabout in the dark.

"Psssst," I heard, and turned to see a tall figure, the red tip of a cigarette. I heard the rustling of skirts in the grass and identified the bride, hiding in a dark corner of her wedding, drinking a beer and sneaking a forbidden smoke. "Hey, baby," she said as I joined her. "How's it hanging?"

I looked at her cigarette and wished that I wanted it. "I can't stand the smell of those anymore," I said.

"I know," she said. She took a long inhale. "Me neither."

"Doesn't Adam think you quit?"

"That's why I'm *sneaking*," she said, inflecting the word like Gollum in the *Lord of the Rings* movies. We were closet fantasy nerds—a weakness for the mythological was part of our bond, both of us still mourning the end of *Buffy the Vampire Slayer*. "But this is the last one. After this I'll lead a life of purity and openness."

Why is it that when you have a secret, everything anybody says seems to be about that secret? "That's nice," I said. "And Adam will, too."

"Oh, he'd better," she said. She looked past me as something caught her eye. "Hey, there's Smith and Holly. I do not get that combination."

I turned to see Smith, Nathan's other best friend, and his latest girlfriend. Smith was the arts editor for the local free weekly. He was slender and angular and spiky-haired, and might have been an arrogant hipster type if he hadn't been brought up southern and polite. I sometimes had the impression he didn't quite like me. The girlfriend was, as near as we could tell, a bitch, the sort of person whose mood shifts freeze the atmosphere.

"Well, you know he likes those icy blondes," I said. "It's very Hitchcock. He likes women who may or may not be dead, who attract homicidal birds."

"You and your metaphors," Alex said. "What are you, some kind of poet?"

"Ha ha ha," I said. And then for no reason I said it again.

"She looks like a homicidal bird," Alex said.

"Mmmm," I said. The girlfriend was so skinny, so childlessly skinny, or skinnily childless. I was suddenly cold, and couldn't recall what I'd done with my sweater.

"Speaking of metaphors," Alex said, "I really did love your toast."

"I'm glad," I said.

"So this procreation thing," she said. "You really want me to do it, huh?"

"You know I do," I said. "Misery loves company. Oh, wait—I mean, it's one of life's transcendent experiences."

She laughed. "Should I get knocked up on my honeymoon?"

"Maybe," I said. Nathan and I had been talking about kids when we conceived Mattie, but we hadn't meant to conceive her. "Is this an OK time?" he'd asked, and I'd breathed, "Yes," into his ear, without giving any thought to whether it really was, without giving it a second thought. But Binx we had planned. Binx we'd conceived in late June during a rather bloodless episode of let's-make-a-baby sex, and then his father left me at home, cells dividing in my uterus, and went off to fuck another woman. "Here's the thing about having kids. It's kind of exhausting trying to do the right thing all the time, and then half the time you get sabotaged. You know, breast is best and all that, so I nurse them both and take my ginormous prenatal vitamin and eat right and sterilize all the pain-in-the-ass pump equipment and take the pump to work and close my office door and sit there at my desk with my breasts hanging out of my shirt, the pump whirring away, and then after all that it turns out the bottles I was using leak chemicals into the milk."

"This is the story you want to tell me?" she said.

"So I'm feeding my baby chemicals," I said. "Cancer-causing chemicals? Early-onset puberty chemicals? Delayed-onset puberty chemicals? I can't even remember. Fuck-them-up-somehow chemicals."

"They fuck you up, your Mum and Dad," she said, and I supplied the next line, "They may not mean to, but they do."

It was true, wasn't it, and I was not exempt. As if it wasn't enough to worry that, as one parenting book said, if I picked my baby up too much, he'd never learn independence, and as another book said, if I didn't pick him up enough, he'd never learn trust, now I had to worry about the effects of divorce. Now my children's faces would be like the ones on the divorce mediation billboard I saw on the way to work—teary-eyed and trembling-lipped—and since I was bound to screw them up, my only hope was to screw them up in a sufficiently dramatic way, a way that led to a best-selling memoir, so they could make big bucks in the psychological freak show circuit.

"Jesus, girl," Alex said. "I thought you were trying to get me to procreate."

"I am, I am," I said. I dimly heard her say something about my needing to step up the propaganda efforts, to make frequent use of the words *cute* and *charming*. I saw the need, in my response, for a comic tone, but I couldn't muster it, stuck on the flip side. "If Nathan and I got divorced," I said, "what would I do about money?"

"What do you mean?"

"Divorce is expensive, right? I make fifty-five thousand a year. We have the mortgage, and the car payment, and Mattie's preschool. We're living paycheck to paycheck as it is. In fact we dip into the savings a little every month, and we only have that savings because of Nathan's book money. I'm embarrassed to tell you how much credit card debt we have. I don't know how this happened. Why have we been living like this? Why do I have cable? I shouldn't have cable."

"I thought you had satellite."

"I do, but that's not the point. I shouldn't have TV at all."

"What would you do with Mattie when you're trying to put Binx down for a nap?"

"I don't know. People did *something* before television. Not just at naptime. In general."

"They embroidered." She frowned. "How much credit card debt do you have?"

"Twenty thousand."

She let her jaw drop. "Holy shit. You've kept *that* secret." She took a big swig of her beer, as if to wash the information down.

"If we had to give back Nathan's advance, I don't even know where we'd get the money."

"Why would you have to give back Nathan's advance? Is there a problem with the book? I thought they were super gung-ho about it."

I looked at her. "Yes," I said. "They are."

"And why are we talking about divorce?"

"I miss Austin," I said.

"You haven't lived there in years."

"I know," I said. "I just realized I've been missing it for years. We had this great porch swing."

"You could get a porch swing here, couldn't you?"

I shrugged. "We don't really have a porch. Not a proper porch. It's just a fucking carport with a wall around it."

The look on her face said I'd been too emotional about this. "I like your porch," she said. "You have a hammock."

"Why do the same things happen to everyone?" I asked.

"What do you mean?"

"You think you're different. And then you find yourself talking about your mortgage."

"You don't have an adjustable, do you?"

"Fixed," I said.

"Thank God," she said. She swiped at her hair, sweaty and slipping from its pins, with the back of her cigarette hand.

"Don't set your hair on fire," I said. That had happened, once, years before, when we were passing a bowl back and forth, and she'd been a little careless with the lighter. She hadn't really set her hair on fire, just singed the tips a little, and it had seemed funny to us then and might have gone on seeming that way to me in memory if I hadn't had children and begun to picture them doing all the stupid things I'd ever done and more, and maybe not having the luck that had kept me from burning the house down or crashing my car at ninety miles per hour on a stretch of country road.

She ignored me. "What happened was, we grew up. And growing up is mortgages and IRAs and . . ." She waved her cigarette in the air, conjuring adulthood.

"You remember that quote from *The Breakfast Club*, 'When you grow up your heart dies'?" I said. "When I was a kid, I remember being like, 'That is so *true*.' You think when you're young it's a permanent state, or that you'll still be you even as you get older, but you're not."

"Sure you are," she said. "You're you with a mortgage and kids, instead of you with an adolescent chip on your shoulder."

"John Hughes is so wrong," I said. "Your heart doesn't die. I wish it did." Maudlin. I was drunk and quoting the movies of my youth and getting maudlin.

She looked at me, and I could see in her face the transition from one mode of behavior to another, as she shrugged off ironic banter in favor of sincerity. She could tell I needed sincerity. The next words out of her mouth were going to be, "Sweetie, what's wrong?" and it was her wedding and I couldn't tell her. I shouldn't even have said as much as I had, but what I had to say wanted out, a bird inside my mouth.

"I'm going to get a drink," I said. "You need a drink?" I left without waiting for her answer. I didn't go to the bar. I had reached the stage of drunkenness where it no longer seems pleasurable to keep drinking, an alarming place I hadn't visited in a number of years. A memory swam upward, of visiting a friend when I was in grad school, having a few too many at a party, then sitting down to e-mail Nathan, who was at home in our house in Austin, our little rental house. *I'm rather runk*, I wrote. *Where are you? Love, Sah*. He was delighted by that e-mail. Maybe it was the idea that my brain, even at its most befuddled, reached out in search of him. Maybe he just found it endearing that I misspelled my own name. He called me "Sah" sometimes after that, and whenever he did, I could count on him to beam at me, flush with love.

I gave the dance floor, all those happy jumping people, a wide berth, swinging out into the dark. I stumbled against a solid male torso, and a hand grabbed my arm. It proved to belong to Smith. "I'm too drunk," I said to him.

"I can't help you with that," he said. He said it pleasantly, but as I looked at him it suddenly occurred to me that he might know what Nathan had done, and that, not liking me, he might not disapprove, and I said, "I've never done anything to you," my eyes suddenly awash with tears.

He looked properly alarmed. "What are you talking about? What's wrong?"

"You don't think we're a good couple," I said. "You never have."

"I think you're happy," he said. "I always have."

"Happy families are all alike," I said. "In that they're all unhappy."

"That's a grim view for a guest at a wedding." He frowned. "What's going on with you?"

I rubbed at my eyes. I sniffed, loudly, like a child. I don't think he wanted to ask me the obvious question—whether we were an unhappy family—but he was too kind a person not to acknowledge my obvious distress. "What's wrong?" he asked again.

"Nathan cheated on me," I said. Just like that, it was out.

He hadn't known. I could tell by the look of horror on his face. Poor guy. He'd believed in Nathan, just like I had.

"I thought we were reasonably happy," I said. "But. Poof." I made two small explosions with my hands. "So you tell me," I said. "Is a happy life always an illusion?" Not that I thought he would know. Not that I thought anyone did.

He didn't answer. His eyes went past me, over my shoulder, and I turned to see that man, my husband, walking slowly toward us, my sweater dangling from his hand.

"Are you ready?" he asked. "It's time to go home."

CHAPTER FOUR

I woke alone. I had a hangover, which made me want to quote to Nathan the line from *Lucky Jim* about a small creature using my mouth first as its toilet and then its mausoleum. But Nathan wasn't there. I imagined, immediately, that he'd decamped to some seedy motel. But why a seedy motel? Why not a perfectly respectable Holiday Inn? I pictured him sitting on the bed in a sterile hotel room, flipping through the little booklet that tells what's on HBO. No one knew where he was, not his wife, not his children, as if he'd become a lonely traveling salesman, reclining in bed after bed next to a phone that was never going to ring. Nathan, I wanted to tell this imaginary figure, don't sit on the bedspread. Don't you remember that story—was it on *60 Minutes*?—about all that besmirches a hotel room bedspread? Don't you remember what horrors glowed beneath the infrared light? I remembered saying to Nathan, when we saw this story, that I would have preferred to live in ignorance, rather than to know that every time I crossed the threshold of a hotel room, I entered a hellhole of bloodstains and sperm.

Nobody would let me be ignorant. Not the Internet. Not CNN, with its relentless, maniacal ticker. Not *Newsweek*, which I'd taken to calling *Everything There Is to Be Afraid Of*.

"Catchy," Nathan had said. "I wonder why they don't change their name to that."

Not Nathan. Him least of all.

At the time when Nathan dropped his bomb, I was already feeling more uncertain, more anxious, more infected with a Thomas Hardy–style fatalism, than I could ever remember feeling in my life. I tortured myself with the horrors of the world. I couldn't stop myself from reading anything with a headline about a child who'd been hurt or killed or just gone missing. I stared at the little photos from Sears with the shimmery blue backgrounds reproduced on CNN.com. I let the cursor hover over the link, willing myself not to click on it, and then I always did. Was I hoping to steel myself, with this endless goggling at other people's misery, against anything of the sort happening in my own life? Was this what it meant to be a mother? Or was I affected by the state of the country, of the world? Had I been this anxious as a teenager in the days of nuclear escalation, when I'd wondered with Sting if the Russians loved their children too? Had I been this anxious after 9/11? I'd always considered myself an optimist—I *hated* Thomas Hardy. Where had that person gone? How was I to be an optimist in a country that seemed heavy with foreboding as the economy tailspinned, the war tumbled on, the terrorists trained, the polar bears drowned, and the president stood at the podium, peevishly squinting. What madness, in the face of all this, to have procreated not just once but twice, and so to square myself against an array of indomitable forces all hell-bent—it seemed to me, in the middle of the night, and sometimes during the day—on harming my children. What madness, now, to be confronted with the prospect of raising those children alone.

I considered getting up to discover where my husband had gone. If I tried to move, there was an excellent chance I was going to throw up.

Someone knocked on the door, and for a moment I thought it was Nathan, which would mean that this room was suddenly not ours but mine alone. "Mommy," Mattie said, "can I come in?" and then she opened the door without waiting for an answer. "Can I get in the big bed?" She clambered up next to me, said, "Hi, Mom!" her little voice ringing out exuberantly, and then she put two fingers in her mouth to suck and began twirling her hair with another, and her face went slack and sleepy.

"You're funny, Mattie," I said.

She took the fingers out of her mouth. "Why?"

"Because you turn on a dime."

She considered this and decided it not worthy of comment. The two fingers went back in her mouth. The one resumed twirling.

"Let's go back to sleep, okay?" I said. I pulled her against me and tucked the covers over her. I knew this wasn't going to work, but I pretended that it might. She snuggled against me, and I closed my eyes. Maybe I could pretend my hangover away, and the sum total of yesterday as well. Mattie's little feet were cold. I cupped one in my hand to warm it.

Mattie squirmed. She wriggled away from me and sat back up. "Daddy had a sleepover with me," she announced. Well, that explained Nathan's absence. The guest bed was in Mattie's room. The events of the night before were bleary.

Had I sanctioned his departure to the guest bed? I might have been concerned about the effect on Mattie of seeing us sleep apart, but maybe I was too drunk to debate it.

"I know," I lied. "He wanted to make sure you were sleeping well."

"Oh," she said. "I was. Did you have a good sleep?"

"Not really," I said.

"Why?"

"Mommy has a headache," I said.

"Why?"

"Mommy drank too much."

"Why?"

"Why indeed," I said. "Never drink too much, Mattie."

"Why you don't want me to?"

"Why?" I repeated. My head throbbed, as if in answer. I wanted to turn to Nathan to say, "I *drank* too much," which he would of course recognize as a line from the opening of "The Swimmer." I was full of literary allusions this morning. Without Nathan, that happy conspiratorial feeling of shared recognition, they weren't much fun, and the way they kept jumping up and down in my brain waving their hands like eager students made me feel dull and flat and alone. I had only my preliterate three-year-old to talk to, and she wasn't yet familiar with the works of John Cheever. "Goodnight Moon," I said to Mattie.

"Moo-night goon," she said, and laughed. This was something Nathan said to her. He liked to switch the first letters of words in phrases. Then she returned to the original topic. Weren't children supposed to be easily distracted? Why was my tenacious little offspring the one exception to that rule? "Why you don't want me to drink too much?"

"It gives you a headache."

"Too much milk?"

"No, not milk. Alcohol."

"*Al*cohol?" Her *l*'s were still *w*'s, so the word came out *Ow*-co-haw.

"Exactly," I said.

"Did Daddy drink too much?"

"Oh, Daddy," I said. "Daddy, Daddy, Daddy. Why don't you go ask him?"

"I want *you* to come."

What I wanted was to pass out, to enter a sensory deprivation chamber. To die, I might have said, but in the hyperbolic mode, not the suicidal one. I really didn't want to go find Nathan asleep in the guest bed, snuggling up to a cliché of estrangement, but it seemed a fine idea to me that Mattie go. I loved my daughter more than life, but I would have liked very much for her and her high-pitched little voice to be in another room. If you have kids, you know that you can say to your child that you don't feel well, but you can't expect any resulting change in her behavior. Small children don't take excuses. When Mattie was two and I was pregnant with Binx, she caught a stomach virus and almost immediately recovered, but not before she passed a far more vicious version to us. All night Nathan and I threw up, me heaving in the bathroom with my swollen belly pressed against the underside of the toilet, and the next day I was in a state of wonderment that I still had to take care of this child. No time off for illness, or hangovers, or severe emotional distress, let alone good behavior.

"Why don't you go by yourself?" I asked.

"I want *you* to come." She turned the volume on her voice up a notch, and I could see by the set of her jaw that my choices were to acquiesce or face down a tantrum. At that moment the baby shrieked. He woke up demanding, unlike his sister, who as a baby had lain in the crib babbling happily to herself until we went in to get her. "Mom," Mattie said. "Your baby's crying."

"Let's just lie here," I said, "and pretend he's not."

She regarded me a moment.

"Ignorance is bliss, little goose," I said.

"But he is crying," she said. "He is."

"I know."

"He *is* crying."

"I know," I said. "I know."

■

I changed the baby's diaper—an operation he protested vehemently every morning, firm in his belief that no activity should come before his milk—and took the kids into the kitchen, glancing, as we passed it, at the half-open door to Mattie's room, through which I could see only a pile of half-naked baby dolls on the floor, a jumble of limbs. In the kitchen I looked for the advance copies of Nathan's book—they had been on the table where we dumped the mail—but there was no sign of them either.

Mattie had some Cheerios and Binx had some milk and then some Cheerios, and I ventured a few tiny swallows of water. Nathan slept on, or maybe he lay there listening to Mattie say that she wanted to wear her striped dress and her party shoes, to Binx bang the tray of his high chair and shout, "Ah! Bwah!"—normal, everyday sounds from the normal, everyday scene that suddenly felt as fragile as a bubble headed for a pin. I was as alert to sounds of Nathan waking as I normally was to sounds of the baby. Part of me waited, and listened, and tried to guess what would happen when he finally emerged, while Mattie chattered happily and my hangover increased in amplitude and the strain of being on watch became increasingly difficult to bear.

Then I heard him stirring. A thump. A rustling. I tried to identify the movements that made the sounds. I heard him cross the hall into the bathroom. The toilet flushed. Footsteps approached. I seemed to be holding my breath, like I was the girl in the closet and he was the guy with the knife.

"Hi, Daddy," Mattie said, as casually as ever. Nathan stood in the kitchen doorway. Instead of his usual morning garb of boxers and a bathrobe he was wearing some of his clothes from the night before, his dress shirt and his suit pants now as rumpled as if he'd first balled them up in his hands. Maybe he'd slept in them. We looked at each other and I saw trepidation in his face. Like I was the guy with the knife.

My voice, when I spoke, was surprisingly neutral. "Good morning," I said.

He took a breath. Surprised? Relieved? Who knew what the hell he was thinking? "Good morning," he said. "How are you feeling?"

"Extremely unwell," I said. He flinched. "By which I mean hungover."

"Oh," he said. "I thought that might be the case. I'm sorry."

"I'll be fine," I said. "Thanks." I'd made no conscious decision to be so formal, but now I seemed to have committed to the mode and couldn't swerve from it. We were like two embarrassed college freshmen in a morning-after dorm room. "How are you feeling?" I asked.

"No hangover," he said, which was not, I noted, an answer to the question. "I didn't drink that much."

"Mommy doesn't want me to drink too much," Mattie said.

"Oh, no?" Nathan said. His eyes darted to her face, like he was relieved to have an excuse to take them from mine. He went to her, moving fast, scooped her out of her chair, and hugged her hard. "Who's my little goose?" he said. "Who's my goose?"

"I'm not a goose!" Mattie said. "I'm a kitty." She meowed, and Nathan meowed back.

I looked at Binx, who was grinning at the two of them, spasming his body in delight. "Ah!" he shouted, and Nathan turned and shouted it back and Binx laughed, and Mattie did, too.

"Nathan," I said. "What happened to your galleys?"

He looked at me, the smile dropping off his face. "I threw them away," he said. My gaze went to the kitchen trash can, and he said, "Not in there. Outside. In the Dumpster."

We didn't have trash pick-up, out in the county as we were, and so we had a big plastic storage bin outside, which we referred to as the Dumpster and treated as such, and when it got full Nathan hauled the disgusting, odiferous bags to the dump. Sometimes in hot weather he neglected this task long enough for maggots to erupt. "Outside?" I repeated. "With the maggots?"

"Yes," he said, and looked at me in such an intense and serious way I understood that throwing the books away was not, as I'd first thought, an attempt to keep me from searching for clues, but an attempt to prove to me that his offer not to publish had been genuine. He would, symbolically, throw the book away. He was willing to say that maggots were what it, and he, deserved.

"You said it was up to me?" I said. "You'll do whatever I want?"

His lips moved like he was saying yes, but he didn't quite make a sound. I felt like the judge addressing the defendant. The whole world hung on my next words.

"I want to work it out," I said. "I don't want anything to change."

He set Mattie down, steadying her with a hand on her shoulder. Then he crossed the kitchen to me and bent to hug me, burying his face in my neck. I put one hand on his back and then the other in his hair, and something inside me let go. My whole body sighed. He dropped to his knees and held on.

"What are you doing, Daddy?" Mattie asked.

"I'm thanking Mommy," he said, and I believed—I believed—that everything would be all right.

■

Here is where we should have had a fade to black. But this was life, and there were no merciful cutaways, only the two of us—his chin pressing rather painfully into my clavicle, his weight bending my upper back forward in an increasingly uncomfortable way—and within seconds of that glorious moment of happy conviction I felt myself drifting back toward the restless ambiguity that characterized my emotional state at that time and for a long time after. Picture a wrestling ring. Around the edge circled relief and love and anger and despair, and every so often a couple of them jumped into the ring and tangled and one of them emerged the victor, but mostly it was just them circling that blank gray ring in the center, the empty battleground.

Still, in that moment, with his breath warm against my skin, my hand in his hair, I wanted relief and love to stay with me. I willed them to. I thought of standing in the backyard with Nathan during a nighttime snowfall, years before, both of us with our faces turned up to watch the snow come down. He said, "Light speed," and I knew what he meant—that the sensation of watching those white flakes fall toward us, catching the light from our bright warm house behind, was like those moments in the Star Wars movies when they jump to light speed and all the stars rush in. But none of that needed to be explained, because we had the same mind.

"Why are you thanking Mommy?" Mattie said, and then, when Nathan didn't immediately respond, she said it again, louder.

"Um," he said, lifting his face. While I'd been watching the snow in our backyard, he'd clearly gone someplace too, a place from which it was a struggle to return. The thing about children, we'd often noted, is that they drag you relentlessly back to the here and now, which in our childless days Nathan and I had spent much of our lives escaping.

Matttie started bouncing on the balls of her feet, chanting, "Ay-ay-ay," in a robotic, unnatural voice. This was a tactic she used to get our attention, because, as much as we tried to hide it, she knew it drove us crazy.

"Hey, Mattie," Nathan said. He pushed off me, and squatted at her level.

"Ay-ay-ay," she said into his face, her teeth bared like a little animal's.

"What would you like to do today?"

This question stopped her. She cocked her head. "Why are we not going to school today?"

"Today is not a school day," he said. "It's Sunday."

"Why is it Sunday?" Without waiting for an answer, she turned and went over to her play refrigerator, whispering to herself as she opened the door. Now that she had his attention, she felt free to wander away. In that we seemed to be alike.

The baby ran out of the Cheerios he'd been happily eating and began to cry. Nathan scooped him out of the high chair and lifted him into the air. "Can you shake your head?" he said, demonstrating, and Binx shook his head wildly in return, laughing, showing his one hillbilly tooth. "So," Nathan said without looking at me, "do you still want to go to that festival, or do you feel too sick? Because I could just take the kids if you want to nap or something."

For a moment I didn't know what he was talking about. Then I remembered—there was a street fair in Chapel Hill, the sort of thing Nathan hated and which, up until this moment, he'd been strenuously refusing to go to, leading to the sort of argument in which I said he was only thinking of himself and not of the children's pleasure and he said I was stressing everyone out by insisting we do so-called fun things with the kids when they'd be just as happy at home. Now he was not only offering to go, but offering to take both kids by himself. I swear if a hair shirt had been available, he'd have donned it in an instant.

"That sounds good," I said. "Let's all go."

"Mattie," Nathan cried, "we're going to a festival!" And she, who probably had no idea what a festival was, caught the excitement in his voice and began to do what we called her happy dance, her little feet flying, and Nathan swung the baby in circles, and the baby shouted, "Ah!" and Mattie and Nathan shouted it back, all three of them laughing. I realized I was holding onto the seat of my chair with both hands, as if to keep myself in it. I looked at this delightful domestic scene—two children and their adoring father—and my heart broke and broke again. I thought, I'm a mother. A mother, a mother, a mother. I thought, Remember this. This is what you're trying to keep.

■

Funnel cakes and African dancers and bongos and beaded necklaces. Mattie was at her most delightful, dancing to the music and announcing to everyone that she was three and obsessed with party shoes, both of our children eliciting from strangers those high-wattage smiles you never see until you go out into the world toting a baby. Nathan pushed the stroller and I held Mattie's hand, and every so often Nathan reached for my free hand, brought it to his lips, and kissed it. The sun was out and the air was crisp. The fatty, greasy funnel cake had helped ease my hangover, and it was hard to remember why I'd ever held anything against anyone. We saw one of the other children from Mattie's preschool, a sweet, shy blond boy who liked to tell Mattie he loved her and hug her tightly, attentions she seemed to accept with a certain amount of perplexity. His parents were about our age, and they had a baby girl about Binx's age, and we stood together chatting in a pleased mirror reflection of each other while the preschoolers ran circles around us. Binx demanded to be picked up, so I held him near the other baby. They smiled at each other and touched hands, and then Binx put both his hands on her shoulders, leaned in, and gave her the gentlest of kisses on the mouth.

"Oh, so you love her, and her brother loves your sister," the father said. "This is going to work out well."

The mother laughed. "Boys start early, don't they?" she said.

"And they never stop," the father said. I laughed, but this more-or-less innocent moment gave me a pang, and for a little while my throat closed up again, and I had to watch the babies intensely because I couldn't look at anyone else, tears behind my eyes. Look at those babies, though. A moment I could live in, watching little fingers meet and part, the joy of those gummy smiles.

When I could join in the conversation again, I looked up at the parents and thought how happy they looked together, noting the fond glances, the casual touches, the way she leaned against him when he made a joke. Hadn't I heard that they'd had problems in the past? That at one point they'd come close to divorcing? Or was I making the whole thing up? I didn't know, but I decided to see them as survivors of a near-catastrophe, now firmly bonded together in the way Nathan and I were from here on out to be. When we walked away from them, in search of the balloon-animal maker they'd told us about, I took Nathan's hand. He had to push the stroller with one hand and hold mine with the other, which made for awkward maneuvering, but he held on anyway, until Mattie spotted our target and ran ahead, and I had to let go.

CHAPTER FIVE

I knew my husband. I was confident of that. No matter what, I knew him. I knew that he didn't like tomatoes until he was twenty-five. I knew that after we saw *The Matrix* he cried out, "Keanu!" in his sleep, and then insisted that I'd misheard. I knew that his voice softened and his jokes grew sillier in the presence of cute girls, and I knew that this was less true now than when I first met him, so that no one but me might detect the change. There was no undoing my knowledge of him. Mattie would be sure to tell me, when she was sixteen or so, "You don't know me!" and she'd be wrong, because I'd always know how her voice sounded—weirdly authoritative despite its high pitch—when she was three and said, "From now on when I'm naughty I want to decide my punishment." And maybe I'd say to Nathan, ten years after our divorce, if we got one, that he didn't know me anymore, and I'd be wrong, because he'd always know what animal sounds I made in labor, he'd always know I was ticklish only in the arches of my feet. We want to be known when we do, and we want to be unknown when we don't, just like we want someone to touch us and kiss us until we don't anymore. We make our bodies off-limits again, but still that other person did touch us, he ran his fingers down our inner thighs, he slipped his tongue inside our mouth.

Nathan, my Nathan. He was so careful, even self-righteous, about what we owe to others, the sort to overpay when it came to splitting the bill, rather than risk shorting someone, or, perhaps even worse, risk confronting them about their own stingy inclination to put in two dollars less than they owed. He'd once refused to eat a thirty-dollar roast he'd accidentally overcooked because he said he'd ruined it. He'd made what should have been rare and tender into something tough and common, he said, and he threw the meat thermometer into the garbage, claiming it had betrayed him, and it was only my intervention that stopped him from tossing the roast in after it. Finally, after much discussion, he agreed to cut it up and use it for sandwiches. Hard to believe that this person could have not only cheated on me but written a book about having done so, and then could go on living with that brand of ruination now, could make oatmeal for everyone in the morning and remember that I didn't want raisins in mine. I was relieved, of course. I ate my oatmeal and watched Nathan read the *Times*, absentmindedly doling out Cheerios to Binx, and debated with Mattie the wearing of sundresses when it was under sixty degrees. I was relieved.

What was it, after all, that could be said to be ruined? I'd rubbed Binx's head and kissed Nathan good-bye and dropped Mattie at preschool with five magic hugs and five magic kisses, and now I was driving the usual way to work, the usual trees flying by outside my window. Life was going on as it always did. In troubled times, I still had my children and my house and my job and apparently my marriage, and as long as no one found out what had happened, Nathan could still have his book, and I wouldn't have to fork over $50,000 like a blackmail victim. I wasn't going to look at the book, I wasn't going to think about the book, the book would be published, the book might bring in some money and so was just a means to an end. Fiction, fiction, it was all fiction. I still loved Nathan, and he said he still loved me. I believed that if Nathan could keep it together, everything would be fine. I didn't give much thought to whether I could keep it together. I was used to the answer to that question being, on a large scale, yes, automatically yes, no need to even ask. The ability to keep it together was my essential quality.

It wasn't as though we'd lived together, in the years before this, in an eternal bliss of peaceful intimacy. I knew as well as anyone the rhythms of life with another person, the days of kisses, casual touches, easy familiarity, the days of snappish voices, rolling eyes, weary familiarity, the way that as one state of being gave way to another, the other seemed distant and fantastical. I'd thought, How could I ever have married you? And I'd thought, How could I ever have been mad at you? And then I'd thought those things again and again and again.

This was different. No, it wasn't different. The offense was larger, yes, than any previous ones. So what? Husbands, wives—countless others had survived it.

He *said* he still loved me. The ruination was in my phrasing. He still loved me. I corrected myself. He loved me. That was what he'd said.

What is *it*, anyway, this thing that we keep together, or lose?

■

And then, at last, I was at my desk, in my safe, functional office with its ergonomic rolling chair, everything I needed to know neatly labeled in a file. I sipped the coffee I'd made an hour ago but not yet tasted—still hot, in the heavy-duty travel mug Nathan had bought me—and watched the e-mail messages pop up on my computer screen. A normal day. At work it was just a normal day.

I had never cheated on Nathan. Why not? I could have. I could have chosen to. Like anyone I'd had those moments—too much to drink, the man lighting your cigarette, meeting your gaze a little too long. There had been that guitar player promising he'd teach me to like Rush, if I just gave him a chance, that French poet murmuring about my eyes, my smile. And there had been Rajiv.

I opened my personal e-mail account. I kept a folder in it labeled "Austin Friends," and though I'd added some e-mails from other people to it—not because Nathan was paranoid but because I was—mostly I kept it to collect the e-mails from Rajiv. *Hey lady*, the last one said. *I've been rereading you, so lately you're in my head. How are you? R.* He'd written it more than a year ago, and I had never answered. Why had I never answered? There was something of the love note, of the secret, in the use of that initial rather than his name. Wasn't there? I looked at all eleven of his e-mails. All signed like that. He'd written ten times over a period of about a year, between the last time I'd seen him and my wedding. And then once about two years ago—a brief, belated congratulations on Mattie's birth. Then, a year ago, *I've been rereading you*. Then nothing.

Dear Fan of Me, he'd written once, in reply to an e-mail

I'd sent, congratulating him on acceptance of one of his films to a festival, a piece of news I'd gotten from Helen. *Thank you for your adoration. Though Central Headquarters of Rajiv Asthana are closed today in observance of Labor Day, I nevertheless labor in this response to cast a little of my light on your life, as do my brief but dazzlingly intense films. If you have not yet experienced the profundity of my work, my wisdom, go now, to festivals across the land, and seek it out. May it be an incredible journey full of twists and turns, peaks, valleys, and plains in between. And may you, in the end, discover that the very thing for which you had been searching was right there in front of you all along. Yours ever so sincerely, R.*

And then he'd written, all alone at the very end, the small word *hi*.

Didn't he have a serious girlfriend now? Wasn't that what Helen had said? I quit the account. I had things to do. At work it was just a normal day.

But, no. There was no normal anymore. There was no safe. Because as I was doing my job, catching up on e-mail, my throat relaxed without my having noticed it, I was all at once visited by the memory of my drunken confession to Smith at the wedding. My throat seized shut again. Smith knew. In my own effort to forget what Nathan had told me, I'd forgotten Smith knew. And who might he have told by now? His Hitchcock girlfriend, that psycho gal? Was the word even now speeding along a network of Web designers and part-time painters and NPR fund-raisers and editors, on its way to everyone I knew? If everyone knew, and Nathan found out that everyone knew, he would crumple, and our fragile experiment would come to an end. There were few things Nathan feared more than other people thinking badly of him, and under the combined weight of guilt and judgment he wouldn't be able to function, he wouldn't be able to stay. He'd realize, if he hadn't already, that publishing the book or not publishing the book was not just about me. He'd realize that he couldn't endure a book tour if everyone knew, couldn't endure standing behind a table piled with books that announced *Infidelity*, couldn't endure the questions about how much was real, how much was true. Or could he? Could he endure that?

I started three or four different e-mails to Smith, but it was too delicate a thing to phrase properly, and finally I surrendered to the inevitable and looked up his number at work. I didn't have it—why would I have it? I'd never before felt the need of any communication with him that couldn't be dispatched by e-mail. We didn't have a phone-call friendship. At home, when I saw his name on the caller ID, I didn't answer. I said, "It's Smith," and Nathan picked up the phone. Dialing his number now, I was as nervous as a twelve-year-old girl calling a boy in her Spanish class with a made-up question about the homework.

He picked up. "This is Smith," he said.

"It's Sarah," I said. "I need to talk to you about the other night."

A brief silence while, perhaps, he absorbed not only what I'd said but the fact that it was me on the phone. Then he said, cautiously, "OK."

"I don't really want to discuss it," I said. "I just want to make sure you don't repeat it."

"Repeat what?"

I had failed to consider that he might have been too drunk to remember. I could have smacked myself in the face for my stupidity. "If you don't know, then we don't need to talk," I said. "Are you saying you don't know?"

"No," he said. "I know."

"Well, then why are you pretending you don't?"

"I'm not."

"Never mind. I just wanted to tell you that Nathan and I are going to work through this, and I think it would make things easier if nobody else knew about it. Otherwise we'll both feel like we're being watched, you know?"

"I won't tell anybody," he said. "You know I won't tell anybody."

"That's true," I said. Of course he wouldn't tell anybody. Smith, Man of Honor, was what Nathan liked to call him. "I should have remembered that."

"I wish I didn't know myself," he said. "I can't believe Nathan would do that. I mean, my God, it changes my whole conception of him. Who is he? How could he do that, when you were pregnant? You were pregnant, for God's sake! Can I even still be friends with him?"

I couldn't answer. I tried, but my throat was so tight now I couldn't even speak, and so, in surrender, I started to cry.

"Hey," he said. "Hey, that was really stupid, I'm sorry."

I took a deep breath. I tried to remember the last time I'd cried—not just teared up at anything on television about children, but really, truly cried.

"I won't tell anybody," he said again.

I couldn't remember. Strange. Before I had children I used to cry out of frustration or anger every once in a while, and now I didn't do that anymore. Had becoming a mother made me tougher? Now it took adultery to make me cry.

"Listen," Smith said, sounding desperate, "can I take you to lunch? We can talk more. Maybe you need to talk."

"I don't want to talk," I managed to say, but he must not

have understood me, because he said he would pick me up at twelve thirty and hung up the phone.

■

My job, as the business manager of the Department of Neurobiology, was one I'd arrived at more or less accidentally, and then proven to be good at. I'd started as a secretary in the department, as a charity hire. The husband of the then-chair was friends with my thesis adviser from graduate school, and my adviser said, "Hey, can you help a starving poet find a job?" It didn't hurt that I could type eighty-two words a minute, a skill that would have been more suited to a fiction writer like Nathan, who still typed with two fingers after years at the computer. I'd never written a poem at eighty-two words a minute. I was slow. I was agonizingly slow. More than once I'd spent a week on a line.

But at work I was fast, and efficient, so much so that when the grants manager left, they offered me his job, and when the business manager retired, they offered me hers. Now all the administrative types in the department were my employees, something that had by this point almost stopped seeming strange. Two of those employees had been working there long before I had, and had, in fact, treated me as upperclassmen treat a freshman when I'd first arrived, alternately teasing me and taking me under their wing. One of the women, the receptionist, Kristy, was actually younger than I was, but she'd grown up faster—married at nineteen, first kid at twenty-one, and now she was pregnant with her third. The other woman, Tanya, who was the chair's secretary, was in her late thirties, but she, too, seemed older, or at least older than my friends seemed at that age. Kristy and

Tanya belonged to a culture that, before them, I'd observed only in passing—they wore fake nails, went to church but drank hard, supported certain NASCAR drivers. Kristy had a Jeff Gordon jacket, which she wore on race days with a hairpin that had his number sticking out of it, a red 24 balanced at the apogee of her curly bleached-blond hair. For years they'd been telling me they were going to take me to a local track and show me how to parade around in a tank top and Daisy Dukes, eating fried bologna sandwiches. Once, on Valentine's Day, they'd taken me to the local sex shop, where they'd debated buying lingerie to please their husbands and I'd marveled at the vast array of dildos, and then to Bojangles for greasy, salty biscuits and fries. They'd both come over strange when I'd been made the business manager, but they were over it now, or at least I thought so. Kristy liked to call me "Boss" when I asked her to do things, to remind me that even if I was in charge she retained the right to tease me.

She wasn't at her desk when I went out at 12:28 to meet Smith. I assumed she was on her lunch break, but she wasn't. She was outside smoking a cigarette, something she persisted in doing even though she was six months pregnant. If I'd smoked while pregnant, I would have done it in secret, ashamed—I didn't even drink wine in public in my third trimester, though I had an occasional glass at home—but Kristy just stood there, three feet from the entrance to the building, puffing away, apparently oblivious to the looks she got. Was she making a statement? Did she just not care? It was hard to say, but I thought it was the latter. I disapproved of her smoking, but admired her "I am what I am" attitude.

"Where are you off to?" she said when she saw me. I

usually packed a lunch and ate it in the tiny break room, next to the tiny fish tank Tanya maintained.

"I'm going to lunch."

"With Nathan?"

"No, he's home with Binx." I was reluctant to tell her who I was going with, and reluctance like that was the sort of thing she was hardwired to notice.

"Who is it, then? Your boyfriend?"

Smith's car turned into the drive, and he waved as he went past us, turning around in the circle to return facing out.

"Cute," Kristy said. "Does Nathan know?"

"Ha ha, Kristy," I said. I couldn't look at her. "Shouldn't you be working?"

"Nothing going on in there," she said. "I've been reading *People* all morning."

"Shh," I said. "Don't tell your boss." I headed for the car, tossing a "See you later" over my shoulder.

"See you," she called.

When I opened the car door, Smith was leaning toward me, but looking at Kristy. I could tell from his face he could hardly believe what he saw. I got in the car and shut the door hard, as though sufficient force could make Kristy and her stomach and her cigarette disappear, and forestall the conversation I knew Smith and I were about to have.

"Should she be smoking?" he asked.

"Of course not." I put on my seat belt with unnecessary care, strangely reluctant to look at him. "She says it will keep the birth weight down."

He reacted with such horror his body jerked backward. "That's why she's doing it?"

"She's doing it because she's addicted. That's a joke she makes."

"You think it's funny?"

"No, Smith, Jesus. I don't think it's funny. I think she should quit smoking. What would you like me to do, call Social Services?"

Smith jerked up the parking brake and got out of the car. It was a mark of his agitation that he didn't turn the car off, seriously as he took the environmental strictures of Al Gore. It was a mark of my shock that I did nothing, just sat there and watched through the window with my mouth hanging open as he crossed behind the car and up the sidewalk to Kristy. She looked at him with a curiosity that hardened into anger as he said whatever he said, and I watched as he gesticulated and she moved her head from side to side in that "Oh no you didn't" way—a pantomime of middle-class liberal righteousness colliding with working-class conservative righteousness. She inhaled elaborately and blew the smoke out in his face, and then he snatched the cigarette and dropped it on the ground. She was yelling, her mouth open, her arms flapping out at the sides, a giant pregnant bird. I reached for the door handle, steeling myself to enter the fray. I had no idea what I was going to say. Did I think she should be smoking? No. Did I think he was right to tell her so? No. The only statement that came to mind was, "I can't handle this right now," which I didn't imagine would be particularly useful. And then, abruptly, her arms stopped flapping, her hands went to her face, and she started to cry. She rocked forward, and Smith caught her, patting her on the back. They stood there a moment like that, strangers embracing on the sidewalk, and he murmured something in her ear.

The sight of Kristy in tears astonished me. I thought of her as brash, tough, the sort of girl who got into parking-lot fights in high school. She was hardly a candidate for a public meltdown, although of course she was pregnant, and there were the hormones to contend with. And really, I had no idea what went on in her life. That thought hit me with the force of a new idea. I knew her husband drove a tow truck but not whether he cheated on her, or hit her, or loved her like there was no tomorrow. Really I had no idea what went on in anyone's life, not even Nathan's. What had made Nathan value the moment over the lifetime? Why was Smith hugging Kristy, a woman he didn't even know, when he hadn't hugged me in my moment of crisis, though he'd known me for years? There he was in full view through the windshield taking her and her extra weight against him and, just for a moment, holding her up. Why wasn't somebody, anybody, holding me right now? Why was I sitting alone in a car watching two strangers embrace?

Abruptly, as if remembering herself, Kristy pushed away. She wiped her face on the back of her hand. She pulled open the heavy glass door, refusing Smith's attempt to help her, and disappeared inside.

Back in the driver's seat, Smith wore an expression of self-satisfaction as he eased the car out onto the road. "You left the car running," I said. "What would Al Gore say?"

"Oh, shit," he said. "I guess I was fired up." He smiled at me, this oddly hopeful smile, and all at once I was furious.

"If you think she's going to stop smoking," I said, "you're batshit insane."

"Maybe," he said. "But at least I said something."

"What you did was upset a pregnant woman and create another problem for me. I called you to talk about a problem, and you made me another one."

"Why would she hold what I said against you?"

"That's a dumb question."

"I think the health of her baby is a little more important than tension between the two of you."

"Which brings me back to my original point. She's not going to quit because you told her to."

"You don't know that, do you," he said. "Sometimes when we realize how other people see us, we see ourselves in a new light."

"Well, what light do you see yourself in if I tell you that you're unbelievably self-righteous?"

"I'd say maybe you should look in the mirror."

"Excuse me?"

"You're self-righteous," he said. "And you're rude."

I stared at him. He stared back, still flush with the proselytizer's zeal. *Rude?* "That's great," I said. "That's just great. Let me out of the car."

Now he looked sorry. "Sarah—"

"Let me out of the fucking car!"

He pulled over. In my agitation I forgot to unbuckle the seat belt and strained against it for a full five seconds trying to climb out, and then he tried to help me by unbuckling it just at the moment I realized and reached for the buckle myself, and I ended up smacking his hand away before I tumbled out of the car, as if this was a first date gone wrong. "Sarah," he called again, but I started to run, and I ran back to the corner where you turned for my building, and then I slowed to a walk in case anyone saw me, running and desperate and disheveled in my professional clothes. Thanks a lot, Smith. You've been a big help.

Kristy wasn't outside anymore, and I hoped she'd be in the break room eating lunch so I could make it back to the sanctuary of my office without encountering her. But when

I walked in she looked up from *People* with a fighting expression. "Who was that asshole?" she said, in a loud and carrying voice.

"I'm sorry about that, Kristy," I said. "He had no right."

"No shit he had no right. Who was he, anyway?"

"He's my husband's best friend."

"Oho." She lowered her voice, beckoned me closer. I stepped up to her desk. "So he's giving me a hard time about smoking when he's running around with his best friend's wife?"

I blanched and said, "No," a reaction that did nothing to persuade her she was wrong.

"What's worse?" She looked around like she was playing to the audience at a talk show. "A cigarette every now and then, or putting it to your friend's lady on the sly?"

"That depends on your point of view," I said.

"Oho, point of view," she said. "Point of *view*. Is that what you call it?"

"Kristy," I said. "Just stop it. Stop it now."

She looked at me in some surprise. "Hey," she said, "I'm just messing with you. I know you and Nathan got a good thing going."

I took a breath. I closed my eyes. I felt my head shake a little, more like a tremor than a *no*. Then I opened my eyes. She was looking at me with a combination of alarm and curiosity. I pushed off from her desk like it was the wall of a swimming pool, propelling myself toward my office. "Hey," she called after me, sounding genuinely worried now. "Hey, Sarah. Look, I was just—"

"It's OK," I said without looking back. I shut my office door.

I'd started an e-mail to Tanya, before the phone call

to Smith. It was still up on the screen. *Remind me*, it said, and nothing else, and I could no longer remember what I'd wanted her to remind me. And it didn't even say *Remind me*, I saw now, but *Rewind me*. An interesting typo, although given the distance of the *w* from the *m*, you couldn't really call it a typo. More of a Freudian slip. Yes, please, rewind me. Be kind, rewind. No fight with Smith. No unwanted honesty from Nathan. No Nathan ever doing what he had done at all. I closed my eyes and pictured casters turning, and the idea of going backward was so compelling that when I opened my eyes I nearly believed I'd achieved it. The mind's experience of the world, that's all that matters. If you smile, you'll begin to feel the corresponding emotion. If you tell yourself something never happened, then it never ever did.

The phone rang. It was Nathan. He wanted to know where the diaper bag was. So I told him, because it was just a normal day, and telling him where he could find what he'd lost was one of the things I normally did. I always knew where his wallet was, his phone, his keys, and when I got sick of his pitiful attempts to locate them—he'd drift around the house picking up objects and putting them down with such an air of hopelessness he might as well have been keening softly—I'd walk right over to the pile of newspaper on the table and lift it up and lo and behold, what should be beneath it but his keys. Sometimes his ineptitude annoyed me, and then when he asked where his keys were, I said, "How should I know?" or "If I gave you a million dollars, could you find them yourself?" Recently, not too long ago, Nathan had spent a Saturday morning struggling with a section of the book he was working on and then, much later in the day than he'd intended, was trying to get out to the grocery store but couldn't find his keys, and when I'd asked that question, he'd snapped, "Why are you being such a bitch?" in front of Mattie, who said, on cue, as if we were all actors in some sort of horrible domestic drama, "Why is Mommy a bitch?" Then Nathan overwhelmed us both with apologies, me and Mattie, who had no idea, really, what he was sorry for, but gleaned from the whole experience that *bitch* was an awfully exciting word.

And these are the ways we drive each other crazy, men and women, husbands and wives. He asks me, for the millionth time, if I've seen his keys. He wants me, for the millionth time, to drop what I'm doing and tend to his needs. And I snap at him. And his feelings are hurt, because all he did was ask me to help him find his keys, and I know he has trouble finding things and why do I have to get so mad about it, when all he's trying to do is go buy groceries for his family, and then he trots out the b-word, and even though he apologizes, none of it goes away, not my irritation, not his. It subsides. Yes, it subsides, unless you become one of those couples for whom it doesn't, who start saying things at dinner parties like, "Well, my wife says I'm a fucking retard," and "My husband calls me Cruella De Vil," dragging everyone around them into an Ingmar Bergman film.

The first year we lived together, Nathan's keys went missing for weeks, until I found them one morning inside a folded umbrella, which was leaning against the hall table where we normally dropped our keys when we came in the door. I had a flash of inspiration, turned that umbrella over, and they dropped into my hand with a satisfying jangle. Nathan had still been asleep. I'd crept into the room and jingled the keys before his eyes until they opened, and then I watched delighted comprehension dawn on his face before he reached up to grasp the keys, to touch my fingers. He said, "You found them?" and looked at me like I was the one who would always know what he needed, would always know exactly where it was to be found. And how would I have ever gotten to be that person, if he had never lost anything?

■

At quarter after seven I walked into a quiet house. Nathan was at the stove, the scent of garlic in the air. "Hey," he said. He handed me a glass of wine.

"You already got the kids down?" I asked. "Wow."

"I thought you could use a quiet evening," he said.

I said that was great and thanked him, though I wished Binx was still awake. Usually I nursed him when I got home, and breasts don't adjust quickly to a change in plans, so I'd have to pump for the third time that day, and I hated pumping. Funny that in the face of paradigm-shifting events I was still capable of annoyance over such a minor thing.

"I'm working on my fifties housewife routine," Nathan said.

"Shouldn't you be in a pretty dress then? With your hair all . . . " I made curls with my fingers in the air. Recently an old magazine article had circulated among our friends on e-mail, one of those shockingly, hilariously sexist pieces featuring advice to women about greeting your husband at the door with a martini, never disturbing him with your problems, keeping every hair in place—one of those things too ludicrous to have ever been something people believed. Who ever took that seriously, this notion that to be a wife was to be a walking mannequin?

"I thought about the dress," Nathan said. "But I thought you might find it disturbing if I raided your closet."

I laughed. "If I came home and you were wearing my black dress . . . "

"High heels . . . "

"Lipstick . . . "

"A thong."

"I don't own a thong."

"Hey," he said. "I havc my own, of course."

"Is it red and lacy?" I asked. "I hope it's red and lacy."

"Of course," he said, "because I—" The phone rang. It was sitting on the kitchen counter. I picked it up and checked the caller ID, saw it was Smith, and without thinking handed the phone to Nathan.

He answered. "Hello?" A beat. His expression changed from lingering amusement to puzzlement, worry. My throat clenched. He gave me an apologetic look, held up one finger, walked out of the room. I heard the door to his study close. I walked over to the kitchen table and sat down. I listened to the murmur of Nathan's voice, which kept spiking louder in ways that did not bode well. I drank my glass of wine. I got up, turned the stove off, and poured another glass. I pictured myself squeezing the stem of the glass until it shattered. I pictured the mess that would make. I imagined the sticky wine, the blood. I waited.

■

"Can I help?" Rajiv had asked, the night before Nathan and I moved away from Austin. He'd been surveying the nearly empty room and drinking a beer while I struggled to pack a box with exactly the number of books that would fit. We had a great many books, and only so many boxes.

"I'm fine, thanks," I said. I glanced up at him, and then

back down. Rajiv, when he gave you his attention, gave it to you entirely. Mr. Intense Eye Contact, Nathan liked to call him. Because of this, and the extremity of his beauty, I'd always been prone to nervous giggling in his company. I wasn't quite sure what he was doing here, on our last night in town. We'd been friendly the last year or so, ever since Helen had introduced us, but he was really her friend. And he wasn't in our program—he was studying film—so I saw him only from time to time. He'd come tonight with Helen, who was in the bathroom helping Nathan sort through the cabinets. I could hear the murmur of Nathan's voice, the words *feminine hygiene*, then her laughter.

"I brought you a going-away present," Rajiv said.

I sat back, surprised. "It's not a book, is it?"

"Well, yeah." He grinned. "It *is* a book. Not just any book. It's *the* book."

"The Bible?"

He laughed. "Kind of." He held out a small black paperback.

"Where did that come from?" I asked, and at his puzzled look, I added, "Looked like you conjured it." On my feet now, I took the book. It was a copy of Denis Johnson's *Jesus' Son*, dog-eared in several places. And why was he giving it to me? I flipped open to the first marked page. *The door opening*, I read. *The beautiful stranger. The torn moon mended.* "It's my copy," said Rajiv. "The one I used to carry on the T." And then a lightbulb—I remembered a long conversation in the corner of a party, me and him, this book and how much we loved it, the two of us quoting lines back and forth. He told me how he used to carry a copy in his coat pocket on his way to the office job in Boston that he'd hated, how it was a comfort to know it was there. I'd never seen Rajiv passionate—he was a relatively quiet guy, the kind who fades a little at a party until suddenly he drops the perfect quip and steals the scene. Did I really think *fades*? No, honestly, I didn't, because his appearance was so striking that when he was in my vicinity I never stopped being aware of him, and I was certain no other woman did either. Look how they giggled. Look how they put their hands on his forearm when he unleashed that dry wit, how they leaned forward so that their breasts brushed against his skin.

"How can you not want him?" I'd asked Helen, not long before.

"I don't know," she said. "I think looking at him too long might blind you."

"Wow," I said to Rajiv. "Thanks." I took my time closing the book. "I'm not sure I deserve this."

He said, "I'm a little in love with you."

"What?" I said. "No, you're not."

His eyebrows jumped. "I thought I was so obvious."

"You? You're not obvious about anything." I thought, but had the sense not to say, that the short film of his I'd seen had been so subtle, I'd struggled to grasp its meaning. At another party he'd described for me the plays of Horton Foote, whose dialogue was entirely about what went unspoken. Maybe that was why he liked me—the same reason Nathan did—because I showed great interest in conversations like this. You'd think everybody in school for film or writing would have, but no, there was too much talk about romance and money and television and posturing about one's own torrid past and heady future. I liked—Rajiv liked, Nathan liked—to stand around and talk about dialogue. "You're never obvious," I said.

"Except right now," he said. "Now I'm obvious." He

waited. He was not going to try to kiss me. He was not going to ask me for anything. I knew that. He was not the sort to press. He just waited to see what I would say. And what would I say? My God, there was nothing to say, was there? And yet wasn't it nice to be loved? And wasn't he beautiful? Wasn't he funny, wasn't he talented, wasn't he smart? Wasn't he not unlike Nathan, the man packing my tampons in the other room?

"You're an amazing guy," I said. The clichés sprouted in my mind: You're a great friend, maybe in another life. But there was no other life, only this one. For a wild moment I thought I should just kiss him. I opened the book again, another dog-eared page. *And you, you ridiculous people, you expect me to help you*, it said.

"So I know the last thing you need is another book," he said briskly, "but it's small, and I think we can fit it in." He crouched, peered into the box, reached a hand up for the book, not looking at me. I handed it to him and watched as he made room. "Just fits," he said.

I'd been unhappy about leaving Austin, though I'd tried not to say so to Nathan. But right then, my eyes on Rajiv, I was relieved. There'd be nothing I could do about what he'd just said, no temptation to consider it at all.

For years I kept the book underneath a pile of junk in one of my desk drawers at home. Not that there was any need to hide it. Nothing about it would have caused Nathan a moment's suspicion. But I liked having it hidden, secret, a talisman. I liked, sometimes, on bad days, or days when nostalgia rose up and briefly seized my heart, to take it out and flip to the dog-eared pages, trying to guess what line Rajiv had meant to mark. When I moved out of my study I put the book on the shelf next to our other copy. "Oh," Nathan said when he noticed it there. "I didn't know we had two copies of this."

"Yeah," I said, and that was all.

■

I found Nathan sitting on the floor in his study, cross-legged with his head in his hand. The phone was in his lap. He'd neglected to turn it off, so the busy signal beeped angrily. He lifted his head when I came in, his face a picture of misery.

"I'm sorry, Nathan," I said. "I didn't mean to tell him."

"Don't apologize to me," he said. "I don't deserve that. I should be apologizing to you, a thousand times a day, a million times a second."

"I don't think that's possible," I said. This was supposed to be a mild joke, but Nathan gasped like I'd punched him in the stomach.

"He said he doesn't know who I am anymore," he said. "He said if there's a side to take, he's on yours."

I didn't know what to make of that statement, or of my reaction to it, which was surprise and gratification and a dash of anger. "There's no side to take," I said. I sat on the floor beside him. His eyes searched my face. "There's no side," I said.

"Are you sure you want this?" he said. "Are you sure you want me?"

"Yes," I said, because although at that moment I really wasn't sure, it was hard to see what good any other answer would do. The only thing I was sure of was that I didn't want every evening to end with him crying. So I touched his cheek, and we had sex, the kind of tender, grateful sex that sometimes happens when you've come very close to believing it's over, and I managed somehow, miraculously, not to think about him and the other woman, what we were doing and what he'd done with her. I found that I didn't much want to kiss him, though. I didn't really want to look him in the eye.

CHAPTER SIX

Why'd you do that? That's what we asked Mattie when she dumped her plate on the floor, or hit the cat, or threw a toy. And she said her food was too hot, when it hadn't been, or that the cat had been about to scratch the couch, when he'd been sleeping peacefully on the floor, or that honk monsters were trying to get the toy, when unless we were very wrong about the world honk monsters didn't exist. She had no clue why she did these things. She was three. But we kept on asking. For some reason *why* was the main thing we wanted to know. We taught her to offer explanations even when they made no sense at all. Maybe it doesn't matter why you do something. Maybe it just matters that you do it. What good does it really do you, the why?

I do wonder, though, I can't help but wonder, why I tried so hard in the days after Nathan's confession to proceed like everything was fine. Wasn't I supposed to throw him out immediately and burn all his possessions in the yard, according to the new story of Western womanhood, the one that doesn't accept infidelity, that doesn't make standing by your man the primary virtue—that, in fact, holds women who stand by their man in contempt? I should say that when my grandmother told me, "You do what you have to do," she was talking about her own mother's efforts to keep her family intact while her husband slept with his secretary and otherwise lived out the masculine cliché. Here I was, eighty supposedly liberating years later, making the same attempt.

But I didn't have to keep him around, did I, not like my great-grandmother had to keep her husband, the provider, the man of the house. I wasn't even reliant on Nathan for financial support, although it would be awfully hard to manage the bills if we had to pay for two places to live. And I didn't know how we'd handle the child care, or how I'd be able to do his chores in addition to my own. How I'd ever get to see a movie, or run out to meet friends for a drink. How I'd pass the lonely evenings. How I'd meet somebody else and bring myself to take off my clothes in front of him. Because I'd want somebody else, wouldn't I? Sooner or later I would. The truth is, it's hard to go it alone. Few of us are exempt from the longing for another. Each of us half of a heart locket, a lonely puzzle piece. If we weren't we wouldn't be so determined to jam ourselves together.

Would it help to know that I'm a middle child? That I'm a Pisces? That my older sister was an agent of chaos, and as a result I am deeply conflict-averse? In grad school Helen and Nathan liked to joke that I had a strangely sanguine temperament for a writer. Where were my debilitating depressions? My wild convictions of genius? Sometimes I worried that my lack of emotional upheaval meant my work wasn't any good. I thought perhaps my sister should have been the poet, though *I hate you I hate you I hate you* was all I could imagine her writing.

It's not that I don't have a temper. It's not that I can't be mean. I am just as capable of it as my sister ever was, and isn't that the horror, the horror? When Mattie reached two, the age of defiance, I started to feel anger at her that strained toward release like a dog that wants off the leash. Once, she bit me, and I bit her back hard enough to leave the imprint of my teeth in her skin. I'd never before hurt her in any way. Before she started to cry, she said, "You bit me," in a voice of utter astonishment, and I knew that I'd radically altered her sense of the world. I'd revealed what I was capable of, to her, my tiny child, and I hadn't wanted her to know.

The incident confirmed what I already knew—it wasn't safe for me to get angry. Nathan used to say I had no cruising speed. I was Princess Pliable or I was Queen Demented Rage. Those were his names, not mine, and you have to wonder why the nice me was only a princess while the nasty me got to be a queen. Queen Demented Rage—only Nathan knew her. I never fought with anybody else. For a long time he saw that as a sign of the health and openness of our relationship, and then he started to see it as a sign that I managed to hold back the worst of myself from everyone but him.

I'm happy to talk more about my family, since we now believe that the family explains nearly everything, which is one reason it's so terrifying to have children. Sometimes I looked at Binx and thought that whether he turned out a diplomat or an actor might depend entirely on whether we chose to have a third child.

I grew up in Cincinnati, in a four-bedroom house in a neighborhood called Mount Lookout. My father is an engineering professor and my mother is a psychologist, which Nathan liked to say was the perfect combination to give rise to a poet. My parents are nice people, my younger brother, too. The only time I ever heard my parents fight was about my sister. My mother wanted to make her see a therapist; my father thought that would make things worse. She was twelve. Don't get the idea that this was about drugs or sex or any of the usual things. At school she was a well-behaved child. She was a good student. But at home she was angry, all the time, at all of us, and nobody knew why. Sometimes when I was off my guard, sitting on the floor watching television, she'd smack me as hard as she could in the back of the head, barely slowing her steps as she passed through the room.

Even now when we're together, the rest of us can spend an hour trying to decide where to go for dinner, everybody trying to suss out the others' preferences before they state their own. Where would you like to go? Oh, I don't care. Where would you like to go? Not my sister. Jesus Christ, she'll say. You fucking people. We're having Chinese.

And we go get Chinese, even if not a one of us want it, because after years of smashed-up chairs and screams of *I hate you!* we are beaten down. We fly under her radar, and I can't speak for the rest of my family, but I know that I'm wary in her presence, guarded, muted, unfunny, not myself. I am detached from her because otherwise I cannot bear to be around her. Was that how I would be, from here on out, with Nathan? Would that be doing what I had to do? To be a wife, to be a walking mannequin.

■

The next night Nathan wanted to go to our favorite restaurant for dinner, and I didn't, but he looked so hopeful when he made the proposal, as if he was trying to recapture the good times, the pleasure on my face the first time he fed me a bite of the specialty of the house, a spicy, chocolaty chicken mole. So I said fine, okay. The Fiesta Grill was one of the few business establishments near our house, along with an ice cream place and a gas station or two, so we thought of it to some degree as ours. Alas, the restaurant's virtues of authenticity and affordability had recently been extolled in the local paper, so that night it was nearly full, and Nathan found the crowd stressful, more so because Binx wouldn't stop screaming no matter how many Cheerios we gave him, and when it came time to pay and the line at the cash register was long, Nathan, my Nathan, ran out on the bill. I learned this when I got outside, hauling both children and their accessories—bib, sippy cups, toys, wipes—and found him already in the car. He had his forehead pressed to the top of the wheel, which he clutched with both hands, as if he were driving without looking, willing or daring himself to crash. I wanted to forgive him. I did. A strong desire rose within me to do him some kind of physical harm.

Instead I buckled the children into their car seats. Instead I lifted the check from where Nathan had abandoned it on the dash. Instead I went back inside and waited in line, counting to ten over and over in English, French, and Spanish, until it was my turn to pay. The Fiesta Grill was our favorite restaurant. I wanted to be able to go back.

■

Ah, but there is a price to be paid for such calm, such relentless accommodation, and I discovered what mine was when I woke later that night, just after midnight. I had an alert, startled feeling, but Binx hadn't cried. No lights danced on the baby monitor. Of course I didn't know that this sleepless night would be the first of many. Even now it frightens me a little to talk about that time, my capital-I insomnia, because of the possibility that to invoke its name is to invite its return. Oh God, I hope that doesn't happen to me again, you think, and then, because you thought that, it will, and you'll wake once more into a bleak, remorseless stillness. You'll wander in a panic through the rooms of your mind and find them just emptied, as if your thoughts were bugs that scattered as soon as you entered.

But I meant to talk about the first night of my insomnia, which in my memory comes after the incident at the Fiesta Grill. I woke and lay there for quite some time in the innocent expectation that sleep would soon return. I felt the reverberations of every move Nathan made, each shift in position a radical upheaval of my terrain. Our queen-size bed seemed far too small. Because more than once I drifted off, only to jerk awake at his inadvertent touch, I did my best not to have any contact with him, camped out on the cliff edge of the mattress. Still I couldn't escape the brush of his foot, the nudge of his backside, as though his body sought me out, groping toward me in the dark. Maybe he just wanted the familiar, soothing intimacy of my body, the rightness of his legs tucked into mine, his right hand cupping my left breast, his breath against my neck. What it felt like was that he didn't want me to sleep. What I wanted was to push him out of the bed. I lay awake and imagined the satisfying thud of his body against the floor. I lay awake and remembered when the two of us, Nathan and I, could sleep together all night in a twin.

What was the point of lying there? I got up. I had the

claustrophobic's choking desire to escape. What I needed were clothes and car keys. What I needed was to drive really fast. I got on the interstate and hit the gas, and before I slowed back down the speedometer had edged up to 100. I felt better. Better enough to get off the interstate in Durham and start making my way back toward Chapel Hill. I drove down 15-501, a road segmented by stoplights that one by one turned red just in time to stop my car. On either side the strip-mall staples: Wal-Mart, Barnes and Noble, Lowe's. On hot days, when cars were packed so tightly together there wasn't room to go on green, and the sun stabbed merciless light through the windshield, it felt like the road through the middle of hell. Late at night, it wasn't so bad. Look, there was the old mall, finally defunct after the long exodus of shoppers and stores to the new mall. Poor thing. Was it jealous of the new mall? It seemed a distinct possibility.

I turned in its entryway, directed by the sign toward stores that were no longer there. There's something eerie about a giant, empty parking lot, but that night the whole place just seemed sad. Waiting for us all to come back, and you know what? We never, ever would. Right after we moved here, Nathan had taught me to drive a stick shift in this parking lot. He'd been so patient. "I can't do it," I said, after an infinite number of stalls, and he said, with total certainty, "Yes, you can."

I circled round the lot for hours until I could ease up on the clutch and push down on the gas pedal with the exact balance of pressure and speed, and now I circled round it again, like I was trying to catch that other car, but I couldn't, and so I couldn't laugh at Nathan's bad gearshift puns or hear him clap when I finally got it right, and I certainly couldn't stall. This car was an automatic.

"Yes, you can," he'd said.

Oh, Nathan, Nathan. Where did you go? Why'd you do that? Why'd you do that to me?

■

Smith lived in Carrboro, in an old mill house. I had little occasion to visit it, but whenever I did, I was struck by how stark the furnishings were. No pictures of people on the walls, only a black-and-white of the dog who'd died five years ago and never been replaced. Smith did not take back his heart.

When I pulled up, he was sitting on his porch, smoking a cigarette. I was surprised for two reasons: I hadn't expected to see him smoking, and I hadn't expected to see him. It was two a.m. Why had I driven to his house if I hadn't expected to see him? Just an urge, an impulse. Why was I driving around at all? There was a moment when I could have kept going, a dark car sliding by on a dark road. He might have squinted through the smoke and the streetlight haze and thought, "Isn't that . . . ?" He wouldn't have risen slowly from his chair, as he was doing as I climbed his porch stairs. He wouldn't have said, with that tone of wary and puzzled surprise, my name.

"You smoke?" I said.

His cheeks pinked. "Sometimes," he said. "Secretly."

"You are a complicated dude," I said.

He put the cigarette out, although it was only half smoked, and moved to a stool so that I could take the solitary chair. "You really are a gentleman," I said. "A complicated gentledude."

"Gentledude," Nathan would have repeated, drawing the word out, pleased and amused.

"What are you doing out?" Smith asked.

"I thought maybe I'd drive to Tennessee," I said.

"What would you do there?"

"Visit the scene of the crime," I said. "Look for clues."

"Clues to what?"

I sighed. "Motive."

Smith said nothing. He stared out at the street, and I stared at him, willing him to speak if he had something to say. "I was a little annoyed with you the other day," I said after a moment. "I told you not to tell anyone, and there you were on the phone with Nathan."

"Why wouldn't I tell Nathan?" he asked. "He already knew."

"Did you mean what you said to him? That you were on my side?"

"I meant it," he said.

"What does it mean to be on my side?"

"It means I think he was wrong, of course."

"Yeah, I know *that*," I said.

He was silent a long moment. "It means . . . I don't know. What should it mean?" He glanced at me, away. "Is there something I can do for you?"

Kiss me, I thought, but didn't say, of course, because why had I even thought it?

"I'm serious," he said. "What can I do for you?"

■

What could he do for me? What could anyone do for me? Turn back time, oh yes please. Turn back time. But where would I stop the clock? I considered this, nursing Binx on the couch at six a.m. I'd walked in the door to the sound of him crying. How long had he been wailing, poor motherless thing? Long enough for his face to be as wet as if I'd doused him with a bucket. Now he ate ferociously while I stared at the seven volumes of Proust lined up on the top shelf of the living-room bookcase. They'd been a gift from Helen when I first got pregnant. She said she figured I might need a lot of reading material for nights when I'd be up nursing the baby—neither of us knew yet that in the early weeks you don't seem to have enough hands to get the baby on the breast and keep her there, let alone hold a book, let alone heft a seven-hundred-pager. She joked that if I ever got through all seven volumes, I'd be a qualified Proust scholar.

"Is that a lucrative field?" I asked.

"Oh, yes," she said. "The people are clamoring."

At the time she herself had been enamored of the prose of Gertrude Stein, whose childlike repetitions seemed to me silly where they were supposed to be profound, a response that Helen said proved something about me, something bad, the particulars of which I now couldn't recall. We'd fought about Gertrude Stein. Helen was the sort of combatant who turns on you suddenly, unexpectedly, like a cat who lets you pet it until it suddenly turns to sink its teeth into your hand, ears back, eyes wild with the jungle. I remembered the lash of anger in her voice, but not what she'd said.

In Austin? Was that where I would stop the clock? Not before Austin, certainly. I had no desire to go back to the person I'd been then, too embarrassed to call myself a poet, sure that it would be seen as presumptuous, pretentious. In the year between college and grad school I worked my first nine-to-five job, tried to teach myself to write without deadlines. When people asked me at parties what I did, I said, "I'm a secretary," and watched them struggle not to reveal their reaction, waiting for me to offer the caveat we all offered in our twenties, *But what I really want to do is . . .* "But what I really want to do is *rock*," a guy had once said to me and a friend at a party. Oh, my Lord. As soon as he was gone, I turned to my friend and said, "What I really want to do is *rhyme*." What I really wanted to do didn't much seem to matter, as I wasn't doing any kind of work not required by my job. I was in a bit of a muddle without teachers to tell me what to do. My sister wanted me to move to Gainesville, where she was in medical school, and live with her. She would take me in, and take me over. I knew just how it would go. I wasn't in that much of a muddle.

And then Austin. Austin. Austin was not a place, it was my dream of another life, my Oz, and for years after I left, whenever I wished for a tornado, that was where I imagined it taking me. Days there were hot and slow. All the coffee shops had wooden porches strung with Christmas lights. A girl wearing a bright green bikini and flip-flops forever rode by on a bicycle. The temperature of Barton Creek was always sixty-eight degrees. I was a poet there. People seemed to take that for granted, and after a while so did I. And I hadn't had to leave. I'd left for Nathan, because he'd gotten a job and we were together. Without Nathan, I could have stayed. I would have stayed. But I never really got to choose.

In Austin I lived a life of late nights and late mornings, sitting at the kitchen counter in the house Helen rented with her cousin Jane, smoking pot and talking about how things seemed and what they meant, the life of an artist, the prose of Virginia Woolf. Sometimes Jane got out the video camera to record these conversations. The lens trained on my face made me self-conscious, made me feel like not just the conversation but the whole way we were living was staged. But still I admired our commitment to that life. That life! We fought about Gertrude Stein. We went out for pancakes at midnight. We watched *Imagine*, about John Lennon, and at the end we cried. We watched a documentary about Marvin Gaye, listened to Smokey Robinson's attempt to explain the singer's troubles: how tortured he was by his fraught childhood, his thwarted desire to be a sweater-wearing crooner like Perry Como. From Smokey, the camera cut to Marvin Gaye's mother, deep-voiced and weary in a hospital bed, who said, "Marvin did a lot of drugs." Cut away. We agreed on the truth of both assessments.

Helen and Jane stayed in Austin after Nathan and I left. I'd go back to visit, and find the house exactly as it had been, a museum to my memories. Fragile pyramids of cigarette butts rose from the ashtrays on the arms of all the chairs, trails of ashes on the floor, the countertops. Dog hair like a plague upon the futon. The sharp, piney smell of pot smoke seeping from the walls. A strong aroma of garbage in the kitchen, flies on the half-eaten pizza left in an open box on the stove—sure, OK, but the point is that Helen and Jane didn't notice, they didn't see it, they were living the life of the mind. Jane repainted the whole house, without the landlord's permission, to give it the color scheme of her childhood home, and over a period of weeks she shot her student film there, both she and Helen living in her childhood on a movie set, headshots on the table of the actors playing her parents, the life and the art twined like DNA strands.

Helen told me that the way we lived for the five or six days of our yearly visits was not the way she usually lived. She had a job with a law firm. Five days a week she put on a suit and went to work in an office building downtown, among the upwardly mobile, where young lawyers with shiny cars and a gleam in their eyes asked her out in the copy room. I couldn't believe that. I didn't see it. I saw the way the lights strung across the wooden railing of a coffee shop twinkled and blurred after a dose of shrooms, and the way time, too, twinkled and blurred, the days not about vacuuming up the dog hair or taking out the trash but about what we were thinking, what we wanted to say, so that by the time I got home from these trips I had a talking hangover, worn out by overindulgence in the sound of my own voice. The world trembles between light and darkness, we said. Between agony and beauty. The agony of beauty. The beauty of agony. Writing about it is hard, we said. The struggle with your own mind. The pursuit of the elusive, ever-vanishing, perfect phrase. Some years Nathan came with me, and one night he made us sit with our eyes closed while he read aloud Barry Hannah's story "Even Greenland," turning the words over in his mouth like caramels. We celebrated the beauty of the sentence. We believed. The light was bright, the weather warm.

CHAPTER SEVEN

"Are you sure you want me to go?" Nathan asked, for the thousandth time. He had a date with Smith, a date that, unbeknownst to Nathan, I'd arranged.

"Yes, you should go."

"You're not just saying that because you think I want to go."

"No."

"Because if you don't want me to go, I won't."

"I think you should go," I said.

"I want you to be happy," he said.

It was the end of a long day, a one-thing-after-another day. The kids were finally in bed. I'd had two hours of sleep the night before. "OK," I said. "I will be."

Old Nathan, my Nathan, my ping-ponging-between-sentimental-and-ironic guy, would have said, "From here on out, you promise? Because this isn't just about whether I go out tonight, it's about our *lives*." This Nathan said, "That's all I want," and I had to say, "I know," and endeavor to sound like I believed it. And endeavor to believe it.

He bent to kiss me, a quick peck on the lips, because we never parted without such a kiss and we both seemed to understand the necessity of doing the things we always did. Then at last he was gone. I had big plans: to lie on the couch and tend to no one, to stupefy myself with guilty-pleasure TV, to go to bed early. I'd given Smith a clear mission—to reassure Nathan, to give him the support and comfort he needed to function. And was I hoping that while so doing, Smith would also learn who this woman was and how Nathan felt about her and why he'd cheated on me, all the answers I couldn't ask for because I had to pretend that everything was fine? Yes, yes, of course. But I didn't say so. This was a delicate operation. Smith was my man on the inside, but he didn't like me calling him that, visibly stiffened when I did. "I'm your friend, and his, too," he said. But doubtless he would learn something, and then the trick would be to get it out of him.

I wandered the house a while. Passing through the living room, I gave the upright spines of Proust's seven volumes, with their refined deep blue coloring and tasteful font, the finger. I considered calling Helen. When was the last time I'd talked to her? She still lived in Austin, with her husband and two small children, and our conversations, which had once been leisurely sightseeing trips through the landscapes of our thinking, were hurried, short, and all about our kids. We had not expected to be women like that. We had thought that we really would read all seven volumes of Proust. We had thought we would always care—care to the point of shouting—which of us liked, and which of us didn't like, Gertrude Stein. We often felt torn between the people we were and the people we had been, or perhaps had never actually been but always thought we should be.

We tended to think that motherhood had changed us, but maybe it had just reduced us to our essentials. This was who we were when we no longer had the time to persuade ourselves we gave a rat's ass about Gertrude Stein.

I would've liked to call Helen, but if I got her on the phone, which was doubtful, and she asked how I was doing, which of course she would, what would I say? Since Alex's wedding I hadn't spoken to any of my friends. Alex was on her honeymoon, so that one was easy, but Erica and Sally had called, and I hadn't called them back. If I told them what had happened, then I would always know they knew, and then how would I be able to forget it? And why would I want to hash out the demeaning particulars of my crisis, so awful, so ordinary, with anyone I knew?

Maybe Nathan, even now, was telling Smith how they'd met, what they'd said. Maybe he was describing the act itself, or acts, because, after all, I had only his word that there had only been one, and his word apparently wasn't terribly good. Maybe he was saying again that he wished he loved her, so that instead of doing the sort of thing we say can never be justified he would have done the sort of thing we say can be justified by love. Maybe he was telling him her name.

Kate.

Here is where I admit that I spent the next hour Googling the name of the writers' conference where he'd met her along with her name. Kate. I wanted to find a photo. I wanted to know if she was a fiction writer or a playwright or a poet. What if she was a poet? What if she looked like me? What if she was a poet and she looked like me but a skinnier, pre-pregnancy me, and she had the time to go around railing passionately against the prose of Gertrude

Stein, and in every way she replaced the me I was now with some version of my earlier self? Or what if she was nothing like me at all? Would that be better or worse? All I got in answer to my questions was a bunch of hits that included both words but not in any helpful relation to each other. A woman named Kate Pyle was a playwright who'd written a one-act with a man who'd once attended the conference. That was the kind of thing I learned.

I suppose once I'd started down this road of technological surveillance the next step was obvious. I knew the password to his e-mail account: *Lovesah*. But there were no e-mails to or from anyone named Kate. There were e-mails from Nathan to his agent, his mother, his friends, written that week, written today, in a tone of dumbfounding normalcy. "Yo," he'd written in greeting, in an e-mail to one of his high school friends. Yo? He was a good actor, I guessed, at least over e-mail. Or this *yo*, this ludicrously jaunty word, somehow captured what he really was feeling. I imagined confronting him when he got home with the evidence of *yo*. "What the hell is this?" I'd scream, and because he was Nathan and we understood each other he'd know why, in the face of his larger transgression, I might fling myself into hysterics over a *yo*. God is in the details. Or is it the devil is in the details? One of those.

Nathan kept his drafts inside a folder called "Fiction." Inside that was another folder called "Infidelity," and inside that were ten different versions of the novel, dutifully numbered. I opened number ten. *It kept happening*, the novel began. Why was I reading it again? Did I expect it to have changed? One of the subplots was about an affair between two people who met at a downscale motel on their lunch breaks from office jobs, and the twist was that the affair wasn't the tragic or seedy or tragicomic situation you might imagine from this setup but a genuine romance, albeit one carried out in the milieu of a noir's doomed deceivers, or an art film's resigned dreamers, looking to escape their Wal-Mart lives. Nathan had given the woman my job, and in the novel she did the job well and that satisfied her. In one scene she and her lover talked about movies that started with an office worker in the process of having his soul crushed by the cubicle doldrums and then followed him on a hero's journey, in which he discovered that he was never meant to be a cog in the machine, but the dude at the front of the pack stopping bullets with his mind, or catching them with his teeth, or whatever it was, these CGI days, that heroes did with bullets.

"I don't want to be a hero," the woman said. "I don't want my life to turn out to be virtual reality. I just want to do a good job."

"Because you're a happy person," the man said. "Unhappy people—they want to think their unhappiness makes them special. You always felt misunderstood and out of place? Well, guess what, it's because you're Jesus. That's why depressed people are so self-involved. They all think they're Jesus."

"Let's make a movie," the woman said, "about an office worker who turns out to be an office worker."

"What would happen in it?"

"He'd spend the whole movie thinking he ought to be able to stop bullets, and then a photocopier would reveal to him that his destiny was to get his report turned in on time. You know how in the movies they always have to get reports in on time? Just what are these reports?"

"A photocopier reveals his destiny?" the man asked. "A photocopier of destiny."

And then she grinned at him, and repeated the phrase in the tones of a preview voiceover, and he began to tickle her, and they rolled around on their tainted motel bedding, on top of the bloodstains and the sperm. Only Nathan left those last details out, not remembering, as I did, the *60 Minutes* with the infrared light.

After I read this part of the novel the first time, I said to him, "You think I'm happy in my job?"

He shrugged. "It's not you," he said.

It wasn't me. I went back and forth over the pages of the book, scrolling up, scrolling down, waiting for something to jump out, to announce, Aha! The truth! I could hardly stand to read it. I couldn't bring myself to stop. If she wasn't me, then no one was. I could see no reflection in any of these characters. For all I knew every one of the women—there were twelve, I counted twelve of them—were variations of her. Kate. For all I knew he'd written about her over and over, and never written about me at all. So many points of view, and not one belonged to a betrayed wife, a cuckolded husband. The cheaters, that's who got to talk. If I wanted to be in Nathan's book, I needed to have an affair of my own.

She kept running into him, I read, *and not just running into him as in crossing paths in the hall, but literally running into him, body against body, collision and retreat. Was she doing it on purpose? He couldn't have said why but he had the feeling that she wanted to touch him. Was that all it took? Action creates an equal and opposite reaction. She wanted to touch him and after a while he wanted to touch her back. Physics, that's all it was.*

But what, I wanted to ask, what about his wife? Was she catalyst, or just casualty?

Rajiv still waited in my in-box. I was in his head. I opened the e-mail, hit reply, typed, *Hey, Can't believe it took me a year to write back. Things are crazy here.* I hesitated. I typed, *I'm hunting for the eject button.* I signed it *S.*

■

I was still awake when Nathan came home, but I pretended not to be. I pretended, even to myself, that I didn't hear the jangle of his belt buckle as he took off his jeans, that I didn't feel the mattress shift beneath his weight, that I didn't feel him hesitate—should he spoon me, the way he always had?—before he settled into place, not touching me, on his side of the bed. I listened as his breathing shifted into sleep. Sleep arrived so easily for him, and yet it wouldn't come for me, like my stubborn three-year-old standing on the other side of the room, shaking her head every time I called her name. Panic fluttered in my throat, splashed hot across my back. And so I got up. I snuck out of my grown-up house like a teenager. By the time I got home, I'd driven a hundred and fifty miles. I could have been well on my way, if I'd actually gone somewhere.

CHAPTER EIGHT

Kate Ryan. An unremarkable name, one that brought up 2,530,000 hits on Google. There was an army of Kate Ryans. More than an army. There was a universe of them. But what about Nathan's—or should I say *our*—particular Kate Ryan? What about her? She was a fiction writer, and as fiction writers often do, she taught fiction writing, at a small college in South Carolina.

There are a number of versions of the literary life. Kate Ryan's was the kind where you publish a few pieces in small journals and then get a job teaching a 4/4 load at an out-of-the-way teaching college and struggle to find time to write between grading an avalanche of composition papers. You hope to get a book published, because if you do, you might get a job at a bigger university, teaching fewer classes, or even better, you might achieve the miracle of selling so many books or winning so many fellowships you can afford not to do anything else. If I'd finished my MFA a single woman, if Nathan and I hadn't decided to put our writing first, make do with part-time jobs, let the chips fall where they may, I probably would have followed this path. If I hadn't stayed with Nathan, if I hadn't yet had children, I would have a life very much like hers. Nathan wanted to be with the sort of woman I'd be if I hadn't been married to him.

I knew her name, I knew she was a fiction writer, because I got Smith to tell me. As soon as I got to work, I called him. He didn't want to tell me anything, of course. He didn't want to betray Nathan's confidence, he said, but more than that, he didn't see how knowledge of the details could possibly benefit me. "You have to at least tell me if she's a poet," I said to him. "Give me her name, rank, and serial number," I said. "Tell me something. Tell me something that will make me feel better."

"He loves you," he said.

"That doesn't help."

He sighed. "She's not a poet."

"Are you sure?"

"I'm positive. She's a fiction writer. Her first book just came out."

"And it's not poems?"

"It's stories."

"What's her last name?"

Silence.

"If you don't tell me I'm going to search Amazon for a Kate with a new story collection. So please just save me the time, Smith, because I really should be working."

"Ryan," he said. "Kate Ryan is her name."

So now I knew. I'd wanted to know, and now I knew. There's what you want and there's what's good for you, and when we're children we don't realize what a luxury it is to have our parents to tell us the difference.

She was no prettier than I was. The two of us were a

couple of reasonably attractive women. She had big, appealing eyes, but so, I'd been told, did I. She had dark hair, like me, but hers was short and plain and mine was long and curly and still sometimes Nathan tugged a ringlet to make it bounce and looked at me like he was a schoolboy and I was the classroom's prettiest girl. Did it make things better or worse that she wasn't prettier, that I had no recourse to that easy, obvious explanation? She wasn't younger, either. She was, in fact, older, though by only a year. She was almost exactly my age. And it wasn't just the circumstances that made me feel that her life was my alternate reality. It was the sensibility. Here, from an interview I found: "I don't write about love so much as intimacy. Because it's so daily, you know, and yet so full of mystery, and that combination fascinates me."

And what about the men you date? the interviewer asks. *Are they looking for themselves in your work?*

"One of them was. And, you know, he was in there, but he didn't recognize himself, which is probably a good thing."

Do you ever feel, as a woman, that you should tackle subjects other than love?

"As a woman? What do you mean?"

I mean, the stereotype is that love is a woman's primary concern. Do you feel the need to defy that?

"I think that in part because of the expectations placed on them, women wrestle constantly with the place of romantic love in their lives, and not just romantic love but ideas of motherhood and women's roles in general, and that even if you reject marriage and motherhood that very rejection in some ways defines you. To be fair, I should say that I see your point—I have sometimes worried that my work would be characterized as particularly 'female' because of its subject matter, and part of me says, 'So what?' Both because, why should we feel there's anything wrong with that? And because it's ultimately ridiculous. Love isn't a female concern, it's a human one. And when I think about what art can do, how it shows us our common humanity, love, and its loss, seem to me to be the primary components of that commonality."

Do you think . . .

"Plus, you've got to write about what you write about. What preoccupies you, I mean."

You're preoccupied with love?

"Well, see, that's my point. Who isn't?"

Kate Ryan. Ah, Kate Ryan. Yes, I agree with you.

■

I ducked out of work early to go to the Regulator, where I found Kate Ryan's book on the new releases shelf. *Yes and No*. That was the title, standing out in white against the red of the spine. I picked it up. The same photo on the inside flap, her rueful eyes. She was at work on a novel. Of course she was. Who wasn't? The blurbs used words like *witty*, *astute*, and *wise*. No doubt the writing of this book had pre-dated her encounter with Nathan—had pre-dated it by months and years. I knew that. I knew how the whole thing worked. And yet I expected to find a story about him in there, among her other stories of love, of *intimacy*. I expected a story that would tell me how Nathan figured in the ongoing construction of the narrative of her life. Maybe he was a meaningless thrill. Maybe he was the man she wanted. Either one was strange to imagine. How her sense of the stakes could be so different from mine. I opened the book to a random page, like you might open the Bible, looking for something—explanation, solace, advice—in the first passage on which your eyes alight.

My mother doesn't love my father anymore. He keeps flinging himself against this fact, like a bird against a window. Everyone but him can see it. What am I supposed to do about it, when he comes to me with his sad eyes? I am busy trying to get my Baptist boyfriend to take my virginity, a suggestion which makes him shake with temptation, sliding away from me on the couch, rolling off me where we lie on the golf course behind my house.

Another page.

"We never talk about anything," he says. "Have you noticed how we never talk?"

"No," she says. "We talk constantly."

He says, "You always do this. Why won't you let me talk to you? There are things . . . I want. Things . . ." He stops, and his arms pump as though he is stopping just short of beating his chest. He says, "Desires . . ."

"Look," Julie says, "why don't you just go to the movies like the rest of us?"

Another page.

It is never clear to the rest of them what they should call Claudia and Bob. Sometimes they are a couple, sometimes they are not, and sometimes Claudia will look at one of them, whoever happens to be the host that weekend, and say, "Why on earth is Bob in another room? Don't you know we're sleeping together?" The poor host will say, "So you're back together?" and Claudia will say, "No," with that gentle scorn that is her special touch. The host will go away thinking that this is it, this is the last time Claudia is invited, and also about that old recurring topic of dis-

cussion, that anyone could have known they were unsuited the first time they heard their names paired. Claudia. Bob.

Sarah. Nathan. No denying those names went together, with their biblical, inevitable ring.

Another.

She wonders how it would feel to discover that all of her memories were someone else's stories, like in the movie Blade Runner. *It could mean that she was free. Or that she was nothing. It would be hard to tell which.*

Another.

There is nothing I want more than him in my bed. Dana says, "You're exaggerating." But she is wrong. I am giving myself over to it. Him, him, him. It is exhilarating, and at the same time I understand how sick it is. How pathetic. I want to write him letters that say I love you, that say please. Please. Pleas, as a word, is awfully close to please. She pleas. Please. She pleas for him to please; she pleases him for pleas. If you think about it, pleas starts to look truncated, as though it's missing something. I wonder why this never occurred to me before.

■

My hand was on the doorknob when Nathan pulled open the door. Behind him in the ExerSaucer Binx was screaming, but I couldn't get to him because first Nathan and then both Nathan and Mattie were blocking the door, standing in my way. "Mommy," Mattie said, "can I wear a sundress?"

"I've been doing some research on insomnia," Nathan said.

"Can I wear a sundress, Mommy?" Mattie asked.

Binx ramped up his screaming to its most ear-shattering pitch, his face a red mask of fury, his fists balled in the air.

"You need to exercise," Nathan said, "but not too close to bedtime, so I think we should all go for a walk now."

"Mommy!" Mattie insisted. "I want to wear a sundress!"

"It's cold out, sweetheart," I said to her. To Nathan I said, "Excuse me," and when he stepped back, I crossed the kitchen to lift the baby out. His screaming stopped. He looked at me reproachfully and said, "Aaahhhh" in a mournful way.

"Aaaahhhh," I said back.

"Huh-huh, huh-huh, huh-huh," he said. He launched himself sideways, screaming when his face met cloth instead of nipple.

"I've got to feed the baby," I said.

"Oh, right," Nathan said. "You feed him, and I'll take Mattie to the potty, and then we'll go walk the drive."

"I don't need to go potty!" Mattie shouted.

"Push the stroller up and down the hill a few times, and I guarantee you'll sleep tonight," Nathan said.

"Guarantee?" I asked, not to affirm his guarantee but because I'd never heard him use that word in that way, with the overeager sincerity of a salesman.

"I don't need to go potty!" Mattie shouted again.

"You haven't been in three hours," Nathan said. He put his hand on the top of her head and steered her down the hall, ignoring her protests.

"Why would you lie about needing to go potty?" I asked Binx. He screamed in response. "What if I don't want to go for a walk?" He screamed at that, too. "I take your point," I said.

Through the lens of my exhaustion the world was both blurry and sharp, as when you're sitting outside on a sunny day drinking too much wine. I sat on the couch with Binx at my breast, his hands kneading maniacally at my flesh, and all the little darkening hairs on his head seemed distinctly in focus, but the room beyond him—my bookshelves, my reflection in the dark television screen—seemed vague and far away. "Oh, baby," I said. "Oh, baby, baby." I rubbed his head. I touched the tip of his tiny nose. He smiled at me around my nipple—why was that the most charming in his repertoire of smiles?—and I pretended he was all there was in the world, the sound of Mattie and Nathan arguing in the bathroom just fading away.

Because we lived on a winding country road with no sidewalk, no shoulder, and pickup trucks swerving around cyclists at sixty miles an hour, since the kids had come along we'd taken our walks on the driveway. It was a long driveway, as I've said, and steep, so pushing a stroller back up the final stretch to our house was good exercise, even if going up and down five or six times lacked a certain excitement. Mostly Nathan and I were working too hard to talk, fighting to keep the strollers from running away with us on the way down, fighting to push them up the hill on the way back. Not talking was fine by me.

By the fourth lap I was lagging behind Nathan. I was too tired for this, and I didn't want to do it, and I suddenly resented Nathan for making me do it, even if his motivations were good. Kate Ryan. Kate Ryan. And Nathan had failed, week after week, to fix the mailbox, which wobbled on its post at the end of the drive, and which he'd insisted I not fix myself, because if I did what he perceived to be his job I'd make him feel bad. I resented that, too. I resented the hell out of the back of his head. Over the crunch of wheels on gravel Mattie was calling my name. Or, anyway, she was calling me Mom. Is that the right word for that appellation? Is Mom my name? I stopped walking and leaned over the top of the stroller to hear her better. Caught in the grip of wheeled momentum, Nathan and Binx kept trundling down.

"What is it, sweetie?" I asked. I was braced for her to say she wanted to get out and walk, for argument.

"Mom," she said, her tone inquisitive, "why did you decide not to be married anymore after your wedding a few days ago?"

A flash of panic, shivery and hot. What did she know and how did she know it? "What do you mean?"

"Why did you decide not to be married anymore?" she repeated.

"We didn't decide that," I said.

"No," she said, frustrated by my stupidity, "why did you decide not to be married when I wasn't born anymore?"

"Oh," I said. Relief chased the panic away. "We got married before you were born. Is that what you mean?"

"No! I mean after your wedding a few days ago!"

"That wasn't our wedding, sweetheart. That was Alex and Adam's wedding."

She looked puzzled. "Alex and Adam's wedding?"

"That's right."

"Oh." She put her fingers in her mouth, got the twist going in her hair. I resumed the walk, the matter resolved, but no. Her misunderstanding about the wedding failed to explain away the original question. I stopped walking. I came around to look her in the face.

"Why did you think we decided not to be married anymore?"

She didn't answer. Children her age are by nature cryptic, unable to explain the assumptions and associations they make, falling back, in the face of questions too frustrating to answer, on silence and refusal. She looked at me with her fingers in her mouth, her eyes heavy-lidded and dull. "Answer me, please," I said. Twirl, twirl, twirl. "Mattie, please answer me, or we're going back inside."

With a wet pop the fingers came out of her mouth. "Daddy," she said, and then opened her mouth to insert the fingers again.

"What do you mean, Daddy?"

She said, around her fingers, "Daddy said you decided not to be married anymore."

"When did he say that?"

"Yesterday," she said. This answer told me nothing. To her yesterday was not the day before this one but anytime in the indeterminate past. And really, why not? What did it matter that Nathan had told me what he'd done five days ago, and that he'd done it more than a year ago? He might as well have done it, be doing it, right this minute, fucking Kate Ryan, short story writer, right here across the gravel drive. Nathan and I had been together ten years. We'd met ten years ago. We'd married four years ago. We'd had our first child three years ago. When was it that, sick with a fever, I lay on the couch beside him through wavering hours as he read to me from books I'd loved in childhood, *The Dark Is Rising*, *A Wrinkle in Time*, and then when his eyes got tired he recited all the poems and scraps of poems his memory retained: "Whan that Aprile with his shoures soote"; "Note the stump, a peachtree. We had to cut it down"; "I want to say that forgiveness keeps on dividing"; "For he on honeydew hath fed, and drunk the milk of paradise"? I didn't know. Yesterday.

"Are you sure, Mattie? Are you sure he said that?"

"Yes," she said, with the polite, precise pronunciation she'd learned somewhere. From her teacher? Not from us, habitual users of the sloppy, casual *yeah*, unless we were angry, and then it was *yes, yes, yes*, squeezed out through the teeth. *Yes*.

Nathan and Binx were at the bottom of the hill, behind the Dodsons' place. Nathan stood with one hand on the stroller, looking back at us. "Come on," he called. "We've got to wear you out."

I started walking. I was walking fast, letting the stroller tumble me forward. I called out before I even got to him, "Did you tell her we decided not to be married anymore?" I kept moving while I said it, so by the time I reached him it was his turn to talk.

"What?" he said.

"Did you tell her we decided not to be married anymore?"

"Of course not," he said.

"Did you tell her something like that?"

"No," he said.

"She says you did." We both turned to look at her, witness for the prosecution. Her face was a blank, her eyes a mystery.

"Well, I didn't," he said. "I said nothing like that. I don't know what she's talking about."

"Why would she say that?"

"Sarah, she's three. She says that honk monsters are trying to eat her. She says she's afraid of going closer to stuff."

"I just don't think she would make that up. Where would she even get the idea to make something like that up? And she said you told her that after the wedding. Don't you think that's a bit coincidental?"

"I can't explain it," he said. "I can only tell you that I didn't say that. For one thing, we didn't decide not to be married anymore, did we?"

"I don't know," I said. "You tell me. *We* don't seem to decide on anything. You decided."

"I didn't decide anything. I acted on impulse, and regretted it."

"You decided to act on impulse," I said. "At some moment you decided. You decided to let yourself."

He took a deep breath. "The point is, I didn't say anything like that to her, and there's nothing like that I want to say to her or you or anyone else."

"Whatever."

"I can't believe you don't believe me."

There is nothing I want more than him in my bed.

"Oh, yeah," I said. "It's fucking shocking."

"Sarah," he said. "The kids."

"The kids!" I said. "The kids! Maybe you should have thought about the kids before you fucked somebody else!" To tell the truth I screamed this last part. My voice shot up on the word *fucked*, spiked higher on the word *else*. "Maybe you should have thought about them before you wrote a book about cheating on their mother. You selfish asshole! You motherfucking prick! You want me to decide? I decide! You can't publish that book! That book is dead. It's dead and dead and gone. So live with that, why don't you. Live with that!" His face became a mirror, and in it I saw a monster version of myself, unleashing my anger like black magic. In front of my children, in front of my neighbors' house. If I'd really been a witch Nathan would have been a column of dust. Not even a lizard, not even a toad. Just nothing. Nothingness.

I decided. I decided then. I couldn't be this person. I couldn't live with him anymore.

■

This is what it's like when your husband leaves, because you've asked him to. He goes out to his car carrying two small bags that, for once, you didn't help him pack, and you follow, but hesitate at the door while he goes on down the porch stairs. You stand at the door with the screen held awkwardly open, which takes a constant application of pressure because the door is broken, something the two of you have been meaning to fix but haven't, because neither of you knows how. He puts his bags not in the trunk but in the backseat, and normally you would ask why but this time you don't, which is another way you know things are different. He shuts the car door. Then he looks at you. He waits to see what you'll do. Will you come down the stairs and say something? Will you hug or even kiss him good-bye? You don't know. You don't know what to do. You're still registering your surprise that he didn't ask you to change your mind, or cry, because he's been known to cry about far less. He did go pale when you told him what you'd decided. He did look like he was going to be sick, or faint, or die. But all he said was that he would go, that very night, because you'd asked him to and it was your right to decide what happened next, and he'd find somewhere to stay and call you the next day and figure things out from there. He did say he hoped you'd change your mind about wanting him gone. But he didn't ask you to. He didn't ask you to change your mind about the book, or even say he hoped you would. He said he'd call his agent the next day. Does it make it easier on you, or harder, his obvious conviction that he deserves this? You're not sure, never having tried it the other way.

You go down the porch steps to hug him, but halfway there you realize that you can't hug him, because letting go again might be too hard. So you stop, practically midstep, and cross your arms over your chest. He understands what all this means, because he knows you so well he could turn you inside out, so he makes no attempt to approach. He looks at you with wet and tragic eyes, and then he says again that he'll call you the next day and then he says, and this really breaks your heart, that he hopes you get some sleep. He gets in the car. And then he backs up, and then he turns to the right and points himself down the drive, and then he goes.

After a moment you follow, hanging back at a distance you hope keeps you too small to see in his rearview mirror. At the bottom of the hill, just before the road curves, the brake lights brighten, and you think that he can't do it after all, he's coming back to beg you to let him stay, and you're glad, you don't really want him to go, you love him, you love him, you don't know what you were thinking. Then you see your neighbor making her dogged way across her lawn to the car, her hand lifted in a motion that's somewhere between a wave and a request to stop. Oh, you think. You hadn't seen her there.

Your husband gets out of the car, leaving his door open, and goes around the front to greet the neighbor. They exchange some words. What are they saying? You can't begin to guess. Then suddenly your husband bends—really bends, because your neighbor is a small and rapidly shrinking woman—and hugs her. You feel a shock of surprise at the sight of her hands on his back. You think he must have told her that he's leaving, and the thought of him spreading your business around angers you, but now that you've asked him to leave you've moved this matter into the public domain, and what the hell do you expect? He releases the neighbor. They talk some more. Then he goes back to the car. Just before he gets in he turns his head to look up at your house, and you step hastily back into the shadow of the trees, not wanting him to see you. You're not sure why it matters if he sees you. He gets in. He shuts the door. He drives away.

You would like to stay there in the woods, a frozen vertical thing lost among the trees. But your children are in bed in the house above, and at this very moment might be crying, might be calling for you. So you go back. You trudge. That's the right word, for this moment, and maybe all the moments after.

And that is what it's like when your husband leaves you, because you've asked him to. In my case, anyway, that is what it was like. I don't know why I framed the experience as universal. I guess it felt too big to have happened only to me.

PART II

CHAPTER NINE

The morning after Nathan left, Mattie woke at six, an hour earlier than usual. I imagine she called for her daddy, as she always did, and when he didn't respond, screamed for me. I didn't hear her right away because I'd only been asleep two or three hours and so was deep in slumber, and because Nathan was the one who got up with her and I wasn't alert for the sound of her voice the way I was for the sound of the baby's. When neither Nathan nor I came, instead of getting up to find us, she lay in bed and screamed, and then she began to kick the wall, and that woke not only me but Binx as well. I dragged myself awake to stereo screaming. What I wanted to do was to keep on lying there, and for a little while I did. Mattie cried, "Daddy! Mommy!" and Binx just cried, and I lay there and revisited a thought I'd had the night before, about irresponsibility. How they made the word ugly so you won't want to embrace the concept. Think of that harsh beginning and seven lurching syllables. Not until you reach the last do you get to make a nice long vowel sound, a relaxation of the mouth, a sigh.

I got Binx first, although picking him up didn't stop the screaming, as what he wanted was his milk and he wanted it now, and then I went into Mattie's room and found her turned sideways on the bed with her eyes squinched shut, her legs up the wall, her feet bang-bang-banging away. "What are you doing?" I had to shout to be heard.

She stopped. She opened her eyes. "You didn't come," she accused. "You left me all alone."

"Aw a-wone? You sure have abandonment issues for a child who's never been abandoned," I said. I said it with a fair amount of irritation, and immediately wished I hadn't taken that tone—hadn't said it at all—when she asked, "Where's Daddy?"

I should have prepped an answer to this question, when I wasn't toting a screaming baby and a head filled with sand. "Why didn't you just come look for me?"

"I can't," she said. "I'm scared."

"Of what?"

"The deepness," she said. "In the night movie, a little girl fell into the deepness."

"The night movie?"

"It played up there." She pointed at the ceiling.

I looked up, like I expected to see this night movie projected there, the little girl, falling and falling.

"Usually you have to turn the TV on," Mattie said, her voice now casual, conversational, although her face remained a swamp of tears and snot. "But with the night movies the TV just comes on."

This was the first time she'd told me about her dreams. I was surprised to find out she was having them, even though I'd read somewhere that babies dream even in the womb and wondered how anyone could possibly know that. What did they dream about? What did they know, before they knew anything? Warm liquid, a rocking motion—their sleeping lives no different from their waking ones. And now Mattie's dreams were scary, her subconscious already turning against her at the age of three. "What happened to the little girl?"

"I told you," she said. "She fell into the deepness."

Remember my recent emotional trauma, how little sleep I'd gotten—I reacted to this like she was talking about me. "Oh," I said. "And she never got out?"

"Once you fall in, you can never get out," she said, her face ominously blank, the littlest prophet of doom.

"Maybe you can," I said.

"No!" she shouted, suddenly enraged. "*You can't!*"

"Don't scream at me!" I screamed, and then I whirled the baby around and stormed out of the room, and Mattie started shrieking, "Mommy! Mommy!" as if I'd abandoned her on the side of the road like an unwanted pet.

So this was single motherhood. And where was my husband? What had I done? My daughter wanted to know that, too. Over her Cheerios she hammered at me like a prosecuting attorney. I put her off with flimsy lies until she asked, "If you go to work, who's going to take care of Binx?"

"Oh, fuck," I said. It seemed unbelievable that I could have failed to consider Binx's care, and my anger at Nathan flared at the thought that he hadn't considered it either, at the conviction that it was his fault I'd just cursed in front of our little parrot of a child. I looked at Binx, who offered me his gummy smile and said, "Ba!"

"You're going to leave him all alone!" Mattie wailed.

I swore again. Mattie cut short her crescendo to repeat the word, looking wicked and delighted. I did not want to have to call Nathan. I did not want to ever have to call Nathan. Although it hadn't been my intention at the time, I found that I wanted our awkward yet politely melancholy parting to be the end, which wasn't possible because we had a legal contract and a house and a three-year-old and a baby who couldn't be left at home—no matter what wild fantasies were flashing through my mind—and couldn't be brought to the office. I was going to have to call Nathan.

The message picked up right away, meaning his cell phone was off. "Hi, this is Nathan," his voice said, sounding to my mind brusque and annoyed. "Please leave a message."

I choked. I hung up the phone. I registered that Mattie was singing, "Fuckity fuck fuck fuckity fuck fuck," to the tune of "Here Comes Peter Cottontail," which Nathan sang to her when she was complaining on long walks and he told her they were bunnies on the bunny trail and had to keep hopping along.

It occurred to me that I could call in sick. Or had I used all my sick days with my maternity leave? Suddenly I couldn't remember how that worked, even though I'd carefully researched the policies beforehand. Anyway no one would question me if I took a personal day. I could say one of the kids was sick, and then spend the whole day in the house, where my husband would normally be, while he enjoyed a little vacation.

This time his phone rang and rang. So it was turned on now, our number flashing on the screen under the little word, "Home." But he didn't answer.

"Nathan," I said at the beep. "I forgot about child care for Binx today. I could call in sick, I guess, but I've got a lot of work to do, so if you could come out here . . . Anyway, just call me when you get this." I waited a beat. "Maybe you're in the bathroom."

I paced the kitchen, patting Binx on the back until he belched and then patting him still, thumpity-thump-thump, while he said, "Ba ba ba" and yanked on my hair. I waited what I thought was more than enough time for all Nathan's morning ablutions, shower, shaving, etc. Where the hell was he, anyway? The night before I'd been aware only of his absence from my house, and not of his presence somewhere else. He'd been antimatter. But I remembered from my science classes that matter is neither created nor destroyed, and so he had to go on existing somewhere, in a hotel, in a pancake house, lying in a ditch beside his suicidally wrecked car.

Again the phone rang and rang. "Just checking back, in case you didn't get my first message," I said. "I need to know if you can come, so I know whether to call in. I don't know why we didn't think of this before. Um. I hope you're OK."

I took Mattie into her room and picked an outfit, which she pronounced ugly. "I don't like pants," she said. "I *won't* wear it." I said she could stay in her room alone until she decided to put it on, so she put it on quickly, almost frantic, asking me the whole time not to leave even though I was just sitting there on the floor with Binx in my lap, staring past her at the wall. She knew something was up, she had to, or why was she so desperate at the prospect of thirty seconds alone in her room?

When I called again the phone was off. He'd turned it on and then off again. He'd sat there, wherever he was, probably looking at our number on the screen. He'd let me leave two messages. Maybe he'd listened to them. And then he'd turned the phone off so that as he continued his sojourn into irresponsibility the sound of my dedicated ring tone—"It's a family affair . . . It's a family affair"—couldn't follow him.

"Why is your phone off?" I said. "Or wait, maybe you're trying to call me. I'll hang up." I hung up. I waited. My phone didn't ring. I called voice mail, just in case it wasn't signaling me like it should. "You have no new messages," the mechanical woman said.

I called again. "Something better be wrong with your phone."

Again. "Is this your way of telling me you don't intend to take care of your children today?"

Again. "You know, you're still their father."

Again. "Fuck you, Nathan. Fuck you."

Mattie resumed her new song, dancing around the kitchen. "Shit," I said. Then I called Smith.

"Hello?" He sounded groggy.

I didn't apologize for waking him. "Do you know where Nathan is?"

"What do you mean?"

"He left last night," I said. "I thought he might have called you."

"No. No," he said. "He left?"

"I asked him to," I said. "But I wasn't thinking about who would watch Binx today, and now I can't find him. He didn't call you?"

"No," he said again.

"I thought maybe he would go to your place."

"He didn't," he said.

I paused a moment to fully absorb the new reality. Nathan wasn't at Smith's. He wasn't answering his phone. I had no way to reach him. I'd asked him to leave, and he'd certainly taken that seriously. There was no anger in my voice, only wonderment and despair, when I asked, "What am I going to do?"

"Um," Smith said. "Do you want me to come over?"

"You?"

"I don't work during the day on Fridays," he said. "I usually work Friday nights, you know. And on Saturdays."

For as long as Smith had been part of my life, I didn't know much about him. "I never knew you had Fridays off."

"Yeah, well," he said. "I do. And I can come watch the baby if you want."

"You don't have to," I said. "I can call in sick. Or I guess I could take him with me but frankly I just can't face the thought of packing up all his stuff and hauling it from the parking lot."

"Do you want to call in sick?"

"I don't know," I said.

"Because if you need to go in, I'm happy to come."

"You don't have to," I said.

"But I can."

"Really?"

"If it would help."

"Are you sure?"

"I'm sure," he said. "I'm more than happy to help."

"You're very polite," I said, though generous was what I meant, or bighearted or unstinting, something more dramatic than that mild word *polite*, and he said, "I know."

I wasn't sure why I'd accepted Smith's help, and even as I walked him around the house—him holding Binx as though he was trying him on before purchase—and showed him where things were and explained that I'd arranged for him to pick up Mattie from school and interjected a thousand things out of order until I was certain he wouldn't remember a word, I kept thinking that I should say, Never mind, that's OK, it's sweet of you, but I might as well stay home. But I didn't. I wanted to go to work because it was what felt normal, and I wasn't yet ready to acknowledge how abnormal things now were. More than that, though, kept me from turning him down. In the end, I was just like Mattie. When I couldn't find Nathan, I had felt all alone. I had just wanted somebody to come.

■

All the way to work I thought about going somewhere—anywhere—else. But I couldn't decide where, and the thought of taking advantage of Smith's virtue gave me pangs of guilt, so while my conscious mind juggled desire and indecision and remorse my subconscious just went ahead and drove me to my assigned parking lot. It was a ten-minute walk from there to the office, past a Walgreens and a Chik-fil-A and the sex shop where Tanya and Kristy had once taken me. I lingered in front of every place I passed, even the sex shop, until it dawned on me that those were embarrassing windows to gaze into with anything approaching longing. My reluctance to go to work clung to my ankles like a child who doesn't like the babysitter. *Please don't go, please don't go, please don't go.* I altered my route to take me to an on-campus cafeteria, where I got a cup of coffee and sat for a while nursing it, the caffeine dragging my thoughts out on the dance floor for a jitterbug while the rest of me sat, inert as the chair beneath me.

I thought, Where is Nathan? And then thought it again, and again, until the question took on the tune of "Frère Jacques"—where is Nathan, where is Nathan, ding ding dong, ding ding dong. My skull was a bell, my thoughts the clapper, my whole body a helpless reverberation. Because of "Frère Jacques," I started imagining he'd been on a plane to France when he shut his cell phone off. He'd had a thing about France—the wine! the cheese! the double kisses!—ever since we'd gone there for a literary festival after his first book came out. The book had been a hit there. He'd even been on TV. He'd said to me once, after a month back at home struggling with an early, failing draft of his second novel, far from the kiss-kisses and the adulation, that sometimes he thought he should leave me and move to Paris.

"Excuse me?" I said. This was before the kids. I was sitting at the kitchen table, reading the paper while he made dinner. He'd had his back to me, reaching up for a mixing bowl on a high shelf, when he'd let loose that line.

"I just mean, like Philip Roth and his cabin," he said. "A lot of people think he's done his best work since he pretty much dropped off the world."

"Going to Paris isn't exactly dropping off the world," I said. "But, you know, if you want to leave me, go right ahead."

"Hey," he said. "I didn't say *leave you*. I said *go to Paris*."

"That's not what I heard," I said. "I heard *leave you*."

"I didn't say that," he said. "I was just talking about getting away for a while to work."

"Really," I said. "Because I was thinking maybe I should move to India to learn all the positions of the Kama Sutra. Just for a while."

"Cut me some slack," he said. "You know I've been having a really hard time with this book, and frankly you've been less than understanding, giving me crap if I want to work at night . . ."

"When have I tried to stop you from working at night?"

"Just last night when I said I didn't want to go to the movies."

"I said I'd go by myself."

"Yeah, but you said it like this." He sighed, rolled his eyes, folded his arms, snapped, "Fine, I'll go by myself."

I threw my hands in the air. "So I don't just have to support you working all the time, I can't ever express an emotion while I'm at it."

"Oh, please. Like you've ever not expressed an emotion."

"What is that supposed to mean?"

"You should listen to your tone half the time you talk to me. 'What are you doing in there, Nathan? Are you planning to take out the trash?' You know, my work takes concentration, it takes hours of—"

"*Your* work? Like it's a foreign concept to me? Funny, I thought I did similar work."

"Well, you wouldn't think so," he said. "Given the amount of time you seem to have free to give me crap about mine."

"You don't think my work is as important as yours," I said.

"What? Where is that coming from?"

"I heard what you said in France," I said.

"What did I say in France?"

We'd been at a restaurant, sitting next to each other but engrossed in conversation with the people on our other sides. And I'd caught my name on the lips of the woman he was talking to, just at the moment when my companion had turned to signal the waiter, and I heard Nathan say, "She writes poetry." I noted that he said, "She writes poetry" instead of "She's a poet," but I wouldn't have thought much about that if I hadn't heard the woman ask, in a flirtatious, joking way, "Is she good?"

"She's pretty good," he said. My husband said. Pretty good. "She just needs to take a leap."

"A leap?" the woman asked.

"You know. A leap." He arced one of his hands through the air, as if he were sketching a rainbow. He might as well have slapped me with that hand. I turned back to the man on my other side and tried to keep on laughing through his attempts at English and mine at French, but all I could think was, "I need to take a leap," and one month later I stood in my kitchen, squared off with Nathan, and said it aloud.

"Oh." He flushed. "I didn't mean in your work, I meant in your career. Like, you just needed something big to happen, like winning a book contest."

"Then why are you blushing? And why did you say 'She's pretty good' if you weren't talking about the quality of my work?"

"I was joking," he said. "That woman was flirting with me."

"Well, that makes everything better," I said. "You sold me out not just for the hell of it but in the service of flirting."

"Come on, Sarah, you know I love your work," he said.

"Sure, when you're alone with me. But when you're drunk on wine with a French woman going 'Ooh la la, you're a genius,' all bets are off. Why didn't you just tell her I was an inferior talent who failed to understand you? Maybe she'll be waiting for you when you arrive in Paris."

Then he laughed. He actually laughed. "This is ridiculous," he said, and, oh, the rage that filled me.

"I'm leaving," I said.

"What do you mean you're leaving?"

I didn't bother to reply. I grabbed my bag, hanging right there on the back of a kitchen chair, and I left, with him shouting, "Where are you going? I'm making dinner!" and me shouting back that I hoped he and Philip Roth would be very happy together, dropping off the world.

I peeled out. What a satisfying sound. What a satisfying jump the car took forward, kicking up gravel behind. I only wished one of those stones had pegged him between the eyes. I drove too fast for our country road and hit the interstate hard, the roar and whoosh of the car an exact replica of my emotions. I was never going back. I said that to myself, and I believed it. That's how I used to give myself over to anger—purely, wholly, with a conviction unblemished by fears for my future or that of offspring who didn't yet exist. I used to lose my temper, and to take pleasure in its loss. I've never been so sure of myself as when anger was the only thing I felt, before the meeker, more nagging voices began to offer justifications and concerns and possible consequences. Sitting in the cafeteria now, I wished for the purifying clarity of anger like that.

I went back that time, obviously I went back. I drove all the way to the coast and walked the beach and spent the night in a hotel and the next morning I went back, to a Nathan vibrating with worry and remorse. I'd accepted his claim that he was talking about my career, not my writing, though I'd never fully believed it. What if I hadn't gone back? What if I'd said, I'll show you a leap, and blown past Chapel Hill on a fast track to Austin? Listen, Nathan, you want to know what I thought about, alone in that hotel room? You want to know the truth? I thought about Rajiv. I considered phrases from the e-mails he'd sent since we moved, a *we miss you* that seemed to me code for *I'm a little in love with you*. Why hadn't I just told you what he'd said? Why had I hidden the book, never made casual reference to an e-mail from him? Because Rajiv—he was like a wishing stone, handed over by a fairy queen in return for some karmic good deed. I'd been saving him, you see, for when I needed him, and sometimes when we fought or when my life didn't seem to be quite what I'd had in mind, I'd turn thoughts of him over in my mind, the way you might reach into your pocket to feel the firm reassurance of that stone. All I had to do was wish.

The truth is, Nathan, I sat on the stained comforter in that cheap motel room, and dialed Rajiv's number on my phone. He'd sent it to me, in one of those e-mails. *Call me when you've finished Denis Johnson's new book.* I hadn't called, but I had programmed the number into my phone. I'd labeled it with the name of a high school friend Nathan would never have any reason to call.

"Hello?" he said.

I took a breath. "It's Sarah."

"Wow," he said. "It really is."

I laughed. "It took me a long time to finish."

"Finish what? Oh, the book!"

"Yeah," I said. "The book."

And so, dutifully, we talked for a while about the book, the writing, the story, the ways it did and didn't resemble the earlier work. I have no idea what I said, what he said. I wasn't even paying attention at the time, distracted by the speed of my heart.

"He's here, you know, doing a visiting gig at UT. He's giving a reading next month," Rajiv said.

"Who?"

"Denis Johnson." He laughed. "What have we been talking about?"

"Him," I said. "We've been talking about him."

"You should come to the reading."

"I *should* come," I said.

"Listen," he said, his voice growing quiet. "You really should."

I could feel my pulse in my throat. "Yeah?"

"Nothing's changed for me, Sarah," he said.

There it was—what I'd wanted to hear. "Why hasn't it?" I asked.

"Because you—you're a grown-up, Sarah. These girls I date here—they say they want to be writers or filmmakers but all they do is get high and talk bullshit, and you, you're serious, you're a real artist. With you I can have a conversation. You connect when I'm being serious, and you connect when I'm making a joke. You don't understand how rare that is."

No, I supposed I didn't, having had that with Nathan for quite some time. With you, Nathan. That connection I thought would stop you from ever doing what you did, just as it stopped me from telling Rajiv I'd get to Austin as fast as I could drive. Me, I hung up the phone. I lay awake imagining I had to choose between the two of you, pick one of you out of a lineup, and over and over it was your face that swam to the surface, even though I wanted to choose Rajiv. Why couldn't I choose Rajiv?

I drove back to you, when I could have driven to Austin. If I'd done that I might, right this minute, be at a film festival with Rajiv, shaking hands with Scorsese, or curled up next to Rajiv in a hammock under the Texas sun, reading Proust, or at work in a study lined with bookshelves, writing a series of sonnets on modern love, instead of sitting in a university cafeteria drinking rapidly cooling coffee and reading nothing at all. If I'd gone to Austin, I might never had had children.

The thing is that writing poetry, making art of any kind, is an essentially selfish act. You could argue about what art brings the world, sure, but there's no guarantee that your own personal art will do that. Your pursuit of it might just annoy the friends and family who wonder why the hell you don't get a job. If I hadn't had children, I might not have taken my job. I might not have cared very much about my credit-card debt. I might still be writing. I might not be racked with worry and fear. I might still be enjoying a cigarette. I might not have changed, while Nathan went on being Nathan. Now, if Nathan got invited to a literary festival in France, he wouldn't take me. He'd leave me at home with the kids. I wasn't a poet anymore, after all. I was a business manager. I was a working mom. If one of the parents was fantasizing about leaving the other and moving to Paris, it wasn't supposed to be me. "Why did she even *have* children?" people ask. Does anyone ask, "Why did *he* even have children?"

I never meant to stop writing poetry. I never exactly decided. Sometime between the birth of my first child and the birth of my second I just slowed to a stop. One day I realized I'd been sitting at my desk for weeks without writing a single line. The poem didn't talk back. The poem didn't laugh with a baby's primal lack of inhibition when I made a funny face, didn't giggle and squirm helplessly if I tickled it. It didn't say "Mama" when it saw me like I was the only thing it wanted to see in the world, like laying eyes on me was, each and every time, the realization of a dream. When I held her at bedtime, and told her that it was time for me to sing her a lullaby, Mattie laid her cheek on my shoulder and collapsed her whole weight against me in obedient release. What could a poem do compared with that?

But maybe it wasn't about the children, or at least not about the children alone. You could argue that motherhood had been the death knell for a poetry career that was already on the decline. The trouble had started before Mattie began to fish-flop around my insides. Could it be I'd stopped writing because of what I'd overheard Nathan say? We'd been of one mind, after all. Learning he didn't believe in me was like learning I didn't believe in myself. And maybe, really, I didn't. Maybe that was why I'd been so angry, because he'd voiced my own fears: that I was only "pretty good," that I needed to "take a leap." I had trouble believing that pretty good was worth much. Maybe I'd needed him to do the believing for both of us. *I've been rereading you*, Rajiv had written. He'd meant the work, of course, but the way he phrased it made it sound like he meant me. And of course he did mean me, he meant the work *and* me, because for him, unlike for me, for Nathan, there was no reason to separate them.

I heard the clanking of metal, and looked up to see the cafeteria workers readying the lunch buffet. A couple of students walked by, arguing in a language I didn't recognize. I checked the wall clock and saw that I'd been sitting in the cafeteria for two hours, when I was supposed to be at work. I didn't really care that I was absent, that I was irresponsible. Funny how the loosening of one commitment had loosened all the others, as if they'd all been tied by the same rope.

CHAPTER TEN

Nothing lasts, so the poet says, and what can we do, helpless as we are, but refuse to believe it. Even the indifference, the numbness that had felt so certain and committed that I didn't go into work at all—even it left me by the time I got home, so that when I arrived, I sat for sometime in the car with the engine running and the radio on, lost in a what-have-I-done reverie. Surely ten thousand e-mails awaited, asking where the hell I'd been. Surely there were puzzled or angry messages on my voice mail, or maybe Smith had answered the phone and I'd have to explain myself to him, justify why I'd wasted his time. Oddly no one had called my cell phone all day. What was worse, if everyone was made furious by my absence, or if no one had noticed it at all?

I opened the kitchen door to the smell of spice and tomato, the sight of Smith at the stove. Binx was in his high chair, sucking on a bottle, Mattie at the table making a chain out of paper clips, both of them concentrating so hard they barely spared me a glance when I came in. On the counter, chips and guacamole in the chips-and-dip serving dish we'd gotten for our wedding and never used. Smith was bent over the oven door, sprinkling cheese across a casserole dish, asking if I'd ever had his enchiladas, saying I was in for a treat—a soap opera actor gamely carrying on with someone else's part.

"Did anyone call today?" I asked.

Smith shook his head. From the sympathetic expression on his face, I gathered he thought by "anyone" I meant Nathan.

No one had called. Well. Had they just imagined I was sitting in my office with my door closed? Maybe they'd assumed I'd scheduled a day off that none of them knew about. I was in charge of vacation time. I could just go in Monday and make vague references to a glitch of some kind. It would be all right. Everything would be all right. Look at Smith and believe it. Observe the quiet dailiness of this domestic camaraderie. Listen to him saying, "Dinner is almost ready," refusing my offer to help, insisting I go sit down.

"What are you making, Mattie?" I asked.

"This," she said, not looking at me. My inability to grasp the obvious was a constant irritant to her.

"I know you're making that," I said. "I mean, what's it for?"

"It's for Smith," she said. She held the chain up, eyed it as if she was only now determining its purpose. "It's a crown," she said decisively. "Smith is a queen. Queen Smith."

"Queen Smith," I said to him. "Is it OK if I address you thusly from henceforth?"

"Please, milady," he said. "I've always wanted to be royalty." He brought two plates to the table and set one in front of Mattie, one in front of me. I cut Mattie's food into bites, blowing on it as she urgently instructed me to do, saying, "See the steam? See the steam? That means it's hot." I pulled some hunks of chicken and cheese out of my enchiladas, tasted them—not too spicy—and then tore them into smaller pieces for Binx, who shoved five of them into his mouth at once right after I set them down. I sat, picked up my fork to bolt my food before Binx started fussing, and only then realized that Smith wasn't coming to the table. I turned to see him loading the dishwasher.

"You're not going to eat with us?" I asked.

"I can't," he said. "I've got to be in Raleigh for a show by eight, and I told Holly I'd meet her for dinner first."

"Oh." I turned back around, sideswiped by the intensity of my disappointment. My enchiladas swam before me. Jesus. Was I going to cry? *Disappointed* wasn't the word for what I felt. Let's try *betrayed*.

I did my best to hide this unseemly reaction, asking Smith about the show, thanking him profusely, insisting he let me finish the dishes, waving and smiling him out the door. My good mood and my appetite went with him. I put a piece of plastic wrap over my plate and stuck it in the fridge.

"He left us aw a-wone," I said to Mattie, who laughed.

"Aw a-wone," she repeated, and laughed again. She forked an enormous bite into her mouth, chewed industriously, swallowed. "This dinner is delicious," she said.

"De-wi-cious," I repeated automatically.

"Usually Daddy makes dinner," she said, and I agreed, and then, inevitably, she asked, "Where is Daddy?"

In lieu of replying I sang, "Where is Daddy, where is Daddy, ding ding dong, ding ding dong." Mattie found this delightful and sang it herself, and continued to do so on and off throughout the next hour and a half while I nursed her brother and bathed them both and left her in the tub to play while I put his pajamas on until, against my instructions, she climbed out on her own to track small wet footprints into his room, where she stood, naked and dripping, singing that song, until she grew impatient with my ministrations to Binx and began to cry that she was cold. When he was finally down and she was finally down, and I closed the door to her room, I could still hear her singing, her little voice and its merciless question trailing me down the hall.

Rajiv had written me back. *Hit eject* was the subject heading. *You should come back to Austin*, the message said. *Every little thing is better here*.

■

Of course I shouldn't have gone driving that night when I couldn't sleep, not with the children asleep in the house and Nathan gone. I'll say so before anyone else can, although I realize that will forestall no one's judgment. What can I say about why? Sometimes an urge comes, and you give in to it. That's what this whole story is about. Nathan gave in to physics, and sixteen months later so did I. At three a.m. I drove eighty miles an hour down Old 86. I'd crashed a car once, on this road, years ago. The stick shift, the one Nathan taught me to drive. I'd gone onto the shoulder, and when I heard the crunch of gravel under the tires I panicked, overcorrected, lost control of the car. I zigzagged into the other lane, yanked the wheel again, shot back through my lane and off the side of the road, spun around, hit a tree, sat there stunned in the new reality. After a while I stumbled out, sat down in the ditch. A couple of men came running across a field. They'd heard the impact. One of them gave me his cell phone and I called Nathan. My memory of this is hazy, except for the clarity of the look on Nathan's face when he arrived and ran toward me, not sparing a glance for the totaled car. I was all he cared about. He came to touch me, to make sure I was real, and his hands on my face, on my shoulders, were both fierce and gentle. "Tell me you're all right," he said.

Now I hit a rise and felt the car lift. It was a scene out of *The Dukes of Hazzard*, except that I was in a Toyota Camry, which was far too reasonable a car for running from the law. But there was the cop, taking his cue, pulling out from the clearing where the cops liked to park, often two of them, cruisers pointing opposite directions so that they could chat out the windows.

For a brief, wild moment I thought about not stopping.

"Do you know how fast you were going?" the cop asked.

"Yes," I said, and even in his impassive face I thought I detected surprise. He was an older man, dark-skinned, with an air of polite weariness. He swung his gaze from my face to the back of the car, where the two car seats sat like stand-ins. I watched him coming to conclusions. "License and registration, please," he said.

I handed them over. He studied the photo on the license, then my face, then the photo again. Any sign of suspicion, and I felt I'd done the thing I was suspected of. I fought a hysterical urge to confess that the photo wasn't me, see if he believed it, see if he hauled me off to jail. "Be right back," he said.

It had been years since a cop had pulled me over, but I recognized this feeling, which was always exactly the same. Agitated suspense and suspension. Scattershot anger at both cop and yourself. The outcome in another's hands, and nothing to do but wait. Funny how some experiences recur and disappear entirely, like bubbles that form and pop.

Most days you forget the feeling of sliding your heels into the metal stirrups at the end of the doctor's table, of a sinus headache just behind the eyes, of the dull, flat drive between here and elsewhere, of lying awake in the eerie stillness of the middle of the night. And then there you are again, back in that bubble, and you think, Oh, *this*. I remember this. Same as it ever was, even as everything else rushes away.

Now, now, was probably when the kids were waking, now that I could no longer choose to go back to them. "Mommy?" Mattie called. "Mommy, the deepness!" And Binx, startled into awareness, cried out his displeasure in consciousness. Lightning hit the house. Windows rattled as a tornado approached. Someone in the woods threw a match, and it arced in a flare of light. A tree began to topple slowly toward the roof. Mattie climbed up her dresser, which pulled in slow motion away from the wall. Binx stuck his head between the bars of his crib. Chokables, chokables everywhere.

The cop was back, passing me my license and registration, and that was all. "No ticket?" I asked.

"No, ma'am," he said. "I think you need to get on home. I don't think this is where you want to be."

"Shouldn't you give me a ticket?"

"You have some other things you need to worry about," he said. "Don't mess up what you've got at home."

"I deserve a ticket," I said.

"Ma'am," he said. "I'm letting you go." He stepped back from the car.

"I deserve a ticket," I said again, but he was done with me, walking sure-footed back to the cruiser. "I deserve a ticket," I shouted out the open window, because I did, I really did. "Come back here!" I shouted, but only after he'd already driven away.

CHAPTER ELEVEN

In the morning, after I called every hotel and hospital within a thirty-mile radius and learned that none of them contained Nathan, at least not under his own name, I went into his study. Binx was taking his morning nap. Mattie was watching *Blue's Clues* in the living room, and as I picked up a paperback copy of *A Sport and a Pastime* that had been lying facedown on Nathan's keyboard, I heard, "A clue! A clue!" burst forth in piping television voices.

I sat down in Nathan's chair with the book in my hand. *Suddenly it is quite clear how acrobatic, how dangerous everything is. It seems not to be his own life he is living, but another, the life of some victim.* A clue, a clue, but to what? Was this about Nathan or me? *A Sport and a Pastime* is a book—a *sens*ual book—about an affair, but so is every third book on the planet, and I'd known for more than a decade that it was one of Nathan's favorites. Nathan liked to ask other writers what book they wished they'd written—it was the fastest way, he said, to learn their sensibilities, the nuances of their ambitions, maybe even something about their very natures—and when they turned the question on him, as they almost always did, he'd sometimes answer that it was this book. Sometimes *The Moviegoer*. Sometimes *The Great Gatsby*. And I knew that when he answered with the Percy or the Fitzgerald he was comfortable with his own accustomed mode, the wised-up romantic still longing for the greater reality of myth, and when he answered with the Salter he was wishing he saw the vicissitudes of love and sex with a colder eye. So what did it tell me, finding this book on his desk, at the end of a time in which he'd confessed an affair and disappeared? That Nathan thought about sex. I already knew that. And what would it have told me to find Gatsby on his keyboard? That sometimes Nathan succumbed to romantic notions at odds with the dailiness of our life, of any life, and blurted out that he wanted to leave me to live in Paris. I already knew that. I even knew that this happened especially when his work wasn't going well and he wanted the excitement he got from high-flown inspiration to be generated by his own life. What did it tell me to sit in his chair, my body against the contours that usually shaped his? That he was taller than me. That, too, I already knew.

Nathan's first book—a short story collection—was about romantic yearning, about sex. This is the book that did well in France. He tried to expand one of the stories—a fable-like thing about a guy who forms a family with his current wife and all his former girlfriends—into his first novel, and ended up with his first major misfire, a book that never saw the light of day, characterized by the intensity of its sincerity about a situation that Nathan just could not render believable outside the compressed, metaphorical confines of a short story. The next book, the one he actually published, the one that spent three weeks on the *New York Times* best-seller list, was about a guy who has to choose between his soulfire love for an artist who doesn't want to procreate and marriage to a lawyer who wants, as he does, to have children. And, of course, the third book—the one he'd written in a delirious rush that had looked like inspiration at the time but now seemed more like rechanneled passion, or an exorcism of guilt—that one was about infidelity.

Now he was working on a book about a missing child—one, unlike the bulk of them, from the father's point of view. He was sensitive about this book, because of the proliferation of novels with the same subject matter, because of their success, and his fear that people might perceive him as trying to cash in. He'd made many a speech to me and to his friends about how his desire to write it had nothing to do with best-seller dreams, how he wasn't going to use the mystery in a cheap or obvious way, how since having children he'd discovered a new seriousness and this book was simply the result of that, an expression of his fears. I hadn't read any of it yet. In fact I'd hardly read his work at all in these, our child-rearing years. The edit I'd done on *Infidelity* was the only exception. That—my lack of knowledge about, of participation in, his work—was another of the many things about our life together that had changed. Time was, he read to me a paragraph he'd just finished. He called me into his study to determine whether "he handed her the flowers" or "he thrust the flowers at her" was a preferable construction. I read draft after draft of his earlier work, and, oh, the knock-down-drag-outs we had about that polygamy book, not the least of which was over my insistence on calling it a polygamy book and his insistence that the book wasn't about that, wasn't about the desire of a man to have multiple sex partners but the desire to maintain connections to those we otherwise lose, the endless possible permutations of love.

I tried to remember the last time he'd asked my opinion, the last time he'd read a paragraph aloud to me moments after it left his brain. I couldn't. I remembered testy exchanges—a couple? several?—in which he'd asked my opinion and then argued with it and I'd said I didn't have time for argument. This kind of thing began to happen after Mattie was born. It was hard to care whether flowers were thrust or handed when I needed to use what little free time I had to get blueberry stains out of baby clothes. So I'd grown impatient. Without my even noticing, he'd stopped asking, and maybe that was what I didn't know anymore—not *him*, not the essential him, but where he went in his mind these days when he was working, and who he saw there, and what kinds of things those people wanted, and what kinds of things they did. Why had he asked me to edit that book? Had he wanted that connection back, the one we used to have? Or had he thought I'd be suspicious if he didn't ask? If so, he was wrong. I'd trusted him, trusted him so completely that a book called *Infidelity* had raised no doubts in me.

The computer came to life when I touched the mouse—still on, of course, because it had been on before I'd asked him to leave, and he hadn't had reason to think he wouldn't perform his usual prebedtime ritual of checking e-mail and the news. I opened the "Fiction" folder again, and then another one labeled "Current." I opened it and saw four files: missing.doc, missingnotes.doc, missingcuts.doc, and ?. "Missing, missing notes, missing cuts, question mark," I said out loud, seeing in the file titles, in the subject matter, some kind of sign. Missing, missing, missing, and a mystery. I clicked on the question mark file, and found one paragraph inside.

I didn't mean to kiss her. Maybe she kissed me first. Let's say that. Yes, she kissed me first. We'd been skinny-dipping in the reservoir. I didn't look when she took off her clothes in the XX dark, I didn't look when she cannonballed into the water, or when she clambered out, slipping and saying, "Whoops!" and then laughing with drunken embarrassment. OK, I glanced up then, at the "Whoops!"—I had to make sure she wasn't hurt—but all I saw was the shape of a body, a body white with reflected light.

I'd read enough of Nathan's drafts to know that when he couldn't find the right word for something he just put *XX* or *??* and moved on. Many times I'd helped him fill in those blanks. "Quiet," I said now. "Thrumming, the thrumming dark. The watery dark. The steamy, steamy illicit-sex dark. The guilty dark. The moonlit dark." I typed that last one in. *She took off her clothes in the moonlit dark.* And she had, hadn't she. That was exactly what she'd done. I hit save.

If you spend any time with a writer there will inevitably come a moment when he tells you a story you recognize from something he's written, or you read something he's written and find a story you've already heard. My own work was not confessional in a blow-jobs-and-suicidal-thoughts kind of way, but it was clearly about me, about my experience of the world, and maybe partly because of that I always made a point of not indulging the temptation to get double duty out of my material. I never wrote an e-mail, as one of my poet friends did, that began *Spring lies heavy upon the doorstep.* Nathan was a perpetrator of this particular crime. It used to drive me crazy when he told a story at a party that he'd used in his fiction, especially when he got confused, as he usually did, about what details came from the true-life source and what were embellishments he'd added in translation.

Or maybe he didn't get confused. He always said he had,

when I pointed out to him, as I could never resist doing, that he'd told an anecdote from one of his novels to people who'd likely read his novels, that by using fictional details rather than the real ones he'd confirmed an impression that every word he wrote was true. But maybe he said he was confused because he didn't want to admit that he knowingly used the refined details, the fictional ones—his social life as much of a performance as his work. Or maybe it was the reverse—maybe the work was as real to him as the life. Why can I summon without effort the emotions of Meg Murry as she shivers in her bed during a storm, fearing for her picked-on baby brother, her vanished father, when there are whole stretches of my own life, my actual life, that have blurred into alarm clocks, cars, staircases and elevators, streaks of color, streaks of light? Stories are experience, dreams are experience, your parents talk about a childhood event until, though the details are vivid in your mind, you no longer have any idea whether you actually recall it. What does it matter what really happened? Sometimes you don't know if you remember the moment, or the photograph.

I was a writer myself, I lived with a writer, I knew some things were lost and some things gained when experience was transmogrified into phrases. I knew that in a writer's work you both find and fail to find that writer's life, and when people asked me whether it worried me that Nathan's work so often featured infidelity and unhappy marriages and ambivalent parenthood I said no, and when they asked me if any of it was true, I said no. No was a much easier answer to give than the actual one, which was that sometimes he might feel something that he wouldn't act on and give that feeling to a character who did act on it, and sometimes he'd take something he actually did or felt and make it bigger, an irritated retort to his mother becoming an argument in which two characters laid bare the resentments of years, and really, just, it's complicated, okay? People never asked me if the things in my poems really happened. Maybe they just assumed they had, and so Nathan had to contend with our friends and families knowing he cried in the parking lot of the movie theater after we saw *Titanic*.

And now I had to contend with this. Not just the knowledge that I'd been wrong not to worry, that he'd transformed a betrayal into fiction, that he'd let another woman inspire him, but this. This paragraph, this snippet of the true. It wasn't in Nathan's usual prose style, which was verbose and exuberant, treading the line between comic and poignant. This was compressed, concise, matter-of-fact, an unadorned rendering of actual experience, a snapshot of the moment when he chose. I wanted there to be more, I wanted details, the way we want to know the nasty things that have been said about us, listening with our stomachs hot and sick, the blood pounding in our ears, and at the same time I was sorry to have read even this, to have seen the moment from his point of view. I didn't want to see his point of view. I didn't want to inhabit him as we inhabit the characters we read about. I didn't want to stand there, wet and naked, and look at that woman and attempt to shore up my loyalties against the tidal wave of yearning. I rejected empathy. I didn't want to see the moonlight on her body, the otherworldly romance of that. Now I knew, as I knew so many other things about him, how it felt to my husband to want someone else.

Listen, buddy, you're not the first, OK? You're not even the first to write it down. I myself have written it down, in a poem I never showed you, about an event I never described to you, because unlike you I know what and what not to reveal. Remember how I came home from that visit to Helen and suggested we get married? You want to know why? Because of Rajiv. I went there knowing I would see him, of course. You and I had seen him the last time we'd gone, but we were together, and he was with a girl who twined herself around him like a vine. But on the next trip he was single again—Helen had told me—and I'd be there alone. I didn't plan for anything to happen. I just wanted to know if anything would.

I couldn't tell, at first, whether he still felt what he'd claimed to feel for me. And then one night Helen took me to a party, and when I bumped into him outside, and said in my best Katharine Hepburn, "Hello, you," he grabbed my hand and pulled me farther into the dark of the yard. He told me—again! and you didn't even know about the first two times—that he was a little in love with me, and, oh, in that moment, drunk on gin and abuzz with desire—my own or his, I couldn't have told you—I believed him. And then I kissed him, and I felt what you felt, and oh, believe me, I wanted to do what you have done. But I didn't. I stepped back, though every nerve ending resisted the stepping back, and on the plane on the way home I thought that if I could resist someone I'd spent years finding attractive, if I could resist what I wanted that badly, because of you, because of you, then I should be your wife.

But I still thought about him, because my experience of him never faded into the everyday the way it did, of course, with you and me. Two months before our wedding I wrote this:

White Christmas lights,
scattershot of stars on a Texas night,

leading me, if not astray
then stranded—

what was that boxwood hedge,
that greeny-scented maze,
doing behind a shabby rental dive
in Austin?

What was that man
doing with his mouth
on my mouth, my mouth
kissing back bourbon and want?

That maze wants so badly
to be an allegory,
rather than a fact

upon whose leaves I pricked
my fingertips
as he pulled me inside—

thinking Christmas, Christmas,
looking for a navigator star,
wishing to be lost.

It was good, too. I knew it was good. I never sent it out. I never showed it to anyone. I'd changed the gin to bourbon, and I hadn't really pricked my fingers or thought about Christmas, but all the rest of it was true, and I'd had rules, you see. I never exposed anything that would hurt you, Nathan, no matter what you sometimes claimed. But now I will. I'll write a poem now, I really will, an unabashed, nakedly true poem about you and what you did. The shoe, the wedding toast, the crying at the Fiesta Grill. The missing, missing, missing. The moonlit dark. There is no point in resisting. That's what the title can be.

I opened a new file. I drummed my fingers on the keyboard. I waited for concentration to settle on me like a cloud, to focus me like a laser beam—oh, my similes had gotten stale. How long had it been since I'd entered that mental space, the one that cannot bear interruption? Interrupted, you try to check your irritation, one part of your brain struggling to hold steady, like a paused screen, on your last thought, another part coping with whatever minor daily concern the person in your space has brought along to trouble you, this person who's crashed through the wrong door into your dream. Nathan and I used to understand that look in each other, the impatience that would sharpen the speech of the interrupted one. Listen, if you came into my study when I was writing and spoke to me, you were stepping into the lion's den, and it wasn't my fault if you lost your head.

You can't be that way with children, though. Or shouldn't be. Or anyway I thought you shouldn't be, and Nathan more or less agreed. Sometimes even when he wasn't working Mattie spoke to him and he didn't hear her, lost in thought, and though when he came back from wherever he'd been he tried not to sound irritable, it was nevertheless true that sometimes she stood by his side saying, "Daddy," five or six times before he dragged his gaze outward and saw her there, and even then it was usually because I'd said, with some sharpness, "She's talking to you. Your daughter's talking to you." Was this something I should hold against him? Would she grow up feeling less than important, would she choose to marry a negligent man? Or was it good for her not to assume that attention was automatically granted, so she wouldn't turn out a princess of entitlement, certain of her eventual fame, like, according to the media, all the young people of today? How was I supposed to know?

The cursor blinked. *You*, I typed. Mattie appeared in the doorway. "You didn't come," she said.

"What do you mean?"

"I called you, and you didn't come," she said. "You never do anything I want."

"Who says I have to do what you want?" I said. "That's not the deal."

"The show was scary," she said. "It had dinosaurs."

"I thought you liked dinosaurs."

"Well, I don't like the scary ones."

"Why don't you go back in there now? Maybe the scary ones are gone."

"They're not gone, actually," she said. "I don't want to. What are you doing?"

"I'm writing a poem."

"Is it scary?"

"Yes," I said.

She advanced on me, cautiously, as though the monster of my poem might at any moment spring forth from the screen. "Lift me up so I can see," she said. I hauled her into my lap. Her hair smelled like peanut butter. "Read the word," she said.

"Mommy, will you read the word, please?" I said.

"Mommy, will you read the word, please?" she repeated.

"I'd be happy to," I said. "It's you."

"No," she cried. "Read *the word*."

"That is the word. The word is *you*." I pointed at the screen.

"That starts with *y*," she said, and I agreed. We sat a moment and looked at that one word, the only word it appeared I would write. Then I deleted it.

■

What I didn't know, I decided later that day, driving around with the kids in the backseat in hope that they would sleep, was what Nathan thought of *me*. It had been years since it had occurred to me to ask. He loved me, I'd assumed. He thought I was "pretty good," he thought I needed to "take a leap." But no—he hadn't quite meant that, or so he'd said, and I'd allowed myself to accept his explanations. "It's not you," he'd said, about the character in his novel with my job, and I'd decided to believe him. But maybe it was me, this woman satisfied with being ordinary. Maybe her story was Nathan's attempt to understand me, the person I'd become. Maybe because he thought I was ordinary, and content to be so, it was OK for the ordinary to befall me, the banality of a drunken husband, a willing woman, a moonlit reservoir.

But, I wanted to say to him, if I could find him, I am not the person this happens to. Don't you remember the bohemian dark, a grad school party, one of our classmates reciting, from memory, Andrew Hudgins's poem "Blur"—*and more than joy I longed for understanding / and more than understanding I longed for joy*—and then a poem of her own, with that line about being as small as a star, and as we listened to her there lived in the two of us, in all of us in the room, the transcendent?

The Nathan in my head said that that didn't matter, the transcendent, the memory of it, up against the facts of my life. As I thought this, my idiotic brain queued up the theme song to the TV show: *the facts of life*, *the facts of life*. We are not special, you know, most of us, no matter what our parents say. We should all sit down and look at ourselves in the mirror and see an ordinary soul. We are going to get married and have children and have jobs. We are not going to be rich. We are never going to be on television. There is no reason for us to have—for us to try to give our children—such unseemly quantities of self-esteem.

Rajiv was at that grad school party. I was almost sure I remembered him there.

"Where are we going?" Mattie asked.

"We're just driving around," I said. "We're looking at things."

"Are we going to see my mother?"

"What do you mean?"

"My mother lives far away."

I glanced at her in the rearview mirror. She had a blank yet rapt look on her face, like a medium channeling a spirit. "I'm your mother."

"You're *not* my mother," she said, her tone so definitive that for a moment I believed her, I felt what it would be like to look at this child and have no connection to her at all, and I wondered how we came to be here together, driving around in this car.

"Why would you say that?" I asked.

"I'm pretending," she said. "My mother lives in Kentucky. Her name is Lola and her cat's name is Sophie. She fixes furniture. She takes me to see grown-up movies. She took me to see a silly grown-up movie. There was a monster and a child and the monster wanted to eat the child but the lion ate the monster before he could eat the child."

"So I'm not your mother?" I asked.

"No."

"Who am I?"

"You're a writer who came to see the movie."

I was not her mother, I was a writer. See—even she knew it was impossible to be both. "Why did I come to see the movie?" I asked. "What kinds of things do I write?"

But she'd lost interest, or lost the thread of her narrative, or both. "Where are we going?" she asked, and then she put her fingers in her mouth and let her face go slack, as though she despaired of the answer.

She was right to do so, because by then I'd begun driving to places where I'd known Nathan to go, in the order they occurred to me: his doctor's office, the Regulator, the coffee shop that served its coffee in a French press and posted descriptions of its beans as full of sensual adjectives as a food and wine magazine. In the coffee shop parking lot, I nursed Binx in the front seat, his head propped awkwardly on my bag, and he pinched my stomach and my breast, rolling the skin between his tiny fingers, and I said, mechanically, "No pinching," but made no effort to stop him, just sat there feeling the tug at my breast, the small sharp pains. A man glanced into the car as he walked by and did a double take, clearly not expecting to witness lactation. He reacted with the mingled pity and embarrassment of someone who's just barged in on you in a public bathroom, and quickened his pace on his way inside.

Mattie began to complain that she was hungry, so when Binx was sated I drove to Weaver Street, a food co-op and café where Nathan liked to go for jazz Sundays, part of me still thinking that if I just went to one more of his haunts, just one more, I'd find him. By the time we arrived both kids had fallen asleep, so I sat in the parking lot and stared at the passersby. From what distance would I recognize Nathan? That guy coming up the street, far enough from me to still be featureless, if he were Nathan would I know it? I would, I believed I would. I knew his gait—the hunch of his shoulders, the hands in his pockets, the way he stared at the ground, lost in thought, giving him a propensity for collisions with poles. I knew the geometry of him, the breadth of his shoulders and the length of his hair. And if I rolled down the window and closed my eyes—like this—how readily would I recognize his voice? Would I know him from a shout? From a laugh? From a sigh? I believed I would. I would. I knew him as a shape. I knew him as a sound.

But she didn't. She didn't know his body, hadn't seen him naked before that night at the reservoir when he shed his clothes. He'd been new to her, each flash of naked back or buttock a glimpse into the mystery. And he'd liked that, I knew that. It hadn't just been about looking at her. It had been about her looking at him.

The shape of a body. The moonlit dark.

White Christmas lights strung along a hedge in the back of a rental house in Austin. The taste of gin in my mouth. A hand catching my fingers, tugging. "Come on," he said. "Come on."

"What is this?" I asked, a little breathless, as though we were running.

"He calls it the secret garden," he said.

"Who does?"

"The guy who lives here. Joe. Didn't you meet him?"

I laughed. "I have no idea."

And then we were through a gap in the hedge, and I saw that a path opened up and then rounded a corner and disappeared, and I said, "A maze!"

And he said, “Told you,” and I said, “I’m amazed,” with the ironic tone that acknowledged I was making a terrible pun but allowed me to make it anyway. But I didn’t laugh, because of the way his hand tightened on mine, not casual anymore, and the inexorable pull, closer, closer, the white lights starry around his face, his beautiful face, his not-Nathan face.

I opened my eyes in the here and now, the sunlight bouncing viciously off a parking lot full of windshields. For a moment I didn’t know if I’d resurfaced from a memory or a dream. It didn’t seem possible I could have been that girl in the maze. Had all my cells replaced themselves since then? What could I say, what could I do, to go back there now and be that girl again?

In the back of the car my children, Nathan’s children, went on dreaming. I risked the slow, quiet extrication of my cell phone from my bag. I dialed Helen. When she answered on the second ring, I murmured into the phone that it was me.

“Hey!” she said. “I’ve been meaning to call you for ages.”

“Me, too,” I said.

“But listen,” she said, “can I—” She was about to ask me if she could call me back, and she’d promise she’d call me right back, but then one of her children would demand a book and the other would want a snack, and her mother would call or the guy would show up to fix the cable, and then her husband would come in asking if she knew where to find his keys and they’d get in an argument about why he could never find them that would evolve into an argument about arguing in front of the kids, and then it would be dinnertime and then bedtime and then Helen would collapse on the couch, washed ashore at last, drained as a shipwreck survivor and certainly too tired to call me back. Meanwhile in the backseat Binx stirred and whimpered in his sleep. I didn't have time to wait. I had no time.

"Nathan cheated on me," I said.

"What?" she said. "Nathan?"

The incredulity in her voice—was that a compliment to me? To him? "You sound surprised," I said.

"I'm beyond surprised," she said. "I'm incredulous. I'm flabbergasted."

"Well, I'm enraged," I said. "I'm enraged, I'm distraught, I'm losing my goddamn mind. I can't sleep, I don't want to eat, I skipped out on work yesterday, I genuinely think I'm going crazy, and right now, right at this moment, I'm sitting in a parking lot staking out a place where he likes to go because I thought he might turn up here. I haven't seen him in two days and he's not answering his phone. For all I know he's dead. Maybe it would be better if he was."

There was a flat silence, one that went on long enough that I thought we'd lost the connection, and I said, "Hello?"

"I'm here," she said. "I'm caught off guard."

"I know," I said. "I am, too." I was losing it, breathing hard. I was the werewolf catching sight of the full moon, feeling the pain and the power of a claw bursting through what used to be a hand.

"I'm so sorry," she said. "I can't believe it. What happened?"

"Oh, he slept with some writer. And then he confessed, and said he wanted to work it out, and I tried for a week or so and then I asked him to leave, and now he's gone, really, really gone. At least before he left I had this illusion of being in control, because he kept telling me what happened next was my decision, but now I've got no control at all because I don't even know where he is. And I'm pissed, I'm just so pissed that I let him stay one day, one minute, after he told me. I can't help but think things would have been totally different before the kids. I wouldn't have just taken it, you know. I wouldn't have tried so hard."

"Oh, Sarah," she said. "I'm so sorry."

I blinked, and spilled tears. "If you sympathize with me, I really will come undone. Let's talk about revenge. Let's talk about raw animal sex."

"OK," she said. "I—" Then I heard her son's voice, as loudly as if he too had his mouth against the phone. "Mommy," he said, "it won't come out."

"It will," Helen said. "You just have to relax and then push a little."

"I'm trying," Ian said. "It won't come out."

"I'm sorry," Helen said to me. "I'm in a public bathroom with Ian. He's having some trouble pooping."

"Oh," I said, amused despite myself, sympathetic, and—no question—deflated.

"No matter what's going on in our lives," Helen said, "there's still the matter of excrement."

"And naps," I said. "And food. And breast milk. And puzzles."

"Yes," Helen said. "But mostly excrement." Her son wailed, and Helen again offered reassurances, if slightly testier ones, and then she said to me, "So on that other topic you should come visit me."

"That's what Rajiv said," I said. "He e-mailed me."

"Interesting," she said.

"Why?" I asked. "I mean, I think it's interesting, too. Do you know something I don't?"

"He's single again," she said. "I know that."

"Is it possible he's still hung up on me?"

"It's possible," she said.

"Can you find out?" I asked. "I know I sound so ridiculous and junior high, Helen, but you have no idea, I really think I'm losing it. I need something, and maybe a guy who's hung up on me is the thing I need."

"I'll find out. I wish there was something else I could do for you."

"I know."

"Mommy!" Ian shouted.

"I really can't believe that Nathan . . ."

"I know," I said.

"What a motherfucker," Helen said, and Ian said, "Daddy says you shouldn't say that!" and Helen said, "Be quiet for a minute," and Ian said, "But Daddy says . . . ," and Helen said, "I know what Daddy says. These are extreme circumstances." I closed my eyes and listened to them argue, back and forth, back and forth, the endless, exhausting exchange.

"I should let you go," I said. I hoped that Helen would say no, I clearly needed to talk, but I wasn't surprised when she said again that she was sorry, that she was in a public bathroom with her constipated child. How could I compete with the immediacy of that circumstance, that need?

"What are you going to do?" Helen asked.

"I don't know. If he's going to disappear, I wish he would die. At least I'd get five hundred thousand from the life insurance if he died."

"Mommy!" Ian shouted.

"I'll call you," Helen said, raising her voice over Ian's increasing caterwaul. "I'll call you as soon as I can," and then I heard her saying, "Stop it, stop it now, you need to calm—" and then the line went dead.

I heard the small wet squeak of finger sucking and turned to see that Mattie was awake, gazing out the window while she twirled her hair.

"Mattie," I said, "did you just wake up?"

She turned her gaze on me, eyes blank and sleepy.

"Mattie?" I reached back and popped the fingers out of her mouth. She made an inhuman sound of protest and lunged for her hand, but I pulled it farther back. "Did you hear Mommy talking?"

"I want to suck my fingers!" she shouted. She strained against my hand, and I let go, and once again the fingers stopped her mouth. I started up the car, my heart careening like a getaway driver's, as though fleeing the scene might save me from accounting for my crime. She hadn't heard.

When we got home, Nathan wasn't there. We went inside just long enough to check the voice mail—nothing—and change Binx's diaper, then I suggested we walk down to the mailbox, clapping my hands, my voice unnaturally bright.

Three or four feet from the road I put the brake on the stroller and left Binx where he could watch as Mattie and I, holding hands, looking both ways, crossed the road to the mailbox. I held Mattie up so she could open the door—nothing there but a solitary piece of junk mail. She reached in to get it, and the mailbox didn't move. "The mailbox is fixed," she said.

"What?" I put her down, leaned over her to try to wiggle it. "You're right," I said. "That's funny. Mr. Dodson must have fixed it."

"Daddy fixed it," she said. She said it with such certainty

I pictured Nathan sneaking back here with a hammer and nails, too tortured to talk to us but still wanting to express his love, a steadied mailbox the first step back toward a steadied life. "He's back," she said.

"Back?"

"At the house," she said. "He's back at the house. He fixed the mailbox this morning."

"I don't think so," I said.

"He did," she said. "He did."

"No, he didn't, Mattie!" I snapped. "He hasn't been here, OK?"

"Where's my daddy?" she shouted, the last word dissolving into a wail. Across the street Binx joined in the screaming. If he'd had words they would have been, "You left me all alone!"

"Jesus!" I shouted. "Will everybody just stop screaming!" I grabbed Mattie's hand and started back into the road, and a car I'd failed to see, a car I hadn't even bothered to look for, just missed us, with a whoosh and a squeal and the long, fading expletive of the horn.

"Oh my God," I said. I was shaking. "Oh my God." I picked Mattie up and she buried her face in my shoulder, clinging to my neck. I looked both ways seven times before I ran across the street back to Binx, Mattie bouncing against me. Binx's face was red, his hands balled into fists, and as I shifted Mattie to one hip and tried to unbuckle his straps with one hand two tiny perfect tears rolled down his cheeks. Still holding Mattie, I wrangled him out of the stroller, and then I sat down in the dirt with the kids on my lap, both of them suddenly, miraculously silent. We watched a bird strut by Mrs. Dodson's scarecrow as though it had never had a thing to fear.

"That car almost hit us," Mattie said. "We would have been squished."

"I know, I'm sorry, I know."

"Will I die?" Mattie asked.

That was the first time, the first time she'd asked me that question, and it was my fault that she was asking it, that I went cold, then hot, then cold again, and that now I had to answer. Yes was the answer, wasn't it, but I could neither say it nor believe it. "You mean if a car hits you?"

"Yes. Will I die if a car hits me?"

"It depends."

"When will I die?" she asked.

I didn't answer. I tightened my grip on both my children.

"If you die," she went on, merciless, "can a doctor fix you?"

"No, honey," I said.

"When will you die?" she asked.

"I don't know," I said.

"Yesterday you said you wanted Daddy to die," she said.

"That wasn't yesterday," I said.

"Earlier," she said, taking a stab. "A few days ago."

"That was today," I said. I knew that what was necessary was a speech on people saying things they didn't mean, perhaps a distracting use of the word *hyperbole*, which would cause her to ask what that meant and in the process steer her off her original course entirely. I just repeated, helplessly, "That was today."

Mattie squirmed off my lap and sprawled in the dirt on her back. "Don't step on the died girl," she said.

CHAPTER TWELVE

I put the kids to bed at six o'clock—one of the perks of having children still too young to tell time—because I just couldn't be responsible another minute. I hadn't been doing such a hot job of it, anyway, so it seemed like a good idea to call it quits. I hadn't touched food all day, and the thought of eating had no appeal for me now, but I wanted a glass of wine, or maybe a bottle of wine, and I wanted to get out my *Buffy* DVDs and sit on the couch and watch them until I passed out. When no one is watching, we can do what we want to do. That is the pleasure of being alone.

I was watching the season-two finale, which is the one where Buffy believes she's lost everything and then realizes she has one thing left and that's herself, and I was thinking that Buffy manages to find that notion empowering but hell if I could, maybe because I was without superpowers, when I heard a car coming up the drive. When you live out in the country and your house is a quarter mile off the road, it's very startling to hear the approach of an unexpected car. Nathan and I had never failed to react to the sound of wheels on gravel with anything less than alarm. Much of the time it was just the mailman with a package, but every so often the sound heralded the arrival of Jehovah's Witnesses. Once it had been a carload of them, and they'd circled the house, two going to the kitchen door, two to the front, one to the side, the door we used as our entrance. Nathan and I were watching out the window of his study. "Oh my God," he whispered. "We're surrounded." I made him go talk to them, and because he was nicer than I was we ended up with multiples copies of the *Watchtower* and, ominously, a promise that they'd return.

Despite the lack of sleep and the lack of food and the abundance of alcohol, I wasn't addled enough to think Jehovah's Witnesses were coming up the drive. I thought it was Nathan. I went into what can only be described as a panic. I turned off the TV, shoved the empty wine bottle under the couch, ran into the bathroom to wash my face, because I'd been crying, because it was very painful for Buffy to have to put a sword through her occasionally evil boyfriend, her one and only true love. I didn't want Nathan to think I'd been sitting around getting drunk and crying over him, as if there were some profit in convincing him that his infidelity and craven disappearance had absolutely no effect on me.

But it wasn't Nathan. It was Smith. When I walked into the kitchen, I saw his face in the glass on the side door. He spotted me, gave me a wry half-smile, and lifted his hand to say hello. I stopped where I was, knocked back by a rush of conflicting emotions too many and too fearsome to identify. I couldn't will myself to go to the door, but I managed to raise my own hand and wave him in, and so he entered. "Hi," he said, closing the door quietly behind him. I noticed that he knew that if he wasn't careful the screen door would slam. Had he known that a long time or just noticed it the day before?

"Hi," I said.

"I'm sorry I couldn't get out here any earlier," he said, setting a grocery bag on the counter. "Busy day."

He seemed to think I'd expected him. I thought about telling him that I hadn't, that he didn't have to feel any obligation to me, but the truth was I liked him feeling it, that his sense of responsibility was strong enough that he assumed I'd take him for granted. No matter what the magazines say, it seems to me we should take each other for granted, husbands and wives, and gift each other with the small, unnoticed pleasure of assuming someone will want to know what you'd like for dinner, someone will be there when you call.

"Yeah?" I said. "What did you do?"

"I had a lunch interview with a guy—maybe you'd know him, he used to be in that group Buffalo Girls? He just split off to start his own band and they're pretty interesting, they combine alt-country with electronica, if you can imagine that. I ended up going back to his place to hear some of what they've been recording, so I was late to meet Holly—she wanted me to go with her to shop for a new couch—and it took a while to, uh, work things out with her." He pulled out a bag of apples and a carton of milk. "Then I went to the grocery store. I picked up a few things for you. Noticed you were running low on stuff for the kids, and I know Nathan does the shopping . . ."

"You are amazing," I said. "You are a freaking saint." I felt indignant at the difficult, reproving Holly. Couldn't she see the effort he made?

"It's just milk," he said. He seemed embarrassed. He

opened the fridge, saw last night's dinner plate in there, with its plastic wrap, and stood there a moment with the fridge door open. "You didn't eat your enchiladas?"

"No," I said. "I'm sorry. I wasn't hungry."

"Did you eat anything today?"

"Eat?"

"You know," he said. "Put food in your mouth. Chew. Swallow."

"I don't want to eat."

"You have to eat something," he said. "You're breastfeeding. I don't know much about kids, but I know a breastfeeding mother has to eat."

I made a face, a childish "bleh" face, like Mattie made when presented with vegetables. Smith looked worried, annoyed, and helpless, which I imagined was about what I looked like when Mattie wouldn't eat. I wasn't playacting exactly, but a small part of me watched the scene at a sociologist's remove, wondering what Smith would do now, what I would do. There was something interesting and entertaining about his consternation. It was kind of fun to play the child.

"There must be something that sounds good," he said. "Let's see. Pizza?"

I shook my head.

"A burger? Mexican? Sushi?"

"A milkshake," I said. "I'd drink a milkshake."

He checked his watch. "I think Maple View is still open," he said. "What flavor do you want?"

"Vanilla," I said.

"Is that your favorite?" he asked.

The question struck me as oddly intimate. "It's my favorite milkshake flavor," I said. "Not my favorite in general."

He nodded. "Got it," he said, and then he said he'd be right back.

Since the whole point of watching *Buffy* was total immersion in a world that was familiar and yet far, far from my own, I didn't want to go back to it knowing I'd be interrupted. I stood in the kitchen, feeling surprisingly hopeless about not knowing what to do with the next ten minutes, and then I was visited by one of those torturing bulletins from my anxious mother-brain, ever prepared to believe that a child-rearing screwup would bring punishment: Your children might be dead, they might have died in their sleep because you sent their father away and brought up death, *his* death, and then you got far too drunk to be able to drive them to the emergency room, even though you were the only responsible adult around.

Binx was a light sleeper, so I snuck into his room like a burglar. As I approached the crib, he twitched—alive!—and I froze, stood there a minute, then slowly, slowly backed out of the room. I closed the door and then released the doorknob as carefully as if a wrong move would explode us.

Mattie I didn't worry about waking, because she was a heavy sleeper like her father. You could lift her out of bed and stand her on her feet and she'd stay asleep, swaying with her hair in her face, her little pink mouth hanging sweetly open. When I went in her room she was asleep on her back, her arms flung open to her sides, as if she'd passed out in the middle of making a snow angel. There was plenty of light in the room, courtesy of a plastic lamp with rotating butterflies she'd insisted on having on at night ever since she entered the age of fear, since she'd stopped saying the fish-chasing sharks in *Finding Nemo* were funny and told me, indignant and accusatory, that they were, in fact, scary.

As were monsters, the dark, the deepness, and, most mysteriously of all, "going closer to stuff." Hard to say if she thought I'd known all this and kept it from her, or if she'd just thought I'd failed to realize it myself. I bent over her, kissed her forehead, whispered in her ear, "You're never going to die," and she took a long, snuffling breath and rolled over onto her side.

I straightened up, caught a glimpse of myself in the full-length mirror that hung on her closet door. It was the only full-length mirror in the house, and because I'd read that girls' poor body images were a result of their mothers' poor body images I'd tried to resist the temptation, when we were playing in here, to examine myself in that mirror in my ongoing effort to determine whether I looked fat, and if I did look fat, just how fat. I looked at Mattie again, still fast asleep. I went close to the mirror. No reason to resist that temptation now.

I stared at myself from the front for a while. The thought of seeing Rajiv again, attractive as it sometimes seemed, became terrifying when I looked in the mirror. If only he were a little less beautiful—indisputably, objectively, terrifyingly beautiful. I was a poet and not a high-school or blog-post poet but a certified poet who should have had all the cliché scorned out of her in workshop, but I couldn't look at his eyes and not think *soulful*, I couldn't look at his body and not think *sculpted* and *statue* and *Greek*. And really, if you're going to yearn toward someone not your perfectly acceptable boyfriend or husband, shouldn't it be someone who can fulfill the surprisingly resilient fantasies inspired by the Brontë sisters, rather than a guy whose eyes don't send you stumbling, all aflutter, into a mire of cliché?

I liked to think that it was my own virtue that saved me,

the night Rajiv kissed me, but it wasn't, at least not entirely. I was right there with Rajiv—the tongues and the belly-to-belly warmth and the hands gripping at clothes and the little smacking sounds that are funny in certain moods but not in that one. His hands were on my rib cage, creeping up toward my breasts, and truth be told all that was in my brain was *yes*, *yes!* and then this other thought came swimming upward. *A little*, was the thought. As in, I'm a little in love with you. A little wasn't very much, was it? If you gave one person a little, you had plenty left to give another, or multiple others, and wasn't that the suspect thing about Rajiv, that his love had come so easy it was hard not to wonder how many other women had inspired it? That he was just *a little* too beautiful? None of that mattered if I was going to indulge my attraction for him, the lure of his for me, and then go back home like nothing had happened. But what if I wanted more, or he expected more? What would happen if I said I was a little in love with him?

I stepped back. I meant to say, "Wait a minute," and "I shouldn't," and "my boyfriend," and all the other things you say—*should* say, Nathan—while you're stepping back from the brink. Instead I said, "You're a lot like Nathan," which was true, perhaps, but not what I'd meant to say at all.

He stared at me a moment, then gave a quick sharp nod. "How so?"

"You have the same sense of humor," I said. "And the same secret sincerity. And the way you were at dinner, making your friend tip more. Nathan would have done that."

"Uh-huh," he said. He shoved his hands into his pockets.

"I just mean—" I stopped.

"Don't worry," he said. "I know."

Since that visit, Nathan and I had been back to Austin, but Rajiv had always found a reason not to accept Helen's invitations to dinner. And so that had been the end. Staring at myself in the mirror now, I wished I hadn't stepped back, hadn't said any of that, and if I could have snapped my fingers and been in that moment again I would have finished what I started. *I'm thinking of making a movie about a romance between a princess and a clown*, he'd written me once. *Don't laugh. They're in love. Love is serious stuff.* That had been a message, hadn't it? A message tucked inside a joke. But what would Rajiv think if he saw me again, as I was now? Was I considerably wider than I'd been before? Would his first thought be "Oh my God, what happened?" My breasts were again bounteously round, having rebounded, temporarily, from the deflating effects of breast-feeding Mattie. Of course, they also spouted milk. I turned to the side, lifted my shirt and examined my stomach. From the belly button up it didn't look so bad, at least not when I stood straight, but from the belly button down it was flabby enough to make a talk-show audience gasp, and when I rounded my back my whole abdomen wilted into wrinkles like a deflating balloon. I rounded and released, poking and pinching my skin, and I must have done that for a while because I was still standing there when I heard the door open again and Smith's voice calling, quietly, for me.

He was standing in the kitchen with a milkshake in each hand. "I couldn't resist," he said when he saw me. We sat at the table facing each other. He sat in Nathan's place—and, yes, I do mean to make something of that, because I couldn't help doing so at the time. Was it so wrong to imagine how much easier my life would be if I could just slot one guy in for another? Was it crazy to compare the value of Rajiv's beauty and Smith's cooking, as though these two men were viable choices? Why did Smith want to know what my favorite flavor was?

The milkshake was the kind that's so thick you have to suck on the straw until your cheeks disappear, then give up and pull the straw out and suck what made it up the straw out the other end. That was the way I liked them, and this one was not only thick but delicious, the vanilla flavor pure and clean. Because it was so good, I took special pleasure in deciding not to drink it. I got up from the table after a minute or two, put the shake in the freezer, said a mental bye-bye to its blue-and-white cup and jaunty straw, and then sat back down.

The look on Smith's face beautifully mingled annoyance and astonishment. "I don't think so," he said.

"What?"

"You're going to drink that." He got up, retrieved the shake, and set it down in front of me.

"You can't make me," I said, but then I started drinking it anyway. "It's not like it would hurt me to lose weight," I said, between sips.

"Don't be ridiculous," he snapped.

"Hey, look, if you weren't in the mood for maudlin self-pity I don't know why you came over here." I swirled the milkshake with my straw. "I'm an unholy mess of a girl," I said.

"That's from something," he said. "What's that from?"

"*The Philadelphia Story*."

"That's right. Good movie."

"Nathan and I used to watch that together once a year."

"Like on your anniversary or something?"

"No," I said. "Actually, we didn't. I made that up."

He stared at me. "Why?"

"I don't know." I shrugged. "I really don't. Clearly I'm going crazy."

He seemed disturbed. Perturbed. Discomfited.

"What's the word for what you're feeling right now?" I asked.

"What?" He frowned.

"Unnerved? Trapped? Agitated?"

"Concerned," he said. "How about concerned. Listen, is Alex back yet?"

I shook my head. "She gets back tomorrow. Why? You want to pass me off to her?"

"Well, frankly, yes," he said. "I think she'd do a better job." He frowned. "I think maybe it's time you told somebody else what's going on."

"I called my friend Helen."

"I mean somebody local," he said. "Like Erica. Somebody who could, I don't know, bring you dinner."

"I don't want to."

"Look, I know you didn't want anybody to know. But Nathan's not here. If that keeps up, people are going to notice. Plus, you need the support."

He was right on both counts. I'd felt bad before he came, better when he was here, and when he was gone I'd felt bad again. Telling more people might make me feel better, but it would also mean that more people would know.

"I can tell people for you, if you like," he said.

"Have it your way," I said, picking my cell phone up off the table. "I'll start calling people." I dialed Nathan. At the beep I said, "Just wanted to let you know I'm going to start filling people in on our situation, as in you cheated on me and now you won't return my calls." I hung up.

Smith sighed. He held out his hand. "Give me the phone," he said. I thought about snatching it away from him, hunkering over as Mattie would have, but suddenly I was weary of playing the petulant child. I put the phone in his hand. He turned it off and we both listened to the chime as it powered down. "I don't blame you for being angry," he said. "But I'm talking about reaching out for support. I don't know if making Nathan feel worse will make you feel better."

"Oh hell yes, it will," I said. "I'm considering rampant promiscuity. The only problem is the mirror." I was so, so tired. I let my forehead drop to the table.

"Have you been sleeping?" Smith asked.

I laughed. "No," I said. "And that's an understatement."

"Well, how about you go to bed now?"

"What's the point? There's no one else to get up with the baby."

"I'll stay," he said. "I'll sleep on the couch."

"Will you breast-feed?"

"I'll give him a bottle. After yesterday I'm a pro."

I shook my head, my forehead turning from side to side against the table. "You don't need to do that. I can't go to bed. I'm afraid of going to bed." I choked out a laugh-cry and said, "I'm afraid of going closer to stuff."

"I'll go in there with you, okay?"

I didn't say anything for a moment. What?

"I mean"—this time the embarrassment in his voice was unmistakable—"I'll tuck you in. I bet that's what one of your girlfriends would do."

"So you're my girlfriend now?"

"You got it, sister."

I lifted my head from the table and looked at him.

"What?" he asked, grinning. "Don't you all call each other sister?"

He did tuck me in. He walked me into my bedroom, one hand hovering lightly near my shoulder in case I needed steering down the hall. I climbed into bed with my clothes on, and he leaned over me and pulled the covers up and then gave them a pat. I thought for a second he was going to kiss my forehead, but he didn't. He said, "Listen to me. Everything is awful now, but it's going to be OK."

I closed my eyes. "How?" I asked.

"That's the way of it," he said, and then he turned out the light.

I fell, for a while, into an alcoholic doze, and then I woke up, headachy and nauseated, and got up to get a glass of water. When I opened my bedroom door I saw the glow of the light from the living room. Smith was still awake, and I could hear the murmur of his voice. He was talking on the phone. I crept down the hall and stood just out of sight, like a child hoping for a glimpse into the mysteries of the grown-up world.

"She needs me," he said. "She's having a hard time of it. She hadn't eaten all day, she . . . No. No. No. It's not like that."

It's not like what? I wanted to ask. It's not like what?

"She's scared," he said. "She doesn't want to be alone."

I was scared, he was right. I had two small children with a long list of needs, emotional and physical, and, apparently, no husband to help me supply them.

"Give me a break, Holly. That's not what I meant. I hardly think that's what she's after right now."

Oh, Smith, I thought. Innocent, innocent Smith. If you came down the hall right now and expressed willingness to keep the lights off I'd take you right into my bed, my marriage bed. Nathan said he still wanted me, but now I can't be sure, and if he doesn't, he whose children did this to my body, then who will? See, Smith, I thought some things belonged to the past—the moonlit night, the sound of a stranger's rapid, anticipatory breath—and that was fine, that was OK, until my husband brought those things back into the present and reminded me of their pleasures, reminded me that those pleasures are sometimes enough to override the rest of your life. And I don't even know if I want the first kiss, the strange body's mysteries, desire's sweep and surrender, I might be too damn tired for those things, but you can't get to what I do want—the familiar, the shared—without having those things first, can you? Unless you want to go on living with me, just like this, I'm happy with this, and maybe Holly can get herself a dog.

"I love you," Smith said. Not, of course, to me. I retreated to my room, gulped water from my hand at the bathroom sink, and got back in bed to dream of poverty.

In the morning he got up with my children, fed them, and made me pancakes. He didn't love me, but two extra hours sleep followed by pancakes seemed superior to love. We were sitting in faux-marital contentment over coffee and the Sunday *Times*—Binx down for his morning nap, Mattie watching *Max and Ruby* in the living room—when we heard the crunch and rustle of a car coming up the drive. We'd been chatting about something on the op-ed page, but as the sound steadily increased in volume, Smith and I both fell silent.

After a moment, I said, "That's probably Nathan."

Smith nodded. "What do you want to do?"

I shrugged. I took a sip of my coffee, looked into the cup,

swirled it. Hot liquid sloshed on my finger. I stuck the finger in my mouth and sucked on it. It wasn't that I had no answer to Smith's question. It was that the answers were manifold, and contradictory, and therefore impossible to express in this brief, suspended time before Nathan walked in the house. I wanted to hide. I wanted to send Smith out to turn Nathan away. I wanted to rush outside and fling myself into Nathan's arms. Outside, the engine stopped churning. A car door shut.

"I wonder if he'll knock," I said.

"I don't know."

"I wonder if he'll knock or just come in."

"I don't know."

Footsteps on the porch stairs. The creak of the screen door opening. The thud of a foot connecting with the door, propping it open. A hesitant knock, which neither Smith nor I got up to answer. Then the jingle of keys. I waited for the door to swing open, for some emotion or another to rush in. I might have imagined any number of possible reactions to the sight of Nathan, but I couldn't have imagined what I did feel, which was that for the first time in our relationship, in my life, I had fallen in love at first sight. Look at him, that man, my husband, the startled, distraught expression, the hangdog posture, the scruffy chin, the disarrangement of his curls that told me he hadn't shaved or showered in days. I was fairly certain the shirt he had on was the one he'd left in. What a reservoir of tenderness I must have had to fall in love, at that moment, with him. What did it were his contacts, which he was wearing despite his dishevelment. He didn't like the way he looked in his glasses—like, he said, a middle-aged accountant—but in the normal course of our lives he'd wear them on a sleepy Sunday morning. He'd put them in this morning, in a small, pitiful effort to look good for me.

"Hi," I said. Smith said nothing. Nathan went on standing there at the door with his hand still gripping the keys, like a man who'd walked into the house he called his own to find the furniture changed, the children grown, his wife at breakfast with another man. He looked beaten, bewildered, utterly lost.

"I'm sorry," he said. There was no disputing that he was.

"Sorry for what?" I asked. I'd felt, as I said, a rush of love for him, and yet the question came out so light, so casual, as to be cold. We are many people, all at once, and all the time.

"Sorry for interrupting," he mumbled, dropping his gaze to his feet. He seemed to feel that I was having an affair with Smith, and that it was no less than he deserved.

"Interrupting is the least of it," I said.

There was a sudden end to the murmur of cartoon voices coming from the other room, and then Mattie appeared in the kitchen. She didn't seem at all surprised to see Nathan. "Hi Daddy," she said, like he'd just gotten back from the grocery store.

"Hi little goose," he said, his voice choked with emotion. He released his death grip on the keys, squatted, opened his arms wide for a hug, and she went willingly, if with no special eagerness, into his arms. "I'm hung-gry," she said into his ear. "Can I have a snack?"

She was hungry, and he obliged her, letting her go so that he could stand and cross the room to the pantry and offer her a cereal bar—no, they were yucky—and an apple—no, it had a snaking bruise—and—jackpot!—a handful of Goldfish crackers, and while she and Nathan performed this ordinary back-and-forth Smith and I just sat there at the table, waiting. I don't know for what.

This is why once you have children you should live a staid and stable life, without affairs and disappearances or moonlight of any kind. For the children, of course, because it's true what they say about them, they thrive on stability, they devote themselves slavishly to routine. But also because with the children there you can't play out a scene like the one Nathan's return should have been, the breast-beating, full-throated drama of betrayal, accusation, remorse. Or at least I couldn't. We couldn't. Some people do, I suppose, and it's their children who go on to write the memoirs.

Smith was the odd man out in this tragic little tableau, and so it was fitting that he was the one to shake us out of the positions we'd assumed. "Why don't you two go outside and talk?" he said. "I'll stay in here with Mattie."

"I want to go outside, too," Mattie said to Nathan. "I want to go with you."

"I need to talk to Mommy," he said.

"Grown-up talk?" she asked.

"Grown-up talk," he said, as though there had never been such a miserable concept.

I walked outside first. I bypassed the chairs and the hammock, where on frisky occasions we had sex. I waited for Nathan in the middle of the yard. He managed somehow to be a good two or three minutes behind me—perhaps he'd paused to comfort Mattie? to say some suspicious words to Smith?—and as I waited I resolved on kindness. Holding him to account, yes, but with sympathy for our mutual distress. I said to myself that our love was bigger than any of this. I felt good about believing it. When Nathan finally arrived, he seemed slightly beside the point. Nevertheless there he was, squaring off with me in the arena of our backyard. "You look like you're getting ready to box me," I said.

"Box you?"

"You know." I jabbed a couple of times, bouncing on the balls of my feet.

He hunched his shoulders, put his hands in his pockets as though to disprove this notion. "Aren't you going to yell at me?" he asked.

I shrugged. "I'm really tired," I said.

He looked away from me, gave himself a shake, looked back, and asked the question I could tell he'd been dying to ask, even as he told himself he had no right to. "What's Smith doing here?"

"He's been helping me out in your absence," I said. "He watched the kids on Friday. Like you were supposed to do." Love, love, I reminded myself, hearing my own bitchy tone.

"He watched the kids?" Nathan seemed as unmanned by this as if I'd announced that Smith had assumed his duties in the sack.

"He did. And meanwhile, you were . . . where were you?"

"I was at Alex and Adam's," he said.

"Ah!" I said, like someone finally given the answer to a riddle. "I never thought of that."

"I had their key," he said. "For feeding the cat. I had the key."

"Right," I said. I paced a little, fighting the anger that rose at this information. "You just stayed at their house without telling them?"

"No, I told them."

I stopped. I stared at him. "What?"

"I called Alex right after I left here."

"You called them on their honeymoon to tell them I'd kicked you out?"

"Yeah."

"Did you tell them why?" I wouldn't have thought it possible for him to make himself smaller, but somehow he did, and I got a glimpse of how he might age.

"Yeah," he said.

"I can't believe you did that. You ruined their honeymoon."

"No, I didn't." He looked worried. "You think I did?"

"Yeah, I think you did. I think they spent the rest of their honeymoon and the whole trip home talking about us, worrying about us, and seeing a bad possible version of their future."

"Well, they didn't say anything like that," he said. "They still told me about their trip, showed me pictures—"

"What do you mean, they showed you pictures? You've seen them?"

"They got back last night."

"I thought they were getting back today."

He shook his head. "Last night."

"They got back from their honeymoon, and you were in their house?"

"I don't get why this is what you're mad about."

"It's not!" I snapped. "I just can't believe you called them on their honeymoon and then were at their house when they got home."

"I couldn't just stay at someone else's place without asking."

"Oh, well, excuse me, I guess I lost track of how *exactly* your morality operates."

He took this like a body blow. "I'm sorry I didn't call you," he said. "I just couldn't. I fell down a well."

"What are you talking about?"

He met my eyes. "When I left here, it was like I'd drifted

out into space. And the phone seemed to be ringing from very far away."

It sounded to me like he'd planned this speech. "Which metaphor are we going with here?" I asked. "Down a well or out in space?"

"They're not exclusive," he said.

"You fell down a well on another planet."

"I'm just trying to tell you how I feel."

"How you feel about cheating on me?" I asked. "Or how you feel about me saying you couldn't publish your book?"

"You think that's all I care about?"

"I think you said I could decide that, but you never thought I would. I think you fell down your outer-space well because I said you couldn't publish the book, and not because I asked you to leave."

"That's not fair," he said. "It's all my life."

"No," I said. "*This* is your life."

"I'm a writer," he said. "Like it or not, that's my life, too. And I'm under a lot of pressure here. My agent—" He stopped. He pressed his lips together.

"Go ahead," I said. "Tell me how your agent's calling you. Tell me how upset she is. Talk about the pressure. I bet you can make me cry."

"I've ruined everything," he shouted. "I want to kill myself. Is that what you want me to say?"

In all my favorite fantasy stories—*Buffy*, *A Wrinkle in Time*—the human, fallible hero always has one thing the villain does not. Love. It's always love, often offered to a person at their ugliest. The ultimate weapon, love. The thing that always wins, always brings the lost one back from the dark side, the whole world back from the brink.

"Fuck you" is what I said.

"Yeah, you're right," Nathan said. "Fuck me."

Neither of us screamed, but we spoke loudly, and our voices echoed. I wondered if Mrs. Dodson could hear us, the way I sometimes heard her visiting daughter arguing with her own kids in the yard. I looked down the hill toward her house. A tranquil scene, the only movement a bird lifting off a tree, landing on a wire.

"I'm sorry about Friday," Nathan said. "From now on I'll take care of the kids like always. If that's what you want me to do. What do you want me to do?"

"I have to make all the decisions," I said, and he said, "Don't you want to?" I looked at him. He'd gone away somewhere since that suicidal outburst, and now he spoke from a very great distance, his voice uninflected. "I always thought you wanted to," he said. "You like people looking to you, counting on you. You like to tell me I screwed up. You like being the responsible one."

I turned away from him, back toward the house, an invisible hand squeezing and squeezing my throat. I wanted to ask, "You think I'm *enjoying* this?" but the hostility I heard in his insinuation robbed me of speech. How could he fail to understand that I, too, was down a well, each of us in our separate wells, barely able to hear the shouts of the other. I was unmoored, undone. Me, the responsible one.

"Why did you have to tell me?" I asked.

"I tell you everything," he said.

On the other side of the glass doors I saw our daughter looking at us, her palms pinking against the glass, her hands up above her head as if in surrender.

CHAPTER THIRTEEN

I meant to go to work on Monday. I really did. I drove to Durham as if I was going to, but then I turned where I should have gone straight. Alex and Adam lived in Durham, on Pickett Road, in the sort of house usually described as "cute," a 1940s-era bungalow with a porch swing and rosebushes in the front yard. "Pickett Road," I'd said when they found the place. "Sounds very American domestic."

"No picket fence, though," Alex said. "Don't get any ideas."

"Does it have an apple tree?"

"No, but there's a taqueria up the street."

"It has a taco tree."

"Exactly," she said.

I'd been the first person of their acquaintance, besides the realtor, to see the house. I'd helped Alex paint the living room purple, the dining room blue. I was at their house so often I kept a bouncy seat, a bib, and a baby spoon there. And of course I had a key, as I'd had a key to every place Alex had lived in the last six years, from the Carrboro mill house with the slowly descending ceiling to the tiny house in Durham that had once been a corner grocery store. And yet Nathan had made me feel like her house was on the other side of a border I couldn't cross. Nathan country.

I don't know what I had in mind when I drove there. Nothing very much, because if I'd thought it through—if I'd acknowledged and considered that intention, rather than just obeying the impulse—I wouldn't have done it. Adam's car wasn't there, which surprised me because it was only nine o'clock and he kept rock-star hours. I parked behind Alex's car in the driveway and took a weird satisfaction at blocking her in. "I've got you now, my pretty," I said aloud, but then I just sat there. I thought about *The Wizard of Oz*, how in the movie they made Dorothy's adventures a dream, when in the book they were as real as the spit-up stain on my shirt, the Cheerio dust covering the backseat of the car. Maybe the filmmakers felt it was too subversive to tell the audience that Oz was an actual place, with its witches and castles and poppy fields, that you could leave black-and-white Kansas and go there, lead a daily life in a place so extraordinary it rendered the ordinary impossible. You can go there in your mind, they said, but then you have to come back home. You always have to come back—you *want* to come back! What does Dorothy want most in the world, after all, but to click her heels and go home? Ah, but I read all the Oz books, even the later ones not written by L. Frank Baum, despite my troubling sense of their inauthenticity, and eventually Dorothy moves to Oz. She takes her family and moves there. No more Kansas. Kansas begone.

The front door opened, and Alex stepped out. She was dressed for work in a skirt and blouse, but her feet were bare. She'd clearly looked out the window and seen my car because she waved, walked to the edge of the porch, and waited. I imagined she was wondering why I didn't get out of the car. I got out of the car.

"Hi," she called.

I didn't say anything. I walked to the edge of the porch and looked up at her. Normally she would have said, "Are you stalking me?" or "What are you doing, you weirdo?" but out of respect for my current situation she said nothing. She held out her hand, like I was in an action movie dangling off a cliff or out a window and she was the one to rescue me. I always wondered, watching a scene like that, how one person could possibly support the weight of another, holding them by the hand over an abyss, and how they could possibly haul them up, as they so often did, except for the times when they let go. Why were scenes like that so common, anyway? The drop, the look of terror, the last-minute grasp of hand on hand. Again and again the hero proves he'll always show up just in time to save you. Again and again he proves his nobility by catching even the tumbling bad guy by the sleeve. We must really like to see people dangling in midair. The moviemakers keep giving it to us. We must really like the look on the bad guy's face when he slips—through no fault of the hero's, unless what we have is an interestingly ambiguous hero—and begins to fall.

There were stairs up to the porch around the corner, but I took Alex's hand and hoisted myself up with one big, awkward step, and then she pulled me into a hug. "Oh, honey," she said.

My head was pressed to her substantial bosom. I could have closed my eyes and let her comfort me. Instead I said, "This is like that scene in *Sixteen Candles* when the foreign exchange student and the tallest girl in school go to the dance."

She stepped back, her hands still on my shoulders. "Sure, make fun of the tall girl," she said, smacking my shoulder lightly. The gesture was not unusual. She was a woman comfortable with physical proximity. She pressed knees, kissed cheeks, squeezed arms, smacked shoulders, and, on particularly drunken occasions, pinched asses. But that time the moment her fingers flicked against my skin, her expression morphed into horror. "Oh God," she said. "I'm sorry. I forgot."

"Forgot what?" I asked. "That you're supposed to treat me with nothing but a respectful pity?"

"I don't pity you," she said. "Pity implies condescension. I feel bad for you. I feel terrible for you. I can't believe this is happening." She pulled me into a hug again.

"Enough with the PDA," I said. "Let's go inside."

Inside the house, I surveyed the scene like a detective. On the coffee table in the living room lay the book Nathan had been reading, a novel that had made the cover of the *Times Book Review* last year. It was splayed open, spine up. "He never does that to hardcovers," I said.

"What?"

"He never leaves hardcovers like that." I pointed at the book. "Only paperbacks." I shook my head. "Poor abused paperbacks."

"Can I get you anything?" she asked. "I think there's some coffee left."

"I'd take a cup of coffee."

We went into the kitchen. There were three coffee cups in the sink. Three coffee cups, telling their story of morning camaraderie. I walked up and peeked inside them. Two were empty, one still half full. I knew from the creamy lightness of the coffee left inside that that one had belonged to Nathan, because Alex and Adam put soy milk in theirs. I opened the fridge and sure enough, right at the front there was a pint of Maple View heavy cream, which Nathan had obviously bought. He was a cream addict—in fact he loved cream so much it was the only reason he drank coffee. He wasn't a coffee drinker before the dairy opened. Then, a couple months after he started, came a morning when we ran out of cream, hours before the dairy opened, and he'd refused to drink his coffee without it, and been surprised to find that he got a headache. I'd been a caffeine addict my entire adulthood, and I laughed at him, but fondly, pleased by the sweet vulnerability of his silliness.

"Did Nathan buy this cream?" I asked.

Alex came up beside me, a fresh cup of coffee in her hand. "Oh," she said. "Yeah. We don't use cream." She handed me the cup.

"I know," I said. I took the cream out, added some to my coffee, put it back. "When did he buy it?"

"I'm not sure," she said. "Why?"

"Because I'm just wondering if it was after I threw him out of the house for screwing another woman, or after we fought about the fact that he'd abandoned his family and he shouted that he wanted to kill himself, that he thought, 'Hey, I know my life is in turmoil and all, but I should pop by Maple View on my way out,' or maybe if during the two days when I had no idea where he was he actually came within a mile of our house and didn't drop by, because your wife doesn't need to know if you're alive or dead but God knows you need your fucking cream."

"I don't think it was like that," Alex said. "I mean, it's not like he's not upset, he's devastated and guilt-ridden and—"

I shut the refrigerator door. "Uh-huh," I said.

"He probably just stopped there automatically, because it's something he'd normally do, like you go to Target for diapers."

"Don't compare him to me," I said.

"I didn't mean it like that."

"Like what?"

"Like you're the same. Like he's not the one at fault." She touched my arm. "I just feel really bad for you guys."

"I know," I said. I went back into the living room, sat on the couch, took a sip, just like Nathan had earlier this morning, sitting here drinking his morning joe and reading that buzzed-about novel to see if it deserved the praise, taking his time, making himself late, when he was supposed to be at our house. At my house. When he was supposed to be with our children. When he was supposed to be with me.

Alex hesitated in the doorway, and I could see in her face her confusion and distress at my behavior, and felt sorry for it, although in a foggy, distant way. I said, "I'm sorry we ruined your honeymoon."

"Oh, sweetie," she said. She sat down beside me and turned so her knee pressed against mine. "You didn't. I wish you'd told me at the wedding. I knew something was wrong."

"I didn't want to ruin your wedding. With my own personal storm," I said. I sighed. " 'Welcome to marriage.' "

"Oh, what the minister said?" Now it was her turn to sigh. "She got a laugh, anyway."

"Kind of uncool, though," I said. "Is my point." I put my coffee on the table, put my face in my hands, scrubbed at it. "I thought you were coming back Sunday," I said through the gaps in my fingers.

"We were," she said. "They canceled that flight, so we moved to an earlier one."

"How come you didn't call me?"

"We got home really late Saturday night, and then Sunday morning was all about Nathan's downward spiral and bucking him up to face you. I kept saying I was going to call you and tell you he was here, and he kept saying he was going to go tell you himself, and then he'd get this pale, hollow-eyed look and start in on how he didn't know what to say—"

"He talked about a well," I said.

"Yeah, he said that to me, too."

"I thought it sounded rehearsed."

"He really seemed to feel that way," she said. "He said he felt like a useless person, like he should just fall off the earth. Has he had trouble with depression before?"

I closed my eyes and leaned back against the couch.

"I'm sorry," she said. "I don't mean to seem like I'm defending him. It's just hard not to feel sorry for someone who's so obviously in distress."

"Even if he distressed himself?" I said. I didn't wait for her to answer. "Why didn't you call me after he came over on Sunday?"

"Well, I wanted to give you time to talk to him, and then he didn't get back here until almost ten, and I thought you might be in bed."

"Almost ten? He left my house like eight hours before that. Where was he?"

"I don't know," she said. "I assumed he was with you."

I shook my head. I didn't explain that Smith had still been there, that because his presence had so obviously upset Nathan I was happy to prolong it, telling Nathan that I didn't want him to stick around that day, that Smith would help me a little while longer. I didn't explain that Smith went to run some errands that afternoon and then came back to help me with dinner, that he held Binx while I put Mattie to bed, and then gave me a good-night hug before he went to meet Holly, his actual girlfriend. I didn't tell her I was entertaining domestic fantasies about Smith, and romantic fantasies about Rajiv, and meanwhile believing, despite everything, that a magic spell would somehow deliver my marriage back to me, intact, Nathan once again the guy I'd always believed him to be.

Normally I would have told her all of this, all of this and more. But I couldn't. Because I was mad at her, and I couldn't bring myself to tell her that. Not mad at her because she hadn't called, because her explanation was reasonable. Mad at her because when he'd showed up, she'd taken him in. Okay, she hadn't even been there when he'd showed up, and Adam had probably taken Nathan's call. But Adam would have asked Alex if Nathan could stay at their house, so she must have said Yes, of course, when she should have said, Hell, no, tell that bastard to get a hotel room. She'd had sympathy for him, even before he went on and on to her about his metaphorical well. And why should she have sympathy for him before she witnessed his distress? Had she known? Had he poured out his heart to her and made her promise not to tell me, and had she agreed? Or did she have sympathy for him because what he had done was understandable? Was it understandable because she, too, knew the strength of such urges, or was it understandable because she thought it would be awfully difficult, after all, to stay married to me?

She'd felt sympathy. She'd taken care of him. Was nobody loyal to me?

"Maybe he went for a walk," she said. "Maybe he just drove around."

"Maybe he climbed down an actual well, like the guy in

The Wind-Up Bird Chronicle. Just to compare his feelings, the fictional representation, and, you know, experience."

She smiled. "How'd he get back up then?"

"I don't know," I said. "Maybe somebody threw him a metaphorical rope."

"He got out of an actual well with a metaphorical rope?"

"It's all blending together," I said. "I'm a little confused."

The amusement fell off her face. "What can I do for you?" she asked. "Is there anything I can do?"

"Turn back time?"

"Barring that. Anything in the present?"

"Turn back time," I said. "Seriously. Drop in on that writers' conference and put Nathan in a chastity belt. Or should that be a chastity jock strap? A chastity strap?"

"Can you make one of those for a man?"

"Add that to your to-do list. Time machine. Chastity strap."

"I'll work on it." She put her arm around me. I leaned my head on her shoulder. It was one more thing to hold against Nathan, this feeling that, despite her words of sympathy, her presence here beside me, the weight and warmth of her arm, she was no longer quite mine. After a moment I moved away, and she stood up.

"You going to go work on it now?" I asked.

"I'm going to the bathroom."

"You can't work on it in the bathroom?" I smiled at her, to make it clear I didn't begrudge her a trip to the bathroom, despite the note of aggrievement I couldn't quite erase from my tone.

She laughed. "You're right," she said. "I should work on it all the time."

"Every minute," I said.

While she was in there I got up and went into the guest room. The room showed signs of Nathan's habitation. Normally the bed was made neatly, the extra quilt folded across the end. Nathan had left the quilt dangling off the bed, the decorative pillows in a pile on the floor. When he'd gathered up his laundry he'd missed a stray sock under the desk. I moved, automatically, to pick it up, and then I stopped and left it there.

I sat down on the bed. It was an old four-poster that had belonged to Alex's grandmother, and it creaked beneath my weight. Alex had had the bed for years, and so I knew from experience that it groaned every time you turned over, in a way that started to make you self-conscious, because you worried that Alex might think the sounds were made by headboard-banging sex. And your husband would say, "So why don't we? I mean, if she already thinks that." And then when you did have sex in that bed, you were so careful, your movements so small, that sex was quieter than simple restless sleep. I lay down. I rolled on my side. The quilt smelled clean yet musty, like everything else in Alex's house. Nathan slept here, I thought, as though that were special, as though I had not spent ten years of nights in a bed that Nathan had slept in. I closed my eyes and listened to the wall clock tick.

I woke an hour later, sleep-drunk and confused, and shoved myself out of bed as if after a shameful one-night stand. I'd left the shape of my body on the quilt, so I smoothed it out, moving frantically, my heart caroming off my ribs, and then I punched the pillow to erase the imprint of my head. I stumbled down the hall to find Alex on the couch, her laptop on her knees.

"I didn't mean to fall asleep," I said.

"I didn't want to wake you," she said. "Nathan told me you haven't been sleeping."

I didn't like the thought of them discussing me. I picked up the book on the coffee table. I read the line, *I don't want to lose you*. Ah, I thought. That story again. I closed the book and set it down, taking a petty satisfaction in the thought of Nathan being unable, however briefly, to find his place. "Aren't you late for work?" I asked.

"I called and told them I wasn't feeling well and I'd be in later. I'm sure they don't believe me, first day back after my honeymoon. Or now they all think I got pregnant on my honeymoon." She gave me a rueful smile. "What about you? Did you call in sick?"

I shook my head.

"Oh no, you're really late then," she said. "Should I have woken you?"

I laughed. "No," I said, and didn't explain the laugh. This was my chance to take her into my confidence, to let her be who she always had been to me, someone I could always turn to. I said, "I'd better go."

■

Smith's office was upstairs in one of the old tobacco warehouses in downtown Durham, resplendent with exposed brick and heart pine timber. I'd been to restaurants in the building, but never up to Smith's office, and I battled nerves as I climbed the stairs. I slipped past the receptionist, who was staring out the window, and peeked into cubicles until I spotted Smith. He was on the phone, cradling it between his ear and his shoulder while he sorted through a pile of papers on his desk. His eyebrows shot up when he saw me. "Hey," he mouthed, and then he held up one finger.

He was going to ask me what I was doing here, and what

was I going to say? I stared out the window myself. Nothing out there but sky, trees, buildings, and power lines.

He hung up. "Hey," he said, this time out loud.

"You shouldn't do that," I said. "It's bad for you."

"What is?"

"Holding the phone like that. Bad for the neck. Bad for the posture. Not at all ergonomic."

"I know," he said. He took a breath. *What are you doing here?* I thought, but instead he said, "You want to sit?" and without waiting for me to reply he got up and pulled a chair over to the side of his desk. I sat. He sat. We faced each other. He waited.

"I've been doing something strange," I said.

"What?"

"You can't tell Nathan."

"I won't. You know I won't."

"I haven't been going to work."

"What?"

"Yeah," I said. "I didn't go Friday and I didn't go today. I called in sick before I came over here. I didn't want them to call the house and get Nathan, you know. I told them I had the stomach flu. And then for some reason I coughed, like that was going to sell it."

"I think you deserve a day off," he said.

"But what if I never go back? What would we do for money?"

"What are your savings like?"

"We've got about fifteen thousand in the bank, but we'll owe some of that in taxes. We pay the credit cards five hundred a month. We were already going to be in trouble if he had to get an apartment, and now we're going to run out of money for the original place. I guess he'll have to move back in. Or I guess he'll have to get a job, or I'll have to get another job." The tightness in my throat choked my voice.

"You didn't quit, though?"

I shook my head.

"So you can just go back?"

"I don't know," I said. "I can't seem to. I know that sounds crazy."

"You don't have to tell them what's really going on."

"You know my boss, the chair, he kills songbirds?" I said. "For his research, I mean. I wonder if he ever has nightmares about it. Tiny songbirds poking at his brain. Let's see what makes *him* tick, tweet-tweet."

"I don't think you should say that," Smith said.

"I'd have to tell them something."

"How about your favorite aunt died and it traumatized you?"

"Smith," I said. "Are you telling me to lie?"

"I'm telling you to consider the possibilities. Maybe you should see this as a chance to find something closer to home. Or get a job more in your field. I mean, you told me last week you'd always thought that job would be temporary. Why not look for something in the arts?"

"I don't know," I said. "I've got two small children. The economy is in the tank. It's not exactly the moment for finding myself."

"Granted," he said. "But you should be able to live on your savings for three months. So if you can't go back to that job, go ahead and apply for whatever job you think you can get, but it doesn't hurt to try for a little reinvention while you're doing it."

"That's true," I said. "That's right." For a moment I imagined myself working here, with Smith, surrounded by warm red brick, popping down to the Greek place for lunch. Or maybe I could work for the documentary film festival, or for the art museum, or one of the university magazines. Then I pictured myself sending out résumés and then I wondered where my résumé was, if I'd even moved the file when I'd gotten a new computer, and then I thought about how I'd have to update it, anyway, and figure out who at my old job was going to be my reference, which would necessitate explaining my disappearance after all, and the thought of all these necessary steps made me very, very tired.

"I'll help you look," Smith said. "And you know, Nathan doesn't have to get a place right away, he can stay with me, or he can move back in without moving back in, sleep in his study or something." He stopped. "Why are you looking at me like that?"

I shook my head, for a moment unable to speak. I managed to say, "I can't believe this is my life." I leaned forward as though I was going to put my face in my hands, but it was like I'd pitched over a cliff and I just kept falling until my head came to rest on Smith's knees. I sobbed with abandon into his jeans. This made him extremely uncomfortable—I could feel the tension in his legs—but nevertheless he brought both of his hands up and cupped the back of my head as tenderly as . . . well, a mother, I'm tempted to say, but why not a father? Fathers can be tender. Fathers like Nathan. He cupped my head as tenderly as Nathan would.

Later that day, I went home to the actual Nathan, except that he wasn't the actual Nathan. The actual Nathan didn't speak to me with sorrowful politeness, didn't put the children to bed and then tell me good-bye. I couldn't have the actual Nathan, the Nathan I wanted, the Nathan who could comfort me.

CHAPTER FOURTEEN

Thursday as I pulled up to the house Nathan was coming out the glass doors, bumping Binx in his stroller down the porch steps. Mattie trailed behind, sucking her fingers and twisting her hair. When she saw me, she brightened up, and did what Nathan and I called her "cavort" up to the car. I got out and picked her up, and she insisted I spin her around, so I did, until we were both dizzy. Nathan watched, standing with both hands gripping the handle of the stroller, wearing a melancholy smile. I put Mattie down and then stumbled in an exaggerated way and she swayed on her feet and laughed. "We're going to check the mail!" she said.

"Great," I said. "Let's go." I offered her my hand and she took it. Nathan started down the drive, and she and I fell in behind him. He hadn't said anything to me. I hadn't said anything to him. I watched the back of his head, lately my primary view of him.

"I've been thinking," I said.

He stopped the stroller and looked back at me, a strange expression briefly contorting his features, gone too quickly for me to read before the blank-faced Nathan-bot returned. Was that an agony of hope I saw? Of fear? Did he think I was going to say he should move back in? That he should get his own place? Which would he hope for, and which would he fear? He'd said he wanted to work it out, but nothing in his behavior this week had suggested that. Interacting with me was just a duty, like all the other ones that dragged him through his days. Maybe he thought I was going to say he could publish his book after all. "Yeah?" he said.

"I don't know what to do about the weekend," I said.

"Oh," he said. He looked back down the drive, started walking again. "What do you mean?"

"Well, should I be alone with the kids all weekend? Should we try to spend it together? We're having trouble maintaining a civil conversation for more than five minutes, in case you haven't noticed."

"That's not my fault."

"Maybe not locally," I said. "But globally."

He kept on walking. Mattie pulled her hand from my grip and stuck her fingers back in her mouth, her brief burst of energy evaporating. She slowed her pace, and Nathan quickened his. I walked a little faster to keep up, calling to Mattie to come on. Then Nathan said, "Why don't you go out of town?"

"What do you mean?"

"Go to the beach. Stay with your aunt. You can get out of here and get some help with the kids and get away from me."

"What about gas prices?" I said.

"You don't have to go," he said. "It was just a thought."

I thought about a three-hour car trip, parenting solo, no one to hand the baby his bottle when he dropped it, no one to pop *My Neighbor Totoro* out of Mattie's player and put in a new DVD. Then I thought about hours alone in the house, parenting solo, with nothing to distract any of us from Nathan's absence, or perhaps his presence, which might be just as bad, or might be worse. "I think you're right," I said. "It would be good to get away from you."

"I wish you wouldn't say things like that in front of Mattie," he said.

"Didn't you just say it?"

"Not in that tone," he said.

"Oh, *tone*," I said. "I would love to never have another discussion about tone for the rest of my natural life."

"The point is—" He stopped. He looked at me again. "You know," he said, "just because I've made mistakes doesn't mean I forfeit the right to the high ground on anything."

I pointed back at Mattie. "She's not listening anyway," I said. She was letting her feet carry her down the road, eyes on the ground, in the oblivious manner that often led her to bonk into people in the grocery store.

"Hey," Nathan said. "There's Mrs. Dodson. What's she doing?"

I looked ahead to Mrs. Dodson's house. She was standing in the middle of the yard by the clothesline, which often flapped with T-shirts and underpants but today was empty. She wasn't hanging clothes, as she often was, or taking them down. She wasn't bending slowly to pluck a weed from her carefully tended garden. She was just standing there. When we came even with her, I saw that her gaze was fixed on a hole in the ground.

"Hi, Mrs. Dodson," Nathan called.

She lifted her face, and her eyes were so blank that I had

the sudden, startling impression that she was blind. She stared at us for a moment before she seemed to register our presence. Then she said, "We've got a mole."

"Oh dear," I said. I found that I often adopted old-fashioned exclamations in her presence. Oh dear. My Lord. Goodness me.

Her gaze moved to the stroller, and then at last her face registered emotion—pleasure at the sight of the baby. "There he is," she said. "Let me see that baby." She started moving toward us, now looking at Mattie. "Let me see that sweet little girl." At the stroller she bent to Binx and said, "Hi there, hi there," and then to Mattie she said, "Ain't you pretty," and Mattie popped her fingers out of her mouth and said, "I wanted to wear a sundress but Daddy said no."

"True story," Nathan said.

"I haven't seen Mr. Dodson lately," I said. "I've been hoping to run into him, so I could thank him for fixing the mailbox."

Mrs. Dodson looked up at me. She blinked, once, twice. She eased herself back up to standing. Then her face collapsed and she began to cry.

I just stood there in blank astonishment, staring at her with as much rudeness as Mattie. Binx began to cry in sympathy, his complaining, keening cry. I didn't move to pick him up. I didn't move to comfort Mrs. Dodson. I just stood there, wholly inadequate. Nathan, my Nathan, he stepped forward and took Mrs. Dodson in his arms.

"He's dying," Mrs. Dodson sobbed. "He's dying. I wanted to let you know but I didn't want to upset you with your new baby."

"He's dying?" I repeated.

"What am I gonna do?" she wailed into Nathan's shoulder. "Oh, what am I gonna do?"

"Mommy," Mattie said, "what does a dead elephant look like?"

I didn't want to answer, but I knew if I didn't she'd just repeat the question, louder and more insistently. I bent to tug her closer so I could whisper in her ear that we'd talk about it later.

"But what does it look like?" she whispered back.

"It depends on how long it's been dead," I said. I expected a follow-up, but this answer seemed to satisfy her.

"He had a cough," Mrs. Dodson was saying. She'd stepped back from Nathan. She pulled a tissue from her pocket and wiped at her eyes. "They took X-rays. It's lung cancer. We had no idea. They said he could live for twenty years or for a month, but now, he's just gotten so much worse, it's been so fast, we have to have this woman in the house, and he's not going to hang on much longer, I know he's not. He's going. He's leaving me."

"I'm so sorry," Nathan said, and I repeated it.

Mrs. Dodson folded the tissue and put it back in her pocket. Her face had resumed its usual stoic lines, though both her mouth and her eyelids trembled. "Will you come inside and see him?" she asked. "I know he'd like to see you."

"Of course," Nathan said, and I echoed him. That seemed to be all I was capable of doing.

We'd never been inside the trailer before. The front door opened directly into the living room, which was small, low-ceilinged, dark, and cool, so that I had the impression we were stepping into a cave. The furniture had obviously been rearranged to accommodate the hospital bed on which Mr. Dodson lay under a white sheet, his upper body propped with pillows, a tube in his nose. His eyes were closed. Mrs.

Dodson went immediately to him, her eyes on the rise and fall of his chest, and I wondered how many times a night she got up to watch him breathe.

There was an old-fashioned brown couch still in the room, and on it sat the nurse, wearing scrubs and an expression that fell somewhere between sympathy and boredom. I gave her an awkward smile, which she returned. I noticed over the course of our visit that she and Mrs. Dodson maneuvered around each other in that small space like pedestrians in a crowded city, enduring the other's presence only by resolutely ignoring it. Behind the nurse, on the wood-paneled wall, hung school portraits of the Dodsons' three smiling children, now adults, older by twenty years than I.

"It smells funny in here," Mattie said, and at the sound of her clear, ringing voice, Mr. Dodson's eyes fluttered open.

"Mattie, shhh." I bent to whisper in her ear. "It does not."

"Yes, it does," she whispered back. "It smells funny."

"Well, be quiet about it," I said. I squeezed her hand. Mr. Dodson gaped, bewildered, at the ceiling, and then he seemed to register that he was still in the world. He pushed himself up on shaking arms to get a better look at us, and his nurse got up and moved with slow deliberation to the bed, pressing a button to raise the back of it higher, staring at a spot on the wall. When I could see him more clearly I realized that he didn't have his teeth in, and that that in part explained the slack-jawed, skeletal look of his face. I'd never seen him before without his teeth. I'd never seen him inside his home, prone in a hospital bed. I'd never seen him dying. He shifted, and the covers did, too, and though the nurse moved quickly to straighten them, I glimpsed the edge of a bed pad, poking out from beneath his lower half, and a flash of his bare, gnarled foot.

"Let me see that baby," Mr. Dodson said.

Nathan obeyed. He took Binx right up to the head of the bed, where he beamed at Mr. Dodson and then lunged forward to grab his glasses. "No, no," Nathan said, extricating the glasses from Binx's grip.

Mr. Dodson laughed. "You're quick, little man," he said to Binx.

Nathan tried to put the glasses back on Mr. Dodson's face, but holding Binx he couldn't manage it smoothly and nearly poked him in the eye with the earpiece. I waited for Mr. Dodson to protest irritably, to snatch the glasses from Nathan's hand—this was a blunt, irascible man, a man who'd patrolled his property with a gun, who'd told me, when I was pregnant, that I was getting fat, and then laughed and laughed, a cigarette in his hand. But he just sat, grinning at Binx, and waited for Nathan to get his glasses on.

"Little man," he said to Binx. "What a little man." He extended his pointer finger and Binx grabbed it, babbling, "Na na na na."

"Na na na na," Mr. Dodson said, and Binx laughed.

Mattie tugged on my hand. "Pick me up, Mommy," she said, and when I didn't immediately respond, "Pick me up!"

I bent and hoisted her up, and she put her hands on either side of my face and said, "I want to tell you something."

"What?" I asked.

"I want to leave," she said. "I don't like it in here."

"Shhh," I said. "We're visiting Mr. Dodson."

"I don't like it," she said. "It's scary in here. I'm afraid of going closer to stuff."

I wanted to reassure her, but also I wanted her to be quiet, to not offend these nice old people in their darkest hour. To my relief Mrs. Dodson, too, was focused on Binx, who was smiling and chattering away, swinging Mr. Dodson's finger—and isn't that the wonder, the grace, of a baby, the way that their profound lack of understanding allows them to be representatives of purity and joy? Mattie, only three, was already old enough to share the discomfort and worry I felt, if not yet old enough to know she shouldn't express those things aloud.

The nurse had moved away from the bed to sit on one end of the couch, and I sat on the other, whispering to Mattie that we wouldn't stay long and that she shouldn't say she wanted to leave because it was rude. She curled up in my lap, squinched her eyes shut, and put her fingers in her mouth. Nathan and Mrs. Dodson talked about Binx and Mr. Dodson talked to Binx, and Binx, sweet Binx, gripped Mr. Dodson's finger and smiled and shouted, "Ba!" I tried not to stare at the nurse.

I wasn't supposed to be thinking about the nurse, who maybe wasn't even a nurse but an aide of some kind. I wasn't supposed to be thinking about whether she was a nurse or an aide. I was supposed to be thinking about death in general and Mr. Dodson in particular, and I was supposed to be thinking about grief in general and Mrs. Dodson in particular, and maybe even reflecting on the trivial nature of the event that might end my own marriage in the face of the unchosen, unavoidable end of this one. I saw nothing in the nurse's face. Nothing about what was it like to enter people's lives at their most grotesque and pitiable moments, about whether you had to be a compassionate person to do this work, or the opposite. How could you endure it, life among strangers, the sound of an elderly soon-to-be widow weeping in the next room? How could you live your life confronted day after day by the losses that await us all? Stranger after stranger, dying in your hands. Was it possible to go on believing, in the way that all of us who manage more or less to stay sane go on believing, that the worst of life won't happen to you? You won't be the man in the bed, so recently up on ladders and tinkering under cars, now unable even to use the bathroom. You won't be the woman who's lived with that man for fifty-three years, helpless to slow his departure. You won't lose your mind, your dignity, your partner, your life. The world is not an abyss into which everything you love must fall. It's a world. You go on home and watch TV.

Eventually Mr. Dodson grew too tired to hold his hand up for Binx anymore and sank back against the bed, and Nathan said we should go. I carried Mattie out. She was clinging to my neck, still feigning sleep. Mrs. Dodson walked outside with Nathan and Binx. "Thank you," she said, her voice trembling with gratitude. "I haven't seen him like that in two weeks. He really lit up when he saw that baby."

"I'm glad we got to see him," Nathan said. "Please let us know if there's anything we can do for you."

"Will you come back and see him again? With the baby? I know he'd be mighty grateful."

"Of course," Nathan said.

"Please," she said. "Please come back."

"We will," Nathan said. "We promise." *We promise*, Nathan said.

I carried Mattie all the way back up the drive, though she grew heavier with every step and my back began to hurt. I liked the warm weight of her in my arms, and I thought that it made sense to crave the embrace of a child in the wake of a visit to death, and that one could write a poem about such a feeling, and that many many people probably had, even if at that moment I couldn't think of one. I said nothing to Nathan about this as we trudged back up to the house, but he, too, must have felt the desire to cling to new life in the face of death, because he carried Binx all the way, pushing the stroller awkwardly with one hand. I was sure that we were going to have a conversation about life and death and love and marriage, that the scene in the trailer—the scene that should have been an epiphanic moment—demanded it. I could hear the dialogue in my head, lines about seeing what was really important. If one of us were writing the scene, we'd try to avoid such clichés, but in actual life we employed them as readily as anyone. The situation called for such a conversation, and we were fully capable of enacting it. I saw all that, I saw the need, and yet I didn't feel it. I didn't actually feel compelled to speak. I was still encased in a weird remoteness.

When we got inside, Nathan said, "That was heartbreaking."

Line, I thought. I nodded. Then I reached for the baby, took him over to the couch to nurse. I could tell that Nathan didn't take offense, that he thought I was too shaken to talk about what we'd witnessed. I could tell this by the gentle way he spoke to Mattie, a gentleness that extended to me.

Over dinner, Mattie was full of death questions, which Nathan answered in a vague yet truthful way, while I poked at my lasagna and tried not to listen. It was a vegetable lasagna out of the Moosewood cookbook, one of Nathan's specialties, and I thought that if we didn't go back to living together, I might never have it again. I almost never did the cooking anymore, though there had been a time when we alternated that chore. What would I do in his absence?

Would I take up cooking again, or would we subsist on a steady diet of cereal and scrambled eggs? Nathan mowed the lawn, took out the trash, went to the grocery store. The thought of taking on all these tasks as well as my own made me want to put my head down on the table. And Mrs. Dodson? Could she live there alone, with no one to help hoe the garden, no one to lie under the truck doing whatever it was Mr. Dodson did under there, no one to steer the riding mower over their three acres of land?

"If Mr. Dodson has been so sick, I don't think he could have fixed the mailbox." I separated a noodle from the cheese with my fork. "Did you fix it?"

"No," he said.

"Stupid question," I said. I dropped the fork on my plate. I looked up to find him staring at me, wearing the expression that presaged a scolding. "Don't look at me like that," I said.

"I can't believe that's what you want to talk about." He rose abruptly from the table, grabbed his plate, and dumped it with a clatter into the sink.

"Be careful," I said. He ignored me.

"Are you all done, Mattie?" he asked her. "Are you ready for your bath?" She said that she was, and he wiped off her hands and scooped her up, bouncing her up and down to make her laugh as he carted her off to the bathroom. I extricated Binx from the high chair, wiped sweet potato out of his eyebrows, and took him to his room. I changed his diaper and prevented him from sticking his fingers in the butt paste and pajamaed him and wiggled him into his sleep sack and plopped him on my lap for a reading of *Owl Babies*, and the whole time I carried on a mental argument with Nathan, that self-righteous man. Surely it wasn't difficult to grasp how much easier it was to focus on the petty and the trivial than on the heartrending, the life-and-death. What did he want me to say, what useless profundities did he want me to offer on the subject of loss? Besides, didn't it matter that he didn't do what he promised to do? Wasn't that the entire problem? The personal is political, it's the little things, for want of a nail, and so forth. You said you were going to be faithful to me, and you weren't. You said you were going to fix the mailbox, and you never, ever did.

I took a long time putting Binx to bed, reading him books until I heard Nathan say good night to Mattie. Then I laid Binx in his crib and stood over him a moment, patting his back while he made the cooing, moaning sounds he made before sleep, plucking at his eyelid in what Nathan and I agreed was a weirdly painful way to self-soothe. I was steeling myself for an argument with Nathan. I was gunning for him. But when I left Binx's room, I found that he wasn't waiting for me in the living room. I went into the kitchen and spotted him on the other side of the glass doors, pointing the key fob at his car.

I followed him outside. "What are you doing?" I said.

He turned. He looked genuinely surprised. "What do you mean? I'm going home."

"You're going *home*?"

He flushed. "You know what I mean. Back to Alex and Adam's." I stared at him. "What?" he said. "The kids are down."

"I thought we were postponing an argument until they were."

"Oh." He looked at the ground. "I don't really want to have that argument."

"Why not?"

"I just think there are some things that don't need to be said."

I felt my eyebrows shoot up. It was clear from his tone that these unsaid things were about me. "Like what?"

"Just . . ." He shook his head. "I'm disturbed you reacted like that."

"Like what?"

"So *coldly*." He looked at me like he couldn't believe what he saw. "I mean, what's happened to you?"

"What's happened to me is you cheated on me," I said. "What's happened to me is you screwed up our lives and wrote a book about it. And then you disappeared for two days, remember that part?"

"I'm talking about before that," he said. "Mrs. Dodson was in terrible pain, and you just stood there. You didn't reach out to her at all."

"Are we talking about you now? That I somehow failed to reach out to you? Because it's hard to reach out to somebody who won't answer the phone."

"No." He sighed. "I knew we shouldn't talk about this." He started toward the car.

I grabbed his arm and dropped it. "You say what you want to say."

"You've changed."

"Excuse me?"

"You used to be different. You used to want to see art films. Now unhappy endings make you squeamish. You used to read books because they were good, or interesting, or challenging. Now you abandon them if the chapters are too long. You used to talk about poetry, not NEH forms."

"NIH forms."

"What?"

"The NEH is the National Endowment for the Humanities," I said. "Do you even know what I do?"

"You sit in an office," he said. "You move some numbers around."

"Once again with a little more scorn," I said.

"You don't seem to care about my writing anymore. You sure don't care about your own. You said you wanted to lead an artistic life, but at the first opportunity you took a job so you could stop worrying about money."

I stared at him. "I took a job for our family," I said. "So we could have health insurance."

"I'm not saying those things aren't important," he said. "But you've got to think about quality of life."

"Yeah," I said. "Like having food in the refrigerator and prescription medicines."

"I just don't think you value art like you used to."

"And Kate does, I suppose? That's your point?"

"No, that's not my point."

"Did you give her the 'my wife doesn't understand me' routine? Did she stroke your ego and your penis simultaneously? What other insights did she have to offer?"

"She said maybe we didn't have the same values anymore."

"What?" My body rocked like he'd punched me in the stomach. "Are you actually saying this to me? Are these words coming out of your mouth?"

"I'm not saying I agree with her."

"But you're not saying you don't. So while I've been working my ass off for this family, trying to think about everybody's future, your interpretation is that I've grown materialistic and shallow. Meanwhile you're keeping the flame alive writing a page every other day."

"I've been writing because I'm a *writer*, that's who I am, and might I add that I've made money doing it. I didn't make you give up writing. It's not my fault you decided the creative life equated to irresponsibility."

"I don't want to feel like that!" I screamed at him. "Don't you get it! This wasn't my idea at all!"

"Whose idea was it?" he asked.

"Yours!" I knew that was unfair. I said it anyway. I lobbed the word at him, hoping that, fair or not, it would knock him flat.

"Mine? Mine? You're kidding, right? I've done nothing but suggest you keep writing."

"Somebody had to change," I said. "And it wasn't going to be you."

He pointed at me. "You," he said, with a jab of his finger. He took a breath. "You chose to change." He hit each word like a drum, the finger keeping time. "I will not let you blame me for that. When we met, your favorite movie was *Last Picture Show*. Now it's *Spider-Man 2*. When we met, you wanted to stay up all night talking about Alice Munro. Now you go to bed at ten o'clock. I try to talk to you about what I'm reading and you say you want to watch TV. You're a poet, for God's sake. When's the last time you read a poem? What's the last poem you read? What do you care about now? What do we have to talk about?"

I stared at him. "You liked *Spider-Man 2*," I said.

"That's not the point," he shouted. "You're so conventional! That's the point! And you were never conventional. That was one of the reasons I—" He stopped himself, but too late. I'd heard him start to make the word *loved*.

"Go ahead and say you don't love me anymore," I said. "You're saying everything else."

Slowly he lowered the accusing finger. He stepped forward. He softened his voice. "I do love you," he said. "What I mean is that I miss you." He reached out to touch me, his fingertips skimming my arm. I looked at my arm where he had touched it. "I know you're my wife, you're the mother of my children, but I miss *you*. And she—"

I snapped my gaze back to his face. He flushed. He hadn't meant to invoke her. He hadn't meant to say the dreaded word *she*. "She what?" I asked. "She was me?" I didn't sound angry, though. I sounded lost. I snatched the keys from his startled hand, ran past him to his car. Maybe gravel shot up behind the tires as I hit the gas. If it didn't, it should have.

I was inches from knocking on Smith's door when I remembered Holly, who might be there, whom it was much easier to forget. So I looked in his living room window, through the space left between the sill and the bottom of the blinds, and I saw the TV, the couch, and Smith, alone. Why wasn't she with him, curled up beside him watching *Last Picture Show* and talking about Alice Munro, as all good women should? I knocked on the window, and he jumped. He came to the door, and when it was open, he looked at me, his expression wary before he conquered it. He wished I wasn't there. "Come in," he said, but I shook my head.

"I just want to ask you something," I said.

"What?"

"What do you really think of me?"

He stepped out on the porch, left the door open behind him. "You mean do I like you?"

"You said not so long ago that I was self-righteous and rude."

He jammed his hands into his pockets, hunched his shoulders. "I was fired up," he said. "I was being self-righteous and rude. That wasn't a general character assessment."

"Nathan says I've changed. That I don't care about art anymore. Basically that I'm bad, bad, bad."

He sighed. "What brought that on?"

"We just found out our neighbor is dying. We visited him this afternoon. And later I asked Nathan if he'd fixed our mailbox."

"Oh," he said. "I did that."

"You did?"

"I noticed it was wobbly that day I was watching the kids."

I stared at him, speechless. He'd fixed my mailbox. It was all I could do not to fall into his arms.

"But I have to say I don't totally follow that story," he said. "From your neighbor to the mailbox."

"Nathan thought I was being shallow and cold, to want to talk about the mailbox after we visited our dying neighbor. He wanted me to be profound."

"Nathan," he said after a long moment, "is in pursuit of self-justification."

"Is that what he's in pursuit of?"

"Sarah," he said. He took a breath. "I have to tell you something."

"Is it what you really think of me?" It made me nervous that he was avoiding that question. I'd asked for his opinion hoping, of course, that he'd weigh in against Nathan's claims, but I also wanted an honest assessment of my character. There'd always seemed to be a fairly clear relationship between what people thought of me and what I thought of myself, but in the wake of Nathan's accusations I was cast into uncertainty. Was Nathan, the person who knew me better than anyone, completely wrong? Or was I, indeed, conventional, materialistic, and cold, and only now cottoning on to that fact?

Some painful emotion contorted Smith's features, but when he looked me full in the face his expression was sincere and calm. "I think you're great," he said. He held my eyes. I leaned in and kissed him on the lips. He didn't move, his hands still in his pockets. He made a startled, muffled sound. I could have just given him a swift kiss, a plausibly friendship-and-gratitude-driven kiss, and then stepped back, but I kept my lips pressed against his too long, as though we were in a clinch out of a 1940s movie, where they just keep mashing their faces together and never get an inch closer. By the time I moved away there was nothing to do but say, "That didn't go well."

He took a breath. "We can't do anything like that." He swung his pointer finger back and forth between us in the universal sign for "you and me."

"Well, we could," I said. "Technically."

"What I mean is that things are complicated enough already," he said. "I do have a girlfriend, you know." There was a silence while I refrained from saying something nasty about her. I wasn't that far gone. Then he said, "I don't think you really want to kiss me."

"Why did I then?" I asked.

"You want to make Nathan jealous, maybe. Even the score. Or maybe you just want to feel something besides what you've been feeling. I know when my college girlfriend cheated on me, the first thing I did was make out with some random girl at a party." He went on talking—"perfectly natural, blah blah blah"—but what I heard was, I don't want you, and what I felt was humiliated. Maybe I didn't really want him. Maybe he was right, and all I wanted was a different emotion. But I felt like I wanted him, and I didn't like being told I was wrong about my own feeling. Even if my explanation meant what had just happened was a humiliating rejection of a genuine come-on, while his explanation meant that it was just the honorable response to the unhinged behavior of a bereft and betrayed wife. Either way it was humiliating. He wasn't attracted to me, or I was crazy, or possibly both.

I interrupted him. "Did I tell you I'm going out of town this weekend? The kids and I are going to my aunt's. She lives in Wilmington. It's a little cold for the beach, but it'll still be nice to walk it, and maybe the kids can play in the sand . . ."

"You're going out of town?" He wore the expression of a patient with a bad diagnosis. "Oh," he said.

"What?"

"This is all just too fucked up," he said. "I really need to tell you something."

"What?" I asked again, and when he hesitated, I said, "What?" again. I had time to guess what the something was, and I thought maybe he was going to confess that he did like me after all. That's exactly how I put it in my head, that he *liked* me, as though I was in junior high circa 1986.

"That woman," he said. "The woman who Nathan—"

I held up my hand. Stop. "I know who you mean," I said.

"She's coming here. This weekend. Or not here, exactly, but to Raleigh. She's giving a reading at Quail Ridge."

"Quail Ridge?" I repeated stupidly. I knew Quail Ridge, of course. Nice bookstore. I liked it. I would have gone there more often if it hadn't been so far away. "Quail Ridge?" I said again.

He nodded.

"You think that's why he said I should go out of town?" I said. I was awestruck by the magnitude of Nathan's perfidy, beyond anything I could have imagined. I stood amazed, like Buffy at the Hellmouth, while a hole in the earth opened up beneath me. I looked down into nothingness. I couldn't see the end. "Oh no," I said, my voice small and insufficient. "Oh no."

"He said you should go out of town?" Smith repeated, and whatever he said next sounded indignant, but I was falling and the words were wind rushing past my ears. I gripped his arm. He was in the middle of a sentence, but he stopped talking. He looked down at my hand. Then he lifted it, gently, and brought it up high, as if he was going to kiss it, and gave it a little squeeze. "I'm so sorry," he said. He made as if to release my hand, but I tightened my fingers on his.

"Can you kiss me?" I asked. "Just kiss me one time."

"I can't," he said.

"Please," I said.

I'd never seen a person look more miserable. "Don't ask me," he said. "I know why you need that, but you have to find somebody else."

"I need you to kiss me," I said. "Just one time right now."

He looked away, expelled a breath, looked back at me. "Just one time," he said.

"That's it," I said. "I promise."

He could have just pecked me on the lips and called it a day, but once Smith committed, he committed. He didn't stint on the kiss. He brought his mouth to mine slowly, and his lips were soft and parted, and the kiss started out tender and then got passionate. I lost myself in it, and, you know, I think he did, too, because his hands came up to cup my face. But it was as if that touch reminded him of everything that was wrong with this picture, because he brought those hands down to my shoulders and he pulled away, just as slowly as he'd approached. He closed his mouth. I should have recognized, when I looked in his face, that a door that had opened in the last week was now shut, once again, against me, that I'd reached the end of what he was willing to give me, what I'd be able to take. Instead I said his name in a pleading way, I tried to pull him back, so that he had to brace himself against me, and the embarrassment I felt at my own clingy desperation fueled my anger at Nathan, without whom none of this would have happened, without whom I wouldn't even have this life. All the way home I cried, cried until my face was wet and sticky, my throat sore from the release of inhuman noise. She was me. That was why he'd done it. She was me, and I was gone.

When I got home that night Nathan was asleep on the couch. He didn't wake. In the study I found the computer on. I e-mailed Rajiv. *Do you remember what you liked about me?*

Within ten minutes I had my answer. *Everything.*

■

I let Nathan think I was sticking to the plan. I packed. He loaded the suitcases into the car. I nursed Binx. I sent Mattie to the potty. And then we were ready to go. Nathan carried Binx outside and strapped him into the car while I was strapping in Mattie. "So when are you coming back?" he asked.

"Never," I said, not looking at him.

"We're not coming back?" Mattie asked. She squirmed, twisting the car-seat strap.

"Hold still," I said.

"We're never coming back?" she asked, volume increasing.

"I was just teasing Daddy," I said. "Ha ha ha." I snapped the last buckle into place.

"When are we coming back?" she asked.

I didn't answer. I stepped away from the car, my hand on the door.

"Tell me!" she cried. "Tell me, tell me, tell me!"

Nathan said, "You're coming back Sunday, sweetheart. On Monday Mommy has to go to work."

I shut Mattie's door. Over the top of the car I could see Nathan, and behind him the tree line where our backyard disappeared into the woods. "I've made a decision," I said. "You can publish your novel."

"Are you sure?" he asked.

"I'm sure," I said. "Publish away."

"You're sure?"

"Don't ask me again," I said. "I'm sure."

Relief on his face, and pleasant expectation. Like I'd told him everything would be better from now on. Like he'd believed it.

"You should also know that I haven't been going to work," I said. "I haven't gone in a week."

He gaped at me. "Where have you been going every day?"

"Shopping," I said. "But don't worry, I didn't buy anything." I climbed into the driver's seat.

"Wait a minute," he said. He pulled open the passenger

door and leaned inside. "Slow down. So did you quit? Are you serious?"

"I didn't quit," I said. "But I won't be surprised if they fire me." I watched the emotions come and go on his face. Ah, yes, Nathan. Confusion. Dismay. The nauseating lurch into a new perspective. And I enjoyed it. I *savored* it. Who doesn't want to punish the person who's punished them? Who doesn't want to hurt the one they love? Isn't that the essential problem with humanity, the kick we get out of spreading the misery around?

"I kissed Smith," I said.

He flinched. "What?"

"I kissed him." In terms of poetic meter, the sentence was an amphibrach, emphasis on the middle word. "Last night I drove to his house, and when he came to the door I kissed him." Where in Nathan's face, and how, would his response reveal itself? Would his eyes widen or narrow, would his mouth tighten or fall slack? He looked sick. He looked like he was going to throw up. Yes, the nauseating lurch. I reached over and grabbed the door handle. I pulled a muscle in my shoulder yanking the door out of his hand. "I had to tell you," I said, though I wasn't sure if he could still hear me. "I tell you everything."

PART III

CHAPTER FIFTEEN

Mattie wanted to stop. She wanted to go home. She was hungry, she said. She wanted french fries. She wanted a different movie. She was hungry. I did not want to stop. Going, going, gone—that was right. That was the thing to be. My hands were made to grip the wheel. I explained that I wanted to get a couple hours down the road before we stopped, because we had to time our drive to avoid rush hour in the various cities we'd be passing through. She wanted to know what rush hour was. I told her it was a bunch of cars blocking your way. She said, "Why do the cars want to block your way?"

Because they're motherfuckers, I thought. "Everybody just wants to get where they're going," I said.

We drove and drove, and Mattie kept up her complaints. Then Binx, who hated the car, decided to express that emotion, and launched into high-pitched screaming, which I knew from experience could last up to an hour. Usually when this happened Nathan was driving, and I was free to jiggle Binx's car seat, or crawl into the back and talk to him, let him hold my finger. Usually this didn't help, and he went on screaming with his face red and his eyes frantic, but at least it made me feel like I was doing something. Now, with him sitting in a rear-facing seat, I couldn't even catch his eye in the rearview mirror. I thought about pulling off at the next exit to nurse him, but in the past this had produced only a temporary cessation of hostilities. As soon as he sensed my intention to return him to the car seat, Binx would stiffen, arch, scream bloody murder again. Before long Mattie started to cry, too, and I gave up on my plan and pulled off at the next truck stop I saw.

"I want french fries!" Mattie said, and Binx continued to scream. I got out of the car and extricated him from his seat, and then I bounced him on my hip outside Mattie's open door while he wiped his wet face on my shoulder and Mattie cried to be let out and begged for fries, and I got Helen on the phone. As soon as she answered, I said, "We're coming there."

"Great! When?"

"Now."

"What do you mean?"

"I mean I'm driving there now. The kids and I hit the road about two hours ago."

"You're serious?"

"We were supposed to go to the beach," I said. "But I'm coming there instead. I took 40 West instead of 40 East."

"Okay," she said slowly. "I'm happy to have you, of course. But you know it's a long way to Austin."

"I don't care," I said. She was silent. She was much better than I was at silence. She could be silent for minutes at a time, and then she'd make the one neat quip that exposed the nervous verbosity of everyone else, including me, for the nattering that it really was. I waited with some anxiety for her to speak again. Believe me, Helen could convince you you were being stupid if she wanted to. She had a particular expression of amused derision—sometimes that was all it took. But that was reserved for ill-considered comments, grandiose claims. True emotional distress brought out the maternal in her. The summer between our years of graduate school, I worked an exhausting waitressing job while Nathan spent six weeks at an artist's colony I'd failed to get into, and after my shift I'd stop at Helen's apartment, worn out with discouragement, and as soon as I sat down she'd pull a Coke from the fridge, pop the pull tab, and hand it to me, and I'd be revitalized by the sweet taste, the sizzle of carbonation on my tongue, her concern for me. Surely she knew how much I needed her to tell me she couldn't wait to see me, and to go put fresh sheets on the guest bed.

She still hadn't spoken. "Remember in grad school when you used to give me Coke?" I asked.

"This is a long way to come for a Coke," she said.

"If you don't want me, just say so," I snapped, and realized only after the words had left my mouth that I'd said, "If you don't want me," when I should have said, "If you don't want me to come."

"Listen," Helen said, "I want you to think a minute, that's all. I'm thrilled to have you come. God knows you could stand to get away, and God knows you could use a hookup with Rajiv. Anything I can do for you I want to do. But you're sleep-deprived and emotionally distraught and you're talking about driving for two days in the car with two small children by yourself, which would be hell on wheels under the best of circumstances. I just want to be sure you're up for that."

"I can't turn around, Helen," I said.

Mattie wailed, "We're going the wrong way!"

"I've got to go," I said into the phone. "I'll call you when we're closer." I hung up before she could dissuade me. "Listen, Mattie," I said, unbuckling her with one hand. "We're going on an adventure. This is going to be fun. When I was a grad student there was this guy who thought he was Kerouac—liked to go around with a cigarette dangling from his mouth and talk about the thrill of the asphalt rolling away beneath him—and I thought he was a big-time loser, but now I see his point. We'll learn, we'll grow, we'll roll with the punches. You'll see." *All right*, *all right*, I was saying in my head. *All right*, *all right*.

"What about gas prices?" she said.

So she had been listening yesterday, when I'd told Nathan I wanted to get away from him. I was traumatizing her. I could only hope that at three she was too young to retain any of this in memory, that in the years to follow I could make up for any future need for therapy I was creating now. Could I? Or would she always have a deep insecurity, the kind that sends people careening from one disastrous romance to the next? And why did I have to live my life obsessed with these kinds of concerns, this constant attempt to control the most uncertain of outcomes, my own effect on somebody else's mind? Parents have always worried about the damage the world might do their children. When did they begin to obsess about the damage they themselves might do? And mightn't that obsession itself lead them to do the damage? "Don't worry," I said. "I get a small rebate for gas on my credit card."

"What does 'roll with the punches' mean?" she asked.

"It means we'll be flexible," I said. "It means Binx will

nap when he naps. We won't worry about it. We'll stop when we get tired. We'll eat french fries. We'll have an adventure."

"Like Jack Care-whack?" she asked.

"You're too little for a motorcycle," I said. "Otherwise exactly the same."

■

The line at the McDonald's counter was long, which was bad news for Binx, who truly, truly wanted his milk. If Nathan had been there, he would have waited in the line with Mattie while I searched out the most secluded table and made an effort at modestly sliding Binx under my shirt. He usually foiled these efforts, grabbing the shirt and thrusting it upward just as I popped the clasp on the nursing bra, as if to say, "Hey, everybody! Get a load of this!" I found this frustrating, but I saw now that it wasn't nearly as frustrating as trying to stave Binx off in a long, indecisive line of people torn between honey mustard sauce or barbecue. I could retreat to a table and make Mattie wait for food, but not only could she cry just as loudly as Binx, with the addition of words, she could get up and march her determined little sparkplug self back to the line, and with Binx attached to my nipple it would be difficult to stop her.

Binx threw himself sideways, aiming his mouth at my breast. When I straightened him back up, he screamed, and when I say he screamed I mean he made a sound like an eagle swooping in for the kill, or perhaps like an eagle who'd just been struck by a spear to the chest. I mean my ears rang. It was loud. As one, America's travelers turned to look upon me and judge. Perhaps they thought I was pinching him. Perhaps they thought I'd put burrs in his diaper. Perhaps they just wanted me to shut my baby up. I stared down a woman who looked like she was from Florida in the most egregiously stereotypical way—too tan, too skinny, too blond, and far too colorful in her splashy floral print. I imagined that she either had no children or had had them so long ago she'd succumbed to the pleasing fantasy that she'd always kept them one hundred percent under control, and I thought that if she kept on glancing at me and then muttering something to her husband, who studied the menu as though he'd never been in a McDonald's before, I was going to march right over and offer to pay her a hundred bucks if she could keep Binx from making that sound for five minutes without smothering him. I put the words, "Fuck you, bitch," into my gaze. Mattie tried to ask me something, but at the same moment Binx screamed again, drowning her out.

"What, Mattie?" I snapped, which was unfair, because she wasn't the one screaming, but I did it anyway.

"I'm hung-gry," she said. She grabbed the chain regulating the line and swung on it. "I want some fries."

"What do you think I'm doing here, Mattie? We're waiting in line."

"But I'm hung-gry."

"What would you like me to do?" I asked. "Would you like me to summon the fries out of midair?"

She considered this. "Yes," she said.

"Well, too bad, I can't. You have to be patient."

"Why can't you?"

"I can't do magic," I said.

"Why can't you?"

"Why can't *you*?"

"Because I'm a human," she said.

"And I'm not?"

"You're a mommy," she said.

"Mommies are human," I said.

She turned to contemplate me. "I want french fries," she said.

When we finally had the food, I surveyed the place, Mattie clinging to my leg, Binx struggling to grab the tray, which I held, one-handed, at an awkward distance, one part of my mind picturing it crashing to the floor and this whole thing starting over. I was looking for a good spot to breastfeed and not finding one. There was an open table right by the line, where I'd be like a tourist attraction on the way to hamburgers and fries. There were open booths right by the enormous windows, where I'd be framed for every beer-bellied dude passing through the parking lot. I picked one of the booths and pointed Mattie toward it. She walked in front of me, stopping every couple feet for no particular reason. "Keep moving," I said, Binx slipping a little in my grip. "Keep moving. Keep moving. That's our mantra now. Keep moving."

"Keep moving," she repeated, and then she said it again and again, so that the words lost their grip on the sound and it became a *chugga-chugga, chugga-chugga*, like a train.

In the booth, Binx screamed while I wrestled with my shirt and my nursing bra, trying not to flash everyone in the place. I got the nipple out and brought his head to it, but he resisted, pushing back against my hand and screaming, drawing all eyes to my exposed left breast. I stuck the nipple in his open mouth and he screamed some more, eyes squinched up, face reddening, until I squeezed my breast with my other hand and milk shot against his tongue. Then he stopped crying, opened his eyes, and began to suck, unclenching his fist so that he could knead the top of my breast. "Oh," I said, in my bad British accent, "jolly good, then. Sorry about that."

"Why did you say that?" Mattie asked.

"I was pretending to be Binx," I said.

"But why did you say jolly good then?"

"I was pretending that Binx was British."

"Binx is not British," she said hotly. "He's a baby."

I thought about explaining that babies could be British, but decided instead to cede the point. "Touché," I said, and when she wouldn't stop asking me what *touché* meant and then, after I used the word *rejoinder* for the hell of it, what a rejoinder was, I reminded her there was a toy inside her Happy Meal, and she wanted to know why. I asked her why did she think, and she said, "Because you summoned it out of midair."

I said, "So you do think Mommy can do magic?" but she had a mouthful of fries and didn't answer. I had a couple bites of salad, dropped a piece of lettuce on Binx's head, wiped the salad dressing off his temple and then noticed that some of it had gotten on his leg as well. Or, no, that wasn't salad dressing on his leg—it was mustard, a watery yellow-brown. Except it wasn't mustard. "Oh, shit," I said.

"Shit?" Mattie asked.

"Yes," I said. "Lots of it." Because it wasn't just on Binx's leg, it was halfway up his back and seeping through the fabric of his onesie. And I saw, when I lifted him away, protesting, struggling back toward my breast, that it was on my leg as well, that it was on the booth, that it was dripping onto the floor. He'd exploded.

I sent Mattie to get napkins, both of us nervous as she

navigated farther from the table, looking impossibly small. She brought back two—not enough, but I couldn't send her out again. I wiped off my hand, bits of napkin sticking to my skin, and then I just stuck the napkins on his leg and left them there. I tried to lift up and over the mess in the booth without adding to the mess on myself, and then I picked up my bag and put it over my shoulder, Binx pressed to my side, sticking us together with that yellowish paste. I carried him to the bathroom, Mattie walking just ahead while I barked orders at her like an animal trainer and tried not to notice the wet cling of my jeans against my thigh. Inside the bathroom I put Binx in the sink and pulled the pants off and the onesie over his head, dragging the mess, despite my efforts, up to the back of his head, and then I dropped those clothes in the other sink. Two teenage girls walked up and then backed away, as if from a rotting corpse. "Remember this," I wanted to say. "Remember this, and use birth control."

The diaper came off next, and I pegged it into the nearest trash can—*swoosh!* I thought—and then I washed Binx in the sink with pink liquid soap as he squirmed and slipped and reached for the faucet, pushing it toward the hot side just as I grabbed his hand. I held him there as tightly as I could with one hand while I wriggled out of my own shirt and rinsed it in the sink on the other side, trying only to rinse out the mess but ending up soaking the whole damn thing, because I had to move quickly to tighten my grip on him. I squeezed the shirt out as best I could and contorted my way back into it. Because he was screaming now, not his horrible death-knell scream, but the piteous one that spoke to me of lifetime trauma, I picked him up and held him naked against my wet shirt, hoping he wouldn't pee on me, while I put each tennis shoe up on the counter, one at a time, to untie and remove it. Then I unsnapped and unzipped and pushed down my jeans with one hand, standing dripping and half-naked in bare feet on the McDonald's bathroom floor. I rinsed the jeans, too, and then reversed the process, the jeans a struggle to get on with the fabric heavy with water, the shoes impossible to tie with one hand, so I just left the laces dangling. Mattie didn't know how to tie shoes yet. How many years away from learning was she? I should have taught her ahead of the curve. "Mattie," I said, "do you think you can tuck my laces inside my shoe?"

"Okay," she said, and she squatted at my feet and tried.

The baby was curled against me, snuffling into my chest. I looked at the gold glinting in Mattie's hair, her industrious little hands. I loved them both so much. Why couldn't that emotion remain at the forefront? Why was it so often shadowed by my troubles, by the irritations of the day? The sublime is always dragged down by the ordinary, like a giant toppled by little men. Or maybe I had it all wrong. Maybe the ordinary makes possible the sublime. How long before Dorothy looked at the Emerald City and saw nothing remarkable at all? "What do you think of this experience, Mattie? Could I write a poem about this?"

"Actually, yes," she said.

"What rhymes with leaky poop?" I asked.

"Sneaky loop," she said. "I got the laces in. I did it! I helped you!" She stood up, beaming, awaiting my approval.

I moved my feet experimentally and my laces tumbled back out. "Peeky dupe," I said.

She laughed. "Beaky soup."

I had no diaper in my bag. I could have sworn I'd put a

diaper in my bag. "This is all about the can-do spirit," I said to Mattie as I pasted paper towels around Binx's crotch, like I was sculpting him an outfit out of papier-mâché.

"Pan-do beer-it," she said.

"You're a poet," I said, and she finished the couplet, "And don't know it." Nathan and I had taught her that. Nathan and I. Mattie clinging to my shirt, I walked back through the McDonald's, soaking wet, my laces dragging on the floor, my half-naked baby shivering in my arms, his balled-up clothes clutched at his back and dripping water down his skin. At the car I dropped the diaper bag on the ground and opened the back door so Mattie could climb into her car seat. "Buckle me in, Mom," she said.

"Just a minute," I said. I said it nicely. I was shivering now, too. I opened the passenger-side door, and there, sitting on the seat, was the diaper I'd thought was in my bag. I put Binx down on the seat, and only then did I see the healthy, unprocessed snacks awaiting consumption in a bag on the floor of the car. Nathan must have packed them for me. At the sight I unraveled. What did it matter if he was a cheating, lying bastard, when he'd remembered to pack the snacks? If he'd been there to tell me about those snacks, I wouldn't have had to go in the McDonald's at all. I peeled the paper towels off Binx, dropping them on the ground, which wasn't like me, I don't litter, and just as I lifted up his butt to slide the diaper underneath it he peed. He peed right in my mouth. I jumped back, and the pee went on arcing out, now landing on Binx's face as he turned his head from side to side, grimacing, trying to avoid this sudden storm. I spit onto the asphalt. I spit again. The baby cried and cried, naked in the front seat of the car. Mattie said something indistinct from the backseat, her voice spiking when I didn't answer, and even though I couldn't quite hear her, I knew the insistent word, "Mom!" I knew it by the insistence.

There was a moment when they seemed to recede from me. I could see that it would be possible to shut the door, to press the key fob and hear the car tweet-tweet, to go inside and hand the keys to someone and tell them to call the police and then to walk out the door and keep on walking. Who would I be, if I were capable of doing that? Who would I become? We pass again and again through these doorways, those of us who decide to stay.

I picked up my baby, my poor baby, and wiped the pee off his face with my shirt. I carried him over to Mattie, and with one hand I buckled her in while with the other I held him close, my shivering baby, and I said, "Shh, shhh, Mommy's here," and both of them were calmed, and neither of them knew how badly I wanted to cry. We can't possibly understand, when we are children, how hard it sometimes is to say the necessary words.

■

Lack of sleep had flattened out my good emotions and amplified the bad ones. In the motel that night, lying in the dark while the children slept, I thought of articles I'd read in *Newsweek* about the brains of drug addicts, how they lose the ability to manufacture the chemicals that light us up with pleasure at good food, at a joke, at sex. Life without drugs is tedious and dull. A cubicle life, a seventh-period-history-taught-by-the-football-coach life, droning and endless. There must be joy, there must be grace, to leaven the despair, or there is only despair. I needed a transporting feeling, a Wizard of Oz drug to saturate the black-and-white with emerald green. I'll tell you what I wanted. I wanted a feeling so easy and liquid and vast I could swim in it, I would have no choice but to swim in it. I wanted to lay eyes on Rajiv, on Austin, and think, Yes, yes! This is where I'm supposed to be.

CHAPTER SIXTEEN

Helen had cut her hair. The last time I'd seen her, toward the end of her second pregnancy, her hair had been long, down past her shoulders, and that was how I'd been picturing her: the image of big-bellied maternity, her thick black hair even thicker, even shinier with pregnancy hormones, even blacker against her flowy white shirt. But she was skinny again, all collarbones and shoulders in her red tank top, and her hair fell exactly to her chin. She looked neat and contained, which was the very opposite of how I felt. There is something about a person's physical presence for which our ability to keep in constant touch can never compensate, and you know that by how startling it is to see them, solid and real, a body instead of a voice, instead of words on a computer screen.

"You cut your hair," I said. We were standing on her front porch, having said hello, having hugged, having discussed how I'd made good time, considering the number of stops the children had required.

"Yeah," she said, and nothing else. Helen, unlike most

people, felt no compulsion to elaborate. If you asked her whether she wanted to come over for dinner and she didn't, she'd say, "No." Just "No," when anyone else would rush in with a thousand excuses. I found this disconcerting when I met her, and then I began to find it admirable. Sometimes your answer wasn't about the cold you couldn't get over, your prior commitments, your long, hard day at work. Sometimes you just didn't want to, and that was what they'd asked, after all, if you wanted to.

Helen looked past me at the backseat of the car, where Binx and Mattie slept slumped over, their heads nearly touching. "So cute," she said. "He's so big. I've been picturing him like he was in the photos you sent when he was born."

"How was he in those photos?" I asked. "I can't remember."

"He was wrinkled," she said. "He was swaddled in that striped blanket every hospital in America must use."

"Oh, right," I said.

"I remember thinking he had really long fingers," she said.

"He did, didn't he," I said. The blanket, the long fingers—I could feel the beanbag weight of him in my arms, the new weight, the slightly scratchy white blanket with its blue-pink-blue stripe, his fingers waving like a sea creature's extremities, moved by their own power or by the elements surrounding them, you can't tell. Did Nathan miss the children right now? Did he miss the way Binx said, "Da-DA," with that emphatic second syllable, as though it had an exclamation point? Did he miss the way Mattie's eyes widened, her expression fixed and distant, when she launched into one of her made-up stories, surreal concoctions featuring babies who could fly, owls who wanted to steal children's eyelashes? Did he remember how our newborn's fingers had moved?

"I can't believe Binx didn't wake up when I stopped the car," I said. "It's a miracle."

"Mine are napping, too," she said.

"Really? This late?" It was nearly five-thirty.

She shrugged. "We were out earlier," she said. "They nap when they nap." She frowned. "Did you hear something?" She backed up into the house, listened, and as she moved I heard flip, flop, flip, flop, because she lived in Austin and she didn't have a job and these days flip-flops were all she ever wore. When we met, she'd just moved from Boston, and she owned seventeen pairs of nearly identical black shoes. I know this because her small apartment didn't have a closet, and she kept the shoes lined up on the three remaining steps of a staircase that disappeared into a wall. "I know," she said, when she saw me examining them, "they all look the same, don't they?" She shrugged and hunted around for her pack of cigarettes. "I have a problem. When I'm in the store, they always seem like no shoes I've ever seen. It's not until I get them home . . ." She lit a cigarette.

"You never take them back?"

She laughed. "Course not."

"You know," I said, "there are subtle but important differences."

"That's right!" She pointed at me with her cigarette. "*Thank* you."

Now she didn't smoke. Now she stepped up beside me, and I looked down at her feet. Red flip-flops, yes, but something else I hadn't expected: a vicious scab across the top of her foot, a mangled nail on her big toe. "Ouch," I said, pointing. "What happened?"

"I got mugged last week," she said. "The guy dragged me a little ways."

"Holy shit," I said. "He dragged you?"

"These guys came up behind us in a parking lot and one of them jumped Daniel and the other one grabbed my bag, but I wouldn't let go, so he dragged me."

"Oh my God," I said. "Did he get the bag?"

She shook her head. "I wouldn't let go. I kept thinking, 'That's *my* bag!' They gave up and ran off."

"Was Daniel OK?"

"Yeah, the guy just kind of held him down. But he totally felt castrated. He kept apologizing for the fact that it happened. I did feel a little like, you wimp, even though I don't think there was anything else he could have done. I kept saying, You did great."

"Must be something primal in those responses."

"I know. It really bugs me. I don't like being subject to biology." She stepped back a couple feet and listened again. "I'll be right back," she said. "And then we can sit on the porch with the door open until your kids wake up."

For the past two days I'd had little in mind but my destination, and now here I was and I wasn't sure why. And why had Helen's story left me with a lump in my throat? It was scary, yes, but this urge to cry wasn't about fear for her, it was about my own self-pity, the feeling that this arrival had not been *arrival*, that I was lost and no one could find me. Helen was trying to shore up her husband's manhood while simultaneously questioning it, and I was—for the moment? forever?—cut loose entirely from such concerns. Maybe that wasn't so bad, because I'd always found the whole topic of manhood or the lack thereof tedious, and just a couple of months ago Nathan and I had laughed and laughed at a line in a Flight of the Conchords song: *Am I a man? Yes, technically, yes.* I hadn't known she'd been mugged. I felt as though I'd missed some significant moment, like her wedding, like all her other friends and family had gathered to watch her hanging tenaciously from the strap of her bag, determined that nobody was going to take what was hers. From her top step I watched my children sleeping in the back of my car. My children. Mine.

I heard Helen approaching. *Flip flop, flip flop*.

She sat down beside me, and I saw that she was holding a tall glass full of ice and Coke. She handed it to me without a word. I felt a gratitude so deep it was almost painful. I took a sip. It was cold and too sweet, and when I said, "Thank you, Helen," my voice shook.

"You're welcome," she said.

■

Nathan had tried to call me not long after I got on the road. I hadn't answered. I hadn't answered any of the times he'd called, or listened to the messages he'd left. I'd thought about it. I thought about it again while I sat on Helen's couch nursing Binx—the three older kids watching *Charlie and Lola*—and listened to Helen bicker with her husband on the phone. Helen had a sectional couch, and the kids flopped across or leaned on various parts of it in the listless, stunned manner of children in front of the television screen. I wanted a sectional couch. It was on my list of things to buy someday, in that magical future when we were out of debt and could buy such things without remorse. But maybe now I'd never buy a sectional couch. Maybe I'd get fired and never find another job, things being what they were in the world. Maybe

I'd end up living in an apartment, too small for such a large and extravagant piece of furniture. Or maybe I'd just rent a room, put nothing in it but a sectional couch, and Mattie and Binx and I would live and eat and sleep on it, tumbled together like puppies in a basket. We could be happy as puppies, if we could manage to be as dumb.

"You told me six o'clock," Helen said. "Yes, you did. That's what you told me."

Helen's husband Daniel had what Nathan and I referred to as a "real job," by which we meant a job that had something to do with business, a job that required professional clothing, that paid an extravagant amount and played some role in the economy. We weren't too clear on what it was. I'd confessed this to Helen a couple months before and she had laughed and offered an explanation I hadn't quite followed. She'd complained at the time that he was working longer and longer hours, even weekends, in anticipation of a promised promotion, and now, tonight, he was late getting back and she was pissed off, as I imagined she was every time, in the usual irritation at each other's ongoing failures that so often characterizes the relationship between husband and wife.

"I'm not cooking, then," she said. "No, we'll go out to dinner." She was close enough that, while I couldn't hear exactly what Daniel was saying, I could make out the placating tone in his voice. He was a nice guy, Daniel, an optimist, someone who knew how to choose a course of action and cheerfully go forth. Helen was a natural pessimist, inclined to brooding and bouts of depression that, in grad school, had manifested as episodes of obsessively watching *Matlock* or *Star Trek: Next Generation*. A yen for Matlock might not seem fitting for a depressive artistic type, but what is depression but the unwelcome conviction that the world will never be what it should? People saw her as a cigarette-smoking cynic dressed all in black, and in some ways she certainly was that, but she craved the honorable, earnest Matlock, the honorable, earnest Picard. She wanted to let the sun shine in, and so she married Daniel, and more than once I'd watched her glower at him and seen him smile back as though there was nothing but love in her eyes. "We'll choose the place," she said. "We're the ones who have to haul all the kids there." She stepped on a toy car, grimaced, kicked it under the couch. "Yeah, well, maybe I'll call you and maybe I won't," she said, and then she hung up the phone.

She came round to the front of the couch and sat, pulling her daughter Abby up into her lap. Abby was twenty months old, between child and baby. She rested her head on her mother's leg, her eyes still fixed on the television. She pointed, babbled some earnest nonsense that lilted up at the end like a question. "That's right," Helen said. She combed a tangle out of Abby's hair with her fingers. To me she said, "He'll meet us at a restaurant. Where do you want to go?"

"Remember how we used to go out for pancakes at midnight?" I asked.

"I don't really want pancakes," she said. "How about barbecue?"

"What was the place that had the brisket?" I asked. "Remember that?"

"Oooh, yeah," she said. "Brisket sounds good. Which place do you like?"

"I can't remember," I said. We sat for a moment and listened to Charlie relate his polite exasperation with his little sister Lola, whose flights of fancy were at once charming and aggravating. I remembered a wooden building—maybe near water? An outside deck, but every place in Austin had that. I remembered Nathan feeding me a bite with his fork. He'd been the one to order the brisket, and it was tender and juicy, while my pork was a little dry, and he'd shared his meal with me. "A lot of my good memories of Nathan have to do with food," I said.

Helen nodded. "Living with someone else is all about food," she said. "What are you going to eat and when are you going to eat it and who's going to cook it or should you go out."

"You told me you knew you wanted to break up with Sam when he asked you whether he should eat a banana." Sam had been Helen's boyfriend in our second year of graduate school. He was a fiction writer, friendly with Nathan, and for a few months we'd enjoyed a paradise of foursomeness. Postbreakup, Nathan and I made one or two awkward attempts at hanging out with Sam, and then we stopped, because no matter what you say in the wake of a breakup, you almost always choose. Who would choose me? Who was I going to lose? Maybe Alex and Adam. Maybe Smith, who'd be angry I'd told Nathan about that kiss. But I didn't want to think about that. Those people were hundreds of miles away.

"I don't remember that," Helen said. She sounded like she didn't believe me.

"We were standing in your kitchen, in that house on Thirty-second. You said you didn't care at all whether he ate a banana, and you couldn't stand being asked to care about things like that anymore. I think you also said you didn't like knowing what he had in his medicine cabinet."

"I remember the part about the medicine cabinet," she said. "There was nothing strange in there, I don't think. I just didn't want to know what his *prescriptions* were." She was stroking Abby's hair, her gaze fixed unseeingly on the television. "That house had a stained-glass window."

"That's right. When the sun came through, there were colors on the walls."

"What I remember is having a fight with Sam because he said he was sick of Korean food." She frowned at me as if I had said it. "Koreans eat it every day."

"I remember that one, too." I sighed. "Not only do I remember my own squabbles, I remember yours."

"Once you and Nathan had a fight about falafel."

"Did we?"

"I can't remember the details."

"A fight about falafel," I said. "Falafel. Crunchy outside, chewy inside. What could we have fought about?"

"Maybe he thought it should be chewy outside, crunchy inside."

"Oh, I doubt it. We always agreed about falafel."

"On our first date Daniel and I had ice cream sundaes, huge ice cream sundaes. He ate his and then finished mine." She shifted Abby a little, grimacing. I imagined some sharp point—a tiny chin, an elbow—was digging into her thigh. "I know working late is not really his fault, but it still pisses me off," she said. "I can't seem to stop being mad about it." She lowered her voice. "He's been refusing to have s-e-x. He says it's because he's tired and I'm pressuring him, but I think he's punishing me for being mad."

"Wow," I said. "That's not the usual configuration for that problem."

"I know," she said. "I should have brought that up when he was fretting about his manhood."

"What happens?" I asked. "Do you do the rub-and-touch thing, and he gives you that look, that oh-no-not-now look?"

"Yes," she said. "It's exactly the reverse. It's exactly the look I've given." She demonstrated, her expression a wary recoil. "It's exactly the look you've given, I bet."

"Why do we all give the exact same look?" I said. "It's depressing."

"Depressing is getting the look," she said. "It's my job to give the look."

"Nathan likes to pretend he just wants to snuggle up, you know, but then his hands start creeping—" I heard my use of the present tense and stopped. For a moment I'd forgotten I was now outside of the normal conversations of wives, the complaints about husbands that again and again reveal the surprise of our commonality, the ordinary sameness of our lives. The looks we all give. The arguments we all have.

"I guess it gives me more sympathy for them, to be the rejected one," she said. "But I'd like to go back to being the woman. If I'm going to get the look, I think he should do the child care."

Daniel was a good-looking guy—he had bright green eyes and the lithe build of an actor—and it was odd to picture him with that look on his face, as I did as soon as I saw him. He was waiting at a table when we got to the restaurant. Helen and I had sat on the couch a long time feeling already exhausted by the steps necessary to departure—the trips to the potty and the diapering and the gathering of bottles and bibs and sippy cups and toys. He expressed no annoyance at our late arrival. He had two high chairs waiting, and crayons and kids' cups of milk, and after he kissed the tops of his children's heads, Helen's mouth, my cheek, he said he'd gone ahead and ordered assorted items off the children's menu so the kids wouldn't have to wait. These days I counted such thoughtfulness as a seduction technique. Helen seemed jostled out of her bad mood. When she leaned across Ian to kiss Daniel again, I found, suddenly, that I could hardly look at them. For the first time it occurred to me that it might be difficult to be around them, engaged in their own version of the more or less happy life I had so recently thought I had. We had so much in common, Helen and I, we had for so long, and now my life had jolted right off the track that hers continued to chug along.

They kissed. She was talking to me, but just for a moment she let her hand rest on his shoulder. He fed her a bite of his food. They retained the necessary ability to move in and out of irritation and companionability, offense and forgiveness, distance and intimacy, the ability that keeps a marriage going, the ability I perhaps no longer had. To know something and yet live as though we don't know it, the way we all do, friends, parents and children, husbands and wives. How many secrets had I been told about the marriages of my friends and my friends' friends? The couple who shoved each other in a drunken argument. The couple who confessed to each other they were sorry they'd ever had the children. The husband who told his wife he was paying the bills, until she came home to an eviction notice on their apartment door. The one who threatened suicide. I glimpsed the depths of other people's lives, in which they nearly drowned, these wives who told me these stories, and then we all struggled back, gasping, to the surface. How do you know when to leave? Is it after one drunken shove? After two? Does it matter who shoved who first?

■

I called Nathan after the kids went to bed. Helen and Daniel were still upstairs with their children. I paced the kitchen while his phone rang, my heart hammering in my throat. "Sarah?" Nathan said. I heard relief in his voice. Relief and gratitude. I was both sorry and glad for the way I'd made him worry.

"Hi," I said.

"Are you OK?" he said. "Are the kids OK?"

"Everybody's fine."

"Where are you?"

"Austin."

"You're kidding."

"Nope."

"Why would you go all the way there?'

I shrugged, though he couldn't see me. "You wanted me to be unconventional."

"That's not exactly what I meant."

"Well," I said. "That's what you got."

There was a long silence. Was he struggling, on the other end of the phone, against the urge to yell at me? Or was he just stunned? "We're at Helen's," I said.

Another silence. "How is Helen?" he asked, finally.

"She's fine. She's good. She got mugged last week."

"Really?"

"Yeah, but she's fine. Her foot is scraped up. She actually refused to let go of her bag and the guy dragged her."

"Somehow that doesn't surprise me," he said.

"That's our Helen," I said. In the silence that followed I felt certain we were both thinking the same thing, hearing the echo of that loaded word *our*. "How's Kate?" I asked.

"I don't know," he said. He sounded miserable. "I didn't see her."

"Oh. I thought that was the whole reason I was going out of town. So you could see her."

"I didn't want you to find out she was here."

"Obviously."

"No, I mean, she was insisting on seeing me, and I was afraid . . ."

"That she'd boil my bunny?"

"No," he said.

"But you were planning to see her, right? Before I left."

"Not to . . . not for any . . ." He took a breath. "I just wanted to make sure I didn't have any feelings for her. I wanted to know why . . . why I let things happen."

"Things?" I said. "Things with an *s*?"

"If that's why I let *something* happen," he said. "It was only one time."

"Only one time," I repeated, and he met me with silence again. "I don't know whether to believe anything you say anymore. Do you know that I just used to assume you were telling me the truth? And now I can't?"

"I'm sorry."

"That might be the worst thing about this, the thought that maybe everything you've ever told me was a lie."

"It wasn't," he said. "You know it wasn't."

Everything that I'm trying to achieve, I'm trying to do with you or for you, he'd said once, when we were making up after a fight. *I want you to think well of me. Without you my accomplishments don't mean a thing*. "Did you tell them to go ahead with the book?"

"Yes."

"So that's it, then."

"That's what you told me to do. And then you left. I don't know if we're going to have any other source of income. And I can't keep jerking them around."

"I know all that."

"So what do you mean, that's it then?"

"I mean that's it. Everyone will know."

"It's fiction, Sarah. I mean, yes, OK, but essentially it's fiction."

"Apparently," I said.

"Apparently what?"

"It depends on what the definition of *it* is."

He sighed. "I'm just doing what you told me to do," he said. "I don't know what else—"

"I don't want to talk to you anymore," I said, and I hung up the phone. I stood there in somebody else's kitchen, in somebody else's house, in somebody else's town. He wanted to know if he had feelings for her. He thought he might. He'd said nothing to suggest he'd decided he didn't. He hadn't even asked me when I was coming home.

I heard Helen's footsteps on the stairs. I put the phone down on the counter and went to meet her. "Let's go get cigarettes," I said. "Let's sit outside and smoke. Or let's go to a bar and sit at the bar and smoke and drink martinis."

"Martinis?" Helen said. She picked up the remote and collapsed on the couch, and half an hour later we were still there, staring at the television with the same stunned expressions that had earlier decorated our children's faces. Daniel had yet to emerge from putting Ian to bed, and Helen said he'd probably fallen asleep himself. We were watching the news, and the news was bad. "Everybody talks about how complacent Americans are," Helen said. "But I didn't really grasp that until lately. How complacent we've been. What if Daniel lost his job? What would we do?"

"I don't know," I said. My throat was tightening, tightening. "Can we watch something else?"

She clicked the TV off with a sigh, tossed the remote on the coffee table.

"Cigarettes," I said. "Don't they sound good?"

"Can't," she said. "Was too hard to quit."

"The thought made you lose your pronouns," I said.

"Daniel would kill me," she said. "Daniel in a state of self-righteous anger is a terror to behold."

"He seems so easygoing," I said. "It's hard to picture."

"Oh yeah," she said. "You have no idea."

"No," I said. I just didn't know Daniel, did I. Not like I knew Helen. Not like she knew Nathan, the three of us bonded by common experience, classes and classmates and parties and late-night pancakes, the sort of drink- and pot-fueled conversations that make you feel you've traveled the highways and byways of somebody else's mind. "You seem happy together," I said.

"I think we're a pretty good fit." She sat up, adjusted a pillow behind her back, snuggled back down. "You can check the liquor cabinet and see what we've got, if you want a drink."

"I don't want to drink by myself," I said. "I wanted mutual debauchery."

"Ooh," she said. "I could make iced lattes."

The last thing an insomniac needs is an evening latte, but I said OK, because she'd offered it with the same anticipatory excitement with which she used to offer me a joint. She smiled more easily when she was stoned, her eyes got small and her grin got wide, and when she was drunk her skin flushed, redness creeping up her face to spread along her hairline, and I knew those things even though I couldn't remember the last time I'd seen her stoned or drunk.

"I got an espresso maker," she said. "It's awesome." The thought of the coffee had rejuvenated her. She walked into the kitchen with a bounce in her step, and I followed, thinking of grad school, afternoons at our favorite café, coffee and cigarettes, a melancholy mood we both wished away and welcomed. Nathan never smoked, but he did occasionally join us for coffee. "In the time you two have spent bitching," he said once, "you could have written a poem or three."

"When's the last time you wrote a poem?" I asked Helen now, leaning on her kitchen counter while she fiddled with her shiny new machine.

"Like, worked on one, or finished one?"

"Either."

"I worked on one yesterday," she said. "I finished one last week."

That was not the answer I'd expected. "Oh," I said.

She scooped espresso beans into a grinder, counting under her breath. "You sound surprised."

"I guess I assumed you didn't have time to write."

"I didn't, until we hired the babysitter."

"You have a babysitter?"

"I didn't tell you that? She comes three mornings a week, and I go off to a coffee shop and write."

"When did that start?"

"About six months ago." She pulled two tall clear glasses from the counter. "It was weird at first. It felt really weird to sit and do nothing, you know? To sit and think. To pay someone ten dollars an hour so I could sit and think. I still feel guilty on the days when I don't actually produce anything."

"That's part of the process."

"I know," she said. "But it didn't use to cost me ten dollars an hour."

I wanted to ask more questions—I knew I *should* ask more questions, how it was going, what she was working on. But I was still struggling with the inaccuracy of my assumptions, my notion that we had similar failures of ambition or energy, the feeling of inadequacy produced by the revelation that we weren't, after all, the same. Ian had been born three months before Mattie, and Helen had been one of my primary sources of support and reassurance. It was OK that I sometimes cried for no reason. It was understandable that when older women urged me to enjoy this time, I felt a flash of anger. It was normal to find the first months of motherhood so hard. Making chitchat with other mothers on the playground, I'd found myself retreating from the ones who refused to complain, the ones who did not seem to feel like a bomb had gone off in the middle of their lives. If they could stand around glowing with love like a figure in a Mary Cassatt painting, then what the hell was wrong with me?

Helen was holding out the glasses to me. They were still empty. I didn't understand.

"Can you put ice in these?" she asked, and so I took them, and obeyed. As I stood at the freezer, ice cubes sticking to my hand, she asked, "So what do you want to do about Rajiv?"

"What do you mean?"

"Well, I told him you were coming here."

"Oh," I said. "You did?"

"I thought you wanted me to. He really wants to see you. I said maybe we could have him over for dinner tomorrow night."

"Here? Really? But I don't know if I want the kids to meet him."

"They wouldn't be meeting him as your boyfriend. It'd be just like meeting us."

"I know, but it's also, I don't want to mix up flirty mode and maternal mode. I don't want to be thinking, 'Oh, baby. Now I have to go breast-feed.' I want him to see me without the kids."

"You want to be Sarah, not somebody's mother."

"Not somebody's mother," I said. "Not somebody's wife."

"Wife," she said. "I hate that word."

"It's not a good word," I said. "Girlfriend was better."

"I can watch the kids tomorrow night. You could meet him out somewhere."

"That would feel so datelike," I said. "Is that too much?"

"Well, the other option is to go to his house," she said.

"You mean just show up there?"

"Show up there, say, 'Hello, I'm here for the sex,' and ask him where the bedroom is," she said. "What are we talking about here? Did you drive across the country for this guy or what?"

I brought her the glasses, and she dumped in the dark espresso, the white milk. We watched the colors swirl. Did I really drive across the country for Rajiv? Was that why I had done it? I didn't know. But if so, wasn't that—really, truly—a little on the crazy side? "What *are* we talking about here?" I asked.

"Sex?" she said. "Marriage? Motherhood? No longer being twenty-two?" She handed me my glass, lifted hers. "Cheers," she said, and we clinked.

We wandered back to the living room. I said, "My mother was twenty-two when she had me."

"My mother was twenty-five."

"Can you imagine? That was when we were in grad school. Can you imagine having had kids at that age? I didn't even know who I was."

She settled back into the couch cushions. "Don't you think knowing who you are makes it harder? I mean, you know who you are, and then it becomes really hard to be who you are."

"That's true," I said. "Excellent point." On her bookshelf she had the same set of Proust she'd given me. "Have you read these?"

"What?" She leaned forward to see those elegant, reproachful spines. "Oh, God, no."

"Me, neither," I said, and I sat down beside her, relieved.

"Someday," she said. "Maybe."

"Someday maybe," I said. "Do you miss graduate school?"

"What do you think? Don't you remember Janelle and her sisterhood circle?"

"I totally forgot about that! She really wanted you to be her sister."

"Did she ever. Goddess this, goddess that. She used to come up behind me at parties and start braiding my hair."

"Remember when Tony kept trying to romance you by suggesting you both sign up for karate?"

"What an idiot. Karate isn't even Korean. He should at least have said tae kwon do."

"If only you'd succumbed to his charms. You could be a black belt by now."

"Remember when Brian implied he'd been a male prostitute?"

"Was he hitting on you, too?"

She shrugged. "Kind of a misguided approach, if he was."

"Did we ever find out whether that was even true?"

"I don't know. It made his poems seem cooler, which was what he was going for."

"I remember all the gossip after his reading, everybody trying to parse what his poems meant. They were elliptical in the extreme, but we were all convinced we saw truth in them." I sighed. "I think back then I had a tendency to confuse the art and the life."

"A lot of people did." She smiled. Then suddenly she intoned, "I rode a great sadness today."

I stared at her. She looked back at me, solemnly. "Are you trying out a poem on me?" I asked.

"You've got to be kidding." She leaned forward. "You don't remember that? The party at Brian's house, everyone sitting around stoned, and suddenly out of nowhere he pipes up and says—"

I finished the thought: "I rode a great sadness today." The scene rushed back, the dimly lit apartment over a liquor store, the orange velour couch and extensive vinyl collection. Brian had once worked for a museum, and along the hall he had put up detergent and tinfoil and cookie boxes alongside typed descriptions of each object and its significance. *An ironic facsimile of a box of tinfoil, this box of tinfoil challenges us with the question: Did I or did I not once contain tinfoil? Hung nonchalantly on the wall, much like a box of tinfoil in someone's home, this box of tinfoil is, remarkably, indistinguishable from an actual box of tinfoil. Asking where life ends and art begins, this box of tinfoil is a box of tinfoil.*

"And you . . ." She grinned, and I grinned, and then she started to laugh, her laughter bumping her words along. "You said . . ."

I was laughing, too, the laughter catching me up. " 'What?' "

"And he said, and this time he seemed a little sheepish, 'I rode a great sadness today.' And again you said . . ."

I was laughing hard now. "I really didn't hear him," I managed to say.

" 'What?' You made him say it a third time! Then, poor guy, he just rushed it out as fast as he could, 'Irodeagreatsadnesstoday.' And just dead silence."

"Well, what are you supposed to say to that? I rode a unicorn?"

"Oh, that poor guy," she said, laughing.

"I felt a great human emotion tonight," I said.

"Oh, me, too," she said. "Me, too."

"I really didn't hear him," I said again, no longer laughing, suddenly visited by remorse. For the first time I felt sympathy for Brian, who wanted so badly to be a certain kind of person that he ended up an actor on his own carefully designed stage. It seemed to me now that there had been pathos even in the way he wore his hair, like Bob Dylan circa 1965. No doubt he had been depressed that day. I remembered him as a depressive guy. But how genuine was his emotion if he could transform it so readily into a line, display it like an accomplishment? How great could his sadness have been if he could say it aloud?

"Do you miss graduate school?" Helen asked.

"I don't miss the place, or, really, most of the people, or, God knows, workshop. I miss, you know, conviction. My youthful conviction."

"Which youthful conviction?"

"I don't know," I said. "Maybe all of them."

■

That night I couldn't sleep. I lay there for a while listening to my children breathe. Binx had a phlegmy rattle in his throat. In her sleep Mattie murmured something about doorways. I got up. In the living room I brought the set of Proust over to the couch, and for the next three hours I flipped through the volumes, reading a little bit here and there. Proust was an insomniac, a piece of information that startled and unnerved me. How eerie it felt, in the middle of the night, to have a hundred-year-old voice tell me exactly how it felt to be awake in the middle of the night. Proust couldn't sleep. He retreated from the world to ruminate on the minutiae of its pains and pleasures, our experience of art, of nature, of other human beings. He elevated that minutiae, he made it the only thing. A phrase of music, played again, less transient than love. Who, after all, can hope to hold all of her life in her mind, with so much forgotten, so much given away? There is no *life*, in the way we often mean the word, as one person's story, a coherent narrative. There's this moment and before it another one and after it another one and layered behind it another one. Experience echoes and retreats, a Coke when I needed it ten years ago, and another now, offered because the original experience endowed it with meaning. But only when the Coke passes from Helen's hand to mine does it have that meaning. Without Helen it's just a drink, liquid bubbling in a glass, a sweet taste, then gone.

CHAPTER SEVENTEEN

In the morning Helen found me on the couch with the first volume of Proust on my chest. "This is quite a sight," she said, gesturing at the rest of the books, splayed around me. "You got drunk on Proust."

"I don't know if you can get drunk on Proust," I said. "He's too detail-oriented for that. You can get stoned on Proust." When I sat up, my brain seemed to shift inside my head. "Did you know he was an insomniac?" I felt awful. The day loomed before me like an obstacle course. "Are my kids awake?"

Helen shook her head. "I haven't heard them. Abby's up." She nodded toward the kitchen, and I peered around her to see Abby wandering by with a piece of toast in her hand. She had half of it stuffed in her mouth and she didn't seem to be chewing it, just carrying it around like a dog with a bone. "Abby's always up."

"What time is it?"

"Just after six. I'm sorry I woke you. I wasn't expecting to find you here."

I shook my head to say, don't worry about it, and she

asked if I wanted a latte, and I nodded to say, Yes, please God, I do. She started to walk toward the kitchen, but I stopped her with her name. She waited. "Let's invite Rajiv to dinner," I said. If I had been her, I would have teased me about my change of heart, about this being the first thought I had upon waking.

"OK," she said.

"I love you, Helen," I said, but I wasn't sure if she heard me.

In the late morning we took the kids to IKEA and Helen bought things while I chased the children, for whom the place represented not a frenzy of consumerism, not a cavalcade of fabulous deals, but an endless playground of beds and chairs and tables, a dollhouse big as life. We ate meatballs for lunch. We took the kids home and put the babies down for naps and read to Ian and Mattie and then turned the TV on for them and drank some more iced lattes. All day I thought about the end of the day, which would bring Rajiv. Helen had called him that morning, and he'd been delighted to come. "Did he really use the word *delighted*?" I had asked, more than once, and more than once Helen had confirmed he did. Delighted. A positive word, of course, but also a slightly silly one, with its overtones of foppish effusion. Or perhaps he'd said it ironically, in a faux-uppity way. Had he said it ironically?

"No," Helen said.

"You're getting sick of this already, aren't you," I said.

She shrugged. "I remember what it's like."

"I haven't done this in a long time," I said. "It feels really weird to be doing this."

"There doesn't have to be a *this*," she said. "It can just be dinner, if that's what you want."

What I wanted was to click my heels three times and return to the maze where he'd kissed me, the one and only time he'd kissed me, the white lights twinkling above us, around us, behind. What I got was a seat on the floor among the strewn pieces of a puzzle, Binx with a puzzle piece dampening in his mouth and me gently trying to tug it out while I also reached for Mattie, who was picking up the other pieces and throwing them, screaming because Binx had come crashing through her puzzle like Babyzilla after she'd spent a painstaking half hour constructing it. I never failed to be surprised by how strong Binx was, his hand and the puzzle piece incredibly difficult to tug away from his mouth as he made the guttural sounds of an animal disturbed at the food dish. Ian was watching with interest, plinking at an electronic toy piano in a desultory way. "Mattie," I was saying, "Mattie, stop that right now," but she couldn't hear me over her own frustration and despair, and I'd failed to hear the doorbell, or notice that Helen had gone to answer it, Abby at her heels, and so when I looked up to see Rajiv standing just inside the living room, it was as though he'd appeared out of thin air. I recognized the look on his face as the shell-shocked one I used to wear years ago when confronted with a chaos of children. There was no yes, yes!, no swept-away feeling. There was screaming, and a look of alarm, and me cross-legged on the floor with my stomach pooched out over my lap, looking far far fatter than I did standing up.

Mattie noticed Rajiv seconds after I did, and abruptly her screaming stopped, although for a moment the air still seemed to ring with it. I hauled Binx to me, wrested the puzzle piece from him, and handed him a toy phone at the same time. Then I stood, held Binx in front of my stomach, and said, "Hi."

"So . . . ," Helen said, and then Daniel called from the

kitchen, "Helen, that pot is boiling!" and she broke off and exited at a jog. Abby toddled along behind her, arms held out, crying, "Mama, Mama, Mama."

"Hi," Rajiv said. "Long time no see." His eyes were on mine, and then they flicked away, to Mattie. He wore a small, odd smile that might have been nervous, might have been secretive, might have been . . . oh, who knows. It didn't seem good. He wore a white, short-sleeved button-down shirt, just see-through enough to show the ribbed undershirt clinging to his stomach, which looked, yes, as taut as ever, like you could press your palm there and feel the ripples of muscle underneath the warm, dark skin. I was wearing my favorite shirt, one that augmented my milk-amplified breasts while falling in loose generosity over my stomach, and I'd taken care with my hair and borrowed a pair of Helen's earrings, and still I felt slatternly, slovenly, exposed. Carrying extra weight felt like wearing my weaknesses on the outside. You could tell by looking at me that I had succumbed to too many pints of ice cream. I had stopped going to the gym. I had failed to be, as a book I'd seen recently exhorted me, a "yummy mummy," and, of course, there was the small matter of my straying husband. Maybe Rajiv thought, No wonder, when he looked at me. Maybe he thought, Good Lord, what was I thinking? Maybe he looked at me with pity, a copy of a copy of someone he once knew.

He crouched before Mattie. Her tear-streaked face had a post-tantrum placidity. She regarded him. "Hi," he said. "I'm Rajiv." He held out his hand for her to shake. She looked at it. "That's your hand," she said.

"Are you sure?" he asked. He turned his hand palm up and wiggled the fingers. "Are you sure it's not an overturned beetle?"

She laughed. "No, it's not a beetle! That's your hand!"

"Oh," he said. "Well, in that case can you give me five?" He held his hand out and waited.

She backed closer to me. "Mommy, what is five?" she asked.

"Five fingers," I said.

"You can't take my fingers," she said to Rajiv in the crisp, adult voice she used when scolding.

"You're right," he said. "I have my own." He straightened up and smiled at me again. This time the smile was better, brighter, a little bit conspiratorial. "And this is Binx," he said. As he bent to smile at the baby, to play peekaboo, which made Binx laugh, I thought I'd made a terrible mistake. I should have gone to his house. I should have just shown up there with a bottle of wine, I should have taken his hand and led him without a word to the bedroom, making sure the lights were out. I should have pretended we were in a movie, or a fairy tale—love, or at least lust, with no preliminaries. Or maybe I should have left it all to my imagination, maybe I preferred it that way. Because now we had to get to the bedroom from a beginning of tantrums and puzzles and peekaboo, polite chitchat over dinner, a segue that one of us had to be brave enough to make, the question of willingness hanging over our heads, unspoken, as we pressed on through the ordinary. This was all backward, the cinematic embrace normally coming before the screaming children, as it had, of course, with Nathan. And I had no idea what to say. I'd been envisioning kisses, twinkling lights, a rush of emotion. Oz, I'd been envisioning Oz. I'd never considered that I might need to begin by asking him about his day. I didn't even know if I cared about his day. A few e-mails, one brief kiss—what did I really know about this guy? What good had I thought seeing him would do?

Binx squirmed to get down, so I bent and set him on the floor, kept my eyes fixed on him as he crawled toward a stuffed animal and flung himself upon it. "He's fast," Rajiv said.

"He's like a little bug," I said. "He scurries." I risked a glance at Rajiv, found him looking at me.

"It's good to see you," he said. I wanted it to be good to see me, of course, so why did I feel disconcerted by the emphasis with which he said this, almost as disconcerted as I was thrilled?

"It's good to see you, too," I said. He was standing awfully close to me. I looked at his stomach, could practically feel the warmth of it beneath my palm. My gaze went back to his face. My God, I'd just given him a once-over, like a pervy old man on the subway, and he knew it, too, his eyebrows up, his mouth cocked on one side in a knowing way. I grinned at him, caught, surrendering. "Hi, beautiful," I said.

He looked surprised. He looked delighted. Yes, *delighted* was the word. Had no one ever pointed out his beauty before? "Hi," he said. He leaned in like this was our first greeting and kissed me on the cheek, and now I could feel what I'd been waiting to feel, that reckless thrumming beneath my skin, that silent, magnetized acknowledgment of mutual desire.

But Helen was calling from the kitchen, asking what we wanted to drink, and Mattie and Ian had started squabbling over the toy piano, and Binx decided to chime in, too, crawling toward me and crying in the way I recognized as a demand for milk. I'd spent nearly four years learning to subvert my own needs to somebody else's, but desire, new desire, competes mightily with a little girl who wants a turn with the toy piano, with a baby who wants his milk. So I tried to set it aside. I sent Rajiv to answer Helen, I moderated over the piano, giving the usual speech about taking turns, and then I sat down on the couch and attached Binx to my breast. I didn't even think about this latter action until Rajiv returned with two glasses of red wine and his steps faltered at the sight of me in that most maternal of poses. He recovered, handed me my glass from a respectful distance, started a conversation about a novel he'd been reading with his gaze fixed resolutely on my face. I hoped I hadn't flipped a switch in his brain, so that now he'd think "mother" when he looked at me. There are many uses to which you can put the body, I wanted to say to him. They don't have to be exclusive, no matter how it sometimes feels.

■

At home, Nathan and I were as schedule-oriented as Supernanny could ever want. Bedtime was between seven and seven thirty, and every night we repeated the ritual of baths and songs and storybooks. Helen and Daniel were much more casual; their children often stayed up snuggled against them on the couch until they carried them, asleep or half asleep, up to their beds. I was experimenting, rolling with the punches, and so I let my kids stay up, too, Mattie and Ian watching TV while we ate, Binx passed around from lap to lap, putting his fingers in people's mouths and laughing. Would Jack Kerouac have put his children to bed on time? A ridiculous question, which made me smile in a way that Rajiv noticed. "What?" he asked.

"I was just thinking how cute Binx is," I said, because the truth would require too much explanation, and Rajiv might not grasp how funny it was anyway, the whole idea of *On the Road with Kids*. Before Nathan and I had children, we had the usual difficulty understanding why our friends who procreated became, to our minds, incredibly uptight. Why we had to eat dinner at five. Why we couldn't flush the toilet after the kids went to bed. Nathan and I said to each other that when we were parents we wouldn't be like this. Nor would we let our children monopolize a guest, insisting on constant horsie rides that said guest felt obligated to supply, all the while longing for a seat on the couch and a beer. Nor would we let our children talk back to us, or refuse to eat vegetables, or a whole host of other things that seemed, in retrospect, like the rose-colored hopes of crazed idealists. Once, we'd gone to the beach with kid-toting friends, and we were astonished when they got up to leave after only an hour, after all the effort it had taken to sunscreen the children and load up the gear. The children needed to nap, they said, and Nathan said, "Why can't they just nap on the beach?" And our friends the parents gave him a weary smile, a smile I now recognize as saying, If you have children you'll understand, and until then I'm too tired to explain it to you. Sunlight and sunburn and sand in the diaper. A baby who won't stay where you put him, who flips right over and crawls away. A little girl who can't sleep without her covers over her head, the stuffed octopus she's named Bob.

Two hours past his bedtime Binx grew fussy, wanting to nurse constantly, finally falling asleep at my breast, milk running out of his slack mouth. I carried him into the room we all were sharing and put him gently in the Pack 'n Play, and then Helen came up the stairs carrying a sobbing Mattie, and it took me a long time and three books to console and calm her down enough that she could go into the room with the sleeping baby. "Nap on the beach," I whispered in her ear, and she repeated the phrase and laughed.

When I came back down Helen and Daniel were doing the dishes, their children dozing against each other in front of the television, and Rajiv was standing by the back door staring out into the yard. He turned when he heard me. "I'm going outside for a smoke," he said. He waited. My God, he was good at waiting.

"Can I come?" I said.

It was a starry, starry night. Without discussing it, we walked to the back of the yard, just outside the pool of light spilling from the windows, where no one glancing out from the house could see us. Of course I didn't tell him I no longer smoked. He handed me a cigarette and I took it, and then when he held up his lighter I put the cigarette in my mouth, my hand trembling a little, and he leaned forward and lit it for me. Nathan had never been a smoker, but he wasn't the only man I'd ever dated, and I'd known the pleasure of having a man light my cigarette, of feeling for a breath of time like Lauren Bacall in black and white, wielder of a sultry gaze. I'd forgotten that feeling, and I enjoyed its return. What a shame that the cigarette tasted terrible, that I inhaled too heartily and the smoke assaulted the back of my throat, making me sputter and cough like a teenager failing in an attempt to seem worldly wise.

"Are you okay?" Rajiv asked.

"Fine," I said, and though I coughed out the word he seemed to accept that response. I held the cigarette and watched the smoke rise upward and hoped he wouldn't notice if I didn't inhale again. Why did I think I had to pretend for him? I thought that to get what I wanted I had to be the old me, and at that moment I remembered the old me as one in tune with the rhythms of smoking, drinking, flirting. The old me was the girl in the maze, the girl he'd loved a little, and even though I was five years and ten pounds and two kids heavier than that girl, I wanted him to see her when he looked at me. I wanted to be her. She hadn't had a husband who'd chosen another over her. She'd been a poet. She hadn't had a husband at all. Rajiv didn't ask me about Nathan, or recent events, or what I planned to do next, questions surely almost anyone else would have posed. Only later did it occur to me that he wanted to pretend, too.

What did we talk about? I have no idea. It was a stream of pointless chatter. I was talking in a nervous, hiccupping way, my sentences stop-and-start, my voice rushed and high-pitched, my laugh too quick and too loud. All the alcohol I'd consumed seemed to be rushing through my head like whitewater.

"You know," he said after a while, and I knew by the way he hesitated that something honest was coming. "I thought about you a lot, after the last time I saw you."

"You wrote great e-mails," I said.

"Oh, those." He grinned. "I slaved over those."

"No, you didn't."

"Hours and hours!" he said. "Checking every word in the thesaurus. Because there might be a better word."

"You're kidding," I said, and he gave me his secret smile. "Well, I have a little microphone right here"—I touched my ear—"telling me what to say."

"Interesting. Who's on the other end?"

"Hmmm. I haven't thought this joke out enough. James Bond? The president? Shakespeare?"

He laughed. "I can't imagine a more schizophrenic combination than that."

"One minute it's poetry, then it's spy talk, then it's a bunch of nonsense about coexisting with fish."

"Pretty much," he said. He inhaled, exhaled. I watched the smoke drift upward. "So what I'm gearing up to tell you," he said, "is that I made a short film about you."

"This time you sound serious."

"This time I am serious. It was sort of a losing-the-dream-girl thing, but, you know, the importance in your mind, the ongoing importance . . ." He sighed. "Now I'm babbling."

"No, sir," I said. "I know babbling, and that was not babbling." I was inches from saying more about babbling, the sounds Binx made, and then I remembered, no babies, not with him.

"Anyway," he said.

"Anyway," I said. "Can I see it?"

He laughed. "Oh God no, it's terrible. I'm embarrassed by it now. It's really overwrought."

"I don't think of you as capable of overwrought. Or," I said, remembering, "of obvious."

"Obvious," he repeated. He dropped his cigarette and rubbed it out. "Yeah, but sometimes I am." He looked up. And there was the intense eye contact. And there, oh no, was the nervous giggle.

"I don't think of myself as a dream girl," I said, and hoped that it was only to myself I sounded high-pitched and breathless.

"Maybe that's what makes you one."

"Hmmmm," I said. "If that were the only requirement a lot more people would be dream girls."

He laughed. "There are other requirements," he said.

"What are they?"

He smiled. He stepped closer. He didn't answer me. Nathan liked to explain things. We had that in common. If he had been the one with me in the garden, he would have made an effort to explain. He might have listed my good qualities. He might have made a joke about big bazongas. He might have done both, because we had in common, too, a tendency to conclude a bout of sincerity with a joke. You couldn't just let the emotion lie there, all naked and newborn and strange.

Rajiv explained nothing. Rajiv, I was beginning to see, had a weakness for the inexplicable, the ineffable, the sweet abandonment to things beyond our ken. He kissed me. Though I responded, for a moment my thoughts hovered with Nathan: Did Nathan really want to undercut emotion with a joke? Or was that just me? Had I made him uncomfortable with sentiment, the way he always made me late?

Rajiv was kissing me. I stopped thinking about Nathan. I stopped thinking about anything.

■

"Your mouth is all red," Helen said.

Rajiv was gone, Daniel upstairs with the kids. Rajiv had left not long after we'd returned from our kissing interlude, for which I was grateful, because it was a struggle to stand there making chitchat with him and Helen when all I wanted to do was touch him again.

"Really?"

"Mmm-hmmm," Helen said. "Actually, half your face is red. He must be quite the kisser."

I went to the mirror. She was right. I looked like a teenage girl who'd been out in the car with her boyfriend, my mouth bright red and the skin around it pink, like I'd worked my lips so hard they'd dissolved into the rest of my face. You just don't kiss that vigorously once you've been together for ten years. You go much faster to the sex. "Wow," I said.

She laughed. She seemed a little excited herself—if you're married, and you're faithful, you get your thrills vicariously. "So what happened?"

"He kissed me."

"Well, your face tells that story," she said. "But what did he say?"

"He said he'd made a film about me, but it was terrible."

"Huh," she said. "Never saw that one, I don't think. Unless you were the carny in the one about the amusement park."

"The carny, huh? Is that what I am to you? Because your friend used the words *dream girl*."

"And you just bloomed like a flower, didn't you?"

"That kind of talk—it's like a drug, Helen."

She started reminiscing about a guy she'd dated in college who'd been prone to courtly speeches about how wonderful she was. "But his metaphors were bad," she said.

I was only half listening, my mind still on Rajiv. I wanted to ask her if he was so romantic, so certain, about every woman he dated. I suspected the answer would be yes, because if Helen thought his feelings for me were as revelatory and particular as he claimed, surely she'd be worried about the damage I might do him, so obviously indulging the urge to make myself feel better. But I didn't want to hear a yes. So I didn't ask.

"So what now?" Helen asked.

"Well, I like him," I said. "Really, you know, for a lot of the things I first liked about Nathan, the way we connect about books and movies and music, the fact that he gets my jokes."

Helen said nothing, but she looked at me. Oh, she looked.

"It's not weird," I said. "We're attracted to the same qualities over and over. Daniel's got some things in common with the other guys you've dated."

"Sure," she said. "But you don't want to go after Rajiv because you want to get back some version of Nathan."

"Get back, or get back at?" I asked.

She shrugged. "Either one."

My cell phone began to play "Family Affair," which meant Nathan was calling me. The sound was muffled and seemed to come from behind Helen. She leaned forward, pulling a couch cushion with her, and my phone tumbled out. One of the kids must have been playing with it. I looked at the screen, though I knew who the caller was. "It's Nathan," I said.

She made an "uh-oh" face. "Are you going to answer?"

"I don't know," I said. I closed my hand over the phone.

"I'm going to go check on Daniel," she said.

The phone vibrated once more in my hand and then stopped. The sound of the ring had been like an alarm clock snatching me out of a dream. Nathan. Oh, right. My husband. The whole reason I was here. What was he thinking, what was he doing, while I was outside in the arms of another man? I was sure he missed the children. A few weeks before all this we'd gone to the movies, a rare night out, and there was a scene in which a man leaned close to a baby, letting the baby grab and squeeze his nose, and the baby looked exactly the age of Binx, who loved to grab our noses, look at us inquisitively when he did so, then laugh. As I watched, my eyes filled up with tears, as they did these days at any media mention of children—happy children, sick children, missing children—and I could feel the goony, lovesick smile on my face. I glanced at Nathan. He watched the onscreen baby with the same smile, and the love I'd been feeling for Binx wrapped itself around Nathan. We loved each other, we loved our children, and we were of the same mind, and at that moment those states of being seemed to stretch forward unstoppably into the future. Why wouldn't we always feel what we felt at that moment? Why not?

I called him back. Where before he'd been chastened and prone to silence, now he'd worked himself up to angry. "You haven't called," he said.

And I said, "I've been busy," my own anger spiking in response. Austin was my world now, however temporarily, Helen and Daniel and Rajiv the people who populated it. Nathan—who was Nathan, this asshole on the other end of the phone? Not the man who'd so recently kissed me in the garden, that was for sure. Not the man who'd called me his dream girl. This voice on the phone, sharp with accusation—it belonged to someone very far away. I was here and he wasn't, and if experience is entirely the mind's perception of the moment, then he didn't even exist.

"Busy doing what? What's going on there?"

"What do you mean?" I went cold.

"I mean, how long are you planning to stay? When are you bringing my children home?"

I didn't answer. I had no idea. I couldn't imagine. I couldn't look past the next day.

"Hello? Are you listening to me?"

"Yes," I said.

"Because I'm not exactly talking about what I had for lunch."

"No," I said. He was referring to an argument we'd had a month before, or maybe longer. "No, you're not." I paused.

"Hello?" he asked. "Are you there?"

"I'm here," I said. "I'll call you tomorrow, okay?" And then I hung up the phone. How strange that he was still thinking about that argument, given everything that had happened since. I'd been having a bad day and he'd called me at the office, interrupting me in the middle of some task that had, at the time, seemed important. He'd started telling me about his morning, then he took a breath and I assumed he'd finished, and I said OK, I'd talk to him later. "I wasn't done," he said.

"What," I snapped, "you weren't finished telling me what you had for lunch?"

Because he had a tendency to do that, you know. If he had half a can of lentil soup, I knew about it, and, alas, I didn't particularly care. He likes details, Nathan. He thinks a story should start at the beginning—of course, of course, but many times we've differed on what the beginning is. To understand the story I'm telling now, he might think you needed to know about the first girl he loved, what she wore to the prom, what her face looked like when she broke his heart. He once told me that the driveway of his childhood home sloped down at a thirty-seven-degree angle. Sometimes we could laugh about his predilection for minutiae, but not that time when he called me. That time he was furious. That time he said, "You could at least pretend to give a shit about how I spend my time."

I said, "I do."

He said, "You do give a shit, or you do pretend?"

"Both," I said, which was the accurate, but unwise, answer, and the fight went on from there, to such places as whether it took longer to do the laundry (my job) or the dishes (his). If there's anything we've learned from the endless parsing of everything, it's that nothing is ever about what it seems to be about. Depending on what the meaning of *is* is. There's subtext to the subtext, every argument a rabbit hole. Do we know why we're angry? Do we know what we're fighting about?

"You are self-absorbed and inconsiderate," he said, and I said, "Funny, that's what I was thinking about you."

For every good memory there's a bad one. And the reverse. The reverse is also true.

CHAPTER EIGHTEEN

It had been so long since I'd lived outside the regimented world of work that I still found it disconcerting to wake up on a weekday morning without any sense of what the day would hold. Was it possible I missed going to work? That I liked my job after all? Yes, it was possible. There was satisfaction, wasn't there, in the daily accomplishment of tasks, in the neat organization of files and spreadsheets. And I missed Tanya and Kristy, who continued to believe, or at least pretended to, that my family and I had been struck down by the rotavirus. "Nasty stuff, the rotavirus," Kristy said when I talked to her that morning, and I agreed that it was. "Don't come in and give it to me," she said, and I promised I wouldn't. It never ceased to amaze me, how easily all of us were fooled.

"How are things there?" I asked.

"Falling apart without you," she said. And then she laughed.

"Hey," I said.

"No, seriously, we miss you. I'm working a lot harder

than usual. And Tanya and John are pissed at each other. He wants her to print out his e-mails and put them on his desk, then he dictates his answers for her to type. Then she's supposed to print them out so he can correct them, then make his corrections, then send the e-mails from his account. I am not making this up."

"Jesus." I could hear her sucking on a drink, probably Bojangles sweet iced tea. The straw made that pool-draining sound, a squeak against the plastic lid. I could picture her pulling it in and out, looking for more tea. "Seriously, Kristy," I said. "Refills are free."

"Shut it," she said. "I'm only allowed one. That's the diet I'm on. I'm fat as a cow."

"You're pregnant," I said.

"Yeah, I noticed," she said. "Plus, I can't be running off to Bojangles every five minutes, what with having to do your job. If you don't come back soon, Tanya might start sending crazy e-mails from John's account."

"Like what?"

"Dear Professor Buttface," Kristy said. "Please join me in an experiment to enlarge my penis."

"Do you think he could get the NIH to fund that?" I asked.

"He probably already has," Kristy said. "They're probably spending half their day enlarging their penises."

"Who's they?" I asked.

"The faculty. The professors so-and-so."

"What about the women?" I asked.

"Oh shit, it's John," Kristy said. "I've got to go." She hung up, just like that. She had to work, you know. And what did I have to do? Sit around with Helen drinking coffee, idly debating what to do next. And that was strange. It was strange, walking a wide trail through a park, pushing the babies in their strollers while the older kids ran ahead, without the beat of my to-do list in the back of my brain: *return e-mails*, *weed garden*, *make phone calls*, *clean stove*. Around us college kids played Frisbee golf, and I watched them, their laughter, their investment in the game, the way nothing about them suggested that they might have homework or troubles waiting at home. I'd spent my high school and college years, and then my twenties, trying to get somewhere, and then at some point, without quite noticing the change, I'd begun to assume there was nowhere left to get. I had two kids and a job and a marriage and a house. I lived on a plateau and went around busily maintaining it. Now here was a new reality, the path ahead disappearing under golden trees, like paths do in fantasy novels, on their way to magic and swordplay. What would happen next in my life? In the world? I couldn't even pretend I knew. We never really know, do we, and yet we manage to live as though we do, as though there is some permanence to our routines of waking and breakfast and school and work and afternoon coffee and television and bedtime and the same person sleeping every night on the other side of the bed. What a shock it is, that there is no permanence. But it has to be a shock, right? Without the magic trick of belief, it would be too hard to live.

"So tomorrow the babysitter comes," Helen said.

"Oh, right," I said.

"Do you want me to ask if she can watch your kids, too? I mean, you'd have to pay her."

"I don't know. What would I do?"

Helen shrugged. "You could go to the coffee shop with me and work."

"Hmmmm," I said. "What are you working on?"

"A series of poems about my parents—hey!" Ian was waving a large stick in the air, dangerously close to Mattie. "Stop that right now, or no TV time!" Ian shot her a mutinous look but dropped the stick.

"Do you have trouble going back and forth between TV time and work? I mean, switching from kid mode to writing mode?"

"Um . . ." She was still watching Ian, who lingered near the stick, looking back from time to time to see if she was still watching. "Don't you dare," she called to him. Ian turned and stomped off down the path. Mattie ran after him, and we quickened our pace to keep them in view.

"Kids just make you so present in the moment," I said. "When I'm with them, I feel like I've never been so attuned to what's going on around me in my life. Because you have to be. You always have to have half your mind on them."

"That's true," Helen said. "Some days I can't concentrate, and instead I'm wondering how Ian's doing at school, or whether the babysitter remembered to give Abby her morning snack. But there were always days when I couldn't concentrate. I was just thinking about different stuff."

"But the ability to concentrate is still there," I said. "You can still lose yourself in your work."

"I found it harder when I was still breast-feeding," she said. "Maybe it was the hormones. But now, yeah, that's back, like it used to be. On good days I look up and see it's time to go and I have no idea where the hours have gone. I enjoy the experience even more than I used to because that kind of time, when you can just get lost in your mind, is so rare these days."

"I don't know if I can do it anymore," I said. "Let go like that."

For a moment we walked in silence. Binx had fallen asleep, his head lolling to one side like he had no bones in his neck. Abby sucked contentedly on the collar of her jacket, watching the world go by. The older kids were chasing each other, laughing, around a tree. Helen said, "You know how you said you used to confuse the art and the life? Maybe you're still being too romantic about your work, like you have to live a certain way to produce it. Maybe you're making it black and white: you have this kind of life or you have this kind of life."

"When would I write?" I asked. "I've been at work, or I've been with the kids. And don't say at night, because I know you know I don't have the energy for that."

"I get why you haven't been writing. I'm just saying you act like you've given it up for good, and that I don't get. What you need is time, but you seem to think it's something more than that. It's like you've bought into the idea that a mother can't also be an artist. Or shouldn't be."

"I just find it hard to go from breast milk and peekaboo and diapers to, you know, bigger things."

"But that's saying breast milk and peekaboo and diapers aren't bigger things, or don't represent bigger things, which seems like a very male point of view. A fixation on your mother is a subject for literature, but actually being a mother isn't? Well, guess who set those rules? If obsessive interest in your own penis wins you the Pulitzer, then what's wrong with obsessive interest in your own breasts?"

"Are you writing about your breasts?"

"No, but I could," she said. She glanced down at them. "At this moment I can't think of what I would say."

"Poopy!" Abby suddenly shouted from her stroller. "Poopy, poopy, poopy!"

Helen sighed. "That's Abby's contribution," she said.

"She's a fan of the trochee," I said.

Helen pulled off the trail and unfolded a changing pad from her diaper bag. I corralled the older kids, I joked, I smiled. But I was hurt and angered by this characterization of myself, as submitting to the views of the oppressor, surrendering my identity. I'd been busy—I'd been, often, overwhelmed—and so the activity for which I had no time and made no money had fallen by the wayside. Did Helen agree with Nathan, that I no longer cared about art, that my values had changed? It was as though I made them uncomfortable not writing anymore, like my quitting called into question the necessity of the whole enterprise, like they no longer quite knew who I was.

Helen's cell phone rang while she was in the middle of changing Abby's diaper. She held Abby's feet in the air with one hand and picked up the phone with the other, tucking it between her ear and her shoulder. I wasn't really listening, watching the kids planting a stick in the ground, talking earnestly about how it would grow into a tree, and then suddenly Helen said, "Here," and thrust the phone at me. I assumed it was Nathan. I'd left my cell phone at home, and maybe he was no longer willing to wait for my calls. I braced myself and said, "Hello," and a voice much deeper than Nathan's said, "Hey, lady," and I knew it was Rajiv.

"Lady" was what he'd called me in the e-mails he'd written after the visit when he'd kissed me, e-mails always addressed *Hey lady* just like he'd said and which I'd been able to hear him saying when I read the words on the screen—*lady* not with an angry edge, the *lady* of a New York City construction worker, but with a caress. The first time I met him he had a girlfriend, and I'd heard him refer to her as "my lady," and so when he used the word for me I saw it as a coded endearment, just one small pronoun away from being his.

"Hi," I said. It wasn't Nathan. Thank God it wasn't Nathan. Why wasn't it Nathan?

"I've been thinking about you all day," Rajiv said.

"You have?"

"And all last night."

"I'm with my children," I said, "or I'd ask what you were thinking."

He laughed. "Do you think you could come by tonight?"

"Tonight?" I looked at Helen, and she nodded. *Tonight.* A word that rang with anticipation, that spoke of living in the now. A word for Grace Kelly and Cary Grant, for Fred and Ginger, for pop songs, for swooning into his arms despite everything, because of the stars and his eyes and of course the champagne. A word for what I wanted. "Sure," I said.

■

The house was one of those low-slung southwestern houses that looks like it's all roof. It was set back from the road and had a big front yard, the grass brown and crisped. Near the house, a red hammock was strung between two trees. Hanging from the roof of the porch was a hammock chair, this one multicolored, and I pictured Rajiv spending his days moving between the two hammocks—was he in the mood for red or rainbow, upright or reclined? I pictured our hammock at home, hanging between posts in our carport-porch. Time was, I used to spend hours lying in it, rocked by the breeze, wind chimes and birdsong the sound track to whatever book I was wandering through. Now it seemed eons since I'd done any such thing. I climbed into the red hammock. Above me the sky swayed. Here I was at last, and I was too nervous to go inside. What if he wanted to sleep with me? What if he didn't? I closed my eyes. I'd just lie here a moment, and then I'd go knock on the door. Or maybe I wouldn't. Maybe I wouldn't do that at all.

Except the door opened and closed, all on its own. And I didn't move. I heard footsteps on the porch, and then on the grass—how would I describe the sound of his approach? Was *rustle* the right word? I kept my eyes closed. Every nerve ending in my body seemed to anticipate his touch. He stopped beside me. I could hear him breathing. Then I sensed movement, I felt the approach of warmth, and he pressed his lips to mine. The hammock swayed as he braced himself on it, and I tilted toward the ground, grabbed at the webbing, opened my eyes. He steadied the hammock, one arm on either side of me. There he was, smiling, dark curls falling forward around his face. "Sleeping Beauty," he said.

"Well, hi," I said. I'd never considered before how easily the Sleeping Beauty position could segue into the missionary position, what with the woman already supine on the bed.

"Hi," he said.

I sat up and scooted over, and he sat next to me. It's impossible to sit together in a hammock without touching. Our legs pressed together. Our arms. I pretended not to notice, though I could think of nothing else. It was like being back in high school, squeezed into the crowded backseat of somebody's car with a boy you like, sitting on his lap, your heart beating fast, your laugh louder than usual as you fake interest in the conversation, and it feels like no part of your body exists except the part that's touching his. "*Sleeping Beauty* was my favorite of those movies," I said. "The early Disney ones, I mean."

"Did you want to be her?"

"I don't know," I said. "I don't think it was that. I think I liked the song she sings." I launched into it—"I know you, I walked with you . . ."—and unbelievably he joined in, "once upon a dream." I stopped. "You know that song?"

"Sure," he said. "I had three older sisters. I loved all those movies as a kid. It was my secret shame." He picked up my hand like he was going to read my palm. Instead he rubbed his thumb over it in a slow circle. "So 'Sleeping Beauty' was your favorite fairy tale?"

"My favorite of those movies," I clarified. "My favorite fairy tale was 'Beauty and the Beast.' "

"Really," he said. "Now that's psychologically interesting."

"I guess it is," I said.

"You're looking to transform somebody. You're looking for the virtue other people can't see."

He seemed a little too pleased with this assessment. "Or a magic castle," I said. "With a talking teapot."

"I don't think the teapot is in the original story." He turned his head toward me, which put his mouth inches from mine. I thought he was going to kiss me again, and I was all for it, under the spell of the hammock and his hand on mine and oh my God was he beautiful. But instead he said, "Come inside."

"So I can see your etchings?"

He laughed. "You should be so lucky," he said.

It was awkward getting out of the hammock. My memory of this time with Rajiv vibrates with desire, but I can't deny there were awkward moments, made more awkward by the investment we both had in maintaining the thrill of new romance. Stars and kisses fit the bill, and scooting out of a hammock and nearly falling and yanking down my shirt after flashing a pooch of belly did not. As he got out, he accidentally pressed on my hand and pinched my finger, and the way it throbbed was not romantic, but what about the way he brought it to his mouth as he said he was sorry? It sounds like nothing, it sounds almost silly, like he was offering to kiss my boo-boo the way I did for my children, but we all know that when you're in the grip of desire there's nothing silly about eyes meeting your eyes, lips on your finger, murmured words, the warmth of breath. If Nathan had pinched my finger I probably would have said so, and probably in an aggrieved tone, and depending on his mood and how irritably I spoke and how well we were getting along that day he might have said, "Oh, honey, I'm sorry, are you all right?" or he might have snapped, "I'm sorry, OK? It was an accident." When Rajiv did it, I said nothing, just winced, and he noticed without my speaking, and made his apologies. I said nothing, I felt no irritation, and at the time I didn't wonder how long we'd have to be together for the way I reacted to Nathan to become the way I reacted to Rajiv. There's the appeal of the new romance, when you're so accustomed to the old one. It's not just that you don't snap at each other, that you're so ready to forgive offenses you barely notice them, that you look at each other with starry, starry eyes. It's that the snapping, the irritation—they don't even seem possible. Nothing that happened before will happen again. Can't you see that this is a different life?

Rajiv's furniture had the scavenged, eclectic look of items found at thrift stores and yard sales. He had one of those basket chairs that had been a staple of my friends' postcollege apartments, and an ornate coffee table made of some kind of shiny black stone with an elaborate Asian scene in shiny white stones inset on the top. "Wow," I said, pointing at it.

"Somebody had put that out with the trash," he said. "Can you believe it? It probably belonged to somebody's grandmother. Maybe she even brought it back from a trip to China or something. It just looks to me like the kind of thing somebody loved and displayed proudly, and then it ends up on the street."

"But you rescued it," I said.

He pulled me close, abruptly, looked at me seriously for a moment, and then smiled. "And that was an impressive feat," he said. "It's really heavy."

"I'm impressed," I said. I was as breathless and ready to be kissed as Marilyn Monroe, but again, again, he didn't kiss me. He released me, positioned the basket chair directly in front of the television, ushered me into it, and moved to put in a DVD. He'd invested in his entertainment system—a wide-screen plasma TV, surround sound speakers. His DVD library took up an entire wall. Remote in hand, he stepped back from the television and looked down at me. "You know how I told you I made a film about you?"

"You don't forget something like that."

"So I decided I *should* show it to you." He took a breath. "But I want you to remember it's kind of maudlin and overdramatic and I'm totally aware now that it's not good."

"Be careful," I said. "You'll raise my expectations too high."

"All right," he said. He aimed the remote at the television and looked over at me. I waited. "Oh, what the hell," he said finally, and pressed the button. As the figure of a man filled the screen, he whispered, "I can't watch this," and left me alone with his film.

A man climbed a hill in a desert, alien landscape. He was moving quickly, and the look on his face said he was in pursuit of something, although for a moment I had no idea what. Then he came around a curve, and up ahead a flash of long hair and trailing skirts before the woman who possessed those things disappeared around the bend. The film wasn't yet working its spell on me, and I knew this because I found myself wondering if this woman wore heels in addition to her long and filmy skirt for a grueling trek up a sandy incline. I remembered thinking, once, when some horrifying news story had spun me into a catastrophic mood about the perils facing my daughter, that much of women's fashion was designed, on some level, to make us easier to catch: long hair for pulling you back, skirts for constricting your movements, heels for making you fall. None of these things seemed to slow down the woman in the film. She escaped easily from the man, who quickened his pace after his glimpse of her, his breathing growing louder on the sound track. He stumbled, clambered on hands and knees, and rose again, faster, faster, his eyes fixed on the path ahead where the woman appeared, glanced back, and disappeared again.

Finally he reached a place where the trail narrowed and became only a foot wide. The camera swooped down dizzyingly into the drop on either side. But a few yards away the trail opened into an inviting circle, a resting place where the view became beautiful rather than terrifying, and there the woman waited. Or at any rate, there she was. The camera showed her only from a distance, from his point of view.

Was she looking back at him? Was she looking past him at the vast and gorgeous sky? Was she waiting or was she trapped? Impossible to tell.

He stepped, his foot slipped, sand sliding down the side, and as he wobbled a montage of images filled the screen. The woman dove into waters rippling with moonlight. The woman swooned on a sickbed like a consumptive, a handkerchief fluttering from her hand. The woman stood in front of a window, unfurling a river of long, dark hair. The woman posed in silhouette, smoking from a Holly Golightly cigarette holder. The woman waited at the front of an empty church in a wedding dress. Then back to the man. He'd regained his footing, and he looked, again, at the woman. Now she was naked. He walked toward her, and as he did, the images from the montage flashed. He'd nearly reached her when she took a step backward, and another, spreading her arms in a crucifix pose, and as he quickened his pace she stepped off the edge, as easily as if into a pool. He ran, slipping and sliding, while she floated in midair. Her eyes were closed, and then she opened them and fixed him with an intense and unreadable gaze—was it reproach? regret? invitation? The image faded until she was gone. The film ended on a close-up of the man's agonized face. Roll credits. The end.

Nathan had once said to me, "If there's one thing that women like, it's competence. Don't you think that women like competence?" And I had to agree that we did. It didn't matter whether a man knew how to build a fence or write a love song, there was something undeniably attractive about the successful application of a skill. And Rajiv's images were beautiful. Clearly he knew what he was doing. But different as this film was from the one I'd seen in grad school, with its repressed characters refusing to say what they meant, I still struggled to grasp its meaning. Did he present those iconic images of feminine desirability and unattainability in order to comment on their unrealistic nature? Was that why the woman vanished, because the man had conjured her as an impossible ideal? Or did he want all of that—the beauty, the mystery, the pursuit—to be taken as unabashedly romantic, completely sincere? And was I supposed to go find Rajiv now, or was he coming back? In the wake of the film I suddenly felt that I myself was in a movie. Me. Rapunzel. Doomed Camille. Holly Golightly. A bride. Why a bride? Why were some images of the lost woman, and some of the waiting one? Was that complicated or just confused? And if he knew it wasn't successful, why had he wanted to show it to me? He'd handed me all the power, making me his audience, his critic, his dream girl. I was used to the audience part, the critic part—hadn't I been that for Nathan for years and years? The dream girl part I wasn't used to. I was nobody's idea of an unattainable ideal, a fairy-tale princess. Except, inexplicably, Rajiv's.

I stood, and saw him waiting at the edge of the room. He gave me a nervous smile. "Help me out here," he said. "I'm terrified."

"It's beautiful," I said. "The way you framed the shots . . ." I shook my head. "It's beautiful."

"It's totally dumb, though," he said. His hands were fists in his pockets.

"No," I said. I shook my head. "No." But it had unnerved me, made me feel a little pity, a little doubt—was I looking at a man awash in juvenile romantic fantasies? Or was I the one having one of those?

"You don't have to say anything nice," he said. "I just wanted you to see it."

Why? I wanted so badly to say, and then I saw how he waited. He was waiting, again, for me. He'd wanted to hand me power over him, power to wound him, the power of knowing what he felt. He wanted me to know he'd been waiting.

So now what? Here I was. I'd driven all this way, and here I was, with a man who wanted me badly enough to show me a film like that. If I slept with him—if I really slept with him—would that make me the person I used to be? Would it make me Nathan? Was that why I was doing this, to feel what he felt? Or was it revenge—an eye for an eye? *Maybe*, I thought, and, *maybe*, I thought again, that wishy-washy word. If Nathan hadn't done what he did, I wouldn't even be here, and maybe that meant I should go. But Nathan had done it. And I was here. I was tired of *maybe*. I was sick of myself. I was here, and so was Rajiv.

About the sex, I have to say that it was very, very good. Some of that was sheer newness, the revelations of somebody else's body. But newness could have meant awkwardness, an irritating or uncomfortable touch, collisions of noses and knees, and it didn't. I had to fight the urge to dart under the covers as soon as my shirt came off, or to stop the action and explain the loosening effects of pregnancy on skin, which I assumed he'd never witnessed before. But the urge dissipated with the things he said. Things like, "I can't believe you're real," like "I can't believe I get to touch you," things I was embarrassed to repeat to Helen later, when she wanted details, but which did, indeed, make me bloom like a flower. What had I done to inspire all this devotion? I still had no idea, and by nature I was skeptical of what did not seem earned. But the rush of words formed a current, a rip tide, and I let it pull me under. It felt very much like inspiration.

"So," he said later, next to me in his bed. "Tell me what's going on with your work."

"My work?"

"Your poetry."

"Oh." I'd honestly thought he meant my job, and that right there said something about how I'd redefined myself, for good or bad. "I . . ." *Quit*, I almost said, but the word I'd used often enough in my head sounded so final out loud, as though I'd told poetry to fuck off before I stormed out. I didn't want to say anything so definitive to Rajiv. "I haven't been writing much lately."

"Because of all this turmoil?"

"If by turmoil you mean everything that's happened in the last, let's see . . ." How long, exactly, had it been? When had I last put one word after another and called it a line? "My God," I said. "Two years. It's been two years. I don't think I'm even allowed to call myself a poet anymore."

"Once a poet, always a poet," he said. "That's your sensibility, right? That's your *nature*."

I shrugged. "I don't even know why I wanted to be a poet."

"What do you mean?"

"Why did I ever think I had something to say?"

"If not you, then who?"

"Helen," I said. "She's very authoritative."

"Nobody gives you authority. You just have it," he said. "You just have conviction. You choose them."

"And then you become a crazy loser convinced he's a misunderstood genius, like the guy in my program who used to cry because he was trying to improve our moral understanding, or something like that, and couldn't understand why we were hung up on the fact that his poems were terrible."

"Art is like love," he said. "You have to be willing to make a fool of yourself." He made these statements without quotes around them. How did he do that? Nathan, too, could do that—be sincere without the ironic inflection that allows one to be sincere while acknowledging the joke of sincerity. Nathan and I used to quote an exchange from an episode of *The Simpsons*, between two characters at a music festival: "Are you being sarcastic, dude?" "I don't even know anymore." Nathan and I, we loved that exchange. And at two a.m. the night before this one I'd read Proust's description of a character speaking as though in quotes when he talked of serious things. I'd felt the contemporary nature of that observation like a jolt of electricity. It reminded me again that Proust had actually been alive, that what I was reading was not a calcified history of people whose experience of the world was so different from my own as to, for all intents and purposes, be nonexistent. He was alive. He couldn't sleep. He listened to someone speak as though in quotation marks, and he noticed it, just as I did, and see, Nathan, I still took something from art, this sense that we are all connected, we are communicating, person to person and century to century, this sense that is so easy to lose, caught in the maelstrom of our own involving troubles. Art shows us ourselves, in ways both flattering and not, and it lifts us out of ourselves, like astral projection, and who doesn't crave an out-of-body experience from time to time? The body is, after all, a cage, and if there was anything I'd learned lately, it was that so is the mind.

I touched the inside of Rajiv's elbow, just because I could. "When I was in college," I said, "a lot of my friends wanted to be writers, too. And I remember one time I was walking with two of them—we were actually walking past the student center, right by the ATM, I can picture it clearly—and one of them, the guy, said, 'If you could write something great or be happy, what would you do?' And the girl said, 'I'd write something great,' and the guy said, 'Me, too.' And they both seemed really smug about it, like they were pleased to contemplate their future of tortured and melancholy genius. And I said, 'I'd be happy.' "

"So are they still writing?"

"No. That's my point. I'm the only one who kept writing. Up until recently, anyway."

"Maybe their expectations were too high."

"Maybe. But that's not the point of the story."

"Are you saying you stopped because you were happy?"

"I'm saying that would be a perfectly good reason to stop. I'm saying those two liked the idea of being artists more than the daily reality of working at it. I think the only real reason to keep at it is because you're less miserable when you do it than you are when you don't."

"Less miserable," he repeated. "Is that the same as happy?"

"Haven't you ever heard the Freud quote, that his goal was to help people achieve ordinary unhappiness, rather than hysterical misery?"

"Ordinary unhappiness, is that the best we can do? It's not a very inspiring slogan."

"Maybe if you put it on a big banner," I said. "Like 'Mission Accomplished.' "

"I'd like to do better than that," he said. "I'm going to put 'Extraordinary Happiness' on my banner."

"Yeah?"

"I'll hang it from the cottonwood tree."

"Which one is that?"

"The one at the front of the yard."

"That tree could handle a big banner," I said. "It's a big-ass tree."

"Wait until July, when it lets go of its cotton. It's like movie snow."

July? I thought.

"Do you think you'll write again?"

"I don't know. Do I have to?"

He enclosed my wrist lightly in his hand. "Absolutely you do. I expect a poem before I allow you in my bed again."

"I see," I said. "Maybe I should go do it right now, then. Knock out a sonnet of courtly love, maybe."

"Good idea," he said. He yawned. "There's pen and paper on the desk in my study. And a good view."

"I should just sit there until something comes to me."

"Just let it flow," he said. Suddenly I wasn't sure he was joking. What if he wasn't deadpan after all? What if he was deadly earnest instead?

"*Flow* wasn't exactly the word to describe my process. *Hesitate* was more like it. *Balk. Struggle. Agonize.*"

"I sympathize," he said. "Hey, there's your first two lines. She agonized. He sympathized."

"That's a slant rhyme," I said, and then I got up out of bed, pulled on my clothes.

"Where are you going?" he asked.

"I'm going to write a poem," I said.

"Really?" he said.

"I'm unconventional," I said.

He laughed. "Yes, you are," he said. "You're wild."

I went into his study, sat at his desk, picked up a pen. I looked, as instructed, at the view. The window had an elaborate metal grate like ones I'd seen in Mexico, and the lines of the grate framed the neighbors' back porch, where two men sat, smoking cigarettes, on the other side of a silver Mercedes SUV and a baby blue Vespa. The men were a couple, and I knew that not just because they looked at each other with affection, which they did, but because of the way, when one of them accidentally ashed on his shirt, the other one rolled his eyes. I watched the eye-roller get up and go inside, and I wondered if he was so annoyed by his partner's clumsiness he no longer wanted to sit with him, and then he came back out with a wet cloth, crouched before the other man, and began to wipe at his shirt. All the time he was talking, and though I couldn't hear what he was saying, I imagined he was chiding the other man, as one does a child or a spouse. His partner tipped his face up to the sky and closed his eyes, submitting to the scolding, the cleaning, the gamut of another person's care. He rested his hand on top of the other man's head.

I looked down at my blank page. Perhaps I could write a poem about the men outside. Rajiv hadn't been serious—surely he hadn't been serious—and so what was I doing this for? It felt like I had something to prove. It felt like I was filling out a job application. Taking a standardized test. I wished it were multiple choice. *Do you think of yourself as (a) an artist (b) a former artist (c) shallow and materialistic.* "Good question," I said aloud.

Flow, I wrote across the top of the page, and then I made a cross in the center of the *O*. I turned the *F* into a rectangle bisected by a line. I drew rays off either end of the *L*, I added triangles to the tops of the *W*. Some part of Rajiv, the part that had made that film, was a rode-a-great-sadness-today kind of guy. He might have wanted everyone at a party to contribute to a poem on a typewriter, like the guy Helen and I had mocked in grad school. The guy Nathan had defended. I had to admit that there'd been truth in Nathan's defense; there was a kind of bravery in Rajiv's sincerity. Had Nathan wanted more sincerity from me? Was spontaneous poetry at the window the kind of thing he wished we would do together? Was this what he'd looked for and found in Kate Ryan? If so, why hadn't he ever proposed anything like this? He was just as guilty of letting life become ordinary—*conventional*—as I was, no matter what he'd claimed. If he wanted to recapture the life we lived in grad school and for several years after, why didn't he try to recapture it with me? Maybe we each needed someone who was still living that life, someone to take us by the hand and offer to be our guide to willful ignorance of reality. We couldn't ignore reality with each other. We were each other's reality, each other's history, each other's daily bread. We were each other's most important, most necessary person, the one you lean on when life gives you trouble, the one you take the trouble out on, the one person who can help you through it, the person you sometimes hate, partly because you need them so much and they can't always—who could?—live up to that need. And here I was, being exactly what Nathan said he needed, only I was being it for somebody else. It wasn't fair of him to need it, though, was it? Maybe not. None of this had much of anything to do with what was fair.

Nathan, I wrote. I stared at his name. My poems were never so confessional that I would use his actual name. I tore the paper in half, and then into many little pieces, until there was no chance Rajiv might casually glance into his trash can and recognize a part of my husband's name. Now, again, a blank page confronted me. *Lights*, I wrote. And then I thought, *Camera. Action*. Did I wish that I could write a poem? Yes, I did. I would have liked nothing better than to be exactly the person I thought Rajiv was, right at this moment, imagining me to be: spontaneous and exciting and in tune with the large and spiritual movements of the universe. Was I being sarcastic? I didn't know anymore. I was sincere in missing the rush of inspiration, that brief but pure belief in your own brilliance, the good mood that follows the composition of a good line. I wanted it back. I did. But nothing came to mind.

CHAPTER NINETEEN

"Maybe," I said to Mattie, "I'll write a villanelle."

She didn't know what the word meant, of course, but I said it to her because I took a special pride in her advanced vocabulary and also because I wanted to hear the delightful way she'd mangle the word when she repeated it, as I knew she would.

"OK," she said. She was playing with a naked blond doll with ratty hair, whispering something secret and incomprehensible.

"Can you say villanelle?" I asked.

"Vill-nell," she said. She looked up and flashed me a sweet, shy smile.

"A villanelle is a kind of poem," I said. "It has nineteen lines and a complicated rhyme scheme."

She didn't answer me, again absorbed in her imagined world, and I strained to hear what she was whispering to that doll. What went on in her mind? What did that doll know that I didn't? This itchy urge to interrupt her, to make her focus on me—this was what I sometimes felt when Nathan was working, and this must be what she felt when she couldn't get his attention, or mine. It was a child's emotion. Maybe I really would write a villanelle. I'd agreed to go with Helen to the coffee shop, which meant I'd agreed to make the attempt to write, and I anticipated the blankness of the page with dread. A villanelle, difficult as it was, gave guidance. You had to repeat yourself. You had to find the words.

I'd thought that Mattie would be upset when I told her I was going, after days and days of being together nonstop, but she was unconcerned, and when the babysitter came, even Binx went to her without complaint. Didn't they sense that I was turning toward things other than them, that I was threatening to get lost? Didn't they want me to stay?

Look at Helen, blithely concentrating while I loitered on the outskirts of her private world, longing to intrude. The coffee shop was, like so many coffee shops, a repository of funky artiness, and many of the college-age boys sported serious facial air. What an ongoing confusion there was between art and artiness. I wanted to say so to Helen, Helen the stay-at-home mom in her mall-store T-shirt and jeans. Would any of these tattooed denizens venture to guess she was writing a poem? That was why she frowned, sighed, stared at a painting of a dog in a cowboy hat without seeing it. I couldn't remember how to do that. How to let go so completely of the external world. I saw the bright red eye on a blue mixed-media mask. I saw the girl with the green parrot tattoo who stirred the sugar in her coffee long past the point it needed stirring. I heard somebody say, "You've got to be kidding" and somebody say, "When I get back from Germany . . ." I heard the metallic *thunk*, the steam-engine hiss of a latte being made. I wanted to snap Helen out of her elsewhere state, I wanted to bring her back to those things, and I wanted to let go of them myself. Could I move from the outside in, could I make my features form the exact expression on Helen's face—so focused, so laserlike—and in that way begin to write? She didn't seem at all aware that I was staring at her. If I interrupted her to ask how she was able to concentrate, how she was able to begin, she wouldn't be able to explain. I knew that. It was inexplicable. There is nothing and then there is something. You just begin.

You just begin.

You just begin.

You just begin.

I tapped my pen against the table until Helen looked up with the puzzled frown of the emerging dreamer, and I stopped. And she disappeared back into her work, and oh how I envied her. That disappearance, that submergence—when you knew it would come eventually you could persist in the face of the frustration that preceded it, your own inability to make words appear on the page. And more than that, you could persist when you believed, as I'd once so wholeheartedly believed, that there was a point to the struggle, to the existence of your poetry, to my poetry, to poetry at all.

"Who are your favorite poets?" Rajiv had asked me. Nobody had asked me that in years, what felt like years. Nathan certainly never asked me. He assumed he already knew the answer, and mostly he did, but what if some of them had changed? I gave Rajiv names, a torrent of names. People I knew, people I didn't know. People whose work I'd loved in grad school, when I read all the time, all the time, some whose work I hadn't read in years, didn't even know if I'd like now. He wrote them down, all of them. He laughed at how fast I said them, faster than his pen. He went out the next day and bought their books and read them. I made him close his eyes while I read him Juliana Gray's "The Man under My Skin," and, yes, he looked beautiful like that, and, yes, I wanted to touch him. I wanted to touch him all the time. Listen, I had to have him. If it had been possible I would have flung myself inside him, the way you—if you were someone not me—might fling yourself into a skinny-dipping quarry at night off a twenty-foot drop. In the last week he'd taken me to an art-house showing of *La Belle et la Bête*, which I'd never seen, and when Belle emerged in a glory of fabric out of the wall he turned to me and smiled with the conviction that he'd given me something, that my pleasure would equal his own. We watched the dream episode of *Buffy*, and then he wanted to watch *Persona*, and we debated the merits of the image versus the word in direct representations of the workings of the mind. I thought, *Oh*, this *life.* This *me. Hello*, *me. Where have I been?*

Now here I was, trying to write a poem. The girl with the green parrot tattoo smiled at the woman approaching her table, a quicksilver smile, a nervous smile, a smile that said *Here I am for you*.

"I read an article in the *New Yorker* once," Rajiv had said to me the night before.

"Yeah?" I said. He had his camera trained on my face, and I felt very conscious of my expressions, the way my brow darted in as I waited for his point. "Was it the only one you've ever read?"

"Well, you know, the *New Yorker* is usually so lightweight," he said. "I like my weekly magazines to take at least six weeks to read."

I laughed. "You are quite the intellectual."

"We know that," he said. "But back to my story. That is, if you're done making fun of me."

I bowed, flipped my hand palm up to say, Go on.

"So the article was about this guy, this linguist, who studied some disappearing language—in Iceland, I think. It was an Eskimo language, maybe, and only two or three people, or maybe it was just one, still spoke it."

Two or three or one? I wanted to say. Do Eskimos live in Iceland? But no more joking. I offered the camera lens a nervous smile.

"Anyway, this guy was trying to record it, to make a lexicon and a grammar, and the interviewer asked him why. Why bother?"

"Seems like a reasonable question."

"See, that's the point. He didn't think it was a reasonable question. He looked at the interviewer like she was crazy. And he said, 'I do it because I'm me, and Inarak is Inarak.' "

"Inarak?"

"I don't remember what the language was called." I felt him leaning even closer with the camera. What reaction shot was he hoping for? "But you get the point, right?"

"I get the point." I kept my gaze on his bedspread, which was striped with bright pieces of silk, and I wondered what woman had given it to him, because it didn't look like the sort of thing a straight man would buy. I got the point, but he said it anyway.

"You're you," he said. "And poetry is poetry."

True, true, but still two separate things, and why was he so sure they'd taste great together? He'd read some of the poems I'd published here and there, but there had been none of that in quite some time. What's important, he'd said the other night, is not the product but the production. "Easy for you to say," I'd said. "Mister I Make a Living Doing Film Work."

"Some of that's ads," he said.

"Mister I've Won Awards at Film Festivals. Mister I Got a Grant from the Sundance Institute."

"Wow," he said. "I'm pretty awesome."

And I'd agreed. Easy for you to say, I'd thought. Mister I Hit the Best-Seller List. Mister Poised for Even Bigger Success at the Expense of My Wife. Mister *generous* and *genuine* and *human* and *heart*.

"What if you had to convey how you're feeling in this moment?" Rajiv asked now. "What would you say?"

I looked at him. My, my, he was beautiful. I should do my best to concentrate on that. "In this moment?"

"Yeah."

"Or this one?"

"I'm serious," he said.

"I'd say I wanted you to put the camera down."

"But that could sound full of innuendo, or it could sound annoyed."

"Or both," I said. "How would you convey what you're feeling?"

"I'd try to make the viewer feel what I feel by showing you looking at me."

"Looking at you how?"

"Looking at me how you look at me."

"But how am I looking at you?"

"Just like that. I want to film you."

"You are filming me."

"I mean, I want to put you in a movie."

"But I'm not an actress."

"Don't worry," he said. "You'll be dead."

I laughed. "What an offer."

"And I'll use this footage for a flashback, for the hero thinking back on his lost love."

I didn't like the notion of being filmed, or being dead, or being a lost love. I tried to put him off, but he went on persuading me, long after he'd put the camera away and reached for me, and as I was getting dressed to go, he started up again. All right, I said. Fine. I said the filming had to be at night because I wouldn't leave Helen alone in the day with all four kids. "I always make sure my kids are asleep before I come over here," I said.

"Okay," he said in a slightly puzzled manner, and I realized I'd spoken that sentence too emphatically, as though he were judging me, as though I had to prove something to him. But of course I didn't. Rajiv didn't come close to realizing how hard it would have been for Helen to put four kids to bed alone when she was only used to two. He had no reason to think I was a bad friend, or a bad mother. If anything he might have wondered why I couldn't get to his house any earlier than I did, why I insisted on being back at Helen's by midnight. He had never crept into the room where his children slept, shutting the door as quietly as he could behind him. There—Mattie sprawled on her back, her arms flung wide on either side of her, her hair damp with sweat against the pillow. Abandoned to sleep, like I wished I could be. There—Binx on his stomach, his head turned to one side away from me, the dim glow from the nightlight picking up the bald spot on the back of his head where the mattress had rubbed his hair away. Carefully I'd lay my hand on his back, nothing more important in the world than to feel the gentle pressure of his breathing against my hand. Inhalation. Exhalation. The children loomed so large in my life, and then I crept in to find them sleeping and I saw again, again, again, how small they were.

Rajiv didn't know any of that. He didn't know that the sight of the children sometimes made me want to call Nathan, and that sometimes I followed through on that impulse. He didn't know that Nathan waited up until three in the morning in case I called, that he answered the phone on the first ring, as if he always had it in his hand.

Last night Nathan said to me, "I have to admit I thought you'd have come home by now."

"Yeah, well," I said. "You thought I liked my job."

"I guess I thought you liked it pretty well."

"Like the woman in your motel story?"

"That wasn't about you," he said. "I told you that."

"Has anything been about me?"

"Did you want it to be? I thought you wanted to write your own work, not be immortalized in mine. I'm pretty sure I'm quoting you."

Nathan thought I wanted to write my own work. Rajiv thought I should. But did I? Should I? Why was I sitting here in this café drawing a series of tiny flowers, putting loops in the letters of my name? I'd stopped writing for a reason so prosaic, so petty, it was embarrassing to name it—I no longer saw the point of continuing. What did I gain from all those hours spent? What was the return on my investment? Occasional publication in small journals. The right to call myself a poet. Not money. Not success. And only limited personal satisfaction that, for me, had dwindled without affirmation from the outside, as did my conviction that the work was good. And now I'd put my job at risk, now the economy was crumbling—now we were all on the verge of hopping freight cars with our canned beans and our bindles. Maybe no poem of mine was worthwhile in the face of that.

But poetry was poetry. Inhalation. Exhalation. An irresistible tautology. Look at me how you look at me.

And at last, the external world gave way to the internal one. I sat in that café and wrote. I wrote quickly, in full conviction of the words' necessity, their need to be arranged in just this way, and I thought of nothing, I felt nothing, but that need. What is it like, that feeling? What's the right phrase, the right word? Try this: it's like running, if running is for you a bliss of speed and color, and not a pounding of knees, the strain of ragged breathing. It's like what running looks from the outside when you watch an Olympic race and one of the runners is just so fast, so breathtakingly fast, that there seems no effort at all in the forward motion, and she wins, of course she wins. She has to win. She is the distillation of herself, the embodiment of speed. Look at the exultation on her face. She flew out of her body and yet stayed in it. She has never been more perfectly what she is.

CHAPTER TWENTY

There are distinct categories of what a person will do for love. What had I done for Nathan? Had his children. Matched pair after pair out of pile after pile of nearly identical white socks. Read nineteen different versions of the same damn paragraph. For Rajiv I was lying in a ditch at sunset with my neck at an awkward angle, sticky with corn-syrup blood. Would I have done that for Nathan? No, I would not. Oh, hell no, I might have said, or, You have got to be fucking kidding me, and in fact I would have been hurt that he didn't know me well enough not to ask.

For Rajiv I had written a poem. My first poem in two years. I'd even showed it to him. He'd said it was beautiful, and when I asked him what I should change and he said, "Nothing," I decided to believe him. To believe he meant it, anyway. Another thing I would not have done for Nathan—I would not have believed he really thought there was nothing I should change. Had I ever written a poem for Nathan? I'd written about him, but for him? I had written, he had written. His books were dedicated to me. *For Sarah*, they said, right there on the page. But I was there when he was writing them, and he didn't seem to be writing them for me. The dedication was a thank-you for my support, a gesture of affection. I said as much to him once, and to my surprise he seemed offended. He said the books *were* for me, that I was his ideal reader. I was the one whose opinion mattered the most.

"The light is just perfect," Rajiv exulted. He walked around me, examining my corpse through the lens, and though I was supposed to be dead, I couldn't help the way my fingers twitched out of the way of his feet. "Don't step on the died girl," I said.

"What?" Rajiv said.

"Something Mattie said." I closed my eyes, because it seemed easier to be dead that way. I couldn't help but notice that, where Nathan's interest would have perked up, where Nathan would have asked for the story, would have listened with his eyebrows raised and a smile at her amusing phrasing and a wince that she'd said it at all, Rajiv just said, "Oh, OK," and knelt beside me, studying my face. Because she wasn't his child. And you're just not as interested in the funny things a child says when she's not your child. Why was I thinking about Nathan? I was supposed to be thinking I was dead. What did a dead person think about? The question struck me as humorous, so I tried to think of something sad, because I couldn't be lying here all covered in fake blood with a goofy smile on my face. Let's see. Sad. I could think about the economy, about what would happen to my family if I got fired and couldn't find another job. I could think about Kristy's voice mail from that morning, asking with a note of impatience how I was, and how I had yet to return it. But that wasn't good, that was too upsetting, and if I started down that path I'd set in motion anxiety that would last all night and ensure I didn't sleep.

"You're frowning," Rajiv said.

I opened my eyes. "Sorry. I was having anxious thoughts."

He bent to kiss my forehead, and then my mouth, so that he came away with a little fake blood on his cheek. "All you've got to do," he said, "is be totally still."

"Got it."

"You look beautiful," he said.

Beautiful? I was covered in fake blood. It was matted in my hair. But beautiful, okay, sure, why not. It was nice to know I made for a beautiful dead girl. Rajiv moved away, and after a moment I heard him call, "Action!"

I was lying there with my eyes closed, so I couldn't see Rajiv's actor friend Paul stumble down the road from the car. I could hear his frantic footsteps, I could hear him calling my name. "Sarah! Sarah!" Such desperation in the sound. And then it struck me—it was my actual name. Why had Rajiv used my actual name? If I was going to be somebody else, couldn't I be somebody named Penelope, or Camille? Paul said, "Sarah?" like he'd suddenly spotted me, and then he came running. I felt him drop to his knees beside me and touch my face; he touched me more and more frantically, he shook me a little, and I managed to stay limp as a doll. All the while he said my name, over and over, Sarah, Sarah, Sarah, and then finally he began to scream. "No!" he screamed. "No!"

I started to laugh. I felt the laugh coming, and I tried to repress it. *I'm dead*, I told myself, *I'm dead, and it's not funny*. I kept my mouth pressed tight, but I couldn't keep the laughter from vibrating through my body, I couldn't keep the breath from snickering out my nose. Paul let go of me. "I guess we have to do that again," he said.

"Sorry," I said. I pushed myself up on my elbows. "Sorry about that."

"That's OK," Rajiv said. "It happens. Just take a deep breath and tell me when you're ready and we'll try it again."

I took a breath. *I'm dead*, I thought. *I'm dead*, *I'm dead*. "I'm ready," I said. And it all happened again, the running, the touching, the Sarah Sarah Sarah, and then the "No! No!" and as if on cue the laughter returned.

"Come on now, Sarah," Rajiv said. "Dead people don't laugh."

"I'm not laughing," I said. "I'm not making a sound."

"Your whole body is shaking," he said.

"I'm sorry," I said, but I was laughing even as I said it. I looked at Paul and thought about his shrieking, "No! No!" and I laughed until tears came into my eyes.

"Let's take a break," Rajiv said, and Paul went stalking off, muttering something that I was certain was not complimentary to me. Rajiv offered me his hand, pulled me to my feet. "He's a little bit of a diva," Rajiv said.

We leaned against the bumper of his car, and he offered me a bottle of water. "Laughter's not an unusual reaction," he said.

"I know," I said. "I've watched the outtakes on DVDs."

He nodded. He watched the sunset broadcasting its undeniable beauty, beams of light streaming out from behind distant trees, and I knew he was thinking that we were soon to lose that perfect light, and I wondered if he would say so out loud. I didn't think he would. How long would we have to be together before he would say something like that out loud?

"Can I just ask you something?" I asked. "If I'm your dream girl, why do you want to kill me?"

"What do you mean?" he said, and when I heard the bristle in his voice, I knew I'd sounded accusatory where I'd told myself I only meant to tease.

"Well, this is the second film now that's been somehow about me, right? And for some reason I'm dead again."

"What are you talking about? You're not dead in the other film."

"There's that image of the woman with the handkerchief—it's very Camille, very *Moulin Rouge*. She sure looks dead, or close to it."

"That's not supposed to be real. That's one of the images that represents his feelings about her."

"His feeling that she's dead?"

"His feeling that she's unattainable."

"And then she disappears."

"Right. She's unattainable."

"Well, I'm attainable. I'm standing right here. So how come you're killing me off?"

"I think you're taking this a little too literally." He sighed. "I told you that film was bad."

I wanted to push it, I really did. But I looked at his face and saw a mixture of worry and impatience and apology and irritation at my lack of understanding. This was a look I recognized, a look anybody who's been in a longtime relationship will recognize, but it was the first time I'd seen it on Rajiv's face. As soon as I did, I wanted to erase it. If I wanted to be looked at like that, I could go back to Nathan. Nathan and I could look at each other like that until the cows came home. But not Rajiv—Rajiv looked at me with longing. That was what he did. "You're right," I said. "I'm sorry."

"I want you to get what I'm doing."

"I do," I said. "I do." I looked him in the eye. I tried to project sincerity, and gradually that expression faded off his face. He kissed me. "If you keep doing that," I said, "the blood's going to be all over you."

"It's hard to resist." He touched my cheek. "Are you sure you're okay with all of this?"

"I'm positive. I promise I'll stay dead this time."

And I did. I lay there like a stone while my pretend husband screamed my name, and I thought about my real husband. Not about what he'd do if he found me, a bloodied corpse, at the side of the road, because I figured he'd pretty much do what this guy was doing now, the screaming and the crying and so on. I thought about how much Nathan would appreciate this story, the story of what was happening here, how he'd understand exactly why I found the whole thing strange and disturbing and funny at once, how he'd point out nuances of meaning I hadn't even noticed. I really wished I could tell it to him.

All that wistful longing blinked off like a light when I walked into Helen's living room and saw him sitting there. He was sitting there. Nathan. He'd gotten one of his severe haircuts since I'd seen him last, and as always the sight of his hair close-cropped and curl-less, the sight of his ears, was a shock, on top of the shock of seeing him here. His cheeks were shiny, as though freshly shaved. He was wearing my favorite shirt. He stood up when I came in. He almost, but not quite, smiled at me. He had one of Helen's iced lattes in his hand. Without meaning to I shot her a look full of accusation, and how could she know it wasn't because I blamed her for Nathan's presence but because she'd given him something to drink?

"I've been trying to call you," she said.

"My cell phone was off," I said.

"I left you a message," she said.

"I haven't turned it back on." I was looking at Helen, but still I could see Nathan looming in the corner of my eye. He didn't vanish when I looked away. I hadn't, after all, conjured him. "What are you doing here?" I said, and Helen looked puzzled, but then I turned my gaze to Nathan. I looked him in the eye before I looked away.

"Mr. Dodson," he said. "He died."

"What?" I said, or maybe I said, "He died?" because we always do that, we always repeat the unwanted phrase, we always ask for confirmation, we can't quite believe it, and we hope that in the moment before we admit, yes, we understood the first time, and no, we didn't really need to hear it said again, that the news will disappear, it will not, after all, have been said. I cheated on you. He died. What did you say? What?

Just a month ago—or two? Had it been two?—I'd come upon Mr. Dodson putting up No Trespassing signs along his fence. "I've been wanting to warn you," he said when he saw me. "Some no-good types moved into the house on the corner. The Keeters. My wife's cousins. Caught them skulking around, looking in my shed."

"You think they wanted to steal something?"

"I know it." He shook his head. "My wife's cousins," he said again, as though somehow Mrs. Dodson's relationship to them made her responsible for their skulking ways. The Keeters. It sounded more like a designation for a species of redneck than a name. "Don't get married," Mr. Dodson said. Then he grinned at me. "Too late!"

Nathan was still talking, something about the funeral. I caught the words *bright moment*, *angel*, *important to them*, and I understood he wanted to take my children to the funeral, I understood he was here because he wanted us to go back home. I knew it was me he wanted and not just the children. I'd known that the instant I'd seen the haircut, the shirt, the shave. Only moments had passed since I'd come in the house and closed the door behind me. I could still conjure the sensation of the doorknob in my hand. I took a few steps, reached for the door, and I was outside again, letting the last few minutes vanish with a satisfying click.

Helen had put two metal pinwheels in the rock bed around the front yard's tree, and the wind was just high enough to spin them in a start-and-stop, halfhearted way. They spun. They stopped. They spun. Nathan came outside. "Was this necessary?" I asked.

"What do you mean?" he asked. I didn't answer. He knew what I meant. "They really want Binx at the funeral," he said. "I didn't want to argue about it over the phone." I waited for him to add something aggrieved like, "I'm sorry it's such a blow to see me," but he surprised me. He said in a voice that was wistful and naked, "I thought maybe if you actually saw me, you'd decide to come home."

I looked at him. Did actually seeing him make me want to go home? His sideburns were uneven, and really, now that I looked at him more closely, a little long, given the severity of the rest of the cut. "Where'd you get your hair cut?"

"Great Clips."

"The one by the Harris Teeter?"

"No, the one on North Duke."

"What were you doing in Durham?"

"Talking to Gail about the possibility of picking up a class or two."

"A class?"

"I've been looking for work," he said. His expression when he said this—it reminded me of Mattie's when she handed me a drawing she'd done at school, shyly, hopefully certain of my approval.

"I guess I may have made that a necessity," I said.

"Have you been wanting to quit?" he asked. "Should I have known that?"

"I don't know," I said. "I didn't really know it."

"But maybe I should have."

"How could you if I didn't?"

"Maybe you didn't think about whether you wanted to quit because you didn't think you could. And maybe I didn't think about it because I didn't want to, because your working made my not working possible."

"Wow," I said. "I thought my working was changing my values and generally destroying my soul."

"I'm sorry about all that," he said. "I was being a prick."

"I didn't quit, anyway. I've been calling in sick this whole time, though I don't know if they really believe me anymore."

"It'd be a pain to replace you."

"Well, yes. That's true."

"I didn't mean anything by that," he said.

I surveyed the yard. "Moonlight on pinwheels," I said.

And he said, as he always did, "Are you writing a poem?"

"All the time," I said.

"Have you and Helen been staying up every night getting stoned and talking about all the possible uses of the word *the*?"

"No. We haven't done that once. I have to admit I miss it. I miss feeling like that was important. The word *the*."

"It's still important."

"I miss feeling like it was the only thing. I miss being able to feel like that. And you know what else? I only just realized I miss it." I sighed. "Should I even be talking about such things, such trivial things? Given what's going on in our lives? In the world?"

"I don't know. Since you left, I haven't written a word."

What was I supposed to say to that? Good? Sorry? "Did you miss me?" I asked.

"Of course," he said. "It's been awful without you."

"No, I mean, before all this. Did you miss me talking about the word *the*? Did you miss *that* me?" I looked at him. He looked back, his face a picture of uncertainty. He wanted to say yes, I was almost sure of it, and that would have been the truth. He had missed the older version of me, maybe the older version of himself, and maybe that's what part of this had been about, but if he said that, would I think he was being cravenly self-justifying? Would I get upset? And after all, he'd loved me all this time, hadn't he, as wife, breadwinner, mother of his children. It just hadn't been the same. And sometimes we miss the old days, enough that we try to get them back. Sometimes we all do.

"I want you to come home." He stepped closer. "We could all drive back for the funeral. We could all drive back together. Please . . . just come home."

I looked away, back at the pinwheels, which spun and stopped like they were signaling something.

"Or," Nathan said, "I've got a return ticket, and I could take Binx back on my lap."

"What about feeding him?"

"I can give him formula."

"But then I'd have to stop nursing altogether. I didn't bring the pump."

"Doesn't Helen have one?"

"She gave it away. She's not breast-feeding anymore."

"Well, you could buy one."

"They cost like $200, Nathan. I may not have a job anymore."

Now it was his turn to sigh. I wondered if he was more frustrated because of life's complications or because I was diminishing his dramatic gesture with my petty, practical concerns. "If we all go back together," he said, "problem solved."

"I wouldn't go that far," I said. For a moment nobody spoke. "I need to think about it."

"For how long?"

"I don't know."

"My flight's in two days."

"I guess I need to think about it for two days." And what to do with those two days, besides think? Once again, once again, it was up to me. I knew if I told him to go to a hotel he would go, he would take himself away to a bare and standard room in his bare and standard rental car. No doubt he'd brought a book to read. And if I said he should stay here, he would sleep on the couch if I told him to, he would sleep in the bed with me if I let him. What power someone else's transgression, someone else's longing for forgiveness, gives you. And what would happen if I told him what I had done?

■

"My husband is here," I said into the phone. I said "my husband," not "Nathan," although of course Rajiv knew his name. The important thing in this scenario was not his identity but his role: he was my husband, and Rajiv was my lover, my other man. I was Anna Karenina, I was Madame Bovary, I was hunched over on the toilet whispering into my cell phone, which was tragic only in the way characters on shows about rich and bitchy teens use the word.

A silence so unnervingly long that I thought I'd lost the connection. "Rajiv?"

"I knew this would happen."

"You knew what would happen?"

"Do you know that I'm thirty-three years old and I've never managed a lasting relationship? What does that say about me?"

I hadn't known he was thirty-three years old. How funny. I hadn't known how old he was, or that he was slightly younger than I. Why did that come as such a surprise? "Your Jesus year," I said.

Inhalation. Exhalation. "What?"

"That's what some people say about the year you're thirty-three."

"Why?"

"Because that's how old Jesus was when he was crucified."

"Why would you say that to me?"

"I'm sorry, I didn't mean anything by it."

"But why would you say that to me?"

"It was just a non sequitur. That's how my mind works sometimes."

"I guess you're going to go back to your life now," he said.

"Why do you assume that? You think I'm a dog, he calls me and I come?"

"No, I—"

"And what do you mean, 'my life'? What has this been?"

"Don't go back with him."

"Rajiv . . ."

"Stay here with me."

"With you."

"Yes. Stay. You and the kids can move in with me."

I tried to picture that. His house had a second bedroom, currently his study. The kids would have to share it. That was doable, but how would he feel, really, to have the space he used for his work given over to someone else's kids? And what about his beloved coffee table, shiny and sharp-edged and made of skull-crushing stone? What about the alphabetized DVDs on racks that looked strikingly like fun ladders to climb? If we moved in with Rajiv, so many of his things would have to go. "What are the schools like?" I asked.

"What?"

"What are the schools like?"

"I have no fucking idea, Sarah," he said, and though the words were angry his tone was sad. "Is that really what you want to talk about right now?"

There was an echo to this conversation, and after a moment I realized what it was. Me and Nathan, Mr. Dodson, the mailbox, all our accumulated grievances. "Maybe I'm more conventional than you thought," I said.

"You're not," he said. "Just don't go back with him. Even if you don't stay with me. Don't go back with him."

I closed my eyes. Nathan was asleep in my bed, on his usual side. I wasn't going to say so. I wasn't going to say that it had seemed to me it didn't much matter whether he slept there or not, since I'd been keeping to my own side anyway, that empty half still undisturbed in the morning, the bed already half made.

"He hurt you," Rajiv said. "I would never do that to you."

"Easy for you to say," I said.

"I mean it."

"I know you do. It's just, that's easy to say, isn't it, at the beginning when everything's going well. Why would you ever think you would cheat on me when I'm, you know, looking at you like I look at you? What would happen if we were actually together as long as Nathan and I have been?"

"I wouldn't cheat on you," he said. "Not all men cheat."

"I know that. I'm only saying, it gets harder. It gets complicated. And what you don't understand is that when I wake up in the morning it's early, much earlier than I want to get up, and a little face is right there two inches from mine saying, get up, feed me, and then there's a baby crying, and Nathan gets up, too, and he feeds Mattie while I nurse Binx, and then we rush around, together, getting everybody dressed, and then I go to work and I'm sitting at my desk with the breast pump running while I'm trying to type with one hand, and then I come home and it's just this mad dash of feeding and bathing and reading books and then they're finally in bed. And Nathan cooks the dinner, you know? He asks me what I want, and he cooks it. And then he does the dishes. And then he comes and sits with me on the couch and puts my feet in his lap and asks me what happened at work that day, tells me something funny Mattie said, and then we watch TV."

"You're going back with him because he cooks dinner."

"I didn't say that. I'm just trying to explain. That's what our lives are now. Our days are ordinary, and exhausting, and irritating, but I really care, I really care, what funny thing Mattie said. And nobody besides Nathan cares as much as I do." He was silent. Into the silence I asked, "Can I come see you?" because all I really knew at that moment was that I didn't want to get back in the bed where Nathan slept. Rajiv didn't say he was too tired. He didn't say it was one in the morning. He led a different kind of life. He said yes.

On the way over there I thought about the poem I'd written, the one I'd showed him, the one he'd said he loved.

Loving the word *mystery*,
but finding few occasions
to send it rolling
across my tongue,
let me settle for *secret*
and tell you this:
when you come to me,
my fingers go searching
for the curls at the back of your neck,
the dampness of your bath
held there for hours.
I want to cut a dark, wet curl
and keep it in a locket
like a baby's first ringlet,
or a tender frond of a fern
that grows in a foreign country
I might never visit again.

"I love it," he'd said. "It's beautiful." But that last line—what about that last line, Rajiv, with its suggestion of departure? Why did I show it to you with that last line, and why didn't you say a word? And why, really, did you not want me to go back to Nathan, even if I didn't stay with you? Did you not want to think of me as domestic? Did you want me to stay the version of myself I'd been with you, surrendered to desire, twined in bed until midnight, ruminating on art? I can't blame you. Part of me wanted that, too.

When I was in his arms, he asked me, his mouth on my neck, his speech a little muffled, what I would say if Nathan realized I was gone. "I'll tell him I had insomnia," I said. "I'll tell him I went driving."

"And you did," he said.

"And I did," I said. I closed my eyes. What would happen? What was going to happen now?

CHAPTER TWENTY-ONE

In the morning I woke alone. No Nathan, no kids. For a confused moment I thought maybe I was still at Rajiv's, but no Rajiv either. Understand that this day—this day I had before I had to decide—was all about looking for signs. This was one, maybe, this waking alone. But what did it mean? Yes, there was the obvious loneliness of being alone, but, too, there was the luxury of being alone, the fact that with no child screaming from two feet away I might just be able to go back to sleep. And a bed is a lovely spacious place with no one else in it.

But I couldn't go back to sleep. Was that the sign? I had to get up, because I kept wondering where they were. I wondered, too, if Nathan had noticed my absence in the night. He hadn't seemed to. When I'd gotten back in bed he'd rolled over and spooned me without even seeming to wake, as automatically as if nothing had ever happened at all.

Nathan was in the kitchen with Helen and all four children, and in the chaos I had a minute or two to watch them unnoticed from the door. Nathan chatted with Helen while spooning yogurt into Binx's mouth. Look how expert he was, no hitch in the movements of scoop and insert and swipe the extra yogurt off the lips with the spoon, even as he reached for the box of Cheerios with his other hand to satisfy Mattie's demands. Then Helen saw me and fell silent, and Nathan stopped talking, too, and followed her gaze. Strange that I was the one who silenced the room, as though I were the subject of gossip, a monster, a queen. "Hi," I said.

Nathan stood up, like a courtly gentleman. "Did you sleep well?" he asked. I heard no sarcasm in his tone. I nodded, swamped all at once with shame. *Swamped* was the right word. A marshy feeling, shame, all sticky uncertainty. "We were thinking about going to the zoo," he said. "I thought we could all go, or if you wanted a break . . ."

"I want Mommy to come!" Mattie said.

"We can all go," I said.

He looked as pleased as if that sentence had ended with the word *home*. We can all go, I'd said, and maybe that was foreshadowing. Those words in my mouth were the sign. But I felt no more certain than I had before I'd said them. One day to decide. Going home was an option. Staying here was an option. Fleeing back to Cincinnati and the comfort of my parents' house was an option. Nathan was an option. Rajiv was an option. Single motherhood was an option, if a particularly unattractive one. So many options. So many doors to open. "The Lady, or the Tiger?" How I'd always hated that story. Which, for God's sake? Which? Why would I read someone else's story if I wanted to be the one to decide?

■

Here was the trouble, I thought at the zoo. Nothing about Nathan had changed. I watched him demonstrate with his good humor and willingness to enter into Mattie's childish joy that he was a good father. That I already knew. I watched him demonstrate with his conscientious efficiency about diapers and strollers and snacks that having another parent around was a lot easier than not. That I already knew. I watched him demonstrate with his careful attention to me, his determination not to pressure me with questions, not to appear to notice my peevish and distant mood, that he hoped to win me back. And Nathan himself—he was Nathan. He was my Nathan, just as he always had been, and by that I mean not so much that he belonged to me, although in some way he did, but that he was the person I had always known him to be. My memory had not had him wrong. He was generous and selfish and loving and inconsiderate and attentive and distracted and faithful and not. But what would we have together, he and I, from this point forward, if I went back? That I couldn't answer, couldn't know, and so how could I decide?

Then it was naptime, then it was dinnertime, then it was the children's bedtime, the day just tick-ticking away, Rajiv's calls appearing unanswered on my phone. Nathan had taken the lead on dinner, on herding Mattie toward the bath with threats of tickling, and now we knelt together on the other side of the tub while I washed the children's hair, nothing decided, nothing discussed, and his flight at 2:30 tomorrow.

"Make a loop," Mattie demanded, and so I did, sweeping her soapy hair up and over. Binx laughed in a slightly hysterical way and smacked the water with his hands. "No splashing," Mattie shouted, and then she changed her mind and started splashing herself.

"Hey, hey," I said, leaning away from the tub with my hands up, and then I saw that instead of reacting to the children, instead of intervening, Nathan was kneeling with a lost look on his face, staring at me. "What?" I said.

"I wrote a story about you," he said.

"No splashing, guys," I said. I leaned in and trapped Binx's hands in one of mine and he tried to twist away. Mattie splashed again and caught me in the face. I grabbed her hands as well and she struggled, too, and I felt their tiny fingers straining against my palms, both of them striving mightily to escape.

"It's the only thing I've written since you left," Nathan said.

"Let go!" Mattie shouted, and Binx screamed his high-pitched scream.

"Okay, bathtime's over," I said. I rinsed their hair. I picked up Binx and handed him to Nathan, dripping wet and screaming, and then I hauled Mattie out and wrapped her in a towel. She was complaining that she was cold, that she didn't want me to dry her hair, that I wasn't wrapping her towel right, but I didn't answer, my hands doing their mechanical duty. A story about me? A story about me? I picked Mattie up and put her on the stool and squirted neon blue toothpaste on her toothbrush and handed it to her, and Nathan said, "I know I said I hadn't written anything since you left, but that wasn't strictly true. I wrote this story. It's the only thing I wrote."

"What does it say?" Mattie asked around her toothbrush.

I handed her a cup of water. "Rinse," I said.

"Do you want to read it?" Nathan asked.

I looked at him in the mirror. He was holding our baby

wrapped up in a towel. The whole front of his shirt was wet. "I don't know," I said.

"You said you wanted me to write something about you."

"No, I didn't," I said.

"You implied it."

"I just asked if you ever had."

He took a breath, said nothing, watched me in the mirror until I looked away.

"Let's go put pajamas on," I said to Mattie.

"I want Daddy to put me to bed! I want Daddy to put me to bed!"

"Whatever," I said, and I turned and took Binx from Nathan. The baby was shivering a little, so I held him tight against my chest as we went out of the warm bathroom. I laid him down on the bed to diaper him and he started to cry, so I tickled his belly with the top of my head, and he laughed and clutched my hair so tightly I knew it would be painful if I tried to get away. I'd just stay here forever. He was warm and clean, his laugh was delightful, he was happy, he was mine. The trouble was, I hadn't gotten the diaper on him yet, and if I stayed like this too long he'd pee on me. There was always a drawback. There was always a flaw in the plan. Did I really want to meet the version of myself that lived in Nathan's mind?

"What are you doing?" Nathan asked, carrying Mattie into the room.

"He's got my hair," I said, and Nathan set Mattie down and said, "Here." Gently, gently, he pried the baby's fingers from my hair. I stood. Binx reached, straining, wanting to tug on me again. "My flight is tomorrow," Nathan said.

I wrapped my hand around the baby's ankles, lifted him onto the diaper. "Ba ba ba," Binx said.

"My flight is tomorrow, and you still haven't made up your mind."

I slathered on the diaper cream. I pulled out and fastened the tabs.

"How about we go out to dinner?" Nathan asked. "Helen told me about a place with a great house band and funky cocktails. Hendrick's gin, she said."

"I don't know if we should be spending money on that," I said.

"Sarah. I know we need to save money. I know we have to figure out the situation with your job. I know all that. But can we just not talk about it now? Can we just go out to dinner and talk about you and me?"

"I have to change clothes," I said.

"OK."

"I mean, I have to do it now, before the kids are asleep."

"Can you get Binx in bed first?"

"No," I said. I looked at him. I was wearing him down, I thought. Any minute now he would stop being so patient, stop being so nice. He sighed. "OK," he said.

So I changed clothes while he read first to Binx and then to Mattie, and then sang to them both. I put on a dress. I pulled on tights. I sat on the bed with my shoes in my hand. I put one on and sat staring at the other. The children were fussing. Nathan went back and forth between them, patting Binx on the back, giving Mattie another magic kiss, saying, "Shhh, shhh," to both of them, until they quieted down for sleep, and the whole time I just sat there holding my shoe.

"What are you doing?" he whispered.

And this was the moment to tell him. I knew it was. That was why I hadn't put on my shoe. What would I say? What was I going to say? Would I say, "Nathan, I cheated on you," and would he recognize his own words in my mouth? And would I feel triumphant or despairing? And would he feel sad or angry, would he think I'd done it only to bring us to this moment, to take his betrayal for myself? I could hurt him, I could punish him by telling him, I could punish him by not telling him. I could put us on equal footing of offense and forgiveness, and maybe that would be for the best, but was that reconciliation or just bringing this particular struggle and story to an end? What if he had never told me, what would have happened then?

The moment yawned around me. Anything could happen now. Did I need past tense or present tense for this piece of news? I cheated on you. I am cheating on you. Or would I use that word? Did it still count as cheating if he'd cheated first? I'm seeing someone, or I saw. I met someone else, or am meeting. I had a fling. I flung.

The thing is, you make choices. You do some things and you don't do others and in the end there's not much point in asking what different choices might have gained you, and lost you, unless you have a time machine. You become those choices, you embody them. When you write poetry, you're a poet, and when you have children, you're a parent, and when you marry someone you're a husband or a wife. Whatever else you can quit, you can't quit yourself. What had saved me from temptation when I'd first known Rajiv was my nature, unchosen, irreducible. How had neither Rajiv nor I recognized what the last lines of my new poem meant? I'd known I couldn't stay, just as I'd known years before I couldn't be with him, even as I'd gone on pretending I had a choice. I was who I was, and I wanted what I already had.

"What's the matter?" Nathan asked.

I swallowed what I had to say. I swallowed the truth, I swallowed the words that contained it. “Nathan,” I said.

“What?”

“I wish you hadn’t done it.”

“Sarah, believe me,” he said. “I do, too.”

“I don’t know what’s going to happen,” I said. To Nathan, that man, my husband. And he knew what I meant, the way he so often knew what I meant—that I didn’t know what was going to happen not just in the next few minutes, not just in the next few days, but in the world, in our lives.

“Of course you don’t,” he said.

CHAPTER TWENTY-TWO

Nine days since his wife's car had disappeared around the bend of the drive, taking his wife and children with it. Nine days in a house so full and yet so empty of them: her, and her, and him, or rather Her, and Her, and Him. His people. His family. Gone and gone. And what had he been doing with his time in this enormous empty space? He couldn't account for a minute, not one minute, and yet somehow those minutes had found a way to pass. Now it was indeterminate night and the fireflies would be doing their airborne mating dance, fallen stars, Christmas lights. Or would they? Maybe it was too late in the year for that. His wife would know, if she were there to tell him. How many days had it been since he'd gone outside? Nothing marked the hours. Never mind the clocks.

The doorbell rang and he skyrocketed out of his chair, certain from the millisecond he registered the sound that it was her. Her. She was back—he was certain, certain, never stopping to remember that of course she had a key. He went to the side door off the kitchen, which was the door they always used, but there was no one there but the usual great and tragic moths beating themselves senseless on the window, and only then did he realize that the doorbell was at the front door and therefore the person who had rung it was not, and never had been, his wife.

A girl, though. A person of the female persuasion. A blond with her hair in a ponytail—and here he remembered with a prickling in his eyes that his daughter referred to this hairstyle as "a bundle." This girl had her hair in a bundle, and big, trust-me eyes, and a persuasive smile. She wore some sort of badge around her neck. "Hi," she said. She handed him a small slip of paper which he took without thought. He, like so many others, automatically took things that were handed to him—that's what the people who handed him things were counting on. The girl said, "We're offering homes in your neighborhood a free cleaning."

"Neighborhood?" he repeated. He looked past her at the fields around his house, half-expecting to see cul-de-sacs. Maybe they'd appeared in the last nine days, a flurry of construction happening unnoticed on the edges of his misery. Neighborhood? was the least of what he wanted to ask her. You're offering this cleaning to homes? he wanted to ask. What do the homes say? And where the hell did you come from? He didn't see a car.

"We'll clean one room for free, carpets and upholstery," she said. She looked past him into the house. "Free," she said again. "If I could just come in and take a look."

Well, the right answer was no thank you, wasn't it? That much was obvious. And yet there she was in his living room, proclaiming with great confidence that she could "brighten up" the rug, calling her boss from his phone and uttering the ominous and mysterious words, "I need the machine."

Oh help, he thought. What was the machine? Why was Bundle Girl—whose name, appropriately, was Candice—in his house? Where was his wife? Could he just run out of the house and leave it to Candice and her machine? Would anybody care?

Car wheels on a gravel road, and Candice went outside. He peeked out the window. A car of daunting, old-person enormity, out of which emerged a tall man who had the air of someone with a firm and jocular handshake, and then, a large box which he assumed contained the machine.

He had to admit he was a little disappointed, despite his dread, that the machine turned out to be a vacuum cleaner. An impressively large vacuum cleaner, with the 70s-era silver largeness of the car out of which it had come, and a vast array of attachments, but still just a vacuum cleaner, and not a magical one either, into which his whole life could vanish like something out of a cartoon. Inexplicably Candice insisted on calling it a sweeper.

But why is he going on and on about this? Was it anything, after all, but a visit from a door-to-door seller of vacuum cleaners, in and of itself surprising only because he hadn't realized the species continued to exist? Can he persuade you of his loneliness if he confesses that the girl stayed in the house for almost three hours, executing with practiced flair her endless presentation, and that he never once tried to get her to leave? What if he describes the way she attached black squares of cloth to the "sweeper" as she vacuumed, and then pulled them off and spread them open like a magician at the climax of a trick, and again and again he said, "Wow," and agreed that yes, there was an awful lot of dirt in his house, an awful lot of dirt? What if he admits that he began to use the word "sweeper"? If only you could have seen the room after two hours of this, lined with square after square of black cloth, like a deranged chess board, each square decorated with a star of dust and dirt and, as Candice kept saying, dust mites and their droppings, what it all comes down to, the detritus of our lives. "We shed skin all the time," Candice said, "and that's what they live off of. That's what they eat."

But he couldn't afford the $1,800 sweeper, that's what he told her, with genuine regret, and then he sat and stared at the patterns of dust while Candice had a loud and stagy conversation on the phone with her boss. "I don't know what to do," she said. "I showed him the dirt. They've got a lot of dirt. I guess they want to be dirty. They want their kids breathing that stuff."

He did want his kids breathing that stuff, because that would mean they were here. And what did it matter if they breathed it, if it was their shed skin anyway? He had an urge to dump all that grit on the floor, lie down and make a snow angel in it. This was his life now. This was all he had. And he let Candice take it away. He watched as she folded each square in an aggrieved and deliberate way, as though he had forced her to it, he had made this mess. Her manner had changed and gone on changing after he'd said he wouldn't buy the sweeper. She hardened and hardened before his eyes. She hated him. And didn't he deserve it? Hadn't he let her dump baking soda into the carpet and then vacuum it with their own sweeper one hundred times, breathing hard, sweating at the hairline, to do him the favor of proving the inadequacy of his life? She took the squares away, piling them and the machine and everything else she'd brought with her back into that silver spaceship of a car, and the tall man spared only one glance at him, a glance accompanied by the shake of a head, as if to say he'd failed. And didn't he know that? Didn't he know that? Why else was he following their car at a slow, stumbling pace as the taillights bumped away down the gravel drive? Why was he crying? Why was he calling after them, "Please give me back my dirt! Please give me back my dirt!"

He can't write about his wife. He has tried. It is like trying to describe the air, the earth, the sun. It is like trying to describe the way the heart beats fast without saying pounded, *without saying* skipped a beat. *It is like trying to describe crying, like trying to describe himself. She is elemental, both obvious and impossible to render, and if he says,* I'm sorry, *and if he says,* I love you, *how does that break through the scrim of the ordinary, how does that burst forth and vibrate with the truth?*

All he has is how it was without her. He walked back to the house alone. No fireflies. He sat down in the living room. Should he say he felt as if his heart had been torn out? Should he say he felt as if he'd had a limb removed? What he felt he finds himself unable to describe. He was alone in the house, and it seemed as though the camera pulled back to show him shrinking smaller and smaller as the space around him grew. What would she say if he called her and told her what had happened? Would she be happy that the rug was clean? He wouldn't say I love you. He wouldn't say I'm sorry. He'd say, The rug is clean. I had it cleaned. I did it for you.

CHAPTER TWENTY-THREE

We packed up our things, searching under beds and couch cushions for the inevitable missing toy, the lost baby sock. We buckled the children into their car seats. We hugged Helen and Daniel and their kids, and we thanked them profusely for their hospitality and their understanding, and then while Nathan was talking to Daniel I went to hug Helen again and with my cheek against hers I very nearly cried. "You know you're welcome to stay," she whispered in my ear.

"I know. But." I stepped back and smiled. "We have a mortgage. And can you imagine putting a house on the market right now?" I thought about the line in *Pride and Prejudice* where Elizabeth says she changed her mind about Darcy when she saw his house, and I thought, yeah, she meant it a little, a hard nugget of truth inside the joke.

And then all that was done, and because Abby needed a diaper change and Ian was clamoring for a snack, Helen and Daniel took their family inside. In the old days she would have stood there waving, watching us drive away, and as I stood watching the front door close I felt a little bit wistful about that.

"All right," Nathan said. "Let's go."

He opened the car door and lifted a foot inside, then paused when he saw me still standing there. I wasn't changing my mind, though no doubt it looked that way to him. I was going to go. I was going to put the key in the ignition, and turn it, and back the car out of the drive. I was going to stop for fast food and nurse the baby and pull into a motel parking lot and then eventually, eventually, pull up my gravel drive and notice, as I always did when I came home after some time away, that our house smelled a little like cat pee. I was going to go back to my job and take the children to Mr. Dodson's funeral. I was going to click my heels and go home, where life would be, as it is anywhere, a little bit dull Kansas, a little bit great and terrible Oz. I just wanted to stand here for a minute, first, and fix in my memory the life I wasn't choosing, the way Rajiv looked at me before I told him I was leaving, the cottonwood snow.

Nathan watched me, an uncertain look on his perfectly, terribly familiar face.

"Are you ready?" he said.

ACKNOWLEDGMENTS

My thanks to Juliana Gray, author of *The Man Under My Skin*, for writing Sarah's poems. Gail Hochman and Sally Kim continue to be all I could want in an agent and an editor; I'm lucky to have found them both. Thanks to the people at Harper, especially Maya Ziv, for all their hard work, and to Murray State University and UC's Taft Research Center for their support. And to my family, Matt, Eliza, and Simon O'Keefe, my love and gratitude.

Also by LEAH STEWART

Nearly a decade after the incident that ended their teenage friendship, Cameron receives an unexpected letter from Sonia. Despite her boss's urging, she doesn't reply. But when her boss passes away, Cameron discovers that he has left her with one final task: to track down Sonia and hand-deliver a mysterious package to her. In searing, beautiful prose, *The Myth of You and Me* captures the intensity of a friendship as well as the real sense of loss that lingers after the end of one.

"A smart, exceedingly well-written story about the mysteries at the heart of even the most intimate friendships between women. You'll be reading into the wee hours." —*People*

"An intricately constructed, heartfelt story about the death of an intense friendship." —*Boston Globe*

Available from Broadway Paperbacks wherever books are sold

ISBN 978-1-4000-9807-1
$13.00 (Canada: $17.00)